T0354906

UNDYING

A Novel By
William D. Hoy

Trafford rev. 06/29/2015

 www.trafford.com

North America & international
toll-free: 1 888 232 4444 (USA & Canada)
fax: 812 355 4082

Thanks Jingling for all your support

PART I

SOMEWHERE IN THE RUGGED BLACK HILLS
SOUTH DAKOTA, USA

Chapter 1

It's pitch dark, a cool, late April night. The moon shines brightly down on a valley of boundless ponderosa, spruce, and oak trees in the rugged Black Hills of South Dakota. In the distance, through the tall pines, you can see a gigantic granite head of Chief Crazy Horse sculpted in the rugged mountain top in his honor. This is the Indian chief who orchestrated the famous attack against General Custer's United States Army Seventh Calvary about 150 years ago.

A hungry owl glides through the trees, looking for its next meal. Listen carefully. You can hear the sound of the wind blowing through the tall trees. That is all you will hear. What remains is silence.

A handsome, adventurous, young man named Andre Roberson, born and raised in San Francisco and a graduate of the University of California at Berkeley, is sitting shirtless at an old wooden table in a weathered cabin. His left arm is awkwardly stretched out across the top of the table, and he sits patiently in a rickety old wooden chair nailed together from pieces of tree limbs covered with beaver pelts and the skins of small varmints that live in the forest. The cabin's dilapidated roof is covered by all sorts of vegetation, including blueberry bushes and vines growing in clumps of sod. Leaves falling from the oak trees blend with pine needles in the undergrowth, camouflaging the cabin and isolating it from the rest of the world. A small creek winds past the rear of the cabin, the water making a slight trickling sound as it passes over the rocks and fades into the stillness of the night.

A single candle illuminates the room, making shadows as its flame flickers in the draft coming under the cabin's front door. The ramshackle cabin was built many years ago, probably during the days when fur trapping was still legal in the valley. Several dried logs burning in the rock fireplace keep the cabin warm, making crackling noises and occasionally spitting out hot sparks on the wooden floor.

Chapter 2

Another man sits across the table from Andre. He is an old, wise, Lakota Sioux medicine man who must be older than the old cabin. His dark, weathered face bears the lines of age and wisdom. This tribal elder does the bridging between the natural world and the spiritual world. This spiritual man is referred to as *Wakan Tanka* in the Lakota Sioux language and appears to be doing something odd to Andre's outstretched arm.

The elder is holding a small, shiny, straight-bladed knife in his right hand, its handle made from antler of the plains elk. With a slightly shaky hand, he cuts two small incisions about a quarter of an inch wide and half an inch apart into Andre's left forearm. Andre twists slightly, crossing his feet several times in rapid motion and gritting his teeth, but not making a sound as the medicine man works on his arm. Andre squeezes a small piece of wood in his hand to help him endure the pain. The old Sioux dabs the incisions several times with a cloth soaked in a brine solution to keep the bleeding under control.

With meticulous care, he inserts two very thin animal bones about one inch in length into the two incisions. He softly taps the ends of the bones with the handle of his knife, carefully sliding them under Andre's skin. These bones are from the legs of the *Myotis Lucifugus*, the little brown Myotis bat, which is indigenous to the Black Hills. With the spiritual guidance and teaching of the medicine man, plus his own self-induced meditation, Andre will now have the ability to navigate through darkness. He will acquire the bat's sense of balance and ability to detect objects in the dark.

The old man begins to carefully weave the bones into Andre's forearm, forming an X pattern, which starts the unification of his senses with that of a bat. The sweat beading on Andre's forehead begins to trickle-down his face and drip to his chest. The pain is intense, but thanks to his total concentration, Andre is able to withstand it.

As the medicine man meticulously inserts the bat bones, he mutters sounds that are not familiar to Andre. His muttering and intonations don't sound like a chant, however; he seems to be actually talking to someone. He doesn't look up, but continues with the process. He has intensified his communication with the invisible person who may be his god.

After the bones have been inserted, the old man uses a porcupine quill and animal gut to stitch up each incision. Then he smothers both incisions with special herbs that have been boiling over the fire for several hours. The herbal potpourri seems to have a magical power as it penetrates Andre's skin, leaving no liquid residue on the skin's surface. The old man then takes half a dozen painted gourds from his medicine bag, along with paints he made from berries and herbs picked in the meadows and forest. He places the blessed paints on the table and brings out several crude paintbrushes made from horses' tails, then more porcupine quills. He will use all these to create a detailed tattoo on Andre's arm. He gives Andre a cup of the boiled herbs he had applied to the bat bones and has him to drink it to ease the pain.

In preparation for the tattooing, the medicine man removes the one eagle feather he has in his white hair and tucks it in his bag. He then puts on a small feather bonnet, with about thirty feathers running over the top of his head and down to his shoulders. It looks like the traditional Indian war bonnet, but the feathers do not appear to be large eagle feathers, but the smaller feathers of birds from the forest. These bright colors of these feathers are intriguingly blended with each other. It must have taken the man several moons to assemble something so undulating and beautiful.

Concentrating, the medicine man draws an outline on Andre's forearm of a nondescript heaven-bound bird over the inserted bat bones. Its wings are wide open, as if it's flying to another world. He begins to fill in the details with vivid colors. The sharpness of the bird's head plumage is also painted in bright colors. His palette includes paints of blood red, sky blue, tan to relate to the earth, and the white of the spiritual world. While the old spiritual man is painting and pricking Andre's arm with the sharp porcupine quill, he recites a chant.

Ahhha, Ahhha Ke Ah, Ahhha Ahhha Ke Ah. The chant becomes a mantra continuing in a mesmerizing manner.

Andre controls his agony and begins to drift back in his memory to a time when he was a young boy growing up in Northern California. For many years, ever since he had read about the Indian sculpture in a travel magazine, he has fantasized about coming to the Black Hills. This part of the country is Indian country. There are beautiful mountains, a multitude of fish, thousands of roaming buffalo, clear running streams, wolves, beavers, and herds of elk. The air is clean and fresh.

Chapter 3

While Andre was growing up, he never wanted to be a doctor, which his mother wanted him to be. He always wanted to study and understand the human mind and body. He wanted to search for the answers to unanswered questions. Why does the human body have no energy when a man is sad, yet, when the man is happy, his body has an enormous amount of energy? Are there herbs that accelerate the healing process of a human being? Andre often thought, or maybe he daydreamed, that if he could look within himself, then he could see how it all happens. Find the problem and fix it. That would be a miracle. What can the body do for itself without the assistance of man's medicine? Long before man started using modern medicine, he knows, native peoples used herbs.

Suddenly he starts coming out of his daydream, or was it a daydream? Looking at the old medicine man painting on his arm, he starts thinking. How far can an Indian medicine man go into himself with a spiritual meditation? The Buddhist Shaolin monks of China perform unbelievable things physically and mentally. Their secluded lives are mysterious. Does anyone really know what sort of meditation they study?

Focusing, Andre watches as the medicine man finishes the tedious job. "The bones of the bat will stay in place three days," the old man says. "Then they must be removed and buried in blessed ground."

After the medicine man finishes the tattoo, Andre must go into a self-induced meditation for the next three days. He will drink special herbs to sustain his energy and learn the spiritual guidance.

Chapter 4

The old medicine man warns Andre. "Young brave man," he says, "before starting this spiritual process, you must understand the very dangerous path you walk. Things may happen that have no answers. Dreams will take you to unknown territories. Death may result from the induced process. Do we proceed or do we stop?"

The wise old man focuses his eyes straight into Andre's. His sad eyes radiate a strong spiritual presence into Andre's mind. Andre can sense the medicine man telepathically telling him to go forward, and he says, "Yes." The messages he receives from the old man makes him feel positive and comfortable. Andre acknowledges the warning and directs the old wise man to proceed with the ceremony. He and the medicine man will spend time together in the old log cabin secluded in the woods with no communication with the outside world.

Andre will be able to gaze out the cabin window and see the giant head of Chief Crazy Horse. It appears to him there are majestic powers in the sky, and seeing the chief's head seems to reinforce the spirit.

He is on the verge of an experience that has always been in the back of his mind, a mutuality of some degree with bats. What can a bat really do in the dark? It darts in and out of its cave with thousands of other bats, not running into each other but searching for insects. Each time a bat leaves and returns to the cave, it finds where its babies are hanging. Even with thousands of young ones hanging everywhere, mother bats immediately and in total darkness find their own. Are these senses transferable to a human? He is thinking, *No way. That's impossible.* Can a man run in the dark of the forest using the radar senses of a bat? Not hitting anything, navigating around rocks and tree limbs lying in his path? *I've heard there are caves where millions of bats go out and come in each night without any collisions,* Andre says to himself. *There have to be some minor crashes or wing touches. It's astonishing.*

What can the body do without the assistance of man's medicine? Can one look within himself and study his own body, and the why's, the cannot's, the why not's? Andre's mind is drifting.

Chapter 5

After three days, Andre finishes his self-induced meditation and says good-bye to the old medicine man. He will live in the cabin by himself for the rest of the summer.

He begins taking long walks. There are days when he walks all day and late into the night. He visits the Crazy Horse sculpture on evenings when the moon is full. With his uncanny ability to navigate through the darkness, he never misses a step and senses fallen tree limbs and bushes in his way. His balance is amazing. He can walk on uneven, loose rocks, avoid holes, and jump like a deer without stumbling or falling. *It worked*, he thinks. *It really did work.* He walks through the woods at night, not colliding with anything, his body and feet automatically adjusting when something appears in front of him. The medicine man made it work with the insertion of the bat bones and the tattoo of the spiritual bird.

Andre recalls what the medicine man told him. "If you don't practice your spiritual meditation, the spirits will leave your soul and you won't be able to accomplish what you want to achieve. Slowly you will start to loose your ability of perfect balance, and your night senses will dissipate. Don't panic. Practice your spiritual meditation at least once a month and you will keep the spirit."

Occasionally, tourists hiking off the trails wander into his camp site and disturb his meditation, so he goes further up into the mountains, where he can concentrate and enjoy the peace and quiet. At this point, Andre is ready for the process of advancement in self-induced mediation. He is seeking higher enlightenment. He continues his walks, saturating his senses with as much beauty and tranquility as possible.

The days start to get shorter, the nights to get cooler. Winter is coming. Andre starts to make plans. He will have to leave the beautiful Black Hills for a warmer climate.

8

Chapter 6

One day Andre goes into the small South Dakota town and stops at a café for something to eat. After he sits down at the counter, the waitress comes by and drops off a menu.

"Coffee?" she asks as she fills other customers' cups.

"No, thanks," he replies. Looking over the menu, he decides to have the same thing that he always had when he was growing up. Cheeseburger with fries and a Coke. *But this time*, he thinks, *I'm going to have a strawberry shake. I haven't had one of those for years.*

He is a guy with an unusually versatile personality. Spending months in the mountains, meditating, hiking the trails night and day, communicating with the heavenly spirits, living in dirty clothes, sometime no clothes at all, unshaven, he can change physically and mentally over night. Now, however, he is sitting in a café, clean shaven, wearing Levis and a sweat shirt, ready to eat a burger and fries.

The waitress comes back to him. "Honey, what will you have?"

"I'll have a cheeseburger with fries and a strawberry shake."

"Thank you. It'll be up in no time." The waitress picks up the menu.

Andre glances at her name tag, which says Barbie. "Nice name," he says.

With a flirtatious smile, she replies, "I'll get you some water."

While Andre is sitting at the counter, watching the waitress do her thing, he notices several magazines lying on the stool next to him. Humming to himself, he picks one up and looks through it. It is a travel and adventure issue, and glancing through it, he sees an article about the Shaolin Buddhist monks in southern China. The article describes the strict discipline of their monastery and the experience of enlightenment in their lives and beyond, attained through meditation. It seems a bit peculiar to Andre that there is no telephone number, no address, no e-mail given in the article. All he learns is that the monastery is somewhere in the Limestone Mountains in the vicinity of Yangshuo, southern China. *This is what I've been looking for,* he thinks. *Enlightenment through self-induced meditation. If there is such a thing.*

After finishing his meal and paying his bill, he asks Barbie if he can have the magazine.

"Sure," she says. "Go ahead and take it. It's been around here for along time."

"Oh," he says, "one more thing. Do you have a public library around here?"

"Yes. It's down the street. About two blocks on your left. It's not a big place, but it helps a lot of people. My child uses it all the time."

Chapter 7

Walking out of the café, Andre notices a telephone booth, which reminds him that he needs his passport and a visa to travel to China. *I'll call Stacey, my dad's personal secretary*, he thinks. *She can get it out of the company's safe and mail it to me.* Stacey is about ten years older than Andre and has been a good friend to him. She is an extremely valuable worker at his father's company. She will do almost anything for him.

Picking up the phone, he dials Stacey's private number, collect.

"Hello," she answers.

"Hello, Stacey. This is Andre."

There is a brief pause. "Andre? Is that you?"

"Yes, it's me."

"How are you? It's been a long time. Are you still in the Black Hills?"

"Yes. I'm still here and doing fine. Learning new things to enhance my life." He laughs and says, "Stacey, I need a big favor from you."

"Yes? What is it?"

"I will be going to China within the next month or so, and I need my passport. Can you get it out of the safe and mail it to me?"

"Yes, I can," she says. "Is there an important reason for you to be going to China?"

"No. Not really," he admits. "I want to investigate the life of the Shaolin monks in southern China. I read about living in a monastery and learning kung fu, about their disciplined life with meditation. About the enlightenment of the human body."

"Interesting," she says. "Just be careful in what you do."

"Okay, yes, I will. You have my mailing address here at the general store?"

"Yes, I do."

He pauses again. "Hey, Stacey, how is my dad?"

"Oh, he's working very hard. Busy all day and into the evening. He has to slow down or he's going to have a stroke or something." She pauses, and he hears a bit of stress in her voice. "There's something going on in the company," she finally says. "I really don't know what your father's up to. He won't talk to me about it. But I know it's serious. He's had several meetings with his attorneys, but everything is hush-hush. I honestly don't know what's happening." She pauses again. "Last week, these two very rough-looking men wearing very expensive suits, maybe Armani or something that costs a lot of money, came in and had a meeting with your father. I've never seen these guys before. I don't have any idea why they were here. But they look like trouble, I'm sure of it." She stops and he waits for her to go on.

"When they came into the office," she says, "they didn't have an appointment, so I asked your father if he wanted to see them. He asked me their names. When I told him Mr. Oksa and Mr. Rajid, he suddenly became flushed in the face and looked very nervous. He took a binder out of his personal safe in his office, wrote something down in it, and put it back in the safe. He met with them for about an hour. After they left, he didn't give me any follow-up notes for his internal memos that he normally does after meetings. He did mention they were business associates of Mr. Craiger, who owns a little less than half of the company stock. Mr. Craiger is a very troublesome man. Your father and he have never seen eye to eye on anything."

Andre gives this some thought. "That does sound a bit strange," he replies. "I'm sure if something serious comes up, he'll let you know. You can call whoever you know to quash the problem. If all else fails, I'm here in the Black Hills for another month. After that, I might be in the Limestone Mountains in southern China."

Then Andre's voice becomes more serious. "If Dad gets into trouble, let me know and I'll be there over night. I'm serious. Dead serious."

Stacey assures Andre that there is no immediate danger that he is needed there right now and says she will keep him posted if anything comes up. But, she adds, he needs to keep her updated on his address and phone number if he has one.

"Keeping in touch by cell phone is not as easy as everyone thinks," he replies. "You have to have electricity to keep your cell phone charged and often there are no communication towers in the area. Other times, there is no telephone at all, only a post office box, or a clerk behind the counter at a general store who is also the postman."

"Andre," Stacey says, "I have to go now. I would love to talk with you longer, but business is business. Please keep in touch. I'll tell your father you called. Don't wait so long before you call again."

"I promise," Andre says. "Bye."

Chapter 8

At the library, Andre going down the aisles of books. S. Sha. "Ah, here it is," he says. "Shaolin Buddhist monks." He starts reading. The Zen sect is actually a Japanese version of the Chinese Chan School of Buddhism. It gained popularity among Japanese warriors because of its emphasis on strict discipline of the mind and body. It was introduced into China during the sixth century by Bodhiharma. Scanning the pages of the book, Andre begins humming. The Chan School emphasizes the practice of meditation as the direct way of gaining insight and experiencing enlightenment in this life.

"This is very interesting," he murmurs. He spends most of the day and the next couple of days reading all the information he can find about the Shaolin monks and their temples and monasteries.

He even learns a few words of Chinese. *Ni hao* means "How are you?" *Zai jian* means "Good-bye." There is one thing Andre is having a problem with, however. There is no one in the Black Hills that speaks Chinese, so he can only hope he's pronouncing the words correctly. After several days of visiting the library, he decides to visit the general store in town to find out if his passport has arrived.

"Yes," the clerk says.

It has been several months since Andre and the clerk have seen each other. Andre says that he has been staying at the old trapper's cabin up by the stream.

"Yeah," the clerk says. "That old cabin sure is a nice place. Away from everything."

Andre signs for the certified parcel that holds his passport. Now he will start planning his trip to China.

A month has come and gone and Andre is ready to leave for China.

The last night before Andre is to leave, something strange happens. With his two duffle bags packed sitting in the corner of the freshly cleaned cabin, he decides to go for his last night walk up to the head of Crazy Horse.

After returning from this vigorous walk he enters his cabin. After lighting his candle, he freezes. He gazes around the room. *What the hell has happened here?* The contents of both of his duffle bags have been emptied on the floor and scattered everywhere.

Quickly, he reaches down and picks up one of the logs he burns in the fireplace. Ready to strike anything that moves, he slowly walks around in the cabin, looking to see if anything has been stolen.

After a thorough inspection of his belongings he repacks his bags. Sitting at his table he's thinking. *Why would someone do something like this? Are there some jerks who enjoy destroying things in randomly selected cabins?* Oddly, they waited for the last night and then waited until he left. Maybe he came back too soon, and they had to leave. Whoever they were, they knew his routine.

Only Stacey knows the exact date he would be leaving for China. He knows she had nothing to do with it. Maybe someone at the company found out when he was leaving. Maybe the postman in the village?

Is this a warning of some kind?

PART II

ANDRE ARRIVES IN YANGSHUO, CHINA

Chapter 9

As the China Southern Air 737 jet taxies up to the gate at the terminal, Andre looks out the plane window and sees a large sign above the building. The sign says Guilin, and there is another sign in Chinese beside it. *That other large sign*, he thinks, *must be Guilin in Chinese.* Excited, he speaks out loud. "Yes! I've made it! Yes, I'm here in Guilin, China."

Departing from the plane, he fumbles through his shoulder bag, looking for his English-Chinese translation book. "Ah, here it is," he mumbles to himself. "It's going to be very difficult to read Chinese. I hope there will be signs in English."

Leaving the gate, he sees that the terminal is extremely congested. He decides to follow the group of passengers who have just deplaned with him. Picking up speed, he catches up with them. As he follows them, he also looks around at the stores he passes and sees what they are selling. At the same time, he is also paging through his translation book, trying to find a few key words. Watching for signs in English, he keeps bumping into people and apologizing. *Duibuqi* ("excuse me"). He is feeling a bit foolish and hoping he's pronouncing the Chinese word correctly.

Suddenly he spots a sign right above his head that is in both English and Chinese, directing him down the stairs to the baggage carousel. After picking up his duffle bags, he goes to the information booth to get directions. But this does not go very well. The clerk does not understand him, and he is now totally confused about how to get to Yangshuo. The translation book does not seem to help, either, and a few people he talks to do not understand what he was saying from his book.

Frustrated, he begins walking around in the terminal, looking for someone who can speak English. Finally venturing outside the terminal, he sees a middle-aged man standing beside an old black van parked at the curb. The van has a sign with the word *Yangshuo* printed in English taped to its window.

Andre walks over to the man to see if he can speak English. Taking out his translation book, he looks for the right words to say, but he cannot find them. Using sign language, he manages to negotiate transportation to Yangshuo. At least that's where he thinks he is going. Wanting to make sure he gets to the right place, he feverishly digs through the pages of his translation book and finally finds the words *wo yau qu Yangshuo,* meaning, "I want to go to Yangshuo." The old man smiles and shrugs his shoulders, and Andre assumes he understands. Then the driver takes a piece of paper out of his pocket which has "200 *yuan*" and "three hours" printed on it. He shows this to Andre.

Yes, yes, he understands, Andre thinks with relief.

With some help from the van driver, Andre loads his two duffle bags into the van, and off they head for the city of Yangshuo.

Within the first fifteen minutes, Andre falls asleep. He wakes up for a minute, then falls asleep again, wakes again an hour later, and falls back to sleep. It seems like he hasn't slept for days. He must be experiencing jet lag from the long flight.

Now he's awake, however, and the van is driving through the beautiful countryside with its majestic jagged limestone peaks known as the Karst formations. These odd looking pinnacles shoot up out of the ground and spiral hundreds of meters into the sky. The route continues through numerous farming villages where peasants are working in rice paddies, fields covered with growing taro, abundant fields of orange trees. Every so often, back-packers appear, mostly young people walking on trails that run parallel to the road. Their large, heavy backpacks in bright colors stand out against the green of the countryside. The energetic back-packers don't look Chinese. They are Europeans or Americans.

Arriving in Yangshuo, Andre directs the van to stop at a hotel on the Binjiang Lu, a block from where the large tourist boats tie up. The hotel stands out from the other hotels with its beautiful Chinese pagoda shingle roof tipped upward at the corners. The exterior of the hotel painted jade green with a crimson trim. *Hotel Yangshuo* reads the sign in English lettering. Andre thinks, *The hotel's name has a nice ring to it, and it appears to have an in-house restaurant. I'll just charge my meals to the room. That's easier than working with the Chinese currency, renminbi.*

Chapter 10

The van driver carries Andre's duffle bags into the lobby of the hotel, and Andre generously tips him for the extra service. The driver must have brought other tourists here before. He knows how to make a little extra money by being helpful.

Walking up to the reception counter, Andre says, "*Ni hao.*"

The female clerk replies with a radiant smile. "*Ni hao.* She adds in perfect English, "Good afternoon. Welcome to the Hotel Yangshuo. My name is Jing Ling. May I assist you with acquiring a room today? Do you have a reservation?" She is an attractive Chinese lady with long black hair flowing over one shoulder. She is dressed in a traditional Chinese red jacket with embroidered golden dragons and a black skirt.

Surprised to hear her speaking perfect English, Andre pauses, then says, "No. No, I don't have a reservation. I just came into town."

"Did you come on the tourist boat?" Jing Ling asks.

"No," he replies. "I came in by van from the airport in Guilin."

"Did you have a nice trip?" she asks. "It's such a beautiful drive."

"Yes, I did," he says. "The trip was exciting. I saw such beauty as I have never seen before in my entire life." He is very enthusiastic. "Such stunning picturesque mountains. Jagged peaks entwined with interesting vegetation...." His voice trails off into dream-like whisper as he recalls what he saw, but he quickly recovers from his reverie of the past three hours.

"Will you be staying very long?" Jing Ling asks.

"Yes. I plan to stay for about ten days. How much are your rooms? I would also like to have a private bathroom."

"Okay", she replies. "How many people in your party?"

"I'm by myself. Just one."

"How would you like to have a king size bed? You will have plenty of room."

"Yes, that would be fine."

"The price for your room will be 175 *yuan*, per day," she tells him.

He calculates in his mind for a few seconds. *That's about $28 per day.* "Okay," he tells her. "I will take it." *What a bargain*, he thinks to himself.

"Oh," she says, "I forgot to mention that the room rate includes a bottle of water each day."

"That would be fine."

"Will it be on your charge card?"

"Yes. American Express."

"I will also need to make an imprint of your card." As he hands her his card, she looks at it and says, "Mr. Andre Roberson, you need to fill out the register, including your passport number. I will need to make a copy of your passport, as well, for our records. Government policy, you know." She glances at the photo in his passport while she is making a copy and comments, "That is a nice picture."

"Thank you," he replies with a smile.

"Here is your room key, Mr. Roberson. Your room number is 209. Second floor, down the hall on your left. The elevator is around the corner." Before he walks away, she adds, "We also have an excellent restaurant in the hotel that serves superb meals. It will be open for dinner at 5 p.m. There are many more restaurants located here in Yangshuo. Most of them are more casual, and their menus are limited. They are all located within walking distance on Xi Jie to Diecui Lu. The Chinese word *Lu* means 'road,' and *Jie* is 'street.' I didn't want you to get lost." She smiles at him. "If you go down there, my favorite restaurant is Minnie Mao's. It's on Xi Jie. It's one of the most popular places, with excellent Western and local cuisine. And nightly movies. The stuffed tomatoes and the steamed dumplings are the best."

"Thank you for the tip," he responds, smiling again.

In his room, he realizes that he hasn't had a good hot bath for some time, so he takes a nice hot shower and drinks the bottle of water in his room. After toweling off, he changes into some clean, but badly wrinkled, Levis and an old shirt that has a slight mildew smell (it's been stuffed in his duffle bags for several weeks). Feeling around in his bag again, he finds an old bottle of men's cologne. "Ahh," he says, "this will kill the mildew smell," and he splashes some on his face and on the old shirt. Looking more closely at the label, he tries to make out the name of the brand, but it wore off a long time ago. "But it still smells good," he comments to himself. "I feel great right now. I'm ready to go out and explore a new world."

Chapter 11

Outside the hotel, Andre heads in the direction the receptionist gave him. Before leaving his room, he checked to be sure he has his English-Chinese translation book, and it now resides in his hip pocket. Down the sidewalk he goes, talking to himself, trying to pronounce the Chinese words he sees. He tries to read street signs and make sure he is heading in the right direction. Every few stores he passes, he peers in the front windows. trying to figure out what kind of store it is. The sidewalks are crowed. Everyone is going somewhere, tourists, back-packers, and the local people all crowding onto the narrow sidewalks. *This place seems to be a back-packer's paradise*, he thinks. He remembers seeing hiking trails from the van. They were being used by back packers hiking through the countryside. The downtown streets here are crowed with cars, trucks, motor bikes, and bicycles weaving in and out of the traffic. Occasionally, a hand-drawn cart loaded down with crates of chickens or a bicycle with dozens of wooden boxes tied on to it enters the traffic.

Suddenly he spots something new. *I haven't seen one of those before*, he thinks. He is looking at a bright yellow motorbike with an enclosed metal compartment mounted on its rear end. The compartment has a front door entrance for a passenger to squeeze through to get in for a ride. *I think this modified bike is a taxi. It would be very crowded and difficult if two people got in. I'm sure a fat person would not be able to get in.* Then he sees a man talking with the cycle driver. The man gets into the box and closes its door. The driver starts up his cycle and takes off down the street, weaving in and out of the traffic.

"Be careful," Andre cautions himself as he starts to cross the intersection. He looks in all directions and even over his shoulder a couple of times just to make sure he doesn't get run over by something coming from behind. Pedestrians don't have the right of way when crossing a street here. It does not, in fact, matter where they cross. There are few crosswalks, and if a pedestrian is trying to cross a street, most drivers will not stop. Nor, Andre notices, are there many policemen to manage the traffic. He wonders why this is so. All of the roads are so congested, he tells himself; he's sure he would not be able to drive here in Yangshuo, or anywhere else in China. *If this is the way they drive, it's just too crazy.*

Andre manages to cross the street and comes to Binjiang Lu, which runs parallel to the Li River. *Ahh, what a beautiful river.* He stands beside the imperturbable river, letting his eyes slowly pan across the flowing river as it leisurely goes by and disappears around the bend. The colors are beautiful. Bluish greens fade into dark sapphire blue as the river winds toward the craggy mountains. As it flows, the river gives an illusion of a slow, smooth moving river, yet Andre can tell it is a river that people must respect. Some of the mysterious, creamy colored mountains seem to pop right out of the ground beside the river. They look majestic with their jungles of vines and vegetation hanging all over them. *They are so beautiful.*

It is about eighty degrees, no wind, not a cloud in the sky. Andre couldn't ask for a better day. He continues along the river, passing souvenir shops selling silk scarves, statues, trinkets, handbags, shirts, everything a tourist might want.

He also notices a dozen two-story riverboats tied up at the dock. The boats are tied to each other, side by side, in groups of four. When boarding or departing, the passengers must walk across the other boats to get to their boat. "Whoa," Andre says, "this looks great." He stops to get a better look at the boats. These must be the boats the receptionist at the hotel was referring to when she asked if he had come in on one of them. All of the boats look like they might be able to carry about a hundred to 150 passengers. There are large glass windows on each side, with standing room for passengers who get tired of sitting. Downstairs, a large television is mounted high in the front of the boat so everyone can see it. Andre wonders if they show Chinese movies. *They probably show movies for the children to keep them from getting into mischief.*

At the stern of the boat on the top deck is a large area where everyone can stand and take pictures. Directly below this deck is what looks like the kitchen. Andre sees a man dressed in a white uniform throwing water out the side door. It must be one of the cooks.

"It seems like they're getting ready to leave," he murmurs. Where are they are going and where do they came from? The boats don't seem to provide facilities for sleeping. Perhaps their trips are about eight hours or shorter. He wonders what happened to all the passengers. He doesn't remember seeing large groups of tourists walking around in town tonight. *Maybe I just didn't recognize them,* he thinks. *Where do a thousand or so people go in this town? Maybe it's a seasonal thing?*

Andre puts the tourist thing out of his mind for now and continues walking beside the river quietly enjoying the scenery. As he strolls, he moves away from the hustle of the souvenir stands and the heavy foot, cart, and animal traffic of the city.

Chapter 12

He has been walking for an hour when he passes a young Chinese boy standing beside a big bicycle on the trail. The little boy is skinny and wearing clothes that look almost worn out. The bicycle looks too big for the boy to ride, but it appears to be in good shape. As Andre walks past the boy, he notices the boy has his eyes focused on him and he nods his head.

At that moment the boy says, "Ride bike. Two *yuan*."

Andre says, "*Bu* (no)," and continues his stroll. The boy follows him, pushing the big bike. After a few minutes, Andre stops and turns around. The boy is ten feet behind him. He slowly walks closer to Andre.

"Ride. Two *yuan*." This time he has a big smile.

Andre stands there for a few moments, looking over the bike, then looking back at the boy. *Walking is great*, he thinks, *but a bike will get me a lot further in less time. The price is very cheap, and the bike looks in good condition.* "Okay," he says to the boy.

The boy breaks out into a big smile and pushes the bike up to him. When Andre hands him two *yuan* coins, he looks at them and says something quietly to himself, then puts the money carefully into his pants pocket.

Andre takes hold of the handle bars and swings his leg over the seat. In a flash, the boy jumps on the back of the bike where a carrier is mounted. This surprises Andre for a second, but there is no problem. The boy is small, he tells himself, and won't be any extra weight. The young entrepreneur doesn't want his investment to ride away.

When Andre was a young boy, he had a bike and rode with his friends. Sometimes his friends sat on the handle bars, jumped on the back, or stood on the extended axles, anywhere they could fit. He knows how to ride a bike with someone else on it.

Now he peddles with the young boy on the back of the bike, swerving to miss a few people on the trail and a couple of carts pulled by farmers. After passing several more carts he can see the path opening up, so he picks up speed. *This feels great!* The bike is performing well, the path is smooth, there's nothing in their way. The air is blowing through his long wavy hair and in his face. The boy is also enjoying the ride, not saying a word. They pass numerous fields of rice being harvested and loaded on carts, sugar cane was being cut, and oranges being picked. The trail weaves through large groves of bamboo and under giant trees. Andre thinks they may be banyan trees. He wonders if the boy learned a few words of English by doing business with tourists. Or maybe he learned them in school, or perhaps his parents taught him.

They ride for another half an hour, when suddenly the boy yells out, "Stop! Stop!"

This startles Andre. Did the boy get his foot caught in the spokes? He applies the brakes as fast as he can and stops the bike. "Are you okay?" he asks the boy.

But the boy only jumps off the bike and motions Andre off as well. Puzzled, he gets off the bike, then it occurs to him that the boy wants his bike back. "Oh, no," he says aloud. "That can't happen. It's too far to walk back to the city."

Chapter 13

The excited boy motions for Andre to follow him and heads down a path toward a thick grove of giant bamboo at the edge of the river. It seems to him that the boy wants to show him something, but what? *Maybe I should be careful,* he tells himself, *coming all the way out here in the countryside with a total stranger, and a young boy, at that, and venturing into unknown territory.* The unknown territory is dense, dark, and forbidding. Pushing the bike, Andre cautiously follows the boy along a very narrow foot path. Suddenly the lad disappears into the bamboo. Parking the bike, Andre follows him. The boy is more and more excited, walking faster and faster, and soon he starts to run through the thick bamboo. Andre loses sight of him. He is able to travel through the dense growth because of the training he received in the Black Hills, but the boy is traveling too fast. Where is he going? After traveling a couple hundred feet, he hears noise like water splashing ahead of him. He thinks he is catching up with the boy, but the bamboo is extremely thick and he can't see anything except the narrow trail, which soon dwindles into nothing. He also notices that the water on the trail is getting deeper, at least a half a foot now. What is he doing? Still trudging forward and splashing with every step he takes, Andre keeps one arm up in front of his face. The sharp edges of the bamboo leaves are cutting into the sleeves of his shirt.

Suddenly he comes crashing into a small clearing and almost runs head-on into a giant water buffalo. The buffalo jumps backward with a loud bellowing snort, then its eyes fill with rage. A flock of mallard ducks eating nearby senses danger and immediately takes flight. The air becomes deathly still. The buffalo lowers his head showing his massive set of horns. He starts to paw the water with one hoof. A charge is imminent. Andre freezes. He has no idea what to do now. He looks for the boy, but the boy has disappeared.

Do not startle it, he cautions himself, and he slowly starts to back up. He needs to get the boy and himself out of this dense bamboo grove, but it's hard for him to think right now.

Suddenly, he sees the boy out of the corner of his eye. The boy wading up to the side of this massive monster, slapping it on the butt. The little guy is herding the big bull back into the river with the others.

Has the boy gone mad? Andre asks himself. *How many of them are there?* He franticly looks around and counts six more buffaloes in the river.

After being slapped by the boy, the bull turns away from Andre and looks at the boy, then moves slowly back into the water. The boy shouts, "Mine, mine!" and moves further into the deep water between the behemoths, splashing water on their backs. He pulls a large scrub brush out of the vines and starts scrubbing the sides and backs of these beasts.

The boy turns to Andre. "Come, come." He gestures for Andre to wade into the water and help with the washing.

I don't know, Andre thinks. After a minute, however, he slips off his wet shoes and wades into the cool water up to his knees. Using cupped hands, he starts throwing water onto the backs of a couple of the buffaloes. Occasionally they turn their heads and stare at him, but the young boy slaps their sides and they look away again.

"No like," the little guy says.

After splashing more water on the buffaloes and getting more unfriendly looks from them, Andre thinks he might be running out of luck. Maybe he should do some watching for awhile. He slowly moves backward and out of the water, making sure he doesn't turn his back to the small herd. He doesn't want to alarm these beasts. There's no telling what they might do if they get excited.

He sits on a log and watches as the boy finishes washing the herd. He can see that the boy loves these beasts. He's talking with each one as he scrubs, giving them grass he has in his pocket.

After about thirty minutes, the boy finishes the baths and comes over to sit on the log with Andre. When Andre looks at the boy and smiles, the little guy gives a big smile back and says, "Mine, mine."

Andre nods his head and says, "Yes." Then he asks, "What is your name?"

When the boy gives Andre a blank look and says nothing, Andre takes out his translation book and looks at the front pages, where he has written some words he thought he might need. Here it is. "My name in Chinese, *Wo jiao* Andre," he tells the boy. He points at himself and says it again. "Andre."

The boy nods and points at himself. "Shiao Hai."

Andre repeats the name, "Shiao Hai," and the boy responds with a big smile and a nod of his head.

Then Shiao Hai looks at him and says, "Andy."

Andre he shakes his head. "*Mingzi*, Andre," he says, and he repeats it, "Andre."

Shiao Hai concentrates on what he is going to say, then with a big smile says, "Andre."

Andre laughs and says, "Yes," with a nod of his head.

They sit there together for a few minutes, not saying anything, until Andre looks up into the sky. The sun is starting to drop toward the horizon. He doesn't want to be way out here in the countryside when it gets dark. He would get lost, for sure. He gets up and taps the boy on the shoulder and nods in the direction of the trail, then starts walking up the trail through the bamboo back to where he left the bike. Shiao Hai follows him. When they reach the bike, he starts pushing it up the trail, casually looking back over his shoulder to make sure the little guy is still there.

Chapter 14

On the path back to Yangshuo, Andre swings his leg over the seat and mounts the bike. Shiao Hai takes a big jump and lands on the back.

"Are you on?" Andre asks. When the boy says yes, he starts pumping the pedals and they head into the sunset and back to Yangshuo. They have an hour's ride, and since it's about hour before dark, they should make it back before nightfall.

The trail is almost deserted now. Most of the farmers are finished for the day, and a few other bike riders are scurrying along to get home before dark. As they ride, Andre starts to hum a song. He sings a few verses, then goes back humming again. Shiao Hai tries to hum the song with him, but then he starts singing a song in Chinese, and Andre tries to sing with him. Soon both of them are laughing.

When they come to the area where the big tour boats are docked, Shiao Hai calls out, "Stop, stop," and Andre brings the bike to a halt. The boy jumps off the bike and says, "Finish." Andre gets off the bike, and the boy takes the handle bars. "*Zai jian*," he says to Andre.

"See ya," Andre says, not knowing what he said.

"*Ming tian*," Shiao Hai replies, and he disappears down the dirt path, pushing his bike toward some houses in the distance.

Andre is thinking, *Nice little boy. Where is his family? Will I see him tomorrow? Maybe we can go for another bike ride?* Then he remembers his translation book. He pulls it out of his pocket and looks up the words *Ming tian*. The sun has already gone down and he can barely see the page, but, yes, he finds the word. He says it to himself several times. It means "see you tomorrow."

Chapter 15

Andre starts walking back into town and heading for the hotel. He's thinking about taking a nice shower and eating some good Chinese food. The sidewalks are still crowded, he notices, and he suspects that everyone is heading somewhere, maybe to get something to eat or just wanting to get outside. He manages to get across the street, thinking that his experience in the Black Hills helped him in navigating the crowds and the cars, though he's not sure about the episode with the buffalo.

I wonder where someone so small can get so many buffaloes, he thinks. *They must belong to his parents and he takes care of them.* Then he puts them out of his mind.

Entering his hotel, Andre sees the same attractive woman working at the reception desk who checked him in when he arrived. *"Ni hao,"* he says, and she replies, "Good evening, Mr. Roberson."

He laughs and says, "You remember my name."

"Yes, I do," she replies. "Not too many Robersons are around here."

"Yes," he responds, feeling proud she remembers him. "I think I'm going to eat in the hotel restaurant tonight," he says. "Do I make a reservation or is it open seating?"

"You need a reservation," she replies.

"Oh, by the way," he says, "what was your name again? You told me earlier today, but with so much going on, I'm ashamed I forgot it."

"Yes, I understand," she says. "My name is Jing Ling, which means Jane in English."

"Yes, that's a pretty name," he replies.

"Can I make a reservation for you?" she asks. "It is recommended, for it fills up very fast within the next several hours."

"Yes. Would you make the reservation for one at seven o'clock this evening? Thank you very much, Jing Ling. You are very helpful."

Walking to his room, Andre thinks, *Such a pretty smile she has, and a real nice shape.* He goes into his room and sits down on the bed for a few moments, slipping off his shoes, relaxing, and thinking about the day. His thoughts are rolling through his mind. *What am I going to do after dinner this evening?* After all the traveling he has done during the last couple of days, he thinks a good night's rest would be an excellent idea. After drinking down his bottle of water, he notices that someone has left another bottle of water in his room. *Now that is real nice.* Taking off his clothes, he starts a wonderful, relaxing shower, letting the cool water stimulate him. It makes a thousand tiny prickles dance all over his body. It has been a long time since he's had a nice, soothing shower and slept in a clean, comfortable bed.

"No, no!" he says aloud. *I can't be thinking about going to bed right now, I have to have my first classy dinner in China tonight. Ahh, shortly, I will be having the experience of my life, sitting down and having a first-class Chinese meal in China. I'm going to need some help in deciding what I will be eating.* He stops to think for a minute. *Well, maybe I can ask Jing Ling for help? Or maybe she can join me for dinner? No, that's a bad idea, although it would be real nice. I'm sure the hotel has rules that forbid that.*

Chapter 16

It's seven o'clock sharp when Andre approaches the woman at the restaurant's reservation stand. "Good evening," he says. "I have reservations for one."

"Yes," she says with a nod. "We will have your table ready in a moment. What is your name?"

"Andre Roberson. Room 209."

"Thank you."

"Oh, excuse me," he says before she steps away.

"Yes?"

"Is Jing Ling still working this evening?"

"No, I'm afraid not. She has gone home."

"Oh, that's too bad."

While waiting for his table, he casually looks around the dining room and its connecting rooms. *This place is fantastic*, he thinks. *I had no idea it looked so nice.* The main dining room has twenty or more tables covered with fancy white tablecloths, full place settings, and an arrangement of fresh flowers and orchids on each table. He notices red and gold Chinese lanterns hanging from the ceiling with long flowing golden ribbons dangling from them. The cream-colored walls are covered with painted murals depicting the Chinese culture through the centuries. The murals show exquisite, majestic, snow-capped mountains surrounded by clouds, with pristine valleys and flowing rivers below. One section of the mural attracts his attention. It shows a herd of twenty wild mustangs running in a snow storm through a meadow in the direction of the observer. Their manes and tails flow in the wind, and the steam coming from their nostrils gives them an uncannily natural look. These murals, painted with such artistic beauty and balance, must have been created by a master calligrapher. They cover the walls from floor to ceiling.

"We have your table ready, Mr. Roberson," the hostess says. "If you will follow me?"

He follows the pretty hostess, and she seats him in a booth in the corner, just where he likes it, then she says, *"Dui bu dui."* He thinks what she said means, Is this fine for you?

Andre says thank you to the hostess and waits for the waiter. As he waits, he notices an enormous aquarium across the room. It covers one entire wall and holds the largest collection of fish he has ever seen, fish of every color and shape. Staring at the aquarium for awhile, he notices that there are no sharks, barracudas, octopuses, or seals.

No, he thinks with a laugh, *they wouldn't have those in an aquarium.* But he does see a manta ray gliding through the water, effortlessly swimming near the glass. *If you didn't know what it was*, he tells himself, *it would probably scare the hell out of you.* But mantas are not meat eaters. They only eat plankton and microscopic organisms. He smiles again and thinks if there were sharks and barracudas in this tank, they would eat each other and it would be total chaos. *If I were sitting next to the glass, I'd swear I was dining in the ocean.*

The waiter arrives with the menu and rescues Andre from his aquatic thoughts. "Would you like to have a drink while you are making your food selection?" the waiter asks.

"Yes, I would. A glass of your Cabernet Sauvignon, and the house brand would be fine. I'm sure it will help me sleep tonight."

"As you wish." The waiter walks away.

I didn't think they'd have any Napa Valley Merlot here in China, Andre thinks. *I'll try a Chinese beer tomorrow.*

Looking through the menu, he sees several dishes he immediately puts on his don't try list: dumplings with a choice of chicken brains, chicken intestines, or chicken feet. Snakes and bamboo rats. *I don't think so.*

He soon spots the specialty plate, which is described in both English and Chinese. *It must be something everyone likes*, he thinks. *Hunangliu Laoya.* In English, yellow oil old duck. *I wonder how old the duck has to be to qualify for the dinner?* The dish is described as an inexplicably chewy flavorful duck. *I don't think so.* Next he sees other dishes with English descriptions. *Tian suan rou*, sweet and sour pork. *Jie lan niu rou*, Chinese broccoli with beef. *Mi fan*, cooked rice. *Re cha*, hot tea.

The waiter returns to ask if Andre has made his selections.

"Yes," he says, "I would like to have *tian suan roe, jie lan rou,* and *mi fan* with *re cha*."

"Excellent choice," the waiter replies with a big smile, and he repeats the order back to Andre in English. Sweet and sour pork, Chinese broccoli with beef, fried rice, hot tea. "Would you like brown or white steamed rice?" he asks.

"Brown rice."

"Yes, and will you be in need for a fork with your dinner?"

"Yes, that would be nice."

Then he politely asks if Andre would like to have a dessert or an after-dinner drink, which will be delivered after he finishes his meal.

"Not this evening," Andre replies. "*Xiexie,* thanks." It's odd, he thinks, for a waiter to ask if he wants a dessert before ordering his meal. He supposes every restaurant has its own procedures, and maybe that is customary in China.

Chapter 17

Now that was real good of me, Andre thinks to himself. *I ordered a Chinese meal using the Chinese words. Even though I'm reading them off the menu.*

A few minutes pass, and the waiter brings out a bottle of Chinese wine. "Mr. Roberson," he says, "we are out of the wine you requested. Our wine manager asks if you would like to try one of our house specialty wines. I'm not sure if there is a name in the English language for this wine," he adds, "but it's very similar in taste and body to a Cabernet Sauvignon. If you are not pleased with this wine, there will be no charge." The waiter smiles again. "He also told me to tell you, since we do not have the wine you requested and you are staying at the hotel, the wine is a gift of our appreciation."

"Yes," Andre responds. "I would very much like to try a Chinese wine."

The waiter opens the bottle and pours a glass for Andre.

Ahh. Andre relaxes, letting his breath out as he picks up the glass of wine and inhales its aroma. Then he slowly swirls the wine around in the glass, watching its legs run down its side, analyzing its body. He then takes a couple of sips, slowly savoring its body, letting his palate tell him how it tastes as it melts down his throat. "That is good," he finally says. "I may have two glasses this evening."

Andre remembers when he was young and when his dad was tinkering with the wine business in Napa Valley, California. He used to sneak up to where the wine experts were talking and sampling the wines and listen to what they were saying about the different wines. After everyone else had left, he and his friend, Alex, always tried some of the left-over wines. Sometime they drank a little too much and got a buzz. Then the two boys disappeared for several hours so their parents would not find out they were tipsy. To keep from getting caught with the smell of alcohol on their breath, they always chewed bubble gum.

We got good at blowing bubbles, Andre remembers with a grin. He sighs. *One of these days I'll tell Dad about that. I'm sure he didn't know.* Andre sighs again.

He had learned a lot about wine. Which wines were good and which were bad. Now he is thinking that he is sort of novice wine connoisseur. *And I'm getting better.* With a laugh, he considers the glass of wine he is drinking. It is a naturally smooth, full bodied wine, complimented by hints of spice and vanilla. It leaves an oak taste in his mouth. *This is excellent wine!*

He finishes an excellent meal and thinks that the chef needs to be commended.

On his way back to his room, he cuts through the lobby to see if Jing Ling might have come back to work. Sometimes a person forgets something and returns to pick it up. Andre doesn't imagine she will come back, but is just thinking it would be nice to talk with her a little more. But the clerk at the front desk politely tells him, "She won't be back to work for two days."

In his room, exhausted after an eventful, interesting day, Andre strips off his clothes, and dives into a cool shower, finishing off with a brisk toweling. Then he slips between two soft, clean sheets. In a matter of minutes, he is sound asleep.

Chapter 18

Early the next day, Andre wakes up feeling fresh and energetic. He is soon on his way to breakfast. The front desk told him last night that he can either serve himself from the breakfast buffet or order from the menu. It is 6:30, they are just opening the restaurant, and he is one of the first ones in. The hostess seats him in another booth against the wall. He wants to familiarize himself with the Chinese food and decides to eat from the buffet. He can try different foods before he ventures out and orders another meal, so picks up a plate and starts down the buffet line, trying to figure out what some of the foods are. The green eggs, he tells himself, look terrible, but he remembers reading that they taste very good, so he puts one on his plate. He considers rice porridge, watermelon, and dried nuts, though these nuts don't look like what he eats at home. He also serves himself red bean soup, an orange drink, and hot tea, which he thinks may be green tea. He finishes off the first plate and drinks several extra cups of green tea. The food is not too bad, he tells himself when he gets in line for the second time. *No dumplings, though. I'm not sure what's inside them.* By this time twenty more people have arrived for breakfast and the line is starting to get longer.

Andre now notices some small, round cakes that are smaller in size than donuts, but much heaver, and without icing on them. A small sign beside them says *Moon Cakes.* As he is putting a couple of these on his plate, he remembers someone telling him about the moon cake and the time of year they are mostly sold. But he can't remember any details.

At the end of the buffet line sits a bowl of fortune cookies. As he takes one, he remembers that fortune cookies are popular in the United States, but not so much in China. It's a tourist thing. While he is having more tea and eating his moon cakes, he looks around to make sure no one is watching and slips a couple of the cakes into his pocket to eat later. After charging his meal to his room, he is ready for a new day.

Going out the front door of the hotel, he again heads for Binjiang Lu, which is down by the river. He pauses on the sidewalk, wondering if he has his translation book with him. He opens his backpack and finds it, then heads in the direction he took yesterday, thinking he might meet up with Shiao Hai again. Maybe they can go on a longer bike ride today. He reaches the spot where he left the boy yesterday, but Shiao Hai is not there, so he continues walking beside the river. Half an hour later, he spots Shiao Hai standing beside the path with his bike. He casually walks up and says, "*Ni hao.*"

Shiao Hai smiles back at him. "*Ni hao.*" Then he asks, "Go ride? Go ride?"

"Yes," Andre replies. "You are a very good business boy. I'm going to give you a tip today."

Shiao Hai doesn't know what Andre is saying, but he is still smiling when Andre digs in his pocket and comes up with ten *yuan* and gives him the tip. With serious look on his face, the boy accepts the money, says something quietly to himself, and cautiously puts the *yuan* in the pocket of his worn pants. Then, in a flash, the boy is smiling again. "We go," he says.

Andre slides onto the bike and Shiao Hai is on the back in one jump. "Are you on?" Andre asks over his shoulder, the boy replies, and off they go, Andre pedaling at a nice medium pace. He can feel the morning breeze in his face and the wind blowing through his hair. After riding for a while, Andre calls out, "Shiao Hai! Are you back there? You haven't fallen off, have you?" and starts laughing.

The little boy pokes Andre in the ribs and laughs back. Even though they cannot understand each other, they are becoming friends. They ride past fields where farmers are harvesting their crops of rice, sweet potatoes, and other types of vegetables and continue to ride under the massive banyan trees, all the while dodging workers walking on the trail. Soon Andre notices that they are getting close to where Shiao Hai keeps his buffalo herd.

A few minutes later, Shiao Hai calls out, "Stop, stop!" and Andre stops the bike. The boy jumps off the bike and produces a small bag of greens to feed the animals. He motions for Andre to follow, but Andre signals back to let him know he will be staying on the trail with the bike. With a nod of his head, Shiao Hai disappears into the bamboo

41

grove and a few minutes later, Andre can hear the splashing of water and the boy talking and laughing.

Andre parks the bike off the trail and walks over to a patch of grass under the edge of a giant banyan tree. He finds a nice fresh place on the grass and stretches out on it with his hands cupped under his head. Marveling at how fresh the air is, he closes his eyes. Soon he is asleep.

A short time later, Shiao Hai comes walking out of the bamboo grove. "Mine, mine" he says, and Andre wakes up. They get back on the bike and ride away, further out of town.

Chapter 19

After pedaling for awhile, Andre sees a young man ahead of them. He's wearing an orange robe with trousers of the same color and a black sash. He's fishing from the bank of the river. Andre decides to stop and see how many fish the man has caught and find out what kinds of fish are in the river.

"*Ni hao,*" Andre greets the fisherman, who replies, "*Ni hao.*" Andre gets out his translation book and looks at the front page, where he has written several English words and phrases with their Chinese translations. "*Duo sau yu?*" he asks the fisherman. "How many fish?"

"Six fish," the fisherman replies, and then he looks more closely at Andre. "Do you speak English?"

"Yes, I do."

"You look and sound like you are from the United States," the fisherman says.

"Yes, I am. I am from California." He smiles. "How is it that I'm here in the mountains of southern China, in the middle of nowhere, and I'm talking with a Chinese man who speaks English better than I do?"

"No, no," the fisherman replies. "I'm sure you speak better English than I do."

"Where did you learn to speak such good English?" Andre asks him.

"I'm a graduate of the University of Beijing."

"Great. And I'm a graduate of the University of California at Berkley. Hey, we have something in common!"

They both laugh, and Andre asks, "What was your major?"

"International law."

"Good, very good. With China becoming a superpower in the world economy, international law sounds like a needed profession."

"It is a good profession if you can find a job," the fisherman says with a shake of his head. "But it is very hard to get a decent job here. There are too many qualified people and not enough jobs. In order to find something, I need to go to another country. At the present time, it is very difficult to get a visa to the United States. Or anywhere else."

Andre takes a step closer to his new friend. "I'm a little puzzled," he says. "Does the robe you're wearing signify that you're a monk or something?"

"Yes," the fisherman says. "You are very close in your assumption. I'm in training at the school of the Shaolin Buddhist monastery nearby. I don't think I will become a total monk, though, if that is what you mean. Maybe a couple of years learning kung fu for self defense. And some mental discipline."

"That sounds fascinating."

While the two men are talking, Shiao Hai becomes bored and starts to examine the fish.

"What was your major?" the fisherman asks Andre.

"Microbiology."

"Interesting, very interesting."

"I have always been interested in the human body and the marvelous things the brain can do," Andre adds.

"What are the capabilities of the brain?" the fisherman asks.

"The brain is so mystically strong, a person can take his own life if he has a strong enough will," Andre says. "Not by means of suicide as we know it, but through a self-induced will to die. I have thought about some of the rare herbs and their abilities to trick the brain into doing things for the human body. Some of these herbs have been used for thousands of years. We are starting to learn new things about what they can and cannot do for the body. With the deciphering of the human DNA, there's no telling what lies ahead. For instance, if you have a senior couple who have been married for a very long time, and one of them dies, the pain the other might experience can be devastating. The brain can be so strong that the will to die can be overwhelming to the survivor."

"But," the fisherman interjects, "the brain takes care of the body whether we want its help or not."

"Yes, that's right," Andre agrees. "If a person's hearts stops and the brain is still functioning, legally, the person is still alive." Suddenly he stops and laughs. "Hey, I forgot to introduce myself. "My name is Andre, and this little guy is Shiao Hai." He puts out his hand to shake hands with the fisherman.

"Nice meeting both of you," the fisherman says. "My name is Jing Xian, and it's a real pleasure to meet you." He also turns around and shakes the hand of Shiao Hai.

"You said you're in training as a Shaolin Buddhist monk," Andre says. "Where is your monastery?" He turns in a slow circle, looking for the monastery.

"The monastery is located behind you," Jing Xian replies. "In this beautiful valley, up between those two jagged limestone peaks." He points in the direction of the monastery and tells Andre how to get there. "The dirt road that veers to the left will take you up there. It's about five kilometers. The road winds around these mysterious limestone pinnacles, then you go through several groves of giant bamboos. You also pass rice paddies and cross several streams. They're great for frog gigging and catching crawfish." Jing Xian interrupts himself. "Say— what about you two having lunch at the monastery as my guests? I will not accept a no. We have plenty of food. I'm just catching a few fish to add some fresh protein to our meal."

Andre considers the invitation for a minute. "Please explain to Shiao Hai that we will accompany you to the monastery for lunch," he says.

Jing Xian agrees, and as he tells Shiao Hai that they are going to have lunch at the monastery, Andre can tell that the boy is excited at the prospect of a good meal. "Ya, ya," the little guy says.

Jing Xian packs up his fishing gear and hands the line of fish to Shiao Hai. "Come with me," he says.

Chapter 20

Andre gets on his bike, Shiao Hai jumps on behind, still hanging on to the fish, Jing Xian gets on his bike, and they pedal down the dirt road heading for the monastery. They ride slowly through a dense grove of giant bamboo, some of the plants towering forty meters over their heads, then they pass rice and taro fields being harvested. The path then narrows and winds through dense undergrowth. The moss hanging from the trees and the limestone pinnacles completely obliterate the sun, which gives Shiao Hai a spooky feeling.

As they cross an old wooden bridge, Jing Xian slows down and says to Andre, "This is the creek where you can spear frogs in the evenings."

"I've never speared frogs before."

"Oh, it's easy, I'll show you sometime if you like."

They continue along the trail, and when they come to another stream, they need to remove their shoes and walk their bikes across the flowing water. Shortly before they arrive at the monastery, they approach an ancient bridge made of massive rocks. There is an alcove built into the front section for a guard or a sentry to stand in, but this guard box does not appear to have been used for a long time.

As they begin to cross the bridge, they come face to face with two crouching stone lions, one standing guard on each side. At three and a half meters high, these lions are huge, and Andre can hardly take his eyes off them.

At the entrance of the monastery stands a magnificent banyan tree that Andre imagines must be a couple hundred years old. Its canopy spreads out over a hundred meters, its massive limbs stretching out with tentacles of vines hanging down and attaching themselves to the ground. If this tree could talk, Andre thinks, it would tell some wild and interesting stories. The three new friends slowly ride their bikes through the main gate and under the arch of rocks.

"How old is this monastery?" Andre asks.

"Most of the buildings that are still standing are several hundred years old," Jing Xian replies. "The temple itself is probably five or six hundred years old. Through the centuries there have been many political and religious wars that have taken their toll on the monastery."

"This place is fantastic," is all Andre can say.

They follow a path in front of old, ornate wooden buildings with overhanging shingle roofs in the traditional Chinese pagoda style. Colorful flowers have been planted around the buildings.

"We will be going around the side of this next building," Jing Xian tells Andre. "That's where the kitchen and dining room are located."

Shiao Hai, still on the back of Andre's bike says something Andre doesn't understand. When they notice four or five young boys dressed similarly to Jing Xian going into one of the old buildings, Shiao Hai says something else and points at the boys.

"Hey, Jing Xian," Andre calls out. "Who are those little guys?" Are they Shaolin monks?" he asks with a laugh.

"No, Andre," the fisherman replies. "They are orphans. They have no parents. You might say the monastery is their family. There are seven of them that live here. They have their chores and assigned duties. They can live here as long as they want, as long as they follow the rules and do their chores. They are permitted to train with the older students in some studies, but most of the time they train with their own." He gets off his bike and continues his explanation. "First thing each morning, the monastery has a group tai chi class in the courtyard to stimulate the body and awaken the chi. Everyone is there including the grand master. He made that decision years ago, and it works."

"That sounds good," Andre replies.

"If we didn't have this class," his host continues, "there are some students who would never see anyone in the compound because of the special classes they take."

"What happened to the orphans' parents?" Andre asks.

"Oh," says Jing Xian, "there are many different stories. I know for sure two of the orphans were left at the entrance of the monastery one night. I haven't been here long enough to know about the other five. Like them, I'm in the learning stage here at the monastery."

Chapter 21

Jing Xian and his guests walk up to the front of the dining building, where about fifteen bicycles are parked in racks. "Let's park our bikes here," the monk says, and he tells Shiao Hai to take the fish through the side doors into the kitchen and give them to the cook. The boy says "Ya," and disappears into the building.

"Let's go inside and have a cup of tea," Jing Xian suggests to Andre. "We make our own. You can get creative and add your own ingredients." He takes Andre to a counter where all type of ingredients for coffees, teas, and herbal juices are set out. "We have chamomile flowers, hibiscus, and lemon grass. We have green, black, and oolong teas for people who need a stimulant," he adds. "And some peppermint leaves." He examines one of the herbs more closely. "I'm not sure what this is."

Now Shiao Hai comes out from the back room and joins them, telling Jing Xian that the fish have been delivered to the cook.

"*Xiexie,*" Jing Xian tells the boy. "Thank you." Then he turns to Andre again. "You know, we grow all of our herbs here. The chamomile flowers are the ones that grow around most of the buildings in the monastery. Please, let's sit down at one of these tables until the meal is ready."

Jing Xian points to a table, where they sit. "I can give you a brief description of what happens here at the monastery," he says. "It is open to anyone without a home or a place to stay as long as they follow the rules. No one is eligible for education at the monastery without first establishing a financial or working obligation. I have been told that every once in a while the school will get a student from a foreign country. These students stay for about six months, and then they leave and never return. I think they might stay longer if they prepare themselves before arriving. It's not what they expect," he adds with a smile. "The mental discipline is the hard part. It's not the physical part they can't adjust to. There are times the student wants to rush the process of being able to perform extraordinary feats. In doing so, sometimes they hurt themselves if they are not closely observed and trained correctly. The elder monks say the younger generation is too impatient. We expect things to happen too quickly. These students don't understand the Zen. They read about what some of the grand masters can do and they think it can be accomplished in a couple of months." He shakes his head. "They need to focus and practice meditation. Then things will happen. But enough of this! I think I have talked too much. You are my guests. We need to enjoy our meal."

They stand up, and Jing Xian tells Andre, "The meal will be a buffet, as you can tell by the way the food is being presented."

"Yes," Andre replies. "The hotel I'm staying at in Yangshuo helped me with some selections for breakfast and dinner last night."

"So you must be close to being an expert on Chinese food by now." Jing Xing gives him a big smile.

"Oh, no, no," Andre replies with a laugh. "I'm a long way from that. I will need a lot of help to be even close to being an expert. Most likely, it will be through trial and error." He thinks for a moment and adds, "Practice makes perfect. That's what I will most likely convert to." He laughs again.

"Okay," Jing Xian replies. "We will help."

Then the two young men become quiet.

Chapter 22

"Jing Xian," Andre says after a long minute, "I don't remember if I told you the main reason for my coming to Yangshuo. "I …" he pauses, "I … I was in search of the Shaolin monastery. I read about the school in this ad in the back of an old travel magazine while I was still in the Black Hills of South Dakota on a sabbatical of sorts. Do you know where South Dakota is?"

"No," Jing Xian replies, "I can't say I remember a state by that name."

"I didn't think you would," Andre says. "It's a state in the mid-northern part of the United States. It's a very beautiful state with a lot of open space for their plains buffalo and elk to roam. There's not a lot of people or industry in the state. Mostly trees, mountains, and open plains." As Jing Xian nods, Andre thinks back to the ad he read. "In the ad for the monastery," he says, "there was no address, telephone number, or even instructions on how to get here. Except the article said the Shaolin monastery was close to the Li River in the vicinity of the city Yangshuo in the Limestone Mountains of southern China." He smiles. "So it took me several bus tickets, three airline tickets, several van rides, and some good luck to get here. But I made it! My coming here was not an accident."

Jing Xian has a baffled look on his face. "This is puzzling to me," he says. "You need to tell me more. Why here? And why so far away from home?"

Andre follows Jing Xian and Shiao Hai through the buffet line, along with several other monks who arrive and get in line behind them. As he looks at the food, he notices that the monastery has more fruit selections than the hotel where he ate breakfast. He sees oranges, kumquats, pears, blueberries, bananas, and apples. They make their selections, including some of the fish that Jing Xian caught, and return to their table.

Andre looks over to see what Shiao Hai is eating, but he doesn't recognize it. It's obvious to him that the little guy likes it. He has gobbled down the whole thing. When, Andre suddenly wonders, was the last time the boy had a full meal? The fish Jing Xian caught are very tasty, as the monastery cooks have added a few pinches of herbs.

After they finish eating, Jing Xian asks Shiao Hai several questions in Chinese. Hearing the boy's response, he looks concerned. He asks several more questions, and the answers make him look more troubled. He turns to Andre and asks, "Do you know very much about your buddy, Shiao Hai? Like where he lives? Or anything about his parents?"

"No," Andre says. "No, I don't know anything about him. I've known him only a couple of days." He tries to remember what he and Shiao Hai have been doing together. "On the first day I met him," he says, "we rode his bicycle several miles out of town. He showed me his herd of about half dozen water buffaloes that he keeps in a bamboo grove alongside the river. He told me the buffaloes were his. His English is very broken, and I don't know anything else about them. Or him. Today, I met him again on the trail going out of Yangshuo and rented his bike for ten *yuan*. I felt sorry for him and gave him more than three times his asking price for a ride on his bike. I didn't know he was going to accompany me again, but now I guess we've become something like buddies. All this time, I can't understand him and he can't understand me, so we've been using sign language and a few words I know in Chinese." Suddenly he gives Jing Xian a stern look and says, "You don't think Shiao Hai and I are doing something illegal, do you? Sex or something like that?"

"No, no, no," says Jing Xian. "No, I'm not thinking anything like that. Not even close, my friend. You see, Shiao Hai is an orphan. He doesn't have a home. I was wondering if you knew he didn't have a family. Or where he was staying."

"Oh, thank God. You scared the heck out of me for a moment."

Jing Xian nods. "I just asked Shiao Hai if he remembers his family, you know, mother and father, and he has no memory of them at all. The only family he knows is the guy that is letting him sleep on the floor in his spare room. His friend is a man about thirty years old, no wife. Sometimes he's gone for many days. Shiao Hai told me the man doesn't know anything about him. He feels sorry for Shiao Hai and lets him stay in the small room in the back of his house. Shiao Hai has never been to a school. The Chinese and English he speaks are what he has learned on his own, mostly from the tourists he meets who rent his bicycle. He buys his own food because his friend can't afford food for both of them. The money he's getting from the bike rental is his food money."

"Golly," Andre says, "I feel so bad for him." He looks over at Shiao Hai, who gives him a big smile.

"Do you know what Shiao Hai means in the Chinese language?" Jing Xian asks.

"Well, it's his name."

"Yes, I know it's his name. But do you know what it means?"

"No, I don't."

"It means Little Boy. Someone must have called him that several times, and he assumed it was his name. So now he tells everyone his name is Shiao Hai. Little Boy." Jing Xian pauses. "I don't think he has a real name."

"I feel bad about that," Andre says.

"There's nothing you could have done. You didn't know."

"Yeah."

"It seems there was some kind of tragedy in his life. He lost his parents, and the system lost him, so he's been on his own, just surviving. I wonder if his parents are alive or dead. Sometime the parents just can't afford a child and let him go. Put him out on his own."

"I'm really sorry!" Andre exclaims. Then he asks Jing Xian, "Is there something you're thinking about? You seem very concerned."

"Yes. Considering these unusual circumstances in meeting Shiao Hai, I'm thinking he might qualify for the orphan program here at the monastery. The administration needs to investigate his background to confirm that he really is an orphan. We can send an investigator to where he lives. Not a real investigator, like a policeman, if you know what I mean, but someone will go to where Shiao Hai is staying and talk with neighbors and anyone who knows him to find out what he has been doing. Things like that."

"That sounds like a great idea."

"You're probably wondering how I know so much about this program since I've been here for such a short time," Jing Xian says. "As part of my duties, I assist with administrative duties."

"In just the short time that I have known Shiao Hai," Andre says, "he seems like a wonderful little guy. He has a great personality and is very alert. He's just a little kick in the pants, so full of life."

Jing Xian chuckles. "Considering what you've told me about his business management in renting a bicycle, and his having a small herd of buffalo, he sounds like he's some kind of entrepreneur. He might have some business ideas that we can implement here at the monastery. I asked the little guy what he thought about living here, and he likes the idea. He would have many friends and get three meals a day and a clean bed to sleep in every night. Coming here is not guaranteed," he adds, "because we have to do some paperwork and visit where he lives. I will have to talk with him later to make sure he understands what I told him. This whole thing about him coming here has just occurred to me in the last hour."

Chapter 23

"Now what about you, Andre?" Jing Xian asks, "Are you coming here, too? I think it's great to have both of you coming here at the same time. We need to have a meeting so I can explain everything you need to know before coming to the monastery." He pauses to eat more fish. "Now getting back to Shiao Hai," he says, "I was getting side-tracked for a moment. He has some concern about his water buffalo. I told him we have a large lake further up in the valley, about two kilometers from here, where he might be able to keep them. We also could use them for plowing in the fields, and that's okay with him. Actually I think the buffalo would enjoy a little exercise. Oh, and I forgot—the bicycle he owns is too big for him to pedal. I'm sure we'll be able to get him one that's more his size. He'll be able to ride out to check on the buffalo in his free time."

"Jing Xian," Andre breaks in, "I have a plan that I'm sure will please you."

"Oh?"

"Yes. I have money. Not with me, but I can get it wired here overnight. I want to pay for Shiao Hai's admission, plus room and board until he reaches the age of eighteen or nineteen. Maybe twenty. Then he can make his own decision about what he wants to do. But there's one thing that I insist that the monastery does, or the deal is off."

"And what would that be?"

"I want the monastery to teach him how to read and write his natural-born language, Chinese. And English, too. He must become an expert in mathematics and chemistry. Teach him to be a man of refinement, with the manners and protocol he should know. Who knows? He may stay here for his entire life. But that would be his decision. We can talk about finances later," Andre adds. "The money will not be a problem."

"That sounds great," Jing Xian responds. "I really hope you're not doing this out of pity for Shiao Hai."

"I am, in a roundabout way," Andre admits. "In a way, I feel sorry for him. He was doing the only thing he knew to survive. He has a good head on his shoulders. He wasn't begging or trying to steal from me. Just the thought of him makes me want to do anything I can for him."

"Well, I think you're doing one of the most commendable things I have ever heard of." They both watch Shiao Hai, who is walking around in the dining room and looking at the murals on the walls.

"Andre," Jing Xian says after a minute, "while you're here, you need to start processing your paperwork. Tell me, are you using an investment account to finance your and Shiao Hai's admission?"

"No. My dad owns a large import/export company in San Francisco that is doing extremely well. An expense fund has been set up for me to use until he's ready to retire. Shortly before I graduated, he told me to go out and have fun until he was ready to retire. Then he'll give me the business. I agreed, and now I'm traveling the world."

"I notice you haven't said anything about your mother."

"My mother died of cancer about seven years ago. She and my dad loved to travel all over the world. They always showed me the photo albums from their trips. Some places, I couldn't even pronounce the names." He laughs. "I wonder if they didn't happen to stop by here on one of their voyages."

"Well," Jing Xian replies with a smile, "we can check the records."

Andre continues talking about his family. "When my mother died, my father took it very hard. He almost went nuts. I was getting ready to go away to college, but I decided to postpone it for a year. He occasionally dated, but he couldn't find the right one. Then he told me I needed to go to college and not to worry about him. He said I should have fun. Life is way too short. We talk every once a while. I get along well with his private secretary. Her name is Stacey. She keeps me posted on what's happening with the business and what my father is doing. You will most likely be receiving correspondence from her about my finances. And anything else you need to know."

Chapter 24

"Hey," says Jing Xian, "I think Shiao Hai finished eating a long time ago. If we don't get out of here," he adds with a laugh, "they're going to charge us rent."

Andre calls out to Shiao Hai, and all three of them go outside to their bikes. "You two follow me over to the administration building," Jing Xian says, "so I can start the paperwork for both of you."

He gets on his bike and pedals off, with Andre and Shiao Hai following close behind. The two men continue their conversation as they ride down the street.

"Andre, are you familiar with what is taught here at the monastery?"

"No, I'm not."

"We teach all types of classes. Some are taught by request. There are advanced classes in Shaolin kung fu, and several other advanced classes."

But Andre politely cuts him off and explains the real reason why he wants to be trained. He is searching for his personnel zen.

A few minutes later, Jing Xian stops. "Here we are, guys," he says. "This is the administration building. Park your bike in that rack and come on in." He parks his own bike and starts up the steps to the entrance of the building." Andre and Shiao Hai follow him to his office.

"If you want any tea," Jing Xian says, "it's over there on the table. I'll have some hot water in a few minutes, as soon as I get this tea pot turned on." He makes himself some cold green tea while waiting for the hot water and sits down at his desk. "Andre," he says, "you were explaining your reason for coming to the monastery. Please continue."

"I can tell you more details later," Andre says. "First, let me explain what I've been doing this last year. Then you will understand. I hope." Andre now tells Jing Xian about the Native American medicine man and the spiritual meditation in the Black Hills. He gives his experience in detail, with the insertion of the bat bones into his forearm, which gave him the ability to travel in the dark. He then explains his desire to go spiritually within his body, which is why he is seeking Chinese Zen and the possibility of attaining enlightenment through meditation or other means.

"How," he asks Jing Xian, "how does the body respond to such things as the effects of certain herbs? What basic function does a cell have with the thought pattern of a human mind? How can a human communicate with certain cells in the brain? I came up with this crazy idea years before I went to college. In school, I tried taking classes that would help me develop my idea, but nothing even came close to what I was seeking."

He pauses to make himself some tea and take a sip, then continues. "After hearing about the spiritual guidance I could receive from the medicine man, I went to the Black Hills, where the Indian spirit is very strong. Their spiritual medicine helped me to some degree, but not on the real search. After doing some research in the local library, I decided to see what I can do for myself with the teaching of a Shaolin grand master. I do realize it's not going to be an easy task, and there is going to be frustration. I've been planning for this experience for a long time. I want to see where these teachings will take me. I hope it won't be in vain."

Andre pauses again. "Jing Xian," he finally says, "it's like what you were telling me about the students who come here who think they're going to conquer the world in a couple of months. No way would that happen. I know it. I have been studying and waiting for this opportunity for a long time. I'm not here at the monastery for the physical part of kung fu training. But I'm open to some classes for self-defense to stay in shape if my brain starts to stress."

"You amaze me," Jing Xian replies. "Just listening to you, I'm amazed to hear what you've accomplished and the goal you've set for yourself. It's amazing, what you've just told me. You have a strong conviction to see it through, no matter at what cost. You do know it can get extremely dangerous, I'm sure of that."

"Yes," Andre replies, "but I made up my mind many years ago."

"Who else knows about what you're attempting?"

"Well, I mentioned it to my dad one time, but he thought I was crazy and blew it off. I've also talked with my dad's personal secretary, Stacey. You might say she's my confidant. I remember my father hiring her many years ago. She's quite an attractive woman. Very charming personality and extremely intelligent. I recall the time she told me that my dad was trying to get a little sexy with her. She told me she set him straight, and he never bothered her again." Andre pauses, then looks straight at Jing Xian. "You know, she knows all of my secrets. Some of my most embarrassing moments."

Jing Xian laughs. "Secrets, secrets. Don't tell me any now. Tell them to me another day when we have more time." He pulls a sheaf of papers out of his desk drawer.

Chapter 25

"Okay," Jing Xian says, "here are the papers. Read them, fill them out, and sign them. The sooner you get them filled out, the sooner both you and Shiao Hai will become residents here."

Andre looks through the papers and says, "I can fill them out right now so you can start processing them today."

Jing Xian nods his head. "Andre, I can have someone go to Yangshuo today to get the required information on Shiao Hai and be back here in a couple of hours."

"That's great."

"I think Shiao Hai is in the library looking at some books. I'm going to explain to him what is going to happen. I need to get more information from him. So while you're filling out your papers, I'll be with him. I'll be back shortly."

"Okay." When Andre finishes the paperwork, he relaxes in the office for several hours while an investigating monk from the monastery goes to Yangshuo and returns with the required information about the boy.

When Jing Xian comes back, he finds Andre and Shiao Hai both sleeping on the sofa. "Hello," he says.

Andre opens one eye. "Come back in a couple of hours."

"Come on, guys," Jing Xian replies. "I have all the information we need now. Everything is looking good. I'll be making a few phone calls late tonight because of the time difference between here and the United States, and then you'll be living here. It doesn't appear that Shiao Hai really needs to return to where he was living. We can accommodate him right away. Tonight." He explains this in Chinese to the boy, saying that Andre will have to take his bicycle back to Yangshuo to get his belongings. The boy agrees to this.

Then Jing Xian turns to Andre again. "As for you," he says, "I think you will need to get your belongings from your hotel and check out tomorrow. If everything turns out right, and I don't think otherwise, you will be sleeping here tomorrow night."

Andre and Shiao Hai are thus enrolled into the Shaolin monastery. Shiao Hai will live there until he grows up, at which time he will be able to make his own decision for his future. Andre has provided the financial means for him to stay at the monastery for as long as he wants.

Andre's strongest wish is to receive training in the mental processes of the Shaolin monks. He has always believed the human mind has the greatest power of all living creatures on the earth and beyond. The human mind can think, it has perceptions, it has memory and imagination, and it maintains its own body, which is the human body. Human beings have barely scratched the surface of understanding the mind and its abilities and limitations. It is the imagination, the curiosity, that is the initiator of the brain, which in turn directs the mental behavior of the sentient organism.

Andre has found a place that will take care of Shiao Hai for a long time. What he needs is education, three meals a day, a place to sleep, and the boy will also have friends. He has also signed himself up for one year program, maybe more, if things are what he thinks they will be. His main desire is to learn the basic art of kung fu, and he will also study to obtain personal enlightenment. He has already made a good Chinese friend, Jing Xian, who will help him with the required training.

Andre is still thinking about what a superior mind can do if there are no limitations. He remembers when he learned about Albert Einstein, the German-born American scientist who came up with the theory of relativity, a man whose name became synonymous with the word "genius." He was awarded the Nobel Prize for Physics, and Andre also remembers that *Time* magazine (sometime around 1999, though Andre can't remember the exact year), called Einstein the "Person of the Twentieth Century" and the supreme intellect of all time. Some experts said Einstein used about ten percent of his brain in his lifetime. *Unbelievable*, Andre thinks, *what he could do with his mind, only using a small part of it. If he had used more of his brain, there is no telling what he could have done. And all of Einstein's thinking was generated by curiosity.*

Chapter 26

Andre is sitting in a chair in the corner of the meeting room, looking over some papers that Jing Xian gave him. A tall, elegant, elderly man wearing a full length crimson robe and sandals enters the room. His head is bald, presumably shaven, and he wears wire-rimmed glasses, which sit on the tip of his nose. He appears to be a man who has taken extremely good care of himself. He approaches Andre.

"Hello, Andre Roberson," the man says. "I want to introduce myself to you. My name is Shibo Xin Lin. I'm the Grand Master here."

Andre immediately stands and bows.

"Please, please be seated," says the grand master. He pauses, then continues. There is one other master here, too. I hope this is a good time for you. I wanted to meet you and welcome you to the monastery."

"First of all," Shibo continues, "Jing Xian told me you have taken care of the financial responsibility for the new orphan named Shiao Hai, who arrived here the same time as you. I presume you knew him."

"Yes," Andre replies, "we became friends quite quickly. He sure is quite an entrepreneur with the bicycle business. I'm not sure what he uses the water buffalo for. They were a bit scary to me."

"He is a very smart little boy, and we are blessed to have him here, possibly for a long time if he wants to stay. He will be enrolled in our *tong zi gong* class. It's an exercise class for virgin boys that includes external, internal, and soft exercises. It must be practiced under the supervision of a coach; otherwise the qi inside the body will be disturbed. If the exercise is practiced successfully, the body may become as flexible as springs and as hard as iron. Doing this exercise from childhood will keep a person young and healthy forever. In this class, he will become associated with other orphans and earn their friendship. From there, we will see what sorts of things he is interested in. I have talked with him. He indicated he has not received any type of education, so it will be a challenge for him and for us as teachers.

"You, my friend," the grand master continues, "are welcome to stay at the monastery for as long as you want. You must do what is required, as the other students and monks are required to do."

"That's fair enough," Andre replies.

"Briefly, we teach Mandarin, Cantonese, and some English classes. There have been several requests for a French class, but that may not happen for a while. If we get enough requests, we will have the class, but otherwise it will be put on hold. Students can also choose to study a language full-time, without training in the martial arts. Students must have a good character and adhere to the same rules and regulations as those studying the martial arts.

"Every morning at six o'clock, we wake up for training in qi gong, and tai chi. This is a mandatory session which gets the blood flowing and stretches the muscles. This is important for all students, regardless of their training plans at the monastery. Students can study languages, mathematics, science, and/or astrology half the time, and martial arts the other half."

The grand master pauses, then continues. "I have read on your application what you would like to be taught. I find it somewhat different from most applications from new students. You want to study more of the personal zen and enlightenment than kung fu, which is more physical."

"Yes," Andre replies. He tells the grand master what he experienced while in the Black Hills with the Sioux medicine man and the insertion of the bat bones, uniting his senses through metamorphosis with those of a bat.

"I find the process of transformation extremely interesting," Shibo comments. "You must tell me more at a time that is convenient for both of us." He then continues explaining the basic idea of the personal zen. "You will study and understand the personal zen in more detail in your classes, but right now I will explain briefly what it is. It's the process of absorption and concentration that brings the mind to a point where it may be awakened. A motionless thought results in positive changes to the brain. Decisive changes result in a transformation of the person who is capable of living fully in the now and also feeling conjoined to all things."

"I felt the same feeling when the medicine man taught me his art of meditation," Andre says.

"Yes, I'm sure you had a pleasurable and lasting experience." The grand master continues his brief dissertation on the personal zen. "Regular meditation will elevate the immune system and lower stress levels. There is a section of the human brain that acclimates us to time and space; this is referred to as the parietal lobe. When this part of the brain shuts down during meditation, a translocation, or loss, of your area of senses is attained, resulting in a feeling of unity with the cosmos. Mental restraint achieved by calmness. Tranquility will bring about physiological changes no one has dreamed of before. As teachers, we are limited by words. The physical and mental parts are up to the pupil and his ability to gain strength and confidence."

Shibo pauses and looks at the papers he has in his hands. "You have been down the road with training in meditation with the Sioux Indians in the Black Hills. The training you received, I imagine, was excellent. The training you will receive here will be just as good, and even better. I guarantee it. What you told me earlier about the meditation you were taught by the medicine man I will want to discuss further, but as you can see I'm quite busy now. I hope to get back with you one of these days."

Chapter 27

"I will tell you one thing for sure." Shibo pauses again and studies Andre's face. "When I first saw you come into the monastery, I knew by the way you carried yourself that you were a special person. Your ease and agility create a mystical air about you. How lightly and exactly you placed your feet, and yet so firm and positive connecting to the earth. It is the way your foot falls on the earth that reminds me of how the snow leopard of the Himalayas moves so surefooted and effortlessly through his mountainous terrain. It has been a long time since I have seen someone with your demeanor. I'm referring to a highly praised abbot in northern China. Normally, I don't have in-depth personal talks with my students, but you stood out, and now I'm satisfied that we have talked."

Shibo pauses again. "I think you will enjoy another special class we have. The class I'm referring to is taught outside in the woods and inside on the wooden floor. Studying outside gives the students the ability to learn balance. I'm sure you have perfected that ability. There are few classes taught in the forest environment. They are reserved for advanced students. This special class teaches the art of walking stealthily on rice paper while maintaining perfect balance. Students learn how to place their feet without leaving an impression or disturbance on the paper. They learn control of their hips and feet in conjunction with their balance. The abdominal muscles and the spine are the most important parts of the body, making rice paper walking an act of perfection. And, finally, there is the spiritual guidance the student must obey. As the saying goes, *a walker you do not see leaves no footprints.*"

The old man nods his head. "I'm sure you will enjoy this class. I will be teaching it. Oh, and one more thing, and then I must definitely go. Next month we are having a special visitor, the Grand Master Shaolin Buddhist Monk Da Ming. He is from a monastery in the northern part of the country, around Dengfeng. Da Ming specializes in offensive moves of an extraordinary kung fu art by creating pain, using only his hands. For many years, he has translated and developed the practice through reading the ancient war books. He can pinpoint natural obstructions in the human body and use them to his advantage. This process is similar to acupuncture or acupressure, but much more complicated. Finding the points to use is the opposite of acupuncture."

The grand master thinks a moment, then goes on. "The grand master I'm taking about teaches how to grasp, squeeze, and press these points in certain ways which creates the most unbearable pain anyone could experience. In some instances, he is able to inflict pain on an individual without touching him or using an instrument. I have not seen him perform, but I have heard about him. He is an extremely interesting brother monk. There was an incident where a combatant chose to die rather than continue with the master's process. In ancient times, this technique was used to extract information from the enemy without the use of torture, which is too messy. It was also used when one didn't have a weapon like a club, a rock or a knife to inflict pain and eventually death. I think this would be an excellent class for you. I just have a feeling you are the right person for this class.

"Well, Andre," he concludes, "it was nice to meet you. If you will excuse me now, I have a class to teach. Hopefully, I will be getting back with you in the near future. Please get with Jing Xian for setting up the classes you would like."

"Thank you very much for your time and information." Andre stands up again and bows as the grand master leaves the room.

Chapter 28

"Hello, Andre," Jing Xian calls out as he knocks on the door.

"Come on in," Andre replies. "Please sit down. You look like a busy man."

"Yes. We have two more new students besides you and Shiao Hai. I'm trying to get everyone settled in. Andre, I have the list of classes you can apply for right now, although some of them have a waiting list. You need to wait until those students finish, which could take time, as they don't have a definite completion time."

When Andre nods, Jing Xian continues. "I will explain how the classes are basically taught. There are students who take longer to become physically and mentally challenged before they are tested for the completion of the course. If there are enough students who are slower, they will be grouped into another class learning the same thing, but at a different pace.

"I need to mention that the word 'slow,' as in learning and physical ability, is not used in front of students. Some students take the word as meaning 'slightly stupid,' 'can't learn,' 'a waste of time.' That idea does not exist here at the monastery. Only after everyone is finished will they start the class again. When a student takes longer than normal to accomplish an assignment, it is noted in his file. We evaluate each student by how many times he misses his set dates. Some students are excellent in their studies but take longer to accomplish the physical part. It is not a bad thing to be slow. We want to be sure we don't rush the students. This can be the opposite in some studies, where a student excels and gets way ahead of the others. When this happens, we will remove the student from the class and have individual classes to advance his abilities. If we find more than one gifted student, we will have a small group of advanced students. We do not feel that everyone is equal. Their physical and mental abilities are at different levels. Everyone here will learn, but at his own speed. Okay, Andre, here is the list of some of the words you will be hearing. They will be foreign to you, but over a period of time they will come naturally." Jing Xian hands Andre the list.

"In the evening after dinner," he continues, "some of the students get together in study groups. They review what was taught that day and help each other if they have problems. These study groups are helpful because the older students give advice on what may be taught the next day. This has been going on for a long time, and the masters have not said anything about students giving out the secrets for the next day's teaching. I'm sure the grand master knows what has been happening. He knows almost everything that takes place here at the monastery. As long as everything is going well in the classes, and the students are doing extremely well mentally and physically, there will be no changes."

Jing Xian continues. "Now back to the words you will be encountering. *Wu Shu* in Chinese means 'martial arts.' In the English language, kung fu means 'effort, work time in the martial arts training.' So *Wu* means martial arts, and S*hu* means the skills you will be trained in. When you hear the words *gong fu*, you need to work hard to develop your skill. I know you can't remember all these phrases, but you will over a matter of time as you get more involved with the arts.

"Here at the monastery, we teach the traditional Shaolin qi gong, the traditional kung fu, but we also have special classes if we get enough students wishing to learn something special. We get questions from students who wonder how much are they going to be able to learn. The best answer is this. To what degree a student will learn depends on his physical and mental abilities and his dedication to practice and if he gives one hundred and plus percent. In conducting classes, we use the training hall when the weather is not adaptable to our means. We also conduct classes outside in the yard, where you can breathe in the nice, fresh, clean air. We also have special rooms on the grounds where you can train in total silence. In these rooms, the only sounds you will hear are your heartbeat and the surging of your breath between your lips. These rooms were built with extremely thick walls for meditating and listening to your inner feelings. If you need a room, you need to sign up early. Some students use the rooms for meditation, and others use them for improving their techniques using the mirrors. All the rooms are the same, with a padded floor, a table and chair, and one wall covered entirely by mirrors. The rooms are identified on the sign up list. Are there any questions so far?"

"No," Andre replies. "Everything sounds ideal so far."

"You did mention you're not interested in the traditional kung fu, but more in the direction of less stringent physical exercises. You want to focus on a way of life that encourages clarity of mind in perusing the *modus operandi* of your personal zen, eventually seeking personal enlightenment."

"Yes, that's correct," Andre responds. He also tells Jing Xian that Grand Master Shibo told him about the visit next month of Grand Master Da Ming from the Dengfeng Monastery in the north of China and that he will be teaching the technical process of administering pain. "I told the master I would be interested in his teaching," Andre adds.

"That's fine," replies Jing Xian. "I just heard about the class myself, and we have five students who have signed up. I understand this pain technique was popular with influential people two thousand years ago. The technique seems to have been stopped abruptly about two hundred years ago, though no one seems to know why. I was talking with Master Shibo. He's not familiar with the art, but he's going to try and find its history from the ancient books. He said he will try to have the information for the students by the time Master Da Ming arrives."

"I'm interested in the class very much," Andre says.

"I myself am interested in the physical part of kung fu," comments Jing Xian. "For you, we have several classes in the gentle movements. First is a slow qi gong. The second one is tai chi, which is good for centering and promoting good health. Both of these movements are for people of all ages. When working with tai chi, you may experience a feeling called the *chi*. It's a mystical tingling you will feel in your body if the chi is working. Starting at the top of your head the chi travels down through your body to your feet. The sensation feels terrific once you learn how to create it. Tai chi shouldn't be viewed as merely an exercise. You should imagine yourself at the center of your own universe as you circle around. You expand your body and your mind outwards, upwards, back, and down as to the energy of the universe expands in all directions. Your blood and breath travel throughout the complete you as that universe. I will show you where we conduct the class when we take the tour of the monastery."

"That tai chi sounds terrific," Andre replies.

Jing Xian continues. "There are students who want hard physical classes, but they also take the tai chi class to cool down their inner self and feel its tranquility. Early each morning after breakfast and before classes begin, everyone in the monastery participates in a twenty-minute open session in the courtyard. One individual in the front of the group wearing white gloves is the leader. Just try to do what he is doing. Later, after some practice and concentration, you will start to learn the different movements and you'll start to enjoy it. Eventually you will find the chi."

"There is one more class I would like to sign up for," says Andre. "Master Shibo mentioned it to me. I think he said the name of the class is the stealth walking class."

"Yes, yes," Jing Xian replies. "I'm glad you mentioned the class. Shortly before I came here, Master Shibo mentioned that he will be teaching it. He also mentioned that the classes will be divided into four stages. One class will be conducted in the auditorium, another one will be in the snow and cold weather, the third will be in water, and the fourth will be using sharp objects. There are no scheduled dates for the classes right now. Master Shibo said he would like to see you sign up for the class. He will learn something from you."

Andre hesitates for a few seconds. "I'm totally flattered by his comment. Yes, I will be attending his class. But I will be learning more from his teachings then he will learn from me about my bat movements."

Chapter 29

As the weeks pass, Andre settles into the way of life at the monastery, though at first, it is hard for him to understand the schedule and get to classes on time. He and Jing Xian have become good friends by now, and they take a few classes together, after which they meet and talk with each other. In the evenings, after getting a few pointers from the advanced students in the study group, Andre and Jing Xian ride their mountain bikes to the river. Sometimes they race all the way, which keeps them in top physical condition. Occasionally they also see Shiao Hai with his new friends. The little guy is having a terrific time getting acquainted with his classmates and learning to read and speak Chinese and English. He has also been concerned about how his water buffalo are doing and if they are were being fed.

One day while Jing Xian is driving to Yangshuo in the monastery's truck to pick up supplies, he notices a couple of boys paddling their small boats out to the big tourist boats. He stops the truck to watch them sell Chinese souvenirs. When he tells Andre about this, they decide to build a small boat themselves. This is not an easy task, but with help of older, more experienced monks who have lived on the river all their lives, the young men succeed.

After making one boat, they realize they each need to have a boat because their schedules and destinations on the river are different. After completing the second boat, they are ready to start making money for the monastery. First, they get the approval of Grand Master Shibo, then they make arrangements with the monastery's art department to create statutes of emperors, crouching lions, dragons, warriors, and other souvenirs to sell to the tourists. Several days a week (between classes), they paddle their boats into the river, approach the big tourist boats, and sell souvenirs to the tourists. Occasionally, of course, a crew member of a big tourist boat does not let them hang on. There is no hostility here; it's just that the captains don't want to have accidents with the little boats.

Thanks to the success of Andre and Jing Xian in earning money for the monastery, other students are soon inspired to join the venture.

Chapter 30

One day Grand Master Shibo meets with Jing Xian and asks him to notify the students who are signed up for the pain class that the instructor will arrive the next day.

Early the next morning, therefore, Andre arrives at the room where the class is to be conducted and sits down with seven other students. Shortly after his arrival, in walks a weathered monk dressed in a long, red, grand master's robe. As he walks across the room, shuffling his feet, he looks like a little, frail old man, shorter than any student in the class. He is wearing a pair of rimless glasses, and on the tip of his chin are five gray whiskers about six inches long, which he strokes from time to time. He has no hair on his head except for a scraggly white ponytail hanging down his back. He stops in front of the class and begins to clean his eyeglasses with a corner of his robe. Then he speaks in a soft voice.

"Hello, students. I am Grand Master Da Ming." He pauses and takes a sip of water. "I will be teaching you today, and only today, so pay attention. Most likely, this will be the only time you will have a class of this type in your entire life. I will show you how to administer pain. I will answer all of your questions." Master Da Ming pauses and gives a small smile as he slowly looks over the students. "I find it interesting when I look at students who wish to learn this ancient process of inflicting pain. Some of you look very stern, yet there are others who look like they are in shock. I realize that everyone is nervous the first hour of class. That is normal. After the class is over, you will have a better understanding of your inner feelings. The point is not to think you are a sadistic person who likes to inflict pain, but to think by whose authority the pain is being administered."

The master pauses again. "This technique was an effective tool in its day. It made many emperors happy when they got the information they wanted. But things have changed over time. People still want information and will do anything to get it. It seems that in this last century the human race has gone to using drugs, which can be every effective. But when drugs are used, it often has different effects on people, one of which is the tendency to kill the person who has the information. Just in the last three hundred years, some of the most powerful and not-so-powerful countries on this earth have used drugs. They have used all sorts of apparatuses of torture in dark rooms: water, wooden racks, electricity, and anything else one can think of to extract information from uncooperative people. Most of these people never survive the interrogation."

"That *is* torture," says a student.

"Yes, my son, you are absolutely right. Torture in some countries is a hushed-up thing." The master smiles and nods. "After you have learned the procedure, you will find deep in your soul the foundation of good and bad. Remember this: there will always be a good and a bad. You have to know when you are right. Don't be hasty or abusive with the technique. Remember the values of its application. It is an art. Be proud of what you have learned. Always keep in mind how and when to use it."

The master scuffles over to where Andre is seated. "I'm sure you would like to see a demonstration," he says. Why is he selecting Andre? Maybe because Andre is sitting on the end seat closest to the master. Maybe because of the meeting he had with Grand Master Shibo upon his arrival at the monastery.

Grand Master Da Ming addresses Andre. "I'm sure you would be happy to be my demonstrator."

Caught off guard, Andre can only reply, "Yes."

"Would you please stand?"

Andre immediately obeys.

Master Da Ming shuffles up to about two feet from Andre and shows him and the other students there is nothing in his hands. He then comes closer to Andre until they are almost touching. "Son," he says, smiling as he meekly looks up into Andre's eyes, "if the demonstration becomes too painful, please let me know immediately, and I will stop. Please do not be shy. I do not wish to make anything painful for anyone."

"Yes, Master Da Ming." Andre is feeling a little apprehensive, yet positive, because he has a large strong body compared to such a frail little man. Then he thinks to himself, *Did I make a mistake? No. It's okay.*

It can't be that bad. This little man doesn't appear to be in good health, so what could go wrong?

"Just relax, my son." The master shows the students his bare hands again. He then instructs Andre to raise his arms and place the palms of his hands on his own chest. The master now wraps his thin arms around Andre's waist, clasping his hands behind Andre's back and making sure he is not touching him. A few seconds pass. Andre is thinking, *I know he is going to touch me, but I feel nothing.*

Immediately, as if from nowhere, he gets a sharp, penetrating pain. It feels like someone has just thrust an ice pick into his side. He tries to spin away from the master, but he cannot move. Panic starts to take over. He tries to control it, but there is nothing he can do. He is paralyzed, The severe pain is getting worse. *Maybe I'm having a heart attack*, he thinks, then he starts to become delusional. *Something's gone wrong. Got to get away.* He starts to get light-headed, and his legs become extremely weak. *I'm getting sick to my stomach, going to pass out.* Suddenly the pain is gone, as quickly as it came.

"Are you feeling better?" asks the grand master.

"I'm not sure. ... I think so." Andre's voice sounds sluggish. He touches the spot where the pain came from, rubbing it several times, but there is no needle in his skin, nothing sharp attached to his robe. He looks at his hands. There is no blood. He looks at the master and whispers, "The pain was almost unbearable." Then he corrects himself. "No. The pain *was* unbearable. It was so awful I couldn't do anything. I was starting to panic."

The instructor asks one of the other students to help Andre back to his seat. Then he looks at each student in turn, gazing into their eyes. "Students," he says, "I would like to say that my very brave demonstrator made a comment that I don't think you heard. He said the pain was *almost unbearable.* I beg to differ with him. The pain was at the intensity I wanted it to be at. Moving my hands, squeezing at the right spot, regulating the precise pressure, I was in control in a matter of seconds. I was not sure how much pain my demonstrator would be able to withstand. I made adjustments and was a bit lenient on him."

The master nods at Andre, then surveys the rest of the class again. "So, students, this is what I will be teaching you today. You will memorize all of the instant points and the limited points. This procedure of pain is similar to acupuncture or acupressure, but progresses in the opposite direction. You will not feel any pleasure in this procedure if you are the victim." He gives an ironic smile. "Unless you are a masochist. These points are not in the same locations as the pressure points on your body. No utensils are used. No acupuncture needles.

"I want you to gather into teams of two. Later during the class, I will pair you up with another student to make sure you are learning the procedure correctly. I want to remind you this is an extremely important class, which some day could mean life or death to you. There will be no foolishness tolerated. I may need another demonstrator later, so I will be watching to see who is learning, and who is not."

Chapter 31

Eight months have passed. One day a Western Union telegram is delivered to the monastery. It is addressed to Andre Roberson:

Your father had a mild stroke yesterday. Short time in hospital. Many tests. Not serious. No physical impairments. At home resting. You need to visit him. Get in touch with me. Stacey.

Knowing Andre could be in an area without telephones or cell phones, or even mail, Stacy knew a telegram would reach him.

Grand Master Shibo calls Andre into his office. "Andre," he says, "we are aware you received a telegram from your father's personal secretary."

"Yes, Master. I'm concerned for my father."

"Our policy is that we do not open any mail, but we do read telegrams. Our policy is that everything that takes place at home has a direct effect on the student. Through many centuries of schooling, we have learned that when someone has other concerns on his mind, he cannot think correctly and thus becomes distracted. Your father is extremely important to you, and now he is desperately in need of your help. It doesn't matter how long you are gone. Family is the most important thing in your life, whether you realize it or not. You have been a excellent student, and we do not want to lose you. You have become family to us here, too, and so I am going to give you a leave of absence from the school. You have no choice in this matter. I do hope you understand."

"Yes, Master, I do," Andre replies.

"I will be giving Jing Xian, your brother at the monastery, a leave of absence as well. He will accompany you as you visit your father. Jing Xian will be missed very much, as will you be. He has done so much for the monastery, there is no way we can repay him. He has no choice, either, for as a Shaolin monk it is his duty as a spiritual brother to be there, whether you need him or not. Neither of you," Master Shibo concludes, "need to worry about your home here. It will always be here when you return. Please stay in touch with us and please do not forget us, no matter what.

PART III

GOING TO SAN FRANCISCO, CALIFORNIA

Chapter 32

After a eleven-hour flight from Shanghai to San Francisco, Andre thinks it is good to see the Bay Bridge again as the plane loops around the city, slicing through patches of fog and lining up for the approach over the Bay into San Francisco International Airport. Andre and Jing Xian are taking an unspecified number of days (or weeks or months) away from the monastery in Yangshuo. They will be spending time with Andre's father as he recuperates from his mild stroke. Carrying their bags, they approach a city cab parked at the curb in front of the air terminal.

"Hi, boys! Need a ride to the city?" The cab driver is a voluptuous blonde who has been poured into a pair of Levis and is wearing a colorful Hawaiian shirt. "Where do you guys want to go?"

Andre hands her a card with the address of the Majestic Dragon, the five-star hotel where they will be staying.

"Chinatown," she says. As the young men open the cab door and start to get inside, she says, "Hold up, guys. Here, let me put your bags in the trunk. It might be a tight fit for both of you with your luggage."

Andre pauses for a second, "Yeah," he says. "I wasn't really thinking." He sets his suitcases in the trunk and Jing Xian does the same. "I think my mind is still in the plane." he comments. They both get into the back seat of the cab.

The driver gets in and starts the cab, then turns and looks over her shoulder. "Guys," she says, "will you please buckle up? I feel a lot better when my fares are locked in."

They look at each other and buckle up, and Jing Xian says, "You're a very concerned driver. I wish the cab drivers in China felt the same way."

"That's right," she says as she guns the motor. The cab takes off, slamming both passengers against the back seat and cutting off another car, whose driver is laying on his horn. Moving very fast, the cab comes out of the airport and merges into the freeway traffic, heading north up Highway 101 toward the city. She accelerates to over eighty-five miles per hour while they are still in the right lane. In California, the right lane is considered to be the slow lane on the freeways, but she passes all the cars in a blur. Suddenly there is an opening in the lane of cars to her left, and with a quick precise yank of the steering wheel, she shoots the cab two lanes to the left, cutting off several cars. She continues to accelerate.

Andre and Jing Xian are frozen in the back seat, wondering if they will get to the hotel alive. Andre politely asks the driver, "What is your name?"

"It's Judy. And what are your names?"

"Our names are Andre and Jing Xian." Andre pauses a minute. "Judy, have you been driving cabs for a long time?" He is trying to get a conversation going so she might slow down a bit.

"Yeah," she says, "I got out here to California about a year ago. I used to drive cabs in New York City for about ten years. The drivers out here in California drive too cautious. They scare the shit out of you."

"Yeah, they sure do," he agrees as he slides back against the back seat.

"Jing Xian," Judy asks as she runs her fingers through her cropped blond hair, which is being blown by the wind coming through the open window, "are you from China?"

"Yes," he says. "I'm from Beijing, but I've been spending time in southern China near the city of Yangshuo."

"Is that a big city?"

"Well, yes and no. It would be a gigantic city in the United States, with its population of about a million or so. But it's small for a Chinese city."

"What big city is it near?"

"Well, it's about forty miles down river from Guilin, a much larger city with three or four million in population. Do you know where Guilin is?"

"Not exactly," she replies. "I know it's about a two-hour flight south from Shanghai. A fare told me about the city and recommended I visit it some day. Okay," she adds, "I get the picture in my mind. I hear China is beautiful. Hopefully, some day I'll get over there."

"When you go to China," Jing Xian says, "make sure you see the Great Wall. It was built over twenty-five hundred years ago. Tiananmen Square; and the Forbidden City in the Beijing area are other excellent places to visit. Spend several days in the city of Shanghai, and make sure to walk the length of Nanjing Road in the no-car zone. You will see restaurants, clothing stores, entertainment. Every type of product from every major city in the world."

"Do many Chinese speak English?" Judy asks with a strain to her voice as she maneuvers her cab between two large trucks. "The reason I'm asking is because the last time I went to Germany, I didn't have to know their language. Most Germans in the western part of Germany can speak English."

"You won't find a lot of English-speaking people in China," Jing Xian replies. "There are some spots in the big cities, like Beijing, Shanghai, and Hong Kong, where you will find English-speaking Chinese. From Beijing, most tours go to see the famous Terra Cotta Warriors in the city of Xian. That place is unbelievable. There must be hundreds, maybe thousands, of life-size soldiers restored to almost perfect condition. These warriors date back couple thousand years. It's well worth the trip. And make sure you give yourself plenty of time, because it's almost always crowded."

Jing Xian is telling Judy more about China, when suddenly she yells, "Oops! Hang on, guys!" The cab lunges to the left, then lunges back to the right, snapping the passengers' heads back and forth like bobble-head dolls. "This stupid ass is trying to take off my front fender," she says. "Wait till I get around him." After some surging and quick lane changing, things are momentarily back to normal.

"Okay," Judy yells. "The crisis is over." She then pulls down her sun visor and takes a look at her face in the mirror at the same time keeping her eyes on the bumper-to-bumper freeway traffic. She dabs some cream on her face from a tube she has tucked between her legs. "I need to get better lipstick next time," she mutters. "I bought a tube yesterday and it's smearing all over my face."

All the while her cab is zipping along, hovering in the vapor trail of the vehicle in front of her. Jing Xian yells up to her, "That was close."

"Yeah, it was." Judy takes her foot off the carburetor to change lanes again, and the cab starts to slow down a bit. "Now, as you were saying," she calls out to Jing Xian. She guns the cab again, lurching past the car that annoyed her a few minutes ago. "I think I'm going to need a tune-up on this old beast one of these days," she mutters again. "It just doesn't have that quick surge anymore."

"You're right," Andre says. "It does feel a bit sluggish." He cinches up his seat belt a little tighter.

"Jing Xian," Judy calls out. He scoots up closer to the front seat again. "Here's a notebook and a pencil," she says. "Would you write down those names and places you were telling me to visit in China? Every time I go to a travel agency, they never know what a person should see. All they're interested in is getting you on the trip. Then you figure out what to see and wind up missing the good things. I need someone with real-time experience, someone who really knows what to see." She relocates her cab into a different lane.

"I'll write all of these places down for you," Jing Xian says. "I believe you can find most of this information on their web sites."

Judy sees an opening in another lane and guns it. The cab lurches forward. "Get out of the way, you stupid jerk!"

Her passengers hunker down and hang on. Jing Xian finally finishes listing the places Judy should visit. He also recommends several places she can stay while visiting China. Unbuckling his seat belt again, he slowly slips up close to the front seat to hand her notebook to her. "I hope you'll be able to read it," he says. "That was a rough ride."

"Thank you for your help," she says. "I'm sure I'll be able to make it out." Jing Xian scoots back in his seat and buckles up again, and before they know it, Judy is maneuvering her cab off the freeway and heading toward the hotel, which is not far from Union Square. Taking three or four signals on yellow, just beating out the red lights, she drives the streets as though she's been driving them for years.

"Here's your hotel," she says at last. "The Majestic Dragon. It's not too far from the famous Chinatown. And make sure you go into Chinatown. There are some fantastic restaurants there. They'll make you feel like you're back home in China." She glides her cab to the curb and kills the ignition.

"Ahhh," Andre sighs with relief and hands her his credit card. She fills out the information and hands it back, and he signs the charge slip, leaving a nice tip for her excellent ability to drive through the crowded streets of San Francisco so efficiently.

As Jing Xian gets out of the cab, he hangs on to Andre's shoulder to steady his balance. "Captain Kirk?" he says.

"Yes, Scotty?" Andre replies with a big smile.

"The *Enterprise* has landed. Please beam me up."

Andre laughs and says, "Remember what Captain Kirk said in their second visit to earth when they landed in San Francisco? *Remember where we parked.*" Both of them have a big laugh.

Judy is getting their bags out of the trunk. She smiles at Jing Xian. "You know, it took a lot of years to learn how to drive like that in these crowded streets." She gives him a firm handshake.

"I'm joking," Jing Xian says. "That ride brought back memories of when I used to take cabs in Beijing. Same kind of action." He laughs again.

"Before you guys leave, I want you take my business card, just in case you'd like to go somewhere in the Bay Area. Anytime, any day, anywhere, I'm at your service, twenty-four/seven."

"Okay," Jing Xian says. "We will definitely keep your card. Who knows where we might want to fly to."

Judy gets back into her cab, buckles up, and gives them a big smile and a thumbs up, then she guns the engine. The cab lunges forward, both rear tires screeching and leaving a cloud of black smoke. Coughing, the men fan their faces.

"Damn, I guess that old cab still has plenty of fire power," Andre sputters between coughs.

"I wonder…," Jing Xian is thinking out loud as he watches the cab fly through several yellow signals before it makes a quick right and disappears. He then shakes his head.

"Yeah," Andre agrees, "I was thinking that, too."

After looking at his watch, Jing Xian says, "It's too late to give your dad a call tonight."

"Yeah. I'll call him in the morning. He's an early riser."

Chapter 33

"Gentlemen, welcome to the Majestic Dragon. My name is Danny. I'm the hotel concierge. May I assist you with your luggage?"

"Yes, you may," Andre replies.

Danny loads their gear onto the luggage cart. "I will meet you at the reception desk."

After they complete the registration forms, the clerk says, "You have Rooms 3208 and 3209 with connecting doors, as you requested. Danny will meet you at your room with your luggage. I'm sure you will enjoy your stay at the Majestic Dragon. If you have any needs, require assistance with travel, or have other questions, just give the concierge a call anytime. We have twenty-four-hour room service. Here is a copy of what is offered in case you are hungry tonight. You can look at it while you are on your way to your room. There is also a copy in your room."

"Thank you."

"Here we are at the thirty-second floor," says Andre, watching Jing Xian stumble as he exits the elevator car. "That's a fast elevator. It made my legs sort of wobbly."

They see the baggage cart in front of a room halfway down the hall. "Looks like he's here already," Andre says as they enter into his room. Danny has already opened the drapes and checked the thermostat. Now he puts their gear on the baggage stands in their rooms.

"Welcome," he says. "May I suggest, for your pleasure, our excellent health spa located on the fifth floor? There are inside and outside swimming pools and an invigorating Jacuzzi. If your body is aching, and you are in a dying need for a massage, Bahareh, our masseuse, can take care of your aches. If you need anything or have any questions, please give me a call. Enjoy your stay."

As Danny starts to exit the room, Andre hands him a nice tip for his service, then turns to Jing Xian and says, "It's too late to do anything, and I'm bushed. If you're hungry, you can call the concierge and order something to eat. I'm going to take a nice hot shower and go to bed. Maybe I'll have room service bring up a bottle of wine."

"I think I'll have some wine, too," Jing Xian replies. "I need it. Especially after that cab ride, then that fast elevator. Hey, that sure was some cab driver. In a way, I think she's probably a safe driver, although a pretty wild one."

Andre heads into his own room. "Call me in the morning and we'll eat together," he says, and he closes the door. In his room, he notices the message light blinking on the telephone. He listens to the message.

"Hi, Son," his father's voice says. "I hope you had a nice, uneventful trip from China. I'm sending my limo over tomorrow morning at ten o'clock. The driver's name is Bill. It's too late for a phone call tonight. See you tomorrow."

Chapter 34

At 9:45 the next morning, Andre and Jing Xian are sitting in the hotel lobby waiting for their limousine. They have enjoyed an excellent breakfast in the hotel restaurant, although the food in San Francisco is different from what they were accustomed to in China. Jing Xian, a bit uneasy on his first trip to the United States, has decided to follow Andre's lead.

"Hey, Andre," he says, "what are the plans for today?"

"I'm not sure. I guess it depends on how my father feels," Andre replies. "There are so many places to see in San Francisco, I suppose the best way is to play it by ear." He sees a large black car parking at the curb. "Is that our limousine?"

The limo driver comes into the hotel lobby. He is dressed in a nicely cut black suit, a white shirt, and a tie. He talks with the concierge, then walks over to where Andre and Jing Xian are sitting. "Andre Roberson?"

"Yes, that's me."

"Good morning, sir. My name is Bill. I'm sure you don't remember me, but I'm your father's limo driver."

"It's been a long time since I've seen you. You're looking very good."

"Thank you, sir."

"Bill, I would like you to meet a real good buddy of mine. This is Jing Xian."

"It's a pleasure to make your acquaintance," Bill says as he shakes hands with Jing Xian. "I hope you will enjoy your stay in San Francisco." Andre and Jing Xian start to pick up their bags, but Bill steps forward and says, "Please let me do that for you." He is a classic limousine driver: an expert in driving and a professional in taking care of the needs of his passengers

"Doesn't he remind you of some movie star?" Andre asks Jing Xian as they settle into the limo.

"We don't get a lot of good movies in China," Jing Xian replies. "I can't help you out." As the limousine cruises smoothly down the road, he says, "Hey, I can't feel the limo moving. Are we moving?"

"I think so," Andre says. "I'm not sure. The windows are tinted so dark I can't see outside. And the seats are so relaxing, it almost puts you to sleep."

Bill interrupts the relaxing background music to talk to his passengers via the intercom. "I hope you're enjoying your ride. If you're interested in having a mixed drink, wine, or a soft drink, everything is available a finger touch away. There are also mixed nuts and several selections of candy bars. As you can see, we are ready for passengers of all ages. If you need to call me, just press the small blue light on the panel."

Andre presses the blue light. "Thank you, Bill. We just had a full breakfast."

"As you wish."

"Hey, Andre," says Jing Xian, "wouldn't it have been terrific if Bill could have picked us up at the airport, instead of wild Judy?"

"I didn't want to bother my father about getting someone to pick us up," Andre replies. "Not when he's not well. Next time when we come into town, though, we can plan it that way."

"How long has Bill been driving for your father?"

"I'm not sure. All I know for sure is he drove my mother to the hospital to deliver me."

Chapter 35

After arriving on the forty-fourth floor of a luxury condominium high-rise in downtown San Francisco, Andre rings the door bell, and an attractive, middle aged Chinese woman answers the door.

"My name is Andre Roberson," he says to her. "Is Mr. Roberson home? He's expecting us."

"Yes. Please come in. He is expecting you. My name is Chia Ling. Mr. Roberson insists that you have a drink and be seated in the library. If you please, would you leave your shoes at the door. Here is a pair of house slippers for each of you."

"Thank you." The two young men have already removed their shoes. This is a Chinese custom, and the practice of no shoes inside a building is also standard procedure at the monastery.

The maid continues. "Mr. Roberson was soaking in the hot tub on the balcony. He is getting dressed now. He will be out in a few minutes. Please sit down. Please, what would you like to drink?" She nods at Jing Xian.

"I will ahh ... have a scotch and water with a twist."

"Is there any certain brand of scotch you prefer?"

"No, no special scotch."

She turns to Andre. "And you, sir?"

"Do you have any Napa Valley Merlot?"

"Let me check. I think he may have a bottle somewhere."

After Chia Ling leaves the room, Andre leans over and quietly says, "That's a strong drink for this time of the day."

"Yes, I know. But I couldn't think of anything else to say."

"How about hot tea? Coffee? A soft drink? Wine?"

"Right. Next time."

"Hello, boys!"

They hear the booming voice of Mr. Roberson, who comes walking into the library. He is putting on a posh, full-length, tan, cashmere bathrobe. He finishes towel-drying his wavy white hair, leaving it standing in all directions. A handsome man, he stands six feet one inch tall.

"That Jacuzzi is one of the best investments I've made in a very, very long time," he says. "The old bones don't move like they used to, so I need a little fixer-upper every once a while. I'll get you guys some swimming trunks and we'll enjoy it one of these evenings. Hell, even if you don't have a suit, it's okay. I go skinny-dipping most of the time." Leaning over towards his son and his friend, he lowers his voice. "Watch out for Chia Ling. She gets upset with me. She says I'm an important man and should act like one. I keep asking her, do I have to act like an important man in my own house? She tells me yes. I think she had an extremely disciplined mother and father. They were concerned about her and instilled very correct manners."

Andre greets his father. "How are you, Dad?" He gives his father a big hug and says, "The Jacuzzi sounds like a great idea. I'll definitely take you up on your offer before we leave."

"What a hug you have," Mr. Roberson says. "It almost took the old man's breath away. Do you work out at the gym?"

"Sometimes."

"Yeah. You've got some muscles, just like your old dad. I've been feeling great except for a few minor things and an ache here and there. A couple weeks ago, Stacey set up a doctor's appointment for me. You know, one of those visits with a finger up the ass and take a pint of blood? And you know what happened? The stupid people at the lab lost the results. Somehow they had faxed the report to my office, and Stacey never received it. Then the lab, or I guess it was the lab, sent a report telling me that I'd had a stroke. How in the hell can the lab determine if I had a stroke? Well, to make a long story short, Stacey sent a Western Union telegram to you as soon as she got this message about my so-called stroke. Then she gets with our doctor to find out what's happening, and he's dumbfounded about this whole thing. After talking with the lab, they confirm they *didn't* send out any report that I had a stroke." He pauses and shakes his head. "This whole thing is really strange. Why would someone want my health report? Well, anyway ... Stacey got it all straightened out, and I won't get the finger and give any more blood. It seems almost like someone wants you to be here with me. I don't know why. Well, let's not worry about it anymore. We'll find out what's happening. Let's get back to your visit. I really want this visit to be the best ever."

"You betcha," Andre replies. He looks a bit puzzled. "Dad, I want you to meet my friend, Jing Xian. I met him at the Shaolin monastery in Yangshuo, China."

"Hi, Jing Xian. It is definitely a pleasure to meet you."

"The pleasure is all mine, Mr. Roberson."

"Please, please, won't you call me Tim?"

"Okay, I will try. But I was raised to address the leader of a family by his last name."

"Very polite," Tim says. "But see what you can do about bending the rules. I hear Mr. Roberson all the time. It's nice to hear my first name every once in a while. You know, sometimes I even forget what my first name is because I'm called by my last name all the time."

"Okay," Jing Xian replies with a smile, "I will try."

"Thanks. What I've heard from my son is that you're the best friend he has."

"I try to keep him out of trouble," Jing Xian replies with another smile. "But I can't be a miracle worker."

All three men laugh.

"Sit back down, guys," the father says. "Ahhh, here are your drinks."

Chia Ling comes into the room and tells Andre they do have some Napa Merlot. She hands him his drink, then hands Jing Xian his scotch and water with a twist.

Andre has a serious look on his face. "Dad, it seems a bit peculiar for a medical facility to make a mistake about someone having a stroke. Whatever happened, it must be a serious thing."

"Oh, no, Son. It was a little minor thing. I think my body was probably trying to warn me to start slowing down."

"Well, you should listen to your body every once a while."

"I do, Son, but just recently so many things are starting to happen, it's really keeping me on the edge. I've been having some serious problems with one of the majority stock holders, a Mr. Craiger." Mr. Roberson pauses, and his son sees the uneasy look on his face, his eyes revealing a hint of fear. But the older man quickly recovers, shakes his head, and starts smiling again. "But," he says, "I'm not going to talk shop while you guys are here. We are going to see the big city. And then I have a fantastic surprise for you."

Andre grins. "Watch out, Jing Xian. When my father gets that look and starts to warn us, be very careful what you say. You might find yourself on a tramp steamer going up the Amazon and heading into the jungle. Or starting a hike across the Egyptian desert, looking for fossils. When was the last time you were on a sea plane flying to a remote island off the tip of South Africa?"

"Those places sound like exciting."

"That's not fair," Mr. Roberson says as he goes into uncontrolled laughter. He is laughing so hard tears are coming to his eyes, and the younger men are soon doing the same. After a couple of minutes, he finally gets control of himself. "I'll tell you guys more about our future adventure in a little while. Here, let me freshen up your drinks. I have to go and comb my hair. It's starting to get tangled up in my glasses."

As Mr. Roberson steps out of the room, Jing Xian leans over and whispers, "Your dad is great! I bet he can tell a lot of jokes and has some wild adventure stories."

"You're definitely right about that. Especially after he's had several drinks. Believe me, he can go for hours."

Mr. Roberson, his hair neatly combed, comes back into the room with more drinks. "Chia Ling would have brought out the drinks, but she's making some fantastic Chinese finger foods. I won't tell you what they are, I'll let her surprise you. Sometime I won't eat a regular meal, I'll just eat her finger foods. She tells me it's very healthy. They call them *dim sum*. I never can remember the name, so I always call it finger food because I can't use those chop sticks. Oh, yes, I've tried using them many times. My damn fingers just won't do what I want them to do. I keep dropping the food in my lap or on the floor. It gets embarrassing, so I just use my fingers. After I eat with my fingers for a while, the waitress brings me a fork." He laughs. "Well, anyway, Stacey has warned me several times to slow down. I've decided to take her advice. Sometimes I think she is more the boss then I am."

"Say, Dad, how is Stacey doing nowadays?"

"She is doing fine, Son. She does an excellent job keeping everything going in the right direction."

Chapter 36

"So, you guys have any special place you want to see in San Francisco? I was thinking you might like going to Alcatraz Island. It's a very interesting place with a lot of history."

"I'm not familiar with Alcatraz Island," Jing Xian says.

"It's a rocky island in San Francisco Bay. It was maximum security prison for about thirty years," Andre says. "The island has a nickname, 'the rock,' which is appropriate."

"Yes," Mr. Roberson says. "The place was closed down in 1963. A few famous criminals were housed there during its time. Al Capone, the notorious mobster of Prohibition days, and a guy named Stroud, who they called the Birdman of Alcatraz."

"That's interesting," comments Andre. "I didn't know that."

Jing Xian says, "I remember that in one of my history classes in Beijing we read about the mobsters of Prohibition days. Al Capone was one of the major gangsters. He was a famous mobster who operated in the city of Chicago."

Mr. Roberson says, "To get to the rock, we can catch a ferry from the Thirty-ninth Street pier. It's about a half-hour ride to the island. We can walk all over the island and look into cells. Alcatraz is managed by the State Parks and Recreation Department. But enough of the history class," he says. "Let's go to Pier 39. They have every kind of seafood restaurant you might want, plus all sorts of tourist attractions. If you get tired of eating, we can watch hundreds of seals sun-bathing on those floating docks. We can get a drink and watch the seals. There's always a seal jockeying for a different place on the float, upsetting the others. Some days there are over a hundred people at a time watching them."

"That does sound interesting," Jing Xian says.

"We also can go to North Beach for excellent Italian cuisine in an outdoor restaurant. Union Plaza is a nice place if you want to shop.

And Chinatown for dim sum." He laughs. "I promise I won't eat with my fingers."

Dad," Andre says, "I didn't even remember Bill today. It has been so long since I've ridden in the limo. But he remembered me. He still looks good."

"Yes. He's been with me forever, I hope he'll stay around for many more years. God bless the old guy."

Chapter 37

"Guys, we are going to have three days in San Francisco before we are off on the great trip," Tim Roberson announces.

His son is already grinning from ear to ear. "And what part of the world are we heading off to?"

"We are going to northwest Africa."

"Sounds exciting," Andre says.

Jing Xian doesn't say a word for a few moments, then he says, "That's going to be great. I have always wanted to go to Africa, but I could never afford it."

"Now, guys, we don't have to go there," the old man says. "My second choice was Pamplona, Spain, and the festivities of San Fermin. I know that name doesn't mean anything to you, but the reason thousands of people go to the city is the famous running of the bulls. Ernest Hemingway made the town popular by writing about the running of the bulls in one of his novels. Your mother didn't want to go to Pamplona because she was afraid I would run with the bulls and get hurt. She was right. I would have run with the bulls. What a blast that would have been! Many runners drink too much and get hurt. Those bulls have some mean-looking horns, and they know how to use them. I would probably have gotten gored and stomped by some mad bull. I didn't want to upset her, so we never went there. Maybe you guys are brave enough to run in front of the bulls with all of those other young men dressed in white with red sashes. Don't worry about a thing," he adds. "It is all covered, including all the extras."

"Where in Africa are we going?" Andre asks.

"We will be heading to Marrakesh, Morocco, for a ten-day camel safari across the Sahara Desert. A group of twelve people will be on the safari. We will saddle up on those long-legged desert dromedaries. I wonder if it's like riding an elephant. Probably not as smooth."

"I've heard that camels are not friendly animals to ride," Jing Xian comments. "They spit and may bite you. How do they put a saddle on a one-hump camel? Maybe they use the ones with two humps?"

A puzzled look appears on Mr. Roberson's face for a second, then it fades away. "I think we will be visiting a couple oases and a special kasbah," he says. "We will be hiking to the top of several giant sand dunes, which might be more in your agenda."

"Yeah," the young men both say. "That is going to be fantastic."

"I figured you guys would like that. Everything has been arranged. Tomorrow we will drive to a travel clothing store and pick up a few things. Stacey has already got everything fixed for our passports."

Chapter 38

Finishing off his drink, Mr. Roberson glances down at the newspaper lying on the table. "I have to tell you guys something really interesting," he says. "I love animals, and I know you both love them as well. Let me tell you about this pair of peregrine falcons living on one of those skyscrapers in downtown San Francisco over by Beale and lower Market streets." He pauses for a moment. "You guys have time to hear this story? It's in today's newspaper."

"Yes, Dad. We have all day," Andre replies with a big smile.

"I think the building was the PG&E Building. This pair of falcons has been living on high-rise buildings in the downtown area for several years, producing about a dozen chicks. I guess they live off the pigeons. Damn pigeons—they make a mess out of everything. The city has the right idea about keeping the pigeon population down by using falcons. Well, this pair of falcons moved out of the city. Maybe the pollution from the car exhaust got to them. They built a nest on the Bay Bridge, where there's a constant breeze. You might say they've moved to the suburbs." He chuckles, then continues. "Everyone is concerned for the safety of the young chicks when they're hatched. With the wind so strong out there, they might get blown out of their nest and into the Bay. The article also said the chicks might be susceptible as a meal to larger birds that normally don't fly into the city. I'm not sure who is going to do this, but they are going to steal the eggs from the nest, hatch them, and hopefully relocate them back into downtown, where they will grow up. Someone, I'm not sure who, has nicknamed the falcons George and Gracie. Isn't that funny? Really funny?" When neither Andre nor Jing Xian laughs, he asks, "What's wrong? Don't you like the story?"

"Who are George and Gracie?" Andre asks.

Mr. Roberson pauses to think, then it dawns on him. "George and Gracie were a comedy team. They had a show called *The George Burns and Gracie Allen Show* on early television, over fifty years ago, when television was in black and white. I guess that's too long ago. You boys weren't even born yet." He laughs again. Then he returns to the pigeon story. "It's amazing, all of this is going on just to keep the messy pigeon population down in the city."

"Hey, Dad," Andre says, "why don't we give Stacey a call? Maybe all of us could have dinner together tonight. I haven't talked with her for some time. It's been a couple years since the last time I saw her." When his father nods, he dials his cell phone. "Hey, Stacey," he says when she answers, "this is Andre. How are you? ... I'm feeling wonderful. I'm here in San Francisco with Jing Xian. ... We are at my dad's condominium." After some more conversation, he says, "Let's all have dinner tonight. I hope you have some free time. ... Yes, it's been several years since I saw you."

PART III

ARRIVING IN MARRAKESH, MOROCCO

Chapter 39

Flying from San Francisco after connecting through New York with one stop in Casablanca, Tim Roberson, Andre, and Jing Xian look out the airplane window as it taxis up to a large hangar in Marrakesh. Everyone in the plane is getting exciting. When Mr. Roberson made the reservations with his travel agent, Luis, they agreed that Morocco was the place for them to visit.

"I think Marrakesh is the right place to stay for a couple of days," Luis had told him. "You can be rested and see the town before you depart on your camel ride across the dunes. You can leave all your cares behind."

"Yes," Mr. Roberson said. "A camel ride will bring back old memories of when my wife and I went on an elephant ride in India."

"The difference between riding an elephant and riding a camel is like night and day," the travel agent cautioned him. "Getting on and off a camel is an art in itself. It also depends on who takes care of the camels. Some camels are belligerent and stinky, but otherwise, it will be an unforgettable adventure. You and your boys will enjoy the trip. And, remember, being in the desert, you will need different clothes than you wore in India."

"Thanks for being so concerned. I haven't seen my son for awhile. I want everything to go well. A camel ride will be something very exciting for all of us!"

"You're absolutely right, Mr. Roberson. I know you and your son and his friend will have a great time."

"Thanks again for all your help, Luis."

Reading another glossy travel brochure, Mr. Roberson learns that Marrakesh, "the pearl of the south," was founded in the eleventh century and is one of Morocco's oldest and most beautiful cities. Tourists can see the mountains of the high Atlas in the distance. The city boasts pink Moorish-style buildings and gorgeous gardens that fill the air with the scent of spices. He knows he has made the right choice for this special trip.

"Well, we made it!" he says.

"Yes, Mr. Rob—I mean Tim," says Jing Xian.

"We sure did!" Andre chimes in as he pulls his shoulder bag out from under the seat in front of him. "It sort of felt like we were landing on one wheel. Maybe it was a new pilot or a stewardess landing this thing."

"Can you imagine flying this many hours, and then the pilot has to be ready for a perfect landing?" Mr. Roberson says. "It can be hair-raising sometimes."

"Yes," Andre agrees. "Piloting a large plane with so much responsibility is not for me. Maybe a small plane with no passengers would be easier."

After the three men exit the plane, they stand perplexed, looking in all directions.

"Which way do we go?" Jing Xian asks. "I don't see any signs."

"Just follow the crowd," Mr. Roberson says.

"Do you hear that sound?" Andre asks. "What is that?"

"It sounds like someone is pounding on a drum," replies Jing Xian.

"Are the natives beating their drums?" Andre laughs as he listens to the rhythm. *Boom, boom, pause, boom, long pause, boom.* "Where is this crowd heading to?" he asks, then he looks off to his right and sees a hundred or more people merging into make one huge group. They must have been another plane that landed around the same time, and all these passengers are now trying to get through the gate. The tourists are shoulder to shoulder, shuffling their feet, at best moving only few inches at a time. Most of them are quiet, though if people are talking, their voices are muffled so the sound resembles the wings of a flock of birds fanning the air. The huge crowd makes a slow, wide, left turn through two tall doors into a giant building that looks like an aircraft hangar. They seem to be without a destination and with no idea of correct procedure, and the Robersons and Jing Xian find themselves at the mercy of the crowd. Do they get their bags first? Go through customs? What's going on here?

Mr. Roberson is thinking to himself, *This whole thing is odd. Should I be seeing someone standing high in front of the crowd, chanting something to the people, telling us we should follow him? Will we all be sacrificed to the hungry demon?* Suddenly, he is jolted out of his daydream.

"Hey, look," says Jing Xian. "I know where we're going." He points across the room, where the crowd is slowly forming into several lines leading to glass booths, each with a man sitting inside it.

As usual, someone crowds ahead in the line, and people get into a bit of an argument. *Why does this happen?* Mr. Roberson asks himself. He knows that crowding in line just makes people upset and the person who is crowding in is not gaining anything.

Everyone keeps shuffling along toward that insistent rhythm. It must indicate the way out. Half an hour later, Andre suddenly shouts, "I know what that sound is!" He points at the glass booths. "The drumming sound is coming from the customs agents in those glass booths and reverberating throughout the large hangar." Suddenly, almost as if magic, Andre and Jing Xian are in a line moving toward one of the booths. Andre looks over and sees his dad moving into a line heading to the booth next to theirs. "I see you got in a different line," he calls out.

"Yeah," his father replies, "it just happened. I don't think it will be much longer before we are through here. I'm sure when we get out of here our bags will be waiting."

Sure enough, all three men pick up their bags at the luggage carousel, then they head for the exit.

Mr. Roberson comments, "I'm glad all the bags are here. Did you notice there were no tag checks to prove we have the right bags? And did you see some of those bags on the carousel are absolutely falling apart? They must be a hundred years old. Some people either don't travel often or they can't afford new bags."

With a great degree of relief, the three Americans look for directions to ground transportation. As they stroll along, pulling their wheeled suitcases, they notice many kinds of people. They are lucky enough to find a taxi almost immediately, and they ask to be taken to the Tichka Hotel in the Old French Quarter. On the way, they look in every direction at the new and different scenery. They are almost at their hotel when Andre says in a quiet voice, "Did you notice how many shady-looking guys were hanging around in the airport?" After discussing this in low tones, they decide it must be the difference in clothing and the fact that there are more darker-skinned people than one sees in United States or European airports.

Tomorrow morning they will meet their guide and the ten other people who will be with them on the camel ride into the desert.

Chapter 40

After a refreshing sleep, the trio walk to the breakfast buffet, which is located alongside the hotel's picturesque pool.

"Hey," says Jing Xian as he inspects the food, "look at this layout. So many neat things to eat. There must be five different kinds of tomato dishes. And there are scrambled eggs prepared with mushrooms, olives, and other mysterious ingredients."

"And look at the enticing pasta dishes with olives, saffron, and goat cheese." Tim points these out to the younger men, and they also see that there are some uncooked foods that they suspect could cause some intestinal problems in tourists. They look at each other. "Did we pack the Kaopectate?" they ask simultaneously. Mr. Roberson, the experienced traveler, answers with a resounding, "Yes, I have it." Andre and Jing Xian promise they will take care in choosing their food. Around a corner, they see some more familiar food: scrambled eggs, bacon, grits, and fried potatoes.

"Is this goat or rabbit?" Jing Xian asks. "I haven't had couscous before," he adds.

Having made their choices of some familiar foods and some completely new ones, the three find a table located in the center of the crowded dining area. They enjoy the new taste treats.

Chapter 41

Glancing to his right, Andre sees an interesting Moroccan entering the dining area. His stance and demeanor immediately command the attention of the tourists, as he is tall and lean and has the dusky skin and rugged good looks one often sees in this part of the world. His hooded *djellaba machzania* covers his dark hair but allows his white long-sleeved shirt and khaki pants to show. The loose fitting outer robe (the *djellaba*) comes all the way down to the top of his slippers. To complete his Moroccan attire, he wears a woven, multi-colored rope-like belt with a few ornaments attached to it. He appears to be in his early thirties and is a good looking man except for one thing: his dark, deeply hooded eyes that gaze into the room with a penetrating glare. It's hard to break away from that magnetic stare. When he speaks, it is with a slight accent of a combination of Berber and French.

"Good morning!" he announces. "My name is Ajijine, and I am your tour leader. Are you enjoying our magnificent pool? Our sumptuous buffet breakfast? A beautiful day it is! I believe the temperature is about seventy-five degrees this morning. It may get up to about eighty-five today, which is a nice temperature for traveling in the desert. I hope everyone in our group is here. We are the Camel Express Tour."

He starts walking around the tables by the swimming pool, introducing himself to the members of the group and checking their names off his list. He wears a pair of *balras*, the traditional desert foot covering made of soft, light-colored leather. These slippers are very comfortable and worn by many people who live in the desert.

Starting at the first table, Ajijine meets Tom and Marty, who are from San Diego. After welcoming them to the tour, he continues around the room, greeting the others on the same tour: Charlie and Pai Lien from Shanghai, Allen from Missouri, Jodie from the Napa Valley, Maji and Doshi from Pakistan, and Mr. Roberson, Andre, Jing Xian from San Francisco.

"Good," he finally says, checking off the final names. "Everyone is here." Then he adds, "Don't forget, the most scrumptious pastries with fresh fruit are in the alcove to your left. If you have eaten something that does not agree with you, or have eaten too much, make sure you try our wonderful Moroccan mint tea. The tea is excellent for settling the stomach." He pauses and the tourists politely laugh. "One more announcement," he says, "and I'll let you get back to your meal. At nine o'clock, everyone will meet in the hotel lobby. Be ready to explore the old part of Marrakesh."

Chapter 42

By nine o'clock, everyone has finished their breakfast and the group has assembled in the lobby to wait for Ajijine.

"Okay," he says as he walks into the lobby, "is everyone here?" He looks around to make sure. "Let's go outside and board the horse-drawn surreys. We will go through the Old French Quarter, where you can see some of the city's beautiful French architecture on our way to the famous Derma El Fan Square, which is also called the Medina. There you will see cobra-charmers, watermen, orange juice servers, fire eaters, and other quaint types for your amusement."

As the buggies arrive in the Medina, the tourists get their cameras out and make them ready to take photos.

"We are going to spend several hours in the Medina," Ajijine announces. "At times it will get very crowded, so please stay close to each other. If you lose us, we will meet here beside this fountain in three hours. Please don't be late. If you get here early, just wait, and we will be here." He pauses to make sure everyone is listening. "There is one more thing I need to remind you. This was in the instructions I gave you last evening. I hope you read them carefully. I want you to remember the parts of the Medina that I recommended you not go into. These areas are not tourist-friendly. There have been people who have ventured into these areas, and they were never seen again. This has never happened to anyone in my groups. I hope it never does! Don't wonder off unless you tell me where you are going. Okay?"

Ajijine walks briskly towards the entrance of the *souk*, or market, and into the maze. He calls over his shoulder, "Please keep up. And watch out for pick-pockets." The tourists begin to see the extent of the *souk*. First, there are shoes of every different size, color, shape, style, and material. They continue along the narrow walkways and see more stalls: leather goods, imported cans of exotic foods, scarves, exotic fragrances, and clothing, both modern and traditional Moroccan. There are also plastics, every type of herb one can think of, copper kitchen utensils, wood products of high and low quality, pottery for decoration and cooking, valuable jewelry and trinkets, medicines both modern and from the old world, and even a few witchcraft items. On and on the market goes for what seems like miles. The roof of the maze is made of different types of heavy cloth, wood, or palm leaves. *No wonder this amazing place is called a maze*, Andre says to himself.

While in the *souk* one often hears a loud cry, *"Balek!"* It is wise to get out of the way when you hear this call, because this is a mule-cart driver yelling, "I'm coming through." Many booths have the famous, tightly-woven, colorful Moroccan carpets in sizes from little foot rugs to room-size rugs. There are many beautiful carpets to look at, but the tourists must keep up with Ajijine or be left behind. Shopkeepers, sometimes entire families, hawk their wares to the tourists and local shoppers.

Jing Xian slows down in front of a large stall with a huge variety of items. Stuffed birds, colorful horse tails, piles of stacked bones, stuffed rabbits, foxes, and weasels, dried snakes, spiders, bags of herbs, and other enigmatic items are all hanging from the ceiling or sitting on the shelves. He takes out his camera and is carefully aiming it when a man suddenly steps in front of him and shouts something in Moroccan. Jing Xian's heart begins to pound as he tries to understand the man, who has no teeth and long gray hair and is wearing an old brown robe. The man is very agitated and keeps shouting at Jing Xian, who soon realizes that Ajijine is nowhere to be seen. Not wanting to create a problem in this mysterious place, he stashes the camera, turns, and quickly walks away. A minute later, he sees Andre. Walking up to him, he hastily explains, "Hey, don't take a picture of that medicine man over there."

The strange man continues to stand in front of his merchandise, still glaring at Jing Xian.

"It looks like he'll come after anyone who takes a picture of his magic ingredients and creatures. He might put a spell on you." Chuckling, Jing Xian and Andre catch up with the group.

Chapter 43

Waiting beside a doorway, Mr. Roberson calls out, "Boys! Over here! I just saw Ajijine go up these stairs. He wants us to follow him. Make sure you get a piece of the branches the man is giving out at the entrance."

Andre and Jing Xian look at the man holding the branches. He pulls off pieces of the branch and hands one to each person going through the doorway. As each person accepts a branch, the man says something in Moroccan and swipes his upper lip with his finger.

How strange that looks, Andre thinks. *It's like this guy has a cold and is too cheap to get a tissue. That's all I need, is get a cold.* Following Jing Xian, he cautiously takes his piece of branch, listening carefully as the man speaks and again wipes his lip. Andre wipes the branch on his pants and heads up the dimly lit stairs. He pauses for a moment, waiting for his eyes to adjust to the darkness of the stairwell. Where are they being taken? As he climbs the squeaking stairs, a gust of wind fills the narrow space with a disgusting odor that defies description. *Something has died and is rotting in here*, Andre thinks. The smell is so foul that he soon has a pounding headache.

"What's that smell?" he calls out.

"Wait until you get up here," Jing Xian calls back.

He gets to the top of the stairs, and as he exits into the bright light, he sees Ajijine greeting the group, one by one. When the entire group has arrived, he gave them a quick demonstration of how to crush the leaves of the branch between the fingers and rub the fingers under the nose. "If the smell becomes too unbearable," he says, "crush more leaves and rub them on your upper lip until the smell subsides."

"Ah," Andre gasps, "now the antics of the man downstairs make sense." Feeling a bit sheepish, he chalks up his attitude to inexperience.

Marty and Tom, two other members of the group, were lagging behind and didn't get a branch, and they are now becoming nauseous, so Ajijine quickly fetches branches for them.

Andre sees his father and Jing Xian standing at the edge of the balcony and looking down. As he walks up, his father asks him, "Are you all right, Son? You look a little rough around the edges."

"I'm all right," Andre replies, "The smell caught me off guard. Are we all ready for lunch?" The three have a good laugh.

Mr. Roberson swings his arm over his son's shoulder and the three men look down at the large compound two stories below. What they are viewing is the famous animal hide dyeing yards that date back three or four hundred years. There are thirty large round holes cut into the ground, each of which measures eight to ten feet across and three to four feet deep. Each hole contains a different colored dye.

Men wade into the pools to remove hides that have been completely dyed, and the tourists look down to see stacks of freshly cured hides beside the holes waiting to be lowered into the vats of colors, which range in shades of blue, red, yellow, brown, and purple. The stench rises from the untreated hides.

At first, the tourists think the workers are wearing protective gloves and rubber boots, but soon they see that they have no protection. They wonder just how these dyes might affect the health of the men using ancient methods.

Ajijine walks up to the group. "Are there any questions about what's happening down in the dyeing pools?" he asks.

"Those men are working in the pools with no gloves or rubber boots on," says Allen. "Will they be permanently dyed?"

"Yes," answers Ajijine. "Some of those men are from a long bloodline of dye pool workers that dates back for hundreds of years. The fathers of the workers and their fathers, and so on, have been working in the pools all their lives. You just have to accept the bad breaks from the profession, like dyed arms and legs. The animal hides come from cows, sheep, and goats," he further explains. "Goat hide is the most popular. Occasionally, the dyers will get a large order of only one color with only one type of hide. Then I suppose the tourists don't get the full spectrum of the colors they use."

As the group splits up to take pictures and look more closely at the process below, Ajijine reminds them, "Remember to look at all the leather products they have to sell in the connecting room." Satisfied with their pictures and filled with this new information and the excitement of the day, the group continues their tour of the maze, taking pictures when they can and keeping up with Ajijine. No one wants to be left behind.

As they come around a corner in one of the numerous intersections of the *souk*, Ajijine points up, and as one the members of the group also look up. They see a most amazing sight above their heads. There are a thousand wires stretched across the high ceiling, on which hundreds and hundreds of dyed scarves are drying. This multitude of scarves is a universe of every color and pattern one can imagine.

As Ajijine begins talking with the man selling the scarves, two other men come from behind the curtains of the stall to join in the conversation. All three men have arms of dark purple, all the way down to their fingernails. After many years, the many colors have blended into this dark purple.

Ajijine turns to his group and raises his voice. "Everyone! Pick a scarf you like and it will be yours. You will need this scarf when we get out in the desert to protect your face and head from the blowing sand, the intense sun, flying insects, and any other thing that might bother you. If you put it on correctly, you might look like a ninja warrior." He lets out a short laugh. "We will have a little class on how to put the scarf on when we get to the camels."

Ajijine frequently looks around the corner of his hooded *djellaba* to make sure everyone is following him. He seems immediately that Maji and Doshi, who are from Pakistan, always seem to be putting some distance between themselves and the rest of the group. As a professional tour guide, it is Ajijine's responsibility to keep everyone happy, though he is aware of the many problems that can arise with wandering tourists. When they entered the *souk,* he saw this couple talking with someone who was not a shopkeeper and then he saw them pass a paper to another shopkeeper. *Maybe they made a purchase*, he says to himself.

He hopes they will keep up. He has never lost anyone in a *souk*, but he is always worried. One of these trips, he knows, someone can easily wander off and get lost. They could spend hours roaming through the unmarked passageways, trying to find the exit, and they would most likely wind up going around in circles like a rat in a maze. There are innumerable intersections, and some have six different directions, so a stranger can easily become confused and disoriented. Add to that the fact that English speakers are hard to find, and the problem is compounded because in their confusion and anxiety, lost tourists invariably go in the wrong direction. They might not even be able to find the fountain where they were directed to meet. Eventually, the lost person will find his way out, but this is always at the expense of time and the patience of the other members of the group.

As the group works its way through the maze, they exit at the same spot where they entered. Ajijine starts breathing at a slower pace. Now he can relax. He counts his tourists. "Yes," he says with a smile, "everyone is here."

Chapter 44

The group gathers around their efficient guide, who raises his voice again to be heard over the sounds of the marketplace. "We are now going into the middle of the Medina," he says. "You will enjoy the circus-like entertainment of Marrakech's famous square, Djemma El Fna, which translates as Court of Marvels. Here you will see fire eaters, magicians, snake charmers, storytellers, and more. In the evening, the area is filled with restaurants operating in the traditional way, where you sit on wooden benches shoulder to shoulder around large, hot, steel pot and eat Moroccan soup."

The most famous attractions, he adds, are the snake charmers, who use cobras because of their awesome and sinister look. The cobra has the ability to stand up and sway back and forth, mesmerizing onlookers.

"But I warn you," Ajijine says, "mostly you women. When you are watching the snakes perform, always be aware of what is happening around you. Occasionally, a man will walk through the audience with a snake hidden about himself. This snake isn't a cobra, it's just a big harmless snake, but it's very scary. He will keep this snake concealed. Suddenly, with no warning, he will put the snake around the neck of an unsuspecting woman. Believe me, she will almost die from fright. The charmers hire these men to do this. They think it's a lot of fun. Again, I caution you. Be aware. Also keep an eye out for pick-pockets, especially you women. Hold tight to your purses."

Ajijine puts his hand up in the air again. "There is one more thing," he says in his loud voice. "This is extremely important. I warn you. If you take a picture of a snake charmer, whether he is performing or just waiting around before or after a performance, you will have to pay. Be extremely careful when you decide to take a picture. It doesn't matter where you are standing. There are people roaming through the audience collecting money from unsuspecting tourists."

The tourists also see watermen walking around the Medina with their large water cans strapped to their backs and wearing the same style of clothing that watermen wore hundreds of years ago. For hundreds of years, such vendors have been selling water by the cupful to passers-by in the center of the town.

"Remember," Ajijine says, "these watermen pose for pictures now. They don't sell water anymore because you can purchase bottled water in most restaurants and grocery stores. But if you take a picture and they spot you, they will make you pay. Sometimes their demands lead to violence, so be careful." Ajijine makes eye contact with everyone in the group, except for Maji and Doshi, who are standing away from the group as usual.

The group cautiously heads off toward the snake charmers. If someone loses sight of the group, they usually look for Andre, who is the tallest man there, and rejoin the group in no time. Andre stands out in a crowd, which means that the rest of the group uses him as a beacon. Ajijine is almost the same height as Andre, but not as muscular, and when the tour guide has his hood up, he looks like the locals, so the members of the group always look for Andre.

As Mr. Roberson walks along, he is thinking that there must be thousands of people mingling about, watching different events, going in different directions in the square. Most of the people seem to be local, but he also spots other tourist groups. He sees Berber women wearing their bright, distinctive gowns, which are called *djellabas* and decorated in shiny silver sequins, and matching embroidered head scarves. Some women have their faces covered with a meshed veil sewn into their scarves, whereas others have no head coverings.

Andre suddenly understands that if someone is going to get his pocket picked, it will be here. He quickly takes his wallet from his hip pocket and tucks it into a front pocket. When Jing Xian sees Andre move his wallet, he does the same thing. He also mentions this to Andre's father.

"Oh," Mr. Roberson replies, "I moved my wallet long before we went into the *souk*, but it's good you and Andre are alert to the changes around you. This alertness is what world travel experience teaches."

Andre walks closely behind Ajijine through the dense crowd, and the rest of the group follows close behind.

Soon Jing Xian nudges Andre in the ribs. "Hey, look at those guys over there." He points to a dozen men wearing red hats that stand high on their heads.

Mr. Roberson overhears him. "Those red hats with black tassels are called fezzes," he explains. "I believe the hat actually came from an old fraternal order from the ancient city of Fez many centuries ago. The city is north of here. The hat carries a long Moroccan history."

"Does the fez hat come in other colors?" Jing Xian asks.

"I'm not sure. I've only seen them in red. Thinking about it, I believe I've seen some people wearing these hats in parades in San Francisco. I'm not sure if it would be the same mystical order."

Chapter 45

Mr. Roberson pauses to think about fezzes. "There was a movie long time ago," he finally says, "back in the days when the movies were in black and white. I believe Humphrey Bogart was the star. The name of the movie was *Casablanca*. In the movie, there were several men wearing fezzes. The movie wasn't really shot in Morocco. It was all on a Hollywood set. The movie was supposed to have taken place in the city of Casablanca in Morocco during the early 1940s at the start of World War Two. I've heard there are tourists," he adds with a grin, "who come to Casablanca still want to know where Rick's Café and the Hotel Casablanca are."

Andre comments, "I believe there was a Trivial Pursuit question that had something to do with the movie. Who did Humphrey Bogart play? What was the famous saying in the movie?"

"His name was Rick. Ha, gotcha!" Mr. Robertson says. "And 'Play it again Sam' is what he said to the piano player in his bar."

"I don't think so," says Andre. "The famous saying is said by Ilsa, Rick's old girl friend. She said, *Play it once for old time's sake.*"

Mr. Roberson nods. "You're right. It's been a long time since I've seen that movie.

Andre grins. "Hey, Dad, I'll bet you a glass of real fine Moroccan wine that you can't tell me who's the female star of that movie."

Mr. Roberson grimaces and mutters, "I can see her standing there. Who is she?" Now he has both hands pressed against his forehead, concentrating. "Bogie gives her the famous farewell kiss while they are standing in the dense fog. Oh, I'll remember pretty soon. I'll tell you later."

"Yup," says Andre. "You'll tell me over the glass of wine you're going to buy me and Jing Xian. Did I say a bottle?"

"Okay. You think you're so smart."

"Yup, I think I gotcha back, old man," Andre says with a smug laugh.

Jing Xian looks at them with puzzlement on his face. "Who was Bogie? What is that movie?"

"We'll explain it over a bottle of fine Moroccan wine at the hotel."

Chapter 46

The group slowly approaches one of the snake charmers and joins a larger group of people in a circle around him, every eye focused on the swaying cobra, every ear listening to the pulsating music the charmer plays on his flute. Back and forth, the king cobra sways, dancing to the hypnotic music. The snake's head is flattened into its hood, and it looks ready to strike, not taking his eyes off the charmer for one second. A couple of times during the show, the cobra looks bored or tired and slows down in its swaying. When this happens, the flute player waves his hand back and forth in the air, giving the snake a more comfortable feeling and picking up the pace.

After about ten minutes, the charmer decides the show is over. He moves his left hand away from his body, and the snake focuses on the moving hand. The charmer stops playing his flute, lays it in his lap, and continues to wave his other hand. Then he uses his flute hand to pick up a large, round, metal cakepan. In a quick move, he covers the snake with the pan and lowers it to the asphalt. The cobra does not fight or try to escape from under the pan. The show is over. The charmer has several pans lying in front of him, so it is obvious that he has more than one snake. Maybe the snakes get tired easily?

During the performance several men walk through the crowd. They are carrying small cardboard boxes and demanding money from the audience. Everyone in the group put some money into the nearest box.

Ajijine raises his hand to signal his group and says they are going to another location in the Medina. As he starts walking, he looks over his shoulder and sees a couple of Moroccan men dressed in *djellabas* talking with Allen. He immediately stops and turns his head to see what is happening. Allen has his wallet out and is giving the men some money. He must have gotten caught taking pictures of the snake charmer.

"Excuse me, mister," the bigger of the two Moroccan men is saying to Allen. "We are aware you are here on vacation. We appreciate that very much. But when you are taking pictures of the performance by professionals, it is our right to ask for some kind of payment for that privilege. If you do not agree with our request, we will be forced to take the film out of your camera. If you don't mind, we think it would be appropriate for you to pay nothing less than three American dollars. If you enjoyed the performance, it would be extremely appreciated if you pay more."

Allen takes a five dollar bill out of his wallet and hands it to the big man.

"Thank you very much for your five dollar donation," the man says. "Would you like to have a receipt?"

"No, thanks."

"We wish you an enjoyable vacation in Morocco."

"Thank you."

As the men walk away to look for other people who are taking pictures of the performers, Allen catches up with the group, looking a bit sheepish.

"It's okay," Ajijine quietly tells him. "There are many people who take pictures and never get caught. Then there are others who get caught immediately. I guess it wasn't your lucky day. I hope they didn't charge you too much."

"No, they didn't," Allen replies. "They told me he's a professional performer, and if anyone takes a picture, they should pay for the privilege. I agreed. They politely told me if I didn't pay them, they would take my camera and remove the film, and if I refused, they would usher me to their office somewhere in the alley."

The group moves through the crowd. Everyone is following close behind, except for Maji and Doshi, who seem to be looking for someone. Finally, they spot a Moroccan man standing alone and hand him a note. The man disappears as quickly as he appeared.

Ajijine guides the group around a man who looks like he must be ninety years old, or older, with a long white beard that tapers to a point near his knees. His hair is also long and white, and his eyes are set deep into his skull, which makes him look like a walking dead man. Wearing a long black robe with a hood, he raises a long staff over his head with both hands. Andre recalls seeing someone like this in science fiction thriller movies. The old man gibbering in a peculiar language with such intensity that the crowd starts to gather closer around him. Many onlookers nodding their heads and talking to themselves.

The man is now walking around a cage with a bird of prey inside it, maybe an eagle. A nearby cage holds a large raven. The old man has stacked several piles of bleached bones beside the cages. It is hard for the observers to tell what kind of bones they are, perhaps cows' bones, perhaps human bones. Holding his staff in one hand, the old man picks up one of the bones and starts to yell at his audience. He continues to walk around his cages and getting up close into the faces of his audience.

"He must be some kind of spiritual teacher," Ajijine whispers to Andre as they walk by. The tour guide decides not to hang around this medicine man. He is scaring the tourists.

Eventually, Ajijine gets his group back to the buggies. "We are heading back to the hotel," he tells his charges. "We will be getting a simple lunch along the way. For the adventurous people who would like to stay here in the Medina, look across the way." He points across the Medina toward the Marrakesh Hotel. "That is a nice hotel that, I might add, has a nice lunch, although it might be a bit pricey. But never walk outside by yourself. Always try to walk in pairs or more. And please be careful. You can catch an honest cab back to the hotel. It shouldn't cost very much. Tell the driver the name of our hotel. It is the Tichka Hotel."

As the members of the group nod, he continues. "Tonight we are going to have a real Moroccan dinner at the hotel, starting at seven o'clock. After dinner, you will be entertained by several belly-dancers and acrobatic musicians who wear the famous fez hats. Everyone will be seated in the Moroccan style, which is sitting on rugs and pillows. You will be served one of our fine Moroccan wines by the beautiful women of the Sahara. If everyone who is going back with me will get aboard the buggies, we are leaving soon." He looks at his charges and adds, "Please raise your hands if you will be staying here. I need to make a list to keep track of everyone and where they are going to be. Thank you."

When the buggies stop in front of the Tichka Hotel, it's obvious that the warm sun has taken its toll on the group. They are tired and hot and eager to head for their rooms for a cool shower.

But Ajijine has one more announcement. "Dinner starts at seven o'clock. Please, you don't want to miss this dinner show. Wear something that is cool and comfortable that you can lounge around in, but sort of dressy. No shorts or T-shirts, please. Part of the stage is an open air stage, so you will be able to see the stars and the wonderful night sky. After a nice cool shower and a little rest, you will be rejuvenated for this evening. If you decide to take a nap, make sure you have a wake-up call at the front desk. If you miss dinner, and you might be looking for food at midnight, please be aware that the hotel doesn't serve late meals."

He pauses. "There's a wonderful lounge downstairs, overlooking the pool. It's a great place for a drink and conversation before the show. I believe there is a piano player outside beside the pool. Nice background music. The swimming pool is excellent. Bathing suits are mandatory up to eleven o'clock at night. Some children are still around." He laughs."

"I might add," he says, "that we will be leaving the hotel tomorrow morning for the camel ride. We will not be returning to the hotel. Make sure you have checked out at the front desk and that you are in the lobby with your luggage at nine o'clock. Reminder: wear wide-brimmed hats, plenty of sun block, and long sleeves. See you all at seven for the dinner show." At this point, the tour guide leaves the hotel.

"Let's meet in the bar by the pool in a couple of hours," Mr. Roberson tells Andre and Jing Xian. "Say about six o'clock. That should give you guys plenty of time to get cleaned up. We need a little time to have a drink and unwind before dinner."

Everyone heads up to their rooms.

Chapter 47

It is 5:30 when Mr. Roberson comes into the hotel bar. *Ah*, he thinks, *just a little early. Maybe someone else in the group is here. But I can't sit in my room looking at four walls.* He sits down, and the waiter comes to his table. "I would like to have a glass of Merlot wine," he tells the waiter. "And charge it to my room."

"Yes, sir," the waiter replies.

A few minutes pass, and Maji and Doshi arrive in the bar and approach Mr. Roberson's table.

"Mr. Roberson," the Pakistani man says, "my name is Maji. I would like to introduce my wife, Doshi."

"It is a pleasure to meet you both."

"May we join you?" Maji asks.

"Yes, that would be nice," Mr. Roberson replies. "My son and his friend won't be here for a while. I didn't see you too much while we were walking around in the Medina today."

"Oh, yes," Maji replies. "We were there, but we just didn't stay up in the front of the group."

"I see. Well, if you don't mind, I would like to be called Tim. It's less formal, and we just want to relax and enjoy life, you know. This trip is going to be one of the most exciting times in our lives, to be going across the Sahara desert on camels."

"Have you been on a camel before?"

At the same time Maji asks his question, his wife lights up a long brown cigarette that looks like a cheap cigar. She blows the smoke straight into Mr. Robertson's face. Moving his head out of the cloud, he moves his hands in a fanning motion and coughs.

"You know," Maji says, ignoring the smoke, "camels are demanding, both mentally and physically. I was wondering. It might not be safe for you to be on this camel safari. Are your son and his friend capable of taking care of you if something should happen to you?"

125

Mr. Roberson shakes his head. *How odd this guy is,* he thinks. *What is he talking about? Camels are demanding? The mental aspect of the trip? Odd, very odd.* He does not think he is out of shape, although he has developed a paunch over the past few years. Perhaps some of those years are starting to show. *This guy sure doesn't have any tact,* he thinks. *He's almost insulting. Well, maybe, it's his demeanor. He doesn't realize he's disturbing. I'll try to blow him off.*

Mr. Roberson looks out at the swimming pool as he sips his wine, only occasionally glancing at Maji and Doshi out of the corner of his eye. They are talking and sipping their own drinks. *Who do they think they are?* he wonders. *They have no class.* The Pakistani couple both look out of shape, and it is obvious that they are wearing expensive clothing, *but,* he tells himself, *the clothing doesn't hide their flab. They both have big butts, they breathe heavily, plus they smoke. It's also obvious that Doshi needs a touchup to her blonde hair. And she also needs to hide more of those wrinkles. And she better quit blowing smoke in my face, or I'll change tables.*

"Mr. Roberson," Doshi suddenly asks, "are both of those boys your sons? They are handsome young men."

"Thank you." He is pleased by her question. "The tall boy is mine," he says. "The other boy is his best buddy. They met in China."

"Very interesting. And what sort of business are you in?"

"I'm in the sea-land containers business. I import and export."

"Yes, I see," Maji says. "I understand it can be a cut-throat business."

"Well," Mr. Roberson begins, feeling blind-sided by such a confrontational statement, "I don't feel it's that bad of business to be in." His voice is starting to show some emotion. "I have been enormously successful for the last twenty-some years without any major downfalls. With the strong economy in the United States, and surging business in developing third world nations, the import and export business is very profitable. Everyone has their competitors. The laws we all must abide by in the countries we do business in keep harmony worldwide."

Maji is starting to get under his skin, and so he is relieved to see Andre and Jing Xian coming into the bar. He excuses himself and stands up. "This has been a very interesting conversation," he tells Maji. "We need to get together again sometime when I'm prepared to answer such challenging questions."

He nods curtly and walks across the room to the table where the younger men are sitting. "That man, Maji," he mutters as he sits down, "and his wife or girlfriend, they're very odd characters. This Maji guy tells me my business is a cut-throat business. He says I should be careful because I might hurt myself on the camel trip. He has a nasty disposition. I don't like him, plus he has a chip on his shoulder."

"Hey, Dad. Be nice. No fighting until we finish our drinks."

"Okay, boys. I'm sorry, but we need to watch them. I'm sure they're going to be trouble." The older man takes a long drink from his glass, then tilts his head back and takes in a deep breath.

"Hey, Pop, do you remember who the female star was with Humphrey Bogart in *Casablanca*?"

"I thought you'd forgotten that."

"Nope. There's a bottle of wine riding on the answer."

"I give up," the older man says with a sigh. "I just can't remember her name."

"Ingrid Bergman."

Now he remembers. "Yes, that's right. I remember her very well."

"I think I know what this is about now," says Jing Xian.

All three men laugh and beckon to the waiter to bring the wine list.

Chapter 48

As soon as Ajijine comes walking into the bar wearing his white *djellaba* with the hood down, Maji swoops in on him and starts shooting all sorts of questions at him, including will the camel party be camping the night before they arrive at the kasbah, and where, and when?

"Has either one of you ever been on a camel?" Ajijine asks Maji and Doshi,

"No," they reply. "We come from the big city. We have never ventured out into the deserts. But this time we are on a mission. But it shouldn't be too difficult," Maji says. "Many of my friends have been on camels."

"You see, we are from Pakistan," says Doshi. "Are there security cameras at the kasbah to protect it from vandalism? We are studying the kasbahs of Morocco, and this particular one is high on our list because of its charm and history."

While she is talking, Ajijine thinking to himself, *There is something strange about these questions they are asking me. Having run this trip many times, I know people have all types of reasons for coming. If no one comes, then I would be out of work, so I put up with the strange questions people ask.*

They are almost too demanding as they ask him what the kasbah looks like, while at the same time, they claim to know it very well. *Why are they so interested in when will we be arriving?* the tour guide wonders. They also ask what road they will be coming in on and will they be riding Land Rovers or camels. Doshi has a tourist map they picked up somewhere and asks Ajijine to mark the spot where the kasbah is located. He complies, but he still thinks it is strange that they are so concerned about where and when the group was going to arrive and where they will be camping the night before. It is, he starts to think, as if they are planning to meet someone there.

Chapter 49

"**B**oys," Mr. Roberson says with an excited look on his face, "you remember when Ajijine announced there will be belly dancers at the dinner show tonight? Well, believe me, they're something to watch. We'll be seated on a beautiful carpet and resting against pillows of all sizes, shapes, and colors, some with large tassels. I hope they'll be pouring wine from the long-necked wine pitchers. It's kind of hard to describe, but you'll see what I mean. They pour your wine from two, maybe three feet, away from your glass without spilling a drop. I'm sure they've had a lot of practice pouring. Make sure you get a picture when they do that. Now, depending on the dinner show, some hotels will have several Sahara maidens walking around giving neck and shoulder massages upon request. It's a nice treat for the women in the group as well.

"The belly dancers are amazing to watch," he continues. "They shake their hips and move their bellies while dancing on their toes and heels. You have to be in good shape for that type of workout. In my travels around the world, I've seen some unbelievable dancers."

"What are we to watch for?" Jing Xian asks.

"The more experienced dancers have developed their stomach muscles so well, they can make a visible ripple move from the top of their stomach all the way down past their navel. They do all these stomach gyrations while clapping these brass clickers between their fingers. Or do they call them castanets? Maybe the castanets are used in Spain. I can't remember. Anyway, they dance to this pulsating Moroccan music. All the dancers have long, dark hair hanging over their shoulders, and dark almond-shaped eyes. Amazing." Mr. Roberson closes his eyes and surrenders to his memories. He takes another drink.

"Please continue," says Jing Xian, sounding eager.

"The dancers wear low-cut, silky outfits that reveal half or more of their well-formed, succulent breasts. *That* is worth waiting for. They have to be real!" Pausing again, he takes another drink. "Well, usually they have several scarves tied or wrapped around their necks. And long, silk, dancing bottoms you can see through." He takes a deep breath. "Now remember this. It is really amazing and important. The dancer will have this large ruby, or something like it, stuck in her belly button. This stone never falls out. It must be glued in. Maybe they have developed a belly button muscle." He laughs at his own joke. "Keep your eyes on it. Well, maybe not all the time." He pauses for another sip. "While dancing, they come up close to the men in the audience and shake their flawless breasts in their faces. They also have a sexual smile all the time while they are dancing. They try to get a rise out of the men, and sometime they do. The man may get very embarrassed. Almost always, the dancers will get several men up on the stage and make them tie their shirts up above their hairy bellies and roll up the legs of their pants and dance with them. It really gets everyone laughing.

"The dancers are accompanied by three or four musical acrobats. The guys I saw when I was traveling through Egypt stood on each others' shoulders while playing music, then did back-flips to get down. Have you ever seen a man juggling a saxophone, a trumpet, and a butcher knife? It's amazing. The men will be wearing fez hats and playing some mean Moroccan music. I tell you, you'll be spellbound." He takes another long drink from his glass.

Shortly after this, the host announces, "The dinner room is open now. Tonight, for your entertainment, we will have two special belly dancers accompanied by the acrobatic musicians. Please come in and enjoy yourself.

Later that night, after the dinner and the show, a lone person is cleaning tables and vacuuming the floor and the night clerk at the front desk is processing the day's receipts. He has a small radio playing music to overcome the silence of the late shift. Mysterious shadows come and go as the workers turn lights on and off.

The bartender has cleaned up his bar, locked the liquor in the cabinets, and finished the night's paperwork. He comes to the front desk. "Here is tonight's money," he tells the night clerk. "We did real good tonight. I think that camel tour group helped out a lot. They had a great time at the dinner show. One of the dancers, I think it was Anne, got this white-haired guy out of the audience. A couple of the men were calling him Mr. Tim. Anne got him to tie his shirt up under his arms, showing off his hairy belly, and you should have seen him dance. He got so close to her, he was pressing against her tits. I think he was embarrassing her. After the seductive dance, the old guy slipped a one hundred dollar bill with his room number into her hand. She smiled and nodded. What do you think?"

"I don't know," the clerk replies. "If he has the money, anything can happen."

"This guy was a character," the bartender adds. "He made the show. He must have been to other shows where they have belly dancers. I understand they'll be checking out in the morning. I think the dancers are going to miss him." He finishes his paperwork and hands everything to the clerk. "Good night," he says. "See you tomorrow."

Chapter 50

Shortly after the bartender leaves the hotel, Maji sneaks out of his room and, making sure he is not seen, walks down the stairs. He passes the busy night clerk without being seen and steps out into the warm, muggy night. It is very late, and there are no taxis in front of the hotel. Most of the people coming in from the Medina have already gone to bed.

He spots a man riding a bicycle toward the hotel. Slowly, he steps back out of the dimly lighted street and into the shadow of the hotel, impatiently waiting for the rider to pass. He is obviously keeping a lookout for something else. *Could this be the person?"* he asks himself. *Or maybe it isn't. It is too dark to tell.*

He steps out of the shadow, making his presence known to the bike rider, who sees Maji and swerves his bike, disappearing at top speed down the street. Maji realizes this must not have been his contact and he may have compromised his location. Getting nervous, he reaches down and rubs his trousers pocket, feeling the bulge of his pistol. *The Beretta's here just in case I need it*, he assures himself. Trying to regain his composure, he lights up one of his Arabian cigarettes. Taking a long drag, he feels the strong nicotine relaxing his body. He then reaches into his other trouser pocket making sure he didn't forget his pen light with its red lens. He will use it to make the signal.

Straining his eyes, a few minutes later he sees a dark car slowly rolling through the shadows at the far end of the desolate street. The car's headlights are out. It stops. Maji rubs his eyes, trying to make out the driver. It appears that only one person is in the car. *Must be Akram*, he decides. He quickly crosses the street and starts walking in the direction of the car, looking over his shoulder to make sure no one is following him. Stopping beside a bush, he ducks down behind it and takes out his pen light and blinks two quick flashes at the car. About ten seconds pass, then he repeats the blinks. "Damn it," he says aloud. "This must be the wrong person again."

But then two blinks come from the car, and it slowly moves in his direction. Hardly making a sound, it pulls up in front of him. He opens the passenger door and jumps in. "Where have you been?" he snaps.

"Thanks for saying Good evening, Akram," the driver replies in a sarcastic tone.

"I wasn't sure if you had received my message I had sent you today. I'm just a little frustrated. It's late and I have to be at the front desk by nine thirty." This is Maji's apology.

"Well, maybe you can catch up on your sleep while they are driving."

"Yeah, maybe I can. Okay, here is the location of where the kasbah is located." Maji hands the driver the map. "Attached are the instructions on what you need to prepare the wall. I cannot give you the exact time when we will be arriving. I didn't want to create any more suspicion than we have already done. Doshi is driving me nuts! There are several events that are going to take place."

He pauses for another long drag on his cigarette. "First, I'm not sure if we will be arriving by camel or in Land Rovers. Ajijine was telling me there are some changes because of several sick camels and one of the drivers. What a mess! I certainly wouldn't want to have a damn business like this where you have to make changes on an hourly basis. I will have to wait for you on the last night before we arrive at the kasbah. We will be at the southern tip of Erg Chebbi. That's Morocco's largest sand dune. I had our trip leader put an X where we will camp. I will meet you on the opposite side of the dune at 2200 hours. Hopefully, at that hour everyone will be asleep. Any questions?"

"Yes. How am I going to find this place if it's in the sand dunes?"

Maji glares at Akram. "I think you may want to reconnoiter the area the day before we arrive so you will be familiar with it. You may have to park your Land Rover some distance from the camp site. Noise travels a lot farther at night, and you don't want to get caught. And make sure you wear good shoes. You may have to walk several miles in the sand."

"The hell with that," says Akram, "I don't want to walk miles in the sand at midnight." He is getting a bit testy. "I have to be at the kasbah long before you guys get there and fix the wall and be ready when you arrive. I'm not going to get any sleep. You understand?"

"No, I don't understand." At this point in the conversation, Maji raises his voice and points a finger in Akram's face. "I'll tell *you*. You either shut your damn mouth and do what you are told to do, or you will wind up just like the guy who is going to die tomorrow. Do you understand?"

He jabs his finger again, almost hitting the driver's face. "We have a job to do. It will be done right. No more questions. It will be *done right*." He pauses and takes another drag on the cigarette, then tosses it out the window. "I will be seeing you in a couple of days."

Maji gets out of the car, pausing to make sure no one is around, then quickly crosses the street. He stops to watch the car disappear around the corner, then lights up another cigarette. He keeps looking around, as if expecting someone else. After he finishes his cigarette, he drops the butt on the pavement and grinds it out with his heel.

Being extremely careful not to draw attention to himself, Maji slowly reenters the hotel lobby and listens to make sure the night clerk is busy. He hears faint music coming from the back room. He walks across the large Moroccan rug and makes his way back to his room without being seen.

Or has he been seen?

Chapter 51

Promptly at eight-thirty the next morning, everyone piles their suitcases and backpacks at the spot indicated by Ajijine. Coming down the hotel's spiral staircase, Jodie struggles with her two large bags and a bulky purse. A bell boy comes up to her to see if he can assist her.

"Yes, that would be nice," she says. "There were just too many people waiting for the elevator, so I though the stairs would be easier." She forces a smile. "I guess I was wrong."

"Hello, excuse me, miss." A Moroccan housecleaner comes walking down the stairs to Jodie. "I hate to disturb you," she says. "Your room number was 208?"

"Yes, it was."

"My name is Sharif, I'm your housekeeper. I noticed when I came in your room to clean, you had left a blouse in the closet."

"Thank you so much. I thought I got everything."

"I'm glad I got you before you departed the hotel. The blouse is very pretty. I'm sure you would have missed it."

"Can you do me a favor?" Jodie asks. "Would you slip the blouse into the side pocket of my suitcase? It will be easier than opening it up, and my arms are full."

"Yes. Here in this pocket?"

"Yes. Thanks a lot." She hands the housekeeper a tip for her help, and the woman goes back up the stairs. The bell boy is still standing by, waiting for instructions from Jodie.

"I may have brought too many clothes," she tells him, speaking too fast to the young man, whose English is poor and understands hardly anything she is saying. "I'm in the camel tour group that is departing the hotel this morning. Would you put my bags with the group's bags? I have to check out of my room." The boy reconfirms her room number and as he starts to carry her bags down the stairs, she stops him and gives him several coins as a tip. She goes on with the story of her purchases. "I found a real nice handmade purse at a terrific price in the gift shop. I want to mail it home so it won't get ruined on the trip. Who knows, I might find more things, and I won't have enough room in my bags. Oh, and just a moment, I forgot something, I need to get into one of my bags and find my address book. I recently moved, and I keep forgetting my new zip code." Still talking about her moving problems, Jodie digs into one of her bags. The bell boy is standing still, looking at her, trying to understand what she is saying, and wondering what he is going to carry. "Here it is," she says after a minute. "I found it. I hope I didn't hold you up." With a grin, he picks up her bags and carries them down the stairs.

Charlie and Pai Lin are already at the front desk and telling the clerk, "This has been the best hotel we have ever stayed at in our entire lives. We are planning a return trip to Marrakesh. We want to stay here at the Tichka Hotel again."

"Please take one of our brochures," the clerk replies. "It has our e-mail address on it." As the clerk hands her a brochure, Pai Lin continues praising the hotel. "And the food was unbelievable. I'll have to bring my bathing suit next time. The pool looked so inviting."

Ajijine arrives now and gets the group's attention so he can make another announcement. "Will everyone please go out and get in a Land Rover parked in front of the hotel. Just bring your personal day bag with you. The rest of your luggage will be loaded by the drivers. Don't worry who is sitting with who. We will be stopping several times before we get to our destination, and we can change around if you wish. Okay? Let's get aboard."

Chapter 52

After several hours of driving and a couple of bathroom breaks, the three-vehicle caravan pulls into Quarzazate, the gateway to the Sahara Desert. Here they take a lunch break, and everyone stands up to stretch their legs.

Ajijine talks to his charges about their itinerary. "From here," he says "we will take a rough ride down a winding dirt road through the Tizi-n-Tichka Pass. We will wind up in the Salt River Valley, which was the original caravan route into the Sahara. There will be some spots on the road the Land Rovers will barely be able to squeeze through, and a few rugged cliffs with dangerous falling rocks. Once we get over the pass, it is well worth the view. There we will spend some time exploring the Ait Benhaddou, the best preserved exotic kasbah in Morocco. Many years ago, the movie *Lawrence of Arabia* was filmed here, and more recently the film *Gladiator*, with superstar Russell Crow, was also filmed there. Hollywood has been looking closely at this area for some time, planning more films. Maybe some day it could be Hollywood East," he adds with a chuckle. Then he continues. "We will eat a picnic lunch here. We will serve some Moroccan mint tea for a soothing effect just in case the food is too spicy for your stomach." He gives Mr. Roberson a nod and a smile. "Along our route, we will pass numerous kasbahs, most of which have been abandoned because of severe weather and nomadic wars."

After lunch everyone is treated to mouth-watering fresh dates that Ajijine ordered from a nearby grove of date palms. "These dates you are eating," he explains, "have a history dating back a thousand years. As you know, this road we are on was the road the camel caravan trains used to across the Sahara Desert. The camels carried a lot of salt and other supplies. These same date palms have been growing here beside the trail for hundreds, or maybe thousands, of years. You see, there are all different sizes of palms here." Ajijine looks at the palm trees and says, "There has to be a spring close by. History is being made as we are standing here." He pops another tasty date into his mouth and says, "Make sure there is no trash on the ground. We want to leave this place just as the way it was when we arrived."

With this, everyone climbs back into the Land Rovers for several more hours of grueling driving. Eventually, the convoy starts to slow down. Up ahead, the tourists see a small herd of camels. They slowly drive closer to the camels and stop.

"Here we are," Ajijine announces as he gets out of the vehicle and starts knocking the dust off his *djellaba*. "If everyone will follow me?"

As he walks in front of the group, Pai Lin remembers *Lawrence of Arabia*, which she recently saw in China. She thinks Ajijine looks just like one of the Arabs from the old movies.

The tour guide walks into the shade of the grove of date palms, the group right behind him. "Please be seated," he says. "Make yourself comfortable on the sand. Drink water from your bottles." As his customers begin drinking, he continues. "I would like to explain some things that everyone needs to know before riding a camel. First of all, the drivers of our Land Rovers have several jobs that have to be done on a daily basis. Right now, they are going to start getting our dinner prepared. They will also be setting up our main tent so we will have a place to sit out of the sun. We will also be setting up the individual tents you will be sleeping in at night. Our drivers can speak some English, but I would prefer it if you would not strike up conversations with them. They have a lot of work to do, and if you talk to them, we will not get to eat tonight." Ajijine gives a small laugh.

"Now over there," he points in the direction of the camels, "are our camels. They all have names, but it is hard to remember them, and when you are riding the camel, they don't really respond to their name, anyway. Most likely, you are not pronouncing the name correctly because you need a Moroccan accent." He laughs again. "The only people they respond to are me and the camel leader. We will start riding the camels tomorrow morning, but first, before dinner is ready, we will practice getting on and off the camels. Tomorrow, six people will ride camels, and the other six will walk. Then we will take a short break and switch. The riders will walk, and the walkers will ride. We will be riding all day tomorrow. If you can't walk all the way, or you get blisters or just plain tired, you can ride in one of the vehicles. When riding a camel you must become acquainted with their different gaits. Our camels will not bite you, and they won't spit at you unless you provoke them. They are nice animals. Don't always believe the stories you hear about camels. There are camels that are abused by their owners and become mean. Occasionally a tourist will be mean to a camel, such as kicking or cursing them."

The guide continues his lecture. "Please do not feed the camels under any circumstances, regardless of how you feel about them. If you are eating something, it doesn't matter what size it is, if it falls on the ground, please don't leave it. We have bags here to put all unused food in. We will dispose of it at the right time. If one of the camels eats it, he may become sick, and that will affect our trip. Someone on our last trip either fed something to one of the camels or dropped it on the ground and the camel ate it, and it made him very sick. We had to replace the camel in the middle of the tour, which meant that we lost valuable time. I'm sure it did not make the people on the tour happy. The camel leader does not speak English. If there is a problem, please speak to me." He looks around and everyone nods.

"Oh, and one more thing," he says. "Each evening, the blankets and saddles are removed from the camels, so in the morning, the saddles will feel different when you climb aboard. In past trips, we have noticed that some people prefer a certain camel. Maybe they feel they have a connection in some way and want it every time it's their time to ride. We are sorry, but there may be more than one person who wants this camel, and we can't have squabbles or unfriendly gestures. We are here to enjoy ourselves and have a good time. So please try to rotate the camels and everyone will be happy.

"Now we are going to get some practice time in before dinner." Ajijine leads the group toward the camel herd. "Why doesn't everyone line up right here in front of me. Remember, do not try to get on or off a camel without me or the camel leader with you. Only one person will be riding a camel at a time." He signals to the first six people. "Okay. Now you six people get on a camel. Please listen carefully. I'm going to tell you what the camel is going to do when he starts to stand up. Camels have very long legs and it takes some special moves for them to get fully standing. So you must always be aware of what is happening when you are mounting a camel. First you will notice that his butt end is going to rise high in the air, which will give you a sensation that you are going to be pitched over his head. That is right. You *will* be pitched over his head unless you are paying attention! When his rear end starts to rise, you should lean backwards with a full grip on the saddle or the blanket, whichever one you can hang on to. Then, when his front legs start to extend, he will sort off level off. Then there will be one more back leg extension. Pay attention! There is a possibility you will be pitched off over his head a second time. Now the camel will be fully standing, and you will be roughly about seven or eight feet above the ground. When the camel first starts to step forward, his motion will give you a slight feeling he is not too steady, but don't worry. He is fine. Everything will be great."

Six people carefully climb on to six camels. All six camels stand up. No one falls off. There is a slight scramble on top of one of the camels, however, when Marty loses her grip on the saddle. "Awwww, shiii—No, I have it!" she yells smiling from ear to ear as she recovers her seat. "This is great!" she yells. "I'm ready to go!"

"Good, good, everyone did well." Ajijine smiles and nods and looks at his people. He continues his instructions. "Okay, now the camels are going to sit down. Watch out for the pitch again. There will be two of them. Great! Now everyone off, and the next six people, please stand beside your camels."

Ajijine notices that Doshi does not approach a camel. "Is there something wrong?" he asks her.

She gives him a look that is both frightened and angry. "Yes, there is something wrong! I'm terrified of camels. I'm not going to ride any of them! They look very dangerous. They're too high. I will fall off and hurt myself. Plus they stink and have too many flies around them."

"Doshi, please believe me," the tour guide replies. "The camels are trained very well. You won't fall off."

"I don't care! I'm not riding any of them."

"Okay, Doshi. If you wish, we will have you ride in one of the Land Rovers."

"Fine. I will be a lot safer in a vehicle."

"If you change your mind later on, please let me know and we will rotate you into our cycle."

"Fine," she says.

Mr. Roberson is watching Doshi's tantrum, which makes him think about last night in the hotel bar. She said nothing about being deathly afraid of camels. *She is strange,* he thinks, *and so is her companion. It is also a bit strange that Maji didn't try to say anything about riding the camel. He just stood there and said nothing. Did she plan on not riding a camel from the very beginning of the trip? Or is there a different reason for her not to ride?*

"Okay," Ajijine calls out, "second group up. Remember, you will have two pitches. The first one is the one that gets a lot of riders."

Mr. Roberson, Andre, and Jing Xian mount the camels as if they were professional camel riders.

"Fantastic," Ajijine says. "Everyone was good. Keep that thought in your minds for tomorrow morning, and no one will get bucked off."

Chapter 53

"**P**lease," Ajijine says as he points in the direction of the Land Rovers, "we will have a spot over there where everyone can wash their face and hands before for dinner. There's nothing better than to have twelve camel riders seated around my round table under the brightness of a full moon in the Sahara Desert. Maybe it's something like King Arthur's Knights of the Round Table in the desert," he says with a laugh. He is sitting on his stool with his wide shoulders hunched over and his *djellaba* hood hanging over his face. While they are waiting for dinner to be served, he starts telling one of the exciting stories he always tells of the adventurous of the famous Lieutenant Colonel Thomas Edward Lawrence, better known as Lawrence of Arabia, who participated in the Arab Revolt near the end of World War I. As he tells his stories, the warm air makes a comfortable and pleasant evening. Dinner is a mutton kabob and Cornish hens with bell peppers and couscous, lentil soup, pureed hummus, and freshly baked bread.

Jing Xian tries a kabob. "Now this is all right," he exclaims.

"We also have some tasty green oranges," Ajijine says. "They are extremely juicy and sweet. For dessert, we have a special hot peaches and apples with cinnamon."

After this excellent meal, which everyone declares "filled just the right spot," Mr. Roberson rubs his stomach. *When I get back home,* he says to himself, *I must let Luis know this was an excellent choice for an adventure tour.*

Ajijine has further instructions. "When you are finished with dinner, and, please, there is no rush, go over to where you washed up for dinner. Each person will be issued their sleeping bag and mat. This evening when you pick up your sleeping gear you will be assigned a number tag, which will remain on your sleeping gear for the entire trip. Remember your number! You don't want to be using someone else's sleeping bag." He nods and everyone laughs. "The crew has also assembled your individual sleeping tents. Go and claim one for yourself. Put your personal bags, sleeping bag, and mat inside. Each evening, before the camel riders arrive at the camp site, the crew will have everything assembled. That includes all of the personal tents.

"Make sure you zip up your tent at all times," he continues, "even when you are inside. There are creatures out here in the desert that would love to crawl inside your sleeping bag or tent and share it with you. Try to get into the habit of shaking your shoes and clothes out before putting anything on. Anything that has been lying or hanging in or near your tent, shake it well! Scorpions are what I'm talking about. They love to hide in things and if they get squished by your foot, hand, or any part of your body, they will sting you. A scorpion sting can be very serious. It can make you deathly sick."

Jodie raises her hand. "I'm not sure what a scorpion looks like."

"Jodie, and anyone else who is not sure what a scorpion looks like, I will find one and show it to you." He continues. "Couples will have their tents, and singles will have their own. After you have arranged your sleeping bag and mat in your tent, come back to the same spot where you got your sleeping bags. You will be issued a quarter of a bucket of water so you can wash up before going to sleep this evening. Today we didn't spend too much time outside, so you didn't get too dirty. Tomorrow we will be on the camels all day, visiting a special kasbah called Telouet for about an hour. It's the old, glamorous Glaoui Palace, which is about one hundred and fifty years old. It is now abandoned and half destroyed. You will be on your own to explore its hidden secrets.

"From there, we will continue on our camels for an hour, then we will stop for lunch. After lunch we will continue by camel across a large dry lake and camp for the evening on its outer edge. The lake is about seven miles across, and if you watch carefully while crossing the lake, you will be able to witness a mirage. But don't be fooled. There is no water out there, believe me."

Maji and Doshi are sitting together away from the others, speaking softly to each other so they won't be overheard. "Thank God," Maji says, "we'll be rid of him tomorrow and won't have to ride those damn beasts across that damn dry lake."

"Oh, please, won't you shut up," Doshi says. "You complain too damn much!"

"And you shut up yourself," Maji snarls back. "After that stupid tantrum today about not riding a camel, you made me sick."

"Well it worked, didn't it?" she replies.

"Doshi, have you ever been on a camel?"

"No. And I'm not going to, either."

Chapter 54

Standing in line to get their sleeping gear, Mr. Roberson says to Andre and Jing Xian, "Come on, guys. I have some tips for you. You have to hear this. Back when I was in the Vietnam War," he scratches his head, "I think it was in 1966, I was in an Army Special Forces unit on an extended search and destroy raid somewhere out in the jungle. None of us had a shower for weeks. You can't imagine how bad we smelled. You know, being in the damn jungle, if you didn't improvise, you got your ass in trouble. We would get some water, but most of the time it was cold, but, anyway, listen."

"Okay, Dad," Andre says. "Tell your story."

"Well," he begins, "you would take your helmet over to the immersion heaters...."

"What is an immersion heater?" Jing Xian asks.

"It's a thirty-gallon galvanized can full of water, and if the cooks had gas, they would heat the water to boiling. The immersion heaters were mostly used to make hot water to cook with. You know what I mean, for washing pots and pans, et cetera. Most of the time, they ran out of gas or out of fresh water, and then everyone was forced to use cold water. Well, anyway, you would bring your helmet full of water back to where you were sleeping that night, God only knows where that might be, and then you stripped off all of your jungle clothes and let junior breathe the fresh air. You carefully stepped around your helmet with your feet spread wide apart, being very careful not to knock it over. Oh, I forgot—you never took your boots off. You always took your bath with your boots on."

"Why would you take a bath with your boots on?" Jing Xian asks.

"The reason you left your boots on was you never knew when the enemy might attack. You know how bad a jungle can be. It would be impossible to run in the jungle in your bare feet. If bullets started to fly, or bombs started dropping, you grabbed your clothes and ran. And you always grabbed your rifle before your clothes. It was always within arm's reach, no matter what you were doing.

"Now remember, not everyone did this at the same time, only when you had security and some downtime, and that was a rarity. For convenience, you used your dirty T-shirt as a wash cloth. The reason for that is simple. While you're washing yourself, you're also washing your T-shirt. Some guys used their dirty undershorts as wash cloths, but I always washed them separately. Those shorts were just too nasty.

"When you rinsed yourself off, a lot of the water fell back into your helmet. Maybe a bit soapy, but, hell, you can't be perfectly clean. Do that several times and you are better off than you were before you started. The guys called that bath the horror bath."

"I can imagine," responds Jing Xian.

"Now, after you wash up tonight," Mr. Roberson suggests, "and before you throw out your used water, take your underwear and socks and wash them out. Hang your wash on the tent lines, and in the morning they'll be dry from the desert air. I don't think anyone will steal them out here."

"I'll check that out, Mr. Tim," Jing Xian says. "And thanks for the information."

Chapter 55

"Hey," Andre calls out, "later tonight, let's climb up to the top of the giant sand dune. I'm sure we'll be able to see every star in the universe. I wonder if you can see the big dipper here in Africa."

"Count me out," Mr. Roberson says.

Later that night, Andre and Jing Xian struggle alone to the top of the giant sand dune.

"Man, that was a hard climb, especially in the areas where the sand was really loose," Jing Xian says. He sits down to dump sand out of his shoes. "This dune must be five or six hundred feet high."

"Yeah," Andre says, thinking how out of shape he is getting. But the hike up the dune was easy for him, maybe because of the training he received from the medicine man. The placement of his feet in the sand seemed easy. Did the meditation using the bat bones really work?

"The sky is blacker than black," Jing Xian says, snapping Andre out of his reverie.

"Yeah," Andre whispers. "You can see a million stars out there. The cavernous sky with its majestical emptiness can engulf your mind."

The full moon is showing off its brilliance, highlighting everything it touches. The two buddies sit on the sand and make themselves comfortable, looking out across the dunes as if searching for something in outer space. A warm breeze blowing across the sand and the dead silence give them a totally relaxed feeling. They both doze off for a few minutes.

Suddenly Jing Xian awakens. "Hey," he whispers, "it's late. Let's get back to camp."

Andre wakes up, too. "Oh. Okay."

As they start back down the dune, however, Andre senses something that is not right. He stops and puts his arm out to stop Jing Xian. Not saying a word, he scans the dune in front of them, then points at something slowly moving at the bottom of the dune. What is it? Jing

Xian focuses on the silhouette and nods his head. What they see looks like a human being hunched over, trudging in the sand. Or is it human? They watch it move methodically around the base of the dune, and soon they see a red eye blinking. It looks like a one-eyed demon in a horror movie. Suddenly another mysterious silhouette appears, this one about two hundred feet away and heading in the direction of the red-eyed form. Watching closely, the young men try to clear their sleepy eyes. They do not believe what they are seeing. The new silhouette blinks its red eye several times, then the first one blinks back.

"What or who are those red eyes?" Jing Xian whispers. They continue down the dune, moving slowing and making as little noise as possible, but the two silhouettes disappear into the shadows.

Andre whispers. "I've got it. That's two people meeting each other in secret. Being so close to the camp, one or both of them must be from our camp. Maybe the camel leader and the Land Rover drivers are checking with each other. I wonder why they're using red lights to blink to each other. Do they have problems out here? Do they need security?"

"With the way they were blinking those lights, it didn't seem to me they knew each others' locations," Jing Xian says.

"Where do they keep the camels at night?"

"I don't know, but it must not be too far from the camp," Andre says, and then he adds, "Their meeting on the opposite side of the dunes from where we are camped also seems odd."

Jing Xian nods his head. "We need to let Ajijine know about this. Tonight. Or maybe we should let him know tomorrow."

"No, I don't think that would be such a good idea tonight. What if it's nothing and we wake him up? We would look pretty stupid."

"Yeah, you're right

They move on down the sand dune and make their way back to their tents.

Chapter 56

Early the next morning, a faint orange-yellow glow appears in the sky and creeps along the sand as a mild stiff breeze ruffles the tents. Andre and Jing Xian are soon up and out of their tents.

Andre can see the Land Rovers nearby. "Can you smell coffee?" he says. "Or is that tea? It seems to be coming from that direction. Let's get a cup."

The two buddies head for the Land Rovers. They are early risers, a habit developed during their training at the Shaolin monastery. They learned that early risers develop the day into what they want it to be. It is impossible, they know, to catch up on time; once it has passed, it is gone forever. While getting their Moroccan tea, they also pick up a couple bottles of water to shave and brush their teeth with.

Walking back to their tents, they pass Mr. Roberson's tent, and Andre kicks one of the lines. "Hey, old man," he calls, "is there an old bear in there? I think I can hear him growling."

"What the hell is going on out there? Am I going to have to come out there and whip some ass?"

The boys laugh and head for their tents. Mr. Roberson sticks his head out of the tent and yells after them, "Is it morning yet? I don't see any sunlight."

"They have hot tea and coffee," Andre yells back. "Better get up, or it'll be gone." A few minutes later, Andre is standing in front of his tent in his cut-off shorts, with his shirt off, exposing his muscular frame and the colorful tattoo he got while studying with the medicine man. Taking in a nice deep breath of fresh air, he holds it for almost a minute, then exhales. After several repetitions, he says, "Ahh. This is the utmost of life." He runs his fingers through his hair, letting the warm breeze stimulate the scalp. *If only I could keep this feeling for the rest of my life*, he thinks.

"Uhh, hey, buddy," Jing Xian says, "did you sleep okay last night?"

"Excellent. And with no dreams."

"I dreamt I was dancing with a beautiful belly dancer all night long." Jing Xian says as he pokes Andre's shoulder, almost spilling his hot tea.

Ajijine walks briskly past the boys, carrying a cup of mint green tea with heavy cream. "Are you guys ready for your first big ride on a camel?"

"You bet!"

A third voice comes from the next tent. "Yes, I am," Mr. Roberson's voice booms out as he sticks his bushy white head out. "I've just finished rolling up my sleeping bag and I've got everything else stuffed in the other bag. He crawls out. "Now I'm ready for coffee and breakfast."

"Say, Ajijine," Andre remarks, "I didn't know you had to have security around the camp out here in the desert."

Ajijine looks sharply at Andre. "I don't understand what you are saying," he replies. "We don't have security out here. Our camel drivers sleep with their camels and the Land Rover drivers sleep with their vehicles. I usually have one eye open, just in case. Our entire group was in their tents, except for you two guys. You were up on the sand dune late last night."

"Oh? You knew we were up there?"

"Yes. Why would you ask about security?"

"Last night, when we were starting back down, we saw two people signaling to each other. They must have been using red pen lights. They were at the base of the dune, about fifty meters from each other, when they started signaling. They were on the opposite sides of the dune from where we're camped. When they got together, they disappeared into the shadows. We didn't know what they were doing. We thought we would let you know this morning."

Ajijine is showing a bit of alarm. "About what time was this?"

"I'm not sure," Jing Xian says. "I think it was late. Maybe it was about ten-thirty, or eleven."

"Maybe it could have been people from another group out here," Ajijine says after a moment's thought. "Although I'm not aware of another tour group in this area. As professional tour guides, we all try to alternate the spots out here so our tourists will get the full, open feeling of the desert. I don't think that was anyone who works for me. I'm definitely going to ask all of my employees if they were out last night, especially if anyone was using a red pen light."

Mr. Roberson makes a comment as he walks up. "Maybe someone is trying to steal something. That does sound very strange."

Ajijine nods his head. "I think I will have someone stay up part of the night tonight," he says. "Just in case there is something going on that I don't know about. But, please, let me know as soon as possible if you see anything else that is strange. It does not matter what time it is."

Chapter 57

After everyone has eaten a wonderful breakfast of pancakes and honey, couscous with nuts, fresh peaches, and warm milk, plus other delectable dishes, the tour guide gets their attention.

"Has everyone taken your bags to the Land Rovers? We are going to get an early start this morning. We have a long way to travel. I expect some delays because unexpected things always happen. Something always happens on the first day with new riders and walkers. Some walkers did not bring the correct shoes. They will get blisters. Their shoes will fill up with sand. They may fall down. I have a first aid kit for minor injuries and gauze pads for blisters. If the blisters become too painful, the walker may have to ride in a vehicle. If you have a blister, we will let you ride the camels when it is your turn, if you wish."

As the tourists nod, he continues. "Make sure you bring several bottles of water with you in your day packs. The walkers will hang their day packs on the camels. You don't want to have the extra weight hanging on your back. If you need a drink before our scheduled break, we will stop for a moment so you can get a drink of water. With the warm breeze starting up this morning, I recommend that you use the scarves that were given to you when we were in Marrakesh. The scarf will help keep the sand and dust out of your eyes and the flies away from your face. It will also help to keep your head cool. In the hot desert, your head will perspire, and the scarf will act like insulation, keeping your sweat from drying and thus keeping you cool."

Andre and Jing Xian, both already sitting atop their camels, tie their scarves around their faces. Andre's a bright burgundy, Jing Xian's, dark blue. They look like ninjas from the movies. "We're ready!" the buddies call out.

One ninja is missing, however. Mr. Roberson is still getting his things together. He didn't get a camel this morning because he was a late for breakfast, which means he is in the first group to walk. *It doesn't matter*, he says to himself. *We'll all be changing in one and a half hours.*

All the men have their scarves wrapped around their faces like ninjas. Maybe it gives them a sense of adventure or enhances their testosterone level. The only woman wearing her scarf is Pai Lin, and it keeps falling off.

Andre picked the tallest camel. While waiting for the others to mount up, he is thinking how smooth this scarf feels against his face and how cool he looks. The scarf is definitely going to keep the sand out of his face. It will keep those nuisance flies away, too. Looking out across the desolate landscape, he thinks, *Out here, a person will experience the isolation and silence of the desert. I wonder ... would I experience the same feeling of silence I experienced in the Black Hills?* His mind is still on his meditations in the Black Hills when the camel moves, bringing him back to present reality. He stares out across the desert again. *Out in the desert, you look in all directions and see nothing except sand, large dunes, dry lake beds, and miles of small dark brown and black rocks scattered all over the ground. These rocks must be a million years old.* No wonder the Arabs called the Sahara *babr bila maa*, "ocean without water."

Marty and Tom come up behind Andre on their camels. Tom is trying without success to rewrap his scarf properly and becoming frustrated. He is also swatting at the flies dive-bombing his head. "Where do all these flies come from?" he asks.

"Tommy," Marty says, "quit fussing with those flies. They live off the camels. I'm sure of it."

"They're landing all over everything."

Marty is starting to get tired of listening to his complaints, but suddenly, Tommy coughs several times.

"I think I ate one! I'm sure of it! I need a drink of water."

"Ate what?"

"A fly."

"Well, good for you," Marty replies sarcastically. "That's one fly we won't have to worry about. I hear these desert flies are good protein."

Now Charlie rides up, with Pai Lin following close behind, and Allen behind her. The camels are forming a line, and the tourists are getting ready for the ride of a lifetime across the mighty Sahara Desert. The walkers have also gathered, with their scarves and hats on their heads. Doshi is sitting in a Land Rover.

They set out and travel for an hour and a half, making several brief stops as they approach the majestic Telouet Kasbah, which everyone is excited to see. After dismounting, the group assembles around Ajijine and drinks bottled water and eats dates and nuts.

Ajijine announces, "We will be at the kasbah for an hour. You can take pictures and explore it and enjoy its grandeur."

Chapter 58

As soon as the group arrives at the centuries-old Telouet Kasbah, they begin walking through it, looking at and taking pictures of the decorations on its walls and exquisite floors. Parts of the old palace has crumbled away to the blazing sun and blowing winds. At its highest point, which is three stories tall, its floors retain their enchanting mosaic tiles. Some of the ornate balconies in the courtyard have collapsed, however, and taken the ceilings and walls with them. Steps leading up to some of the large rooms are dangerous to walk on and are chained off. Just standing in one of the large tiled rooms makes the tourists think of its mythic past. Those days are over, possibly lost forever.

The night before, after everyone else in the camel party had bedded down for the night, Maji had made his way towards his planned rendezvous point with Akram. Akram, trudging along in the sand and cursing, arrived at precisely at 2200 hours. Using his red pen light, he blinked in Maji's direction. Maji blinked back to let Akram know who he was.

When Akram greeted Maji, the Pakistani did not reply.

"You like riding that beast all day," Akram said.

"Shut the f--- up, you stupid bastard," Maji said. "My ass is really starting to hurt, bouncing in that truck, then bouncing on the camel. And on top of all that, walking for miles ... and for what?" A minute later, he added, "Akram, let's look at the map. Pull the back of your coat up over your head and open it up so no one will see our lights. We had a long, hard, miserable day, and I need to get some sleep. Let's get this done as quickly as possible so I can get back and go to bed. I can't imagine sleeping on the ground"

"Okay, okay." They both got down on their hands and knees on the warm sand and laid out their map of the kasbah.

Akram and his gang are no strangers to the area. They are Moroccan Berber nomads who have been hired to murder someone. They have done this type of business before, but not in this part of the country and under these conditions. Normally this type of killing is done in the big cities, such as Casablanca, Marrakesh, maybe Fez. But this job is special and requires special attention.

Last night, Maji pointed to a spot on the map. "Akram, you must enter the kasbah through the right side of the second courtyard. This way. You see? If anyone is in the area, you will not be seen. You understand?"

"Yes, yes, I understand."

"Now after you enter the courtyard, there are these old stairs off to the left, going up into this large room. You understand?" Maji looked at the assassin. "Will you quit picking your damn nose while I'm talking?"

"Something was crawling in my nose."

"Listen! Keep quiet. Did you hear something?"

They paused for a few minutes to listen, then Akram said, "That was noise from the camels."

"Okay." Maji looked around. "Damn it, Akram, listen to me he growls. This is the area where he will be killed. These are the stairs." He pointed to another spot on the map. "I want you to work on these steps early tomorrow morning before anyone gets up there. That means *early*. Do you understand me? There's a chain across the entrance to the stairs. It means 'keep out.' Remove the chain. Halfway up the stairs is the spot you will work on. Loosen the bricks that are connected to the wall. Now, remember, when you loosen those bricks, make sure you don't have it collapse on yourself. It would be very sad if you got killed." Maji gave Akram a stern look. "You must have this completed before eleven o'clock. That's the time we will be arriving, give or take half an hour. After you have completed the job, stay there and make sure no one else goes up those stairs. We want to kill *him*. Not some other stupid ass."

Maji gave Akram another hard look. "When we arrive at the kasbah, I will start talking with him and convince him that he needs to go up those stairs with me to take better pictures. Then the mission will be complete. He will be dead. After his demise, I'm sure the camel riders will return to Marrakesh, the trip will be canceled, and we won't have to ride those damn beasts anymore."

Chapter 59

Holding his right hand against the old brick wall to steady himself, Mr. Roberson is now climbing the staircase. Maji has just disappeared around the corner at the top of the stairs.

"Excuse me, sir," Mr. Roberson calls out, "but which way did you turn? I can't see you."

Suddenly he hears a loud cracking sound coming from the wall beside him. Bricks start to pop out and the wall starts to crumble down on him. He lets out an ear-piercing scream as he frantically tries to get out of the way of the falling bricks. He turns to head back down, stumbling on his first step, and suddenly a mass of bricks comes smashing down, hitting him in the back and head and knocking him to the ground below. Then the entire two-story wall gives way and comes crashing down on him.

Andre is just coming around the corner at the base of the staircase when he hears his father's scream and the cracking of the wall. At that same moment, he gets a glimpse of Akram and Maji who are kneeling on the other side of the wall they have just pushed over.

Andre lunges forward, grabbing his father's leg and giving it a hard jerk. He succeeds in moving him partly out of the way. For a moment, he thinks he has his father clear of the falling bricks, but suddenly the other half of the wall collapses. It is going to hit both of them. Andre successfully dodges most of bricks crashing down, though some hit him on his shoulder and back. But within seconds there are too many bricks falling at the same time, all coming too fast.

Jing Xian is taking pictures a couple dozen feet behind Andre when he hears the wall collapsing. He comes running around the corner and starts clawing at the bricks and rocks. When some of them hit him, too, he ignores them and jumps into the mass of clay bricks, calling and digging, looking for his buddy and Mr. Roberson. He digs through the rubble, but with so much dust, breathing becomes difficult, and he starts to gasp for air. He yanks the front of his shirt up over his nose and mouth to filter out the dust. Suddenly, he sees a body part and grabs at it, pulling the body out of the rubble.

It is Andre. Jing Xian can see he is not breathing. His nose and mouth are full of dust and sand mixed with blood. Using his ninja scarf, he wipes the dirt from Andre's face, then sticks his fingers into Andre's mouth to pull more debris. Trying to stay calm, he starts CPR, mouth to mouth.

"Come on. *Come on!*"

Slowly, Andre's head starts to move. He coughs a couple times and expels the rest of the thick dust from his mouth. He spits out blood, too, but he doesn't seem to be able to sit up. He tries to say something to Jing Xian, but his buddy can't hear him. As Jing Xian leans closer, he finally hears Andre's whisper.

"Move the bricks off my legs. I can't move."

Jing Xian stops for a moment and looks at Andre's body. There is nothing lying on his legs. "Relax," he says. "You've been through some trauma." Taking off his day pack, he slides it under Andre's head.

"Andre, how are you feeling now? Here, let me give you some water."

Andre tries to shake his head. "I'm numb all over," he mutters, and he slips into unconsciousness.

Ajijine is beside Jing Xian by now. He looks down at Andre. "How is he doing?"

"He can breathe okay, but he keeps going in and out of conscious. I think there's something wrong with his back." Jing Xian looks at the pile of bricks and rubble in front of them. "I'm sure Mr. Roberson is buried in there. Andre was just behind his father and that other man on our tour, I believe his name was Maji." He cannot say more.

Other tourists are now scrabbling through the rocks and digging as fast as they can.

"There was another man!" Jing Xian suddenly shouts. "Right about over there." He points to where Mr. Roberson should be.

Then someone calls out, "We've found a body. We can't tell who it is. His head's been crushed beyond recognition."

"But by what he's wearing," another tourist says, "he looks like Mr. Roberson."

Jing Xian looks into Andre's face. Suddenly, out of nowhere, someone appears with a stretcher. *Where did a stretcher come from way out here?* he wonders. *Was it stored at the kasbah?*

The stretcher is opened and laid down beside Andre. Gently, but firmly and with the help from Ajijine, Jing Xian slowly lifts Andre unto the stretcher.

Chapter 60

Quietly, his voice steady, Ajijine says to Jing Xian, "Don't move. A scorpion has just come out of the rubble and landed on your left shoulder. It's squeezing itself under your shirt collar."

As Jing Xian freezes, Ajijine slowly moves to his side, not taking his eyes off the scorpion. "I can see it hiding under your collar," he says. "He detects our presence and may strike at any moment."

As Jing Xian hears this, his body reacts. His muscles tense and drops of perspiration start to form on his face. He finds himself thinking back to when he was a boy in China and was stung by a scorpion. The scorpion made him deathly ill. *My parents thought I would die.*

Ajijine is thinking how to get the scorpion out from under the collar. *I could smash the scorpion with a rock*, he thinks, *but what sort of damage would the rock do to Jing Xian? And what if I don't kill it? I've got to get it out from under his shirt collar and down on the ground. And fast! It's too risky for him to take the shirt off.* Ajijine begins looking around for a stick of some kind, but not finding one, suddenly remembers the folding knife with a five-inch blade in his pocket. He pulls out the knife and opens the blade.

"I'm going to take my knife," he says to Jing Xian, "and slide the tip under your collar about four or five inches from the scorpion. I'll try not to disturb him. Then I'll make one quick movement and swing the blade towards him. I'll knock him out from under your collar. I won't miss, but, just in case, immediately after I swing the knife, you rip the shirt off. Okay?"

Jing Xian responds with a nervous blink of his eyes.

Spreading his feet for perfect balance, Ajijine slides the tip of the knife under Jing Xian's shirt collar. His hand is perfectly still. He nods his head. As fast as a cobra can strike, he swings the blade and knocks the scorpion to the ground. Two of the men in the party stomp on it before it can take cover under the fallen bricks.

"*Xiexie, xiexie,*" says Jing Xian, "Thank you, thank you."

Other tourists come closer now. "My friend," one asks, "are you all right?"

"You've got to watch out for scorpions all the time," says another. "Especially when putting on your shoes. They can hide anywhere."

"They're everywhere," says someone else.

"He must have crawled on me while I was digging through the rubble," Jing Xian replies. "People have died from scorpions' stings."

"You are correct," says the tour guide. "Out here in the Sahara, they are feared more than snakes."

Chapter 61

After Ajijine has disposed of the scorpion, Allen and Tom come forward to help carry Andre down to the waiting Land Rover. They will rush him to the Croix Rouge (Red Cross) hospital at Djemma El Fna in Marrakesh. Mr. Roberson's body has already been carried to the other vehicle. It is driving away.

Ajijine turns to the rest of the group. "You will be transported back to Marrakesh as soon as the vehicles return. This tour will be terminated, and your money refunded." He turns to Jing Xian and lowers his voice. "I'm terribly sorry for Andre's father's death and what has happened to Andre. I wish there were something I could do." As the other tourists gather nearer the entrance to the palace, he adds, "Andre's father should not have been going up those stairs. The entire place is very unstable. There was supposed to be signs and a chain across the entrance to those stairs. It looks like someone removed them. I have been through this kasbah many times, and I have always seen a chain across those steps." He looks at his group, counting them under his breath. Someone else is not there. "I understand that Mr. Roberson was walking with another man in our tour at the time of his death. I believe his name was Maji. Where is he, anyway?" Maji has disappeared. The guide shakes his head sadly. "You, Mr. Roberson, and Andre, you all have travelers insurance to take care of everything?"

"Yes, we do," Jing Xian responds. "I'll call Stacey, Mr. Roberson's personal secretary in San Francisco. She'll help us at her end."

Charlie comes running up to them. "Ajijine, Ajijine," he calls, "I saw them—Maji and Doshi. Right after the collapse of the wall, they were getting into a Land Rover, but it wasn't one of ours. It was heading off in a hurry." He points out toward the desert, "Going that way."

Ajijine looks in the direction Charlie is pointing and does not say a word for several minutes. Then he slowly says, "Maybe they are going for help? But I don't know where another Land Rover might have come from. And that is not the direction of Marrakesh." He looks around, then adds, "I had all three of my vehicles here. One has just taken Mr. Roberson to the hospital, and the second is getting ready to leave with Andre. Both of them are going to the hospital in Marrakesh. In that direction." He points in the opposite direction.

"When we arrived at the kasbah," he continues to Jing Xian and the other members of the tour who have clustered around the scene of the accident, "there was no other group here. We were alone. I'm sure there was no other means of transportation here, either, except for a few stray camels. It seems that the new Rover arrived at the same time as the collapsing of the wall. It also seems that two of our riders disappeared without telling anyone of their intentions. Very strange. The mysterious Land Rover arrived conveniently at the time of the accident. I'm sure the police are going to be interested in those two."

Chapter 62

Waiting at the hospital in Marrakesh, Jing Xian thinks to himself, *I can't say I witnessed the collapse of the wall. I came around the corner just seconds after the tragedy happened. Charlie saw Maji and Doshi leaving in a hurry in another Rover. That is very suspicious. But Maji has been acting suspiciously all along. The questions he was asking several nights ago in the bar do not prove he was the murderer.* He shakes his head, as if to clear it. *Maybe the police will say Mr. Roberson was in an area where he was not supposed to be and the wall just collapsed on him. Everything is only speculation. There's no hard evidence to say that Maji and Doshi killed him. Maybe it was an accident.* He shakes his head again. *But I cannot accept that.*

Finally, he takes his cell phone out of his pocket and makes a call he does not want to make. "Hello, Stacey," he says when there is an answer. "This is Jing Xian."

"Well, hello to you, too," she replies. "How are you three amigos doing in the desert?"

After a long pause, he breaks the news to her. "Stacey, there has been a very serious accident. Or maybe it was murder. I'm not really sure right now."

"What happened?"

"Mr. Roberson has been killed. And Andre is in serious condition. He has a possible concussion and maybe a broken back or neck. We rushed them to the Red Cross hospital here in Marrakesh. I'm waiting here at the hospital now to find out how Andre is doing."

"Oh, God! Oh, my God!" she screams. Then she pauses to collect herself. "What do you want me to do? How did Mr. Roberson get killed? Were they in a vehicle? Did it roll over? Fall off a cliff?"

"No, no." Jing Xian's voice is almost dead. "He was killed when a wall collapsed on him in an old desolate kasbah in the middle of giant sand dunes. Andre got crushed trying to save him."

"How terrible." Her voice is quivering. She is starting to cry.

"Please, Stacy, don't cry. I need your help."

"Okay, okay. I'll be all right." She blows her nose and wipes her tears away. "I'll do anything you want or need me to do." She pauses to think of what she has to do first. "I have to notify the board of directors immediately. They'll have to make some immediate changes in the management of the company." Though she is talking business, her voice is still shaking. "If anything happens to Mr. Roberson, the vice president takes over on a temporary position until the board votes on his replacement." She pauses again. "Andre was supposed to take over the business when his dad decided to retire. But now that he got killed, that change will not happen. I have to look into the bylaws to see if there is a clause specifying the status of Andre's inheritance. Mr. Roberson was the founding director of the business and had more shares of stock than anyone else." She blows her nose again and tries to speak more clearly. "There's another man who has almost the same number of shares, but he doesn't work at the company. He and Mr. Roberson were always having arguments on how the company should be run." She pauses again. "Okay, Jing Xian, it's your turn. I'm sorry I cut you off like that. It's just the shock that Tim—I mean Mr. Roberson is dead. It's really hard to think. What do you need me to do?"

"I think Mr. Roberson was murdered," Jing Xian replies. "And Andre got hurt while trying to save his father. I also think Andre got a look at the killer or killers when the wall was collapsing. They may have seen him as well. Andre's life may be in jeopardy if he stays here. I'm positive he won't get the protection he needs. I spoke with the police a while ago. They think it was an accident. They don't want to try to investigate it as a murder. I think they think it's a tourist thing. Will the murderers try to kill Andre if they think their identity has been compromised? Who knows? But I'm not going to take any chances."

Chapter 63

"Stacey, this is what I suggest," says Jing Xian. "Send a corporate jet here to Marrakesh to pick up Mr. Roberson's body and fly him back to San Francisco. Make sure you have Andre and me on the manifest as well, just in case this is an inside conspiracy. Who knows? The wrong person might read the flight plan and know who's returning to San Francisco. But Andre and I will not be on the plane. This is what I'm thinking. Please work with me."

"Okay, Jing Xian."

"Andre and I spent two years at the Shaolin monastery. We got to now each other like brothers. I think I know what he would want me to do for him while he's in this condition. I've listened to his ideas about life and what he wants to do. I firmly believe what the grand master told me. 'There is no choice.'" He squares his shoulders. "I will accompany my blood brother wherever he needs me. The grand master is extremely knowledgeable. I never had the slightest idea I would be so desperately needed as I am needed now. Andre told me all about his trip to the Black Hills and his self-induced spiritual meditations. After our second year of training at the monastery, our grand master has advanced Andre and his personal zen a long way." He pauses to give her time to catch up. "I just got off the phone with Grand Master Shibo. He has agreed with me to have Andre transported to the monastery. You don't have to worry. He'll be taken care of with the most loving hands. He'll have the best protection and the finest means of healing in the world."

Jing Xian thus makes secret plans with Stacey. He is concerned about the lack of medical care for Andre and his safety at the hospital in Marrakesh. Stacey is to make arrangements for a second corporate jet to be flown to Marrakesh after Mr. Roberson's body has been picked up. Andre and Jing Xian will board the second plane and fly to Shanghai, then be taken to Gillian in southern China. From there, they will travel by van to the monastery, which is located fifteen kilometers from Yangshuo.

Finally, Jing Xian tells Stacey about all the strange things that have been happening on the tour, such as Doshi's refusal to ride a camel and the disappearance of the couple after the wall collapsed. He wonders why the police are so casual about Mr. Roberson's death. Maybe they were paid off?

"I think Andre would be safest at the Shaolin temple in Yangshuo," Jing Xian says again. "He can recover there. I could have Andre flown to San Francisco General Hospital, but I don't think he'd be safe there. What Andre has been studying for the last year at the temple can have an enormous impact on his recovery."

"Okay, Jing Xian, I will agree with you," Stacey says, "but I want you to promise me something. If things don't go as well as your grand master anticipates, then you will bring him here to San Francisco immediately. I want you to promise me that."

There is a pause.

"I promise, Stacey. I swear it on my mother's grave."

Chapter 64

"Stacey, hold on for a moment," Jing Xian suddenly says. "A hospital clerk just handed me a report on the x-rays they took of Andre. I'm reading the report from the x-ray technician. It's not good news. Andre's back has been badly damaged in many areas. He is partially paralyzed from his head to his feet. He could sustain permanent paralysis. We have to wait and see. He's already on a respirator to help him breathe. He has four, maybe five, broken ribs for sure, though three are not in an area that would cause any internal damage."

While Jing Xian is reading the report to Stacey, Dr. Hasan, Andre's attending physician, comes walking up.

"Stacey, I'll have to call you back," Jing Xian tells her.

"Yes, please do that," she replies.

"I see you have the x-ray report," the doctor says. "In his present condition, there is little hope that Andre will be able to walk again. He has suffered extreme trauma. There is damage to four vertebrae, and he has five fractured ribs. There is also very likely nerve damage and internal damage as well." The two men sit down together as the doctor goes on. "There is not much a doctor can do for broken ribs except to tape them up and have the patient get plenty of rest. But his vertebrae are pinching the spinal cord. An MRI is required, as well as other things they specialize in at the hospital in San Francisco. Our hospital is not equipped with this sophisticated equipment needed here. He also received a severe contusion on his head, but I don't think it is life threatening." The doctor stands up again.

"I am amazed how well his body has stabilized itself. It appears that he has kept himself in excellent shape. I'm very sorry for him and his father. I wish there were something more I could do for him. We have stabilized his back as best as we can under these conditions. Once you get him to your hospital in San Francisco, they will give him another thorough examination. I'm sure they will give you the same prognosis I have given you. I worked at San Francisco General Hospital for several years, but I left five years ago. They have an excellent staff and several doctors who specialize in damaged backs."

"Okay, Dr. Hasan," Jing Xian replies, "we will have him flown to San Francisco General, hopefully tomorrow morning." Jing Xian feels a little bad about telling the doctor he is going to take Andre to San Francisco when he will be headed to China instead.

Meanwhile, using her personal contacts in China, Stacey secure visas in short notice for Andre and Jing Xian to get through customs in Shanghai. She also calls in some favors from the American Embassy.

It may be difficult to get Andre into China, however, and the journey to the monastery is going to be difficult. Andre may be in a semiconscious condition, but Jing Xian needs to take that chance. Staying in Marrakesh could cost Andre his life. On the corporate jet, Andre will have all the necessary medicine, including oxygen, to keep him comfortable until he reaches Yangshuo.

When Andre and Jing Xian were in San Francisco, they became good friends of Stacey. The three had dinner together several times and enjoyed each others' company. Stacey is several years older than the two young men and has her own private life, which she doesn't talk about. Now when Jing Xian and Andre need her help, she is going to do whatever she can to help them. With his father's death, Andre will be in a very precarious position with the company, and Stacey and Jing Xian are well aware the problems they are facing.

PART IV

AT THE SHAOLIN MONASTERY, SOUTHERN CHINA

Chapter 65

Jing Xian arrives in Shanghai aboard the corporate jet with Andre, who is partly paralyzed. Thanks to Stacey, they clear customs and fly on to Guilin, a picturesque tourist city about two hours southeast of Shanghai and tucked away in the Limestone Mountains straddling the Li River. After an uneventful trip, the plane taxis to the cargo terminal at the Guilin airport and parks on the tarmac. With the help of the flight crew, Jing Xian checks to make sure Andre is secure in his wheelchair before he is pushed onto the lift that will bring him down from the jet. Andre is wearing sun glasses and a hat with a deep brim that hides his face.

Jing Xian looks around the side of the plane and sees an old, faded, red Chevy van driving toward the plane. Two Shaolin monks dressed in their crimson robes are seated in the front seat of the van. The airports ground crew lowers the lift to the ground, and Jing Xian wheels Andre to the van.

"Welcome," one of the monks says. "It is a very sad day that we welcome old friends under such conditions."

"Thank you very much for your kind words," Jing Xian replies.

Each monk lightly touches Andre's shoulder, just to let him know they are friends, even though Andre may not feel their touch.

"Grand Master Shibo is awaiting your arrival," one of the monks says as the other monk opens the back door of the van and starts pulling out a metal ramp they use to roll the wheelchair up into the van.

"Here, let me help you," Jing Xian tells the young monks. "It was a long flight, and I need some exercise."

The other monk jumps up into the van and gets out the tie downs to strap the wheelchair in place for the long bumpy ride to the monastery. When Andre is settled, the driver starts the motor. As the old van motors for several hours down the dirt road, Jing Xian, who is exhausted, looks out the window and thinks about the days when he was studying to become a Shaolin monk. *Well,* he thinks, *maybe not a one hundred percent monk.* He was trying to learn the wisdom of being a monk.

The scenery is beautiful and rich with green trees and bamboo on the jagged mountains, rice paddies in open fields, groves of orange trees and large jack fruit trees, and lazy water buffalo soaking in the Li River. The closest city to the monastery is Yangshuo, where they can buy provisions if needed.

Jing Xian remembers the days when he and Andre took a break from their studies and paddled their small boats out to the big tourist boats on the river to sell souvenirs. It always seemed to him that Andre had such great balance and agility, as if he was half animal. Many times, his American friend would walk on the edge of the little boat or balance on one foot without falling into the water or tipping the boat over as he negotiated with the tourists on the larger boat above them.

Chapter 66

It was during those happy days when Andre met the love of his life. This happened on the day he and Jing Xian tied on to one of the tourist boats and he was trying to get the attention of a group of girls standing toward the bow. A beautiful girl with long brown hair came over to the side and looked down at them.

"Hi," she called. "How much in American dollars for that statue?" She pointed to one of their wares. "Do you take American money? Or does it have to be Chinese?"

Andre, who with his deep tan looked like one of the natives, looked up at her. "Three dollars."

"You speak good English," she said with a smile.

"Thank you," he replied. "Can you detect my California accent?"

She looked surprised. "If I listen hard, I might. Are you from California?"

"Totally. Born and raised by the Bay. And a few years of surfing the waves."

"That is fantastic!" The girl called her friends over to the side where the two young men had tied their boats. "My name is Christina," she called down to Andre. "What's yours?"

"I'm Andre. This is my friend, Jing Xian."

As the girls greeted them, Christina said, "These are my traveling friends. Sophia, Andrea, and Missy."

"How long are you going to be in Yangshuo?" Andre asked.

"Yangshuo? Where is that?"

Andre stopped a minute, realizing the girls were on tour and didn't know the name of the cities they passed, especially the smaller ones. "That's the town where the boat ride ends," he explained.

"Oh, there. We'll only be there for a few hours, then we return to Guilin by shuttle van, and then, I think, we're off to Hong Kong the next morning."

Andre told the girls he had to leave the boat because he was floating too far down stream and it would be very difficult to get back to where he lived. He noticed that her friends were encouraging her to talk with him. Leaning down, she handed him her business card with her personal cell phone number on it. He looked at her address. She was from Chicago.

"Next time you're in Chicago," she said, "give me a call!"

Looking surprised, Andre thanked her and tucked the card into his packet.

Then he and Jing Xian untied their boats, and within seconds the large boat left them bouncing around in the turbulence of the propeller's wake. The girls waved from the railing as they continued downstream.

Chapter 67

The old van makes its way through the entryway into the Shaolin monastery. Half of their friends are there to help Jing Xian settle in while the other half take Andre to the temple where Grand Master Shibo is waiting. As soon as Jing Xian phoned him from the hospital in Morocco, Shibo began preparing for Andre's difficult recovery process. He has already spent several days and nights searching through the library and reading from the ancient Chinese scientific books. The power of Taoism is toward the supernatural and draws its elements from age-old Chinese folk beliefs. He has also read other ancient Buddhist books that advocate the detachment from the existing world.

Yes, the grand master said to himself several times as he inserted another bookmark, *this can help Andre.*

If you want to reach Nirvana, he read, *you must take the eightfold path of the right knowledge of lifestyle, mindfulness, effort, thought, action, and concentration. Yes, yes,"* he thinks again as he sees Andre being wheeled to him, *Andre going into the transition of Nirvana.*

Shibo opened the old book again. *The degree of empowerment. Yes. A similar state in which reunion with Brahma is attained through the suppression of individual existence.* He read on. *The state of absolute blessedness, characterized by release from the cycle of reincarnations and attained through the extinction of the self.* The master has read for hours and hours and written numerous pages of notes and constructed many formulas.

From another book with up-to-date technology, he has made additional notes on proprioception, which relays information of the state of muscle contraction to the brain, and the Muscarinic receptors, which stimulate smooth muscles and slow the heart rate. He has learned through his reading that the mind is electromagnetically connected to the body through meditation and can produce an indigenous opiate that is known to soothe the pain in the brain. *How can that be produced? I must do more research.*

Shibo has searched the monastery's library, looking for books on rare herbs, like a variegated moss that grows on special trees. He has also looked for information about a special wax for the ceremonial candles and how to find the right minerals in the river bed. He has made lists and written down formulas and rituals. He has made lists of herbs. *Lungus Cordyceps Sinensis. Ho Shou Wu*, which enhances longevity and energy. Some of these essential herbs must be fermented for a specific length of time, or they will have no power. They also will not produce their power if not mixed with the right ingredients.

There is one special item the grand master still must find. If he does not, he will not be able to help Andre recover. This essential item is half a dozen dried twigs from the ancient tree, *Thuja Sutchuenensis*, which has scented wood. These special twigs are to be mixed with equal parts of the rare purple hydrangea, which grows a day's boat ride up the Li River, past the city of Yangdi and near the sulfur pools. The grand master decided to have a courier dispatched early the next morning on a search and recovery mission to find these items.

Just three days before Andre's arrival, Xian Zhang, the courier, entered the grand master's room and bowed. "Grand Master Shibo, I am here for your instructions."

Grand Master Shibo returned his bow. "There are some special dried twigs from the *Thuja Sutchuenensis* tree that are extremely important for the formula I must prepare. A brother monk who has been gravely injured and is in danger of dying is arriving very soon. We must act quickly. This tree is indigenous to China and survives in the Chongging municipality in eastern Sichuan. Remember, we only need dried twigs picked up from the ground. In picking up the dried twigs, pay attention and do not pick up any cones. Be very careful. It would be very difficult to explain what we are doing to the government officials who keep watch over the trees. These trees are about eight or nine hundred years old, and I wish them to live a thousand years."

The courier bowed again. "I will be very careful not to endanger either the trees or myself. I will be extremely vigilant and return with what you need. I will not violate any laws. I will return within three days, as you require."

The grand master handed the courier a map showing the exact location of the trees and the location of the rare purple hydrangea.

Chapter 68

Grand Master Shibo's plan is that for the next four months, Andre will dedicate himself to learning the important lessons of the Shaolin way. The grand master will attempt to harness the power of Andre's mind. Now Shibo sits beside Andre's bed, around which are tables stacked with an enormous number of old books. The oil lamps burn and flicker as Andre lies propped on the pillows and listens to Shibo reading from these ancient books. Both men are totally concentrated on the ancient wisdom. The grand master has also set up a blackboard in the room, on which he draws body parts, showing what they are connected to and what purpose they have. Sometimes, Shibo also draws the inside the body as he imagines it, giving Andre ideas about how his body should look in his imagination.

Occasionally, Shibo asks Andre, "Would you like to have a drink of hot green tea?" and Andre answers, "Yes, thank you very much."

Shibo also quizzes Andre on what he has learned, asking him to paraphrase the meaning of the ancient wisdom from the books. This relentless teaching goes on for weeks and weeks, which turn into months. Some days are not good days, and the two men become frustrated, but their frustration always subsides and they trudge on. To help relieve Shibo of the teaching burden, other monks take turns reading to Andre, but only Shibo questions him about what he is hearing and learning.

Thus four months come and go, and the teaching continues. Andre sustains his will to succeed. He is seeking enlightenment. He compiles everything he has studied and comes to understand the human body's functions and recognize the body's interior structure and skeleton. He eagerly recognizes his damaged organs. Shibo also teaches him to lie comfortably in bed for long periods of time and how to manipulate his back muscles to the extent of keeping himself pliable. Through his mental dexterity, Andre stretches his tendons so they won't freeze up while he is bedridden. He visualizes the spine and how the sciatic nerve runs in conjunction with the spinal disks and fluids. He learns to put his white T cells and red blood cells to work repairing the damage to his body.

He also visualizes the displaced bone fragments in his body. He will use his mind to orchestrate the repair of his crushed and ruptured disks. Next he will use his back muscles to bring the bone fragments to the surface of the skin. After each anticipated session of self-induced trance work, Andre will tell Shibo how many pieces he brought to the surface of his skin. With the aid of an assistant, Shibo will search Andre's back, running his hands across the skin to find lumps. After wiping the skin with an ointment, he will use a sharp knife and cut a small incision to remove each fragment, then suture the incision shut.

There is always a possibility that a bone fragment may not reach the skin's surface. When Andre finds a fragment floating in an obscure spot inside his body, he must move it to the surface using a direct approach. If the direct approach is not possible because vital organs are in the way, he will move it to the surface somewhere else in his body.

"The more you know about the human body," Shibo tells him, "especially how it operates within itself, the better you are. The idea of a journey within your body, seeing with the eyes of your imagination and using your mind, leads to amazing results."

This process has to be done right. There are no second chances.

Chapter 69

Some days, the grand master relaxes in his chair beside Andre's bed and reminisces about the days when he was an eager student attending the University of Nanjing. At the university, he studied the famous European painters and the sculptors of the Italian Renaissance. He marveled at the thinking of Michelangelo in his earlier days in Florence. Determined to be the best sculptor, Michelangelo demanded the best marble that could be found. He traveled to quarries throughout Italy and hand picked the perfect slabs of marble for his projects. As a sculptor of the human form, he needed to know how the human body is put together, with its strong, smooth muscles and tendons, its balance, skin tone, and texture. This is why he visited the city morgue and dissected cadavers and sketched muscles and tendons to learn how and where they connected. He also examined the circulatory system and learned how veins and arteries show under the surface of the skin. His monumental statute of David, which now stands in the museum in Florence, shows the muscles, the skeletal structure, the veins, everything in perfect detailed proportion. "How did he do it?" Shibo asks rhetorically. "Perfect planning. The right materials. Patience. Belief in himself."

Andre listens carefully to the grand master's reminiscences. The American student learned to seek his inner zen through his earlier encounter with the Sioux medicine man in the Black Hills of South Dakota. Now at the Shaolin monastery, he is developing a similar, but more advanced, ability to understand human anatomy.

As the two men study the old books together, rare herbs are being gathered from the countryside and being washed and sorted at the monastery. Shibo and his assistants are carefully following the instructions given in the ancient medical books. They have been mixing and boiling the herbs into potions for Andre to drink. The cocktail they prepare has already relieved his pain. It has been four months since Andre was crushed in the kasbah in Morocco, and his physical and mental recovery is astonishing.

Chapter 70

After deliberating for several days, Shibo has decided that now is the proper time for their next step in Andre's process. The tall ritual candles have been poured and set in precisely the right places in the temple. The rare herbs have been found and prepared according to the formulas in the ancient books. The bamboo litter that Andre will be strapped into has been built.

The grand master's assistants start to prepare Andre for the process. They begin by shaving off all of his body hair including his shoulder-length hair and his beard, which have been growing since his accident. Then they dress him in a small loincloth, freeing the rest of his body from the foul secretions that will ooze out of the pores of his skin during the process. Last, the attending monks use their bare hands to smear his body with a sticky, reddish-brown ointment that has fermented for fourteen days and produced the disgusting smell of rotting meat. This concoction must cover every inch of skin on his entire body, including between his fingers and toes and between the cheeks of his buttocks. The fermented mixture has such a nauseating stench that the assistants must wear towels over their noses and mouths. The unbearable concoction acts as a conductor of an electromagnetic field that Andre will use to transmit his mental signals throughout his body. His body will be like a giant road map with roads going in all directions, and his mind will be directing every bit of traffic.

Now Andre is gently placed in a litter, which is constructed of bamboo poles tied together with leather ties. No metal objects, such as nails or wire, were used to build the litter, as metal will interfere with the mental transmutation of Andre's body. The litter has two long bamboo poles extending a foot past on the bottom end so it can be stood up. Two ropes are attached to the head end and wound through two old wooden pulleys attached to a large wooden beam that stretches across the temple ceiling. The assistants will pull the ropes and raise the litter into a standing position. Andre will thus "stand" in this vertical position for the process.

Chapter 71

Sixteen specially poured ceremonial candles are precisely placed on the temple floor at the foot of Andre's bamboo litter in a celestial design called the Great Chinese Green Dragon. The dragon design duplicates the spiritual image that can be seen in the heavens on any given night. The dragon will give Andre the independence and confidence he needs to take his journey within his body. Twelve of these candles are large ones that trace the outline of the dragon. The four shorter candles identify the features of the dragon. If for any reason, any of the candles are not set in the correct location or not the right height or circumference, the process will fail.

Andre is strapped in the litter, with leather restrainers crossing his forehead, his chest, his waist, his legs, and his arms and hands. Under the extreme stress his body will endure during the self-induced process, he must not unknowingly move. Lying in the litter with his shaved head held up by an assistant, he finishes drinking a large cup of freshly brewed ceremonial herbs.

He addresses the grand master. "I'm ready, Master. Pray for me."

Shibo nods his head. "I will pray for you, my son. Remember what I have taught you."

The assistants begin to pull the ropes, and the head of the litter slowly starts to rise. The old wooden pulleys groan and strain under the heavy load, making a squeaking noise like an ox cart carrying a heavy load. The lower end of the litter is dragged across the limestone floor until it stops at the leather bindings it is to be attached to. The litter is now standing on its feet, and one of the assistants secures it to the floor, using the leather tie-down straps. The other assistant slowly starts pushing the top of the litter to a ninety-five degree angle, tilting Andre toward the ceremonial candles and giving him the full spectrum of the light so he can receive their full power. Jing Xian has carefully lit all of the candles using a long rice paper wick attached to a wooden pole and starting with the short candles.

After all the candles are lit, the grand master looks up and addresses Andre one more time.

"Andre, my son, are you ready?"

"Yes."

At a signal from Shibo, an assistant strikes a brass gong and turns the sand clock over. The process commences.

Shibo had read the instructions from the old Chinese medical book while his assistants poured the wax to make the candles. The ingredients had to be mixed perfectly. If there was even a slight error, they will not function and hold their shape while they burn. As the candles burn during the process, they have to be measured at critical times, as they must reach certain heights each time the sand clock is turned. Shibo has used a special beeswax that burns brighter and with more intensity than ordinary candle wax. The outside layer of the candles is made from the wax of a rare white insect called the *Coccus pe-la* of Westwood. A secret herb is added to the white insect wax to harden it and keep it from melting as fast as the core of the candle. This will keep the tall candles standing erect and easily measured at the proper times.

Chapter 72

Strapped in his bamboo litter and hanging from the ceiling in the temple, Andre opens his eyes. Focusing on the massive array of candles, which give out an enormous amount of heat as well as light, he begins his meditation. His body starts to perspire profusely. He brings into his mind what he and the grand master have been studying together for months.

His mind begins to feel like a feather blowing in the wind, he is drifting in and out of consciousness, down, down, he's becoming heavenly light. He senses his body starting to twitch, then it abruptly stops, and suddenly there is now no feeling in his body. Something spiritual is entering his body. He imagines nothing, there are no thoughts racing through his mind, no feelings of panic, his mind is totally blank.

"It's starting to happen," he murmurs aloud.

Now he feels a slight tingling sensation beginning in his chest and slowly inching its way down his body. It almost feels like a snake slithering its way down under his skin. Under his arms, the snake glides, silkily, it winds around his chest, then around his waist, slowly, it moves between his legs and now it's coiled around his ankles. Is this eerie feeling the enlightenment he has been seeking? Is this it? His eyes are heavy, his vision blurry. He is getting very sleepy. He is ready.

At this exact moment, something is also beginning to happen to the ceremonial candles. The flames are beginning to flicker, changing from reddish yellow to a bright emerald green. The flames seem to come to life, growing taller, dancing around, throwing off shadows of live images of the celestial figures painted on the temple walls. Suddenly, the candle flames start splitting in half, as if some mysterious thing is slicing them with a knife. The hot green flames are folding back in opposite directions, as if they are communicating, coiling out like the arms of an octopus and connecting to neighboring candles around the perimeter of the heavenly dragon. The flames become one, long, continuous flame, giving the appearance of a giant fiery snake slithering from candle to candle. Within seconds, the flames are burning flat to the candles. The flames of the twelve candles have united into one bright, fiery pattern.

The Celestial Green Dragon has arrived.

As Andre's body starts shaking violently, he lets out a terrifying shriek, and then, as if on cue, his body goes limp and he is deathly silent. The air in the temple becomes hot and stale. The walls of the temple seem to be speaking to Andre. Grand Master Shibo and his assistants become uneasy as they hear a soft, mournful sound emanating from the temple walls.

"What is happening?" the monks ask.

Watching Andre, Shibo says, "He has sought the help of the supernatural, and now it has arrived. He is in total control of his inner soul."

Chapter 73

Andre's mind starts to navigate through his body.

How eerie, how strange, he gasps as he looks around. *How can I be looking at something I have no idea what it should look like?* He gasps again. *I can move my eyes, yet I have no head or body to move.*

Effortlessly, he drifts around inside his body, using the eyes of his mind to examine the damage in his body. Inspecting his ribs, he looks closely at four ribs that are covered with a greenish-brown glob of mucus. *Must be a healing compound the body produces for repairing bones.* He mentally takes closer note of the damaged ribs as he drifts. There do not appear to be any fragments of bone floating around from his ribs, nor does he see any protruding pieces of rib that may be life threatening.

He looks again. *Ah, there's another rib, a couple down from the others. It appears to be in a state of repair, too.* This rib has a different colored glob attached to it. *Must be damaged as well, maybe it's bruised.* He comes closer. *I'm not sure what a bruised rib should look like. That is some strange looking glob attached to that crack in the rib. It appears to be moving. Is it alive? I wonder what it's doing. Maybe it's sucking bone marrow from the crack? Can it be friendly? Don't want to get too close.*

After this observation, he determines that his rib cage can be wrapped with an adhesive bandage to minimize movement when he inhales and exhales.

Drifting motionlessly through what seems to be a fluid atmosphere, he next comes to his spinal cord. This part of the spinal cord is protected by the unique bones of the spine, but the edges of some of his vertebrae are broken or missing. He notices many bone fragments drifting by, several pieces of which he cannot identify. The disks have not been ruptured, he notices. *That's good.*

This, he tells himself, *is going to take some time. Got to remove these fragments.* Gingerly, he brings his attention to the exposed, smooth part of the spinal cord that is not protected by the vertebrae. Closer observation reveals that the cord has been penetrated through its outer protective padding, the *dura mater*, by several serrated bone fragments. *This must be the spot that paralyzed my body. I think I've found it!*

Carefully, he begins to work. He mentally stimulates the area of the penetration, relaxing the tissue. He begins methodically manipulating the tissue of the *dura mater* where the bone fragments are imbedded, moving it back and forth. Firmly but delicately, he starts palpating the area around the fragments. A slight trickle of a colored fluid starts to seep out from around other imbedded fragments. *Yes! It's working. One more piece is beginning to loosen up.* He can't believe what he is doing. Already, four jagged pieces of bone have been dislodged from his spinal cord and are drifting toward the surface of his skin. He quickly seals the holes in the spinal cord, then examines the rest of the cord to make sure he has removed all of the fragments. *Now, with plenty of rest and the right nourishment, I will be back to normal in good time.*

He moves up his spine. Looking closely at the back of his neck, where the spine connects to the skull, he sees the two splenius muscles, which have been stretched and are partly damaged. They control the rotation and extension of the head and neck. Being only slightly torn but still intact, he decides, they should be fine with proper nourishment and rest. But his head will have to be stabilized a while for proper recovery.

Using what he has learned from the grand master, he begins to gather up some small bone fragments he has found lodged around the edge of a neck muscle. *These must have worked their way all the way up here.* Manipulating the surrounding muscle fibers, he moves the fragments, too, to the surface of the skin, where they can be extracted through small incisions after he comes out of the meditation.

Encountering several areas of uncontrolled hemoglobin flow from some ruptured blood vessels, he repairs these problem areas and reroutes the flow. This injury has produced a large, nasty bruise on his lower back, but the capillaries running along the surface of the skin are showing good signs of recovery. These little veins keep the skin moist and help control body temperature. Using his mental process of tissue repair, he produces needed chemicals to stimulate the growth of certain enzymes. The chemicals he produces are transported through the cell walls via mental osmosis. Repairing soft tissues requires time, he knows, plus proper nourishment and special herbs.

Everything in his body is so compact, and yet Andre doesn't feel crowded. The amazing thing is that he can see without light. It almost seems as if there are a hundred floodlights shining at the same time. He looks at his lungs, heart, liver, and kidneys. *They all look all right*, he tells himself, though his intestines seem to have gas deposits and the airway passage in his throat is slightly swollen, which is normal under these conditions. There are no obstructions to his mental travel except his skeleton, which he navigates around quite easily. He pauses. *No messy fluids in here. Amazing. Nothing to make my movements sluggish.* There is one thing that is very noticeable. He can hear the constant beating of his heart, at least he thinks it is his heart. *Amazing!* As for his being a foreign object in his own body, he has not come under attack by the white cells that defend the body, nor by any other roaming inner guard.

While Andre works inside his body, Shibo is pacing back and forth, rubbing his hands together, gazing up at that seemingly lifeless body. The grand master prays, then starts looking back through all of his notes. *I cannot have skipped anything!* He checks again and again. As he glances at the sand clock again, Jing Xian walks over to comfort him.

"He is fine. I'm sure of it, Grand Master."

Shibo walks away from Jing Xian and mutters, "I must start preparing for his recovery process."

Wait, Andre calls out. But no one can hear him. *Wait! I'm not sure, but I think I can hear someone praying. Yes, it sounds like Grand Master Shibo. I'm not sure if this voice I hear is just a thought, or is it someone actually praying for me. The voice I hear is not loud enough. I'll have to ignore it while I'm on this unbelievable journey.*

When the sand has drained to the bottom of the clock on its third turn, Shibo determines that Andre must start to come out of his trance. Once the clock has been turned the fourth time, the recovery process itself will commence and must be finished before the sand has emptied again. If the ceremonial candles burn down past the wire that Jing Xian has stretched across the floor before the sand clock is empty, Andre will face an excruciating death.

Chapter 74

The sand clock has been turned three times. It's starting to empty for the fourth time. Yes, Andre must complete his journey through his body and come out of his trance. It is written in the ancient Chinese books that if Andre is to successfully recover, he must go through a spiritual branding. The branding must be conducted by the presiding grand master at the monastery.

Here at the Yangshuo monastery, Shibo is the presiding grand master. Following the instructions in the great book, he and his two assistants will extract Andre from his trance. Jing Xian, who has received Shaolin training and is Andre's closest friend, will assist Shibo in the recovery. He will continue to monitor the candles, which must continue to burn in a pattern depicting the Celestial Green Dragon. He has skillfully handcrafted twelve small wooden stands connected by a thin wire that shows the height below which the candles must not burn. If for any reason the candles should burn below the stretched wire and Andre has not received the spiritual branding, he will die.

Shibo walks around in the temple, making sure everything is in the right spot. Every so often, he checks his notes to be sure the sequences are correct. He has one of his assistants move a specially made wooden staircase beside the bamboo litter so he can stand at the same level as Andre. After one assistant moves the stairs, the other assistant immediately climbs up and starts wiping the herbal concoction from the right side of Andre's chest. This is where Shibo will need to brand, yes, brand his student, and so the spot must be perfectly clean. The assistant wipes and wipes, but he is having some difficulty removing the stuff. The thick, gooey mixture seems to have almost become part of Andre's skin. After some intense scrubbing with soap and water, however, the assistant finally succeeds and makes sure there is no residue left. Then he dries Andre's chest with a fresh, clean towel.

Next, the two assistants hurry outside and return, struggling with a large metal bucket loaded with red hot coals. They set the bucket on a wooden platform beside the staircase. The assistants also bring in a bucket of cold water, which they set beside the bucket of hot coals.

Shibo approaches the staircase, making sure the sleeves to his robe are tied completely out of the way. He is carrying a large branding iron, which is normally used to brand cattle on the open range.

Although Andre has been prepped for the retrieval process by the assistants, he is still in the trance and has no idea what is going to happen. Shibo begins to stir the hot coals with a long steel rod. The branding iron must be glowing red hot. Grasping its steel handle, which is wrapped with several layers of buffalo hide, he thrusts it deep into the hot bed of coals. The head of the iron, three inches across, is shaped in a mysterious looking Chinese crouching lion. Waiting for the iron to heat sufficiently, Shibo ties a towel over his face to protect himself from the putrid smell and any flying matter, then he slips on his goggles and a pair of heavy leather gloves. He briefly takes a minute to review his hand-written notes before proceeding.

Now the grand master removes the branding iron from the sizzling coals, holding it carefully away from his body, and climbs to the top of the rickety staircase. At the top of the stairs, he is face to face with Andre.

Trying not to look into Andre's face, Shibo whispers, "It has to be done, my son."

To be sure the head of the iron will be pressed evenly on Andre's chest, Shibo takes a firmer grasp, then raises the iron high up into the air. He aims at Andre's chest.

"Forgive me, my son."

Then he presses the flat tip of the red-hot branding iron against Andre's chest three inches above his right nipple. While he holds it there, his assistant claps his hands four times at the speed of a hopping Chinese bullfrog. The process cannot be rushed, or the spiritual effect will not take place.

Jing Xian can hardly believe what he is seeing. *It's taking too long!* he thinks, feeling the fear and pain in himself. *It's burning him. It's going to kill him.*

Andre's body jumps violently as the heat and shock reverberate throughout his body. The first jump of Andre's chest catches the grand master off guard, almost knocking him off the wooden staircase, but he recovers quickly and continues to hold the branding iron in place. Smoke from the searing flesh drifts slowly upward toward the rafters in the ceiling of the temple. The putrid smoke hangs there like a heavy fog in old Shanghai, making it difficult for Shibo and the monks to breathe. It leaves a thick, pungent smell like a crematorium.

After the monk gives the fourth clap of his hands, Shibo removes the branding iron and unsteadily climbs down the stairs. He plunges the iron into the pail of cold water, producing a loud hissing sound and now a large cloud of steam drifts upward into the rafters.

As the branding ends, the ceremonial candles burning the sign of the Celestial Green Dragon mysteriously extinguish themselves. The temple becomes deathly silent, as the smoke from the extinguished candles drifts upward.

Andre, still entranced and still feeling no pain, shows no facial expression, though his blood-shot eyes flicker open and back and forth.

"Such a ghastly sight, being branded like a wild animal," Shibo mutters to his assistants as he looks at Andre. "But this process has to be done. It is written."

The grand master immediately picks up a clay pot containing the herbal salve he prepared earlier, climbs back up the stairs, and begins to wipe the salve over the branded spot on Andre's chest. Looking at the blackened skin, he feels sick to his stomach, but he forces himself to regain his composure. As grand master, he cannot show any such weakness, especially in front of the journeyman monks. He must concentrate on what needs to be done. While applying the green thick salve, he recites a prayer that seems to cause the temple to reverberate. The repetition of the chant helps to calm Andre's throbbing body. The salve will alleviate the swelling and stop the pain Andre will feel when he comes out of the trance.

After Shibo finishes, the two monks lower the bamboo litter to the temple floor. They meticulously remove the ropes, rolling them up, and hanging them on the wall. The assistants next position themselves at the two ends of the litter and carefully pick it up. As they start to carry Andre into the prayer room, Shibo walks to the side of the litter, stops them, and attempts to talk to Andre.

But Andre, who is slowly coming out of the trance, barely opens his eyes. He looks utterly worn out. Shibo leans over the litter as the two monks wait patiently.

"How do you feel, my son?"

No response.

He pauses. "Are you hurting anywhere?"

Andre still does not respond.

"Is there anything I can do for you right now?"

Shibo directs the assistants to set the litter down and has one of them go and get the special herbal drink for Andre. After Andre takes several sips, he slowly opens his eyes and looks up at Shibo, who leans down so he won't miss a word.

Andre speaks. "It worked."

Shibo smiles.

"It worked," Andre groggily says again. "It really did work! It seemed like I was in a dream. Or something like that." He pauses and takes another sip from the cup, then grasps for the right words to say.

"I wasn't scared. I could see with my eyes and go anywhere with no barriers. I felt like a phantom from another world." Pausing again, he adds, "But I'm so tired."

"Yes, my son," Shibo replies as he gently strokes Andre's forehead. "I will talk with you later and get all the details. Now you must get plenty of rest."

But Andre is already fast asleep.

Shibo nods to the waiting monks. They pick up the litter again and carry it into the prayer room, where Andre will spend the rest of his recovery time. He will sleep for the day or more, and then he will be washed with soap and water to remove the smelly herbal mixture. At that time, Shibo and his assistants will start scanning Andre's back and the other parts of his body, looking for lumps under the surface of his skin. After removing and analyzing the bone fragments, the grand master will be able to determine if a second trance is needed for additional repairs.

Chapter 75

The prayer room where Andre will lie during his recovery is a small, cave-like room next to the main room of the temple. The room was dug out of the limestone mountain by the early monks, over eight centuries ago. As the history of the monastery relates, there have been several death-defying processes conducted in this room over the centuries, all according to the lore in the ancient medical books of the monastery's library. There seems to be no rational or scientific explanation for these recoveries, as all the records say that the procedure was done and the individual recovered. Can we call these recoveries miraculous? What is a miracle? There's no way to know. Andre will stay in this room recovering from the process that gave him the ability to look within himself and begin the task of repairing his injured body.

The process of the spiritual branding can be done just once in a person's life. The spiritual emblem branded onto a man's chest will keep the spirit with him for all of his life on earth. It will also go with him to the world of spirit when he dies. Andre may, however, have to go into the self-induced trance several times to repair his injuries, depending on what he has accomplished the first time. The process has drained his energy to the point of total exhaustion, which can be very dangerous if he is not monitored twenty-four hours a day.

Shibo has of course been monitoring Andre's condition and feels that Andre came through the recovery in excellent condition. He will not have to go back inside himself for another journey of repair. After months of strict rest and the right nutritious foods, accompanied by special herbs, Andre has regained his spiritual energy. In a meticulous physical rehabilitation program carried out under the watchful eyes of the grand master, he has been able to strengthen his body back to what it was before the attack in Morocco. He has also developed more muscle and endurance in his body.

Soon Andre is able to walk. He begins explaining to Shibo the details of his experience. One evening while Shibo is reviewing his notes, Andre comes to his office.

"Master Shibo," he says, "do you have a few minutes? I have something I would like to share with you."

"Yes, Andre. Please sit down."

Andre begins. "Master Shibo, I got this odd sensation when I was inside myself, thinking, *This is me, this is what I look like inside.* But it was difficult for me to see it as *me*, so I just pretended it was a job and I was the repairman doing my job."

"Andre," Shibo replies, "what else could you think about? Of course it was you. But it was so unbelievable, it probably seemed like a dream."

"You're right, Master. That's exactly what I thought. It was a dream. But in this dream, I had total control, and I finished the work. And then you appeared at the end of my dream. All the dreams I ever had, I always woke up in the middle of them. All those odd dreams that never make sense."

"I see." Shibo nods his head in his concentration.

Andre hardly notices the grand master's response, however, as he continues to talk. He sounds like he is still in a dream. "But in this dream, I sensed I had a mission. I accomplished everything I was supposed to. It was totally amazing. Unbelievable!"

"Andre, the information you have been giving me is astonishing. I have been looking at the sketches you have made with the assistance of our artists of what it looked like inside of your body. Some of your drawings actually look like the photos taken of the far depths of the universe using the powerful Hubble telescope. These pictures are what I imagined it looks like inside the human body. I will be spending months writing and documenting all of this information for our medical history books." He smiles. "And you will be the star."

"Grand Master, I have one more question before I leave."

"Yes, what is it?"

"By any chance, were you praying for me while I was in my trance?"

"Yes, I was. Of course I was." Shibo looks slightly embarrassed. Taking off his glasses, he quickly cleans the lenses and puts them back on. "Why would you ask such a question? I wasn't sure if you would be able to hear me because I was thinking only your soul was inside you. I actually felt a bit uneasy talking and praying to a body that was not coherent and yet was still alive."

"Yes, I could hear you," Andre replies. "Your words were not loud enough for me to understand them, however. Maybe, if there is a next time, you can yell, and I may understand you." Now he smiles, too.

"Thank you for that information. It is very important that you remembered it," Shibo answers. "I will definitely put that in my report." He looks down at a book, then looks up at Andre again. "If there is a next time ... then ... yes, we will talk about the possibilities then. Tomorrow, you must meet with Jing Xian and return to your mental and physical program."

"Yes, Grand Master."

"It is incredible. I cannot find anything wrong with you," Shibo comments, giving another rare smile to Andre as he leaves the room.

PART V

A Year Later
Andre and Jing Xian Return to San Francisco

Chapter 76

Shortly after Mr. Roberson's death, a year and a half earlier, Maji and Doshi had returned to San Francisco and reported back to Mr. Craiger, the man who had hired them. Maji spoke while Doshi merely sat next to him, smoking one of her thin cigars.

"The police in Marrakesh will not be able to trace the death of Mr. Roberson to us," Maji said. "There is no proof we were involved. And there are no eye witnesses." He hesitated for a moment. "Well, there is a slight possibility, I mean a very slim one, that Mr. Roberson's son, Andre, may have gotten a brief glimpse of us."

"What the hell are you talking about?" Mr. Craiger demanded.

"I'll explain, sir."

"You damn well better explain."

"Andre came running around the corner of the wall to save his father when he heard him scream. Just at that moment, when Akram and I had just finished pushing it over, we were both in clear view. We're both starting to stand up, when out of nowhere he comes charging into all of those falling bricks and crap, and there's nothing for us to hide behind. Through all the confusion, with the falling of the wall and all the dust, people running everywhere, he may not have recognized us."

"It was that damn Akram's fault that Andre is still alive," Doshi blurted out. "He did a poor job of sabotaging the wall in the first place. He didn't pay enough attention to details."

"Enough, enough," Maji barked. "It wasn't our job to kill Andre, only to kill his father. And that is that," he added, starting to become agitated by Doshi's continuous interruptions. "Andre's friend—I believe his name was Jing Xian—was too far behind to see anything. I'm sure of that."

"Will you both shut up!" Mr. Craiger yelled. "Let me think." He puffed on his expensive Cuban Montecristro cigar. The room began filling up with smoke.

Chapter 77

In Marrakesh, before reporting to Mr. Craiger, Maji had made sure to talk with the doctor who treated Andre and his father. Pretending to be a concerned friend, he had entered Dr. Hasan's office and asked about his two "friends."

"Doctor, can you tell me the condition of Andre Roberson? Did his father survive?"

"May I ask," the doctor had asked, "who are you?"

"My name is Maji. My wife and I were on the camel ride with the Robersons. I presume Mr. Tim Roberson was killed at the kasbah earlier today. I'm deeply concerned about the young man, his son."

"Maji," the doctor replied, "I'm not authorized to give out patients' conditions except to family members. But since you knew him from the tour ... well, the information we received from your tour guide indicated that he had no other living relatives except for his father, who is now deceased. I can say his condition is grave. This is due to the severity of the damage to the young man's back, which has partly paralyzed him. Most likely, he will not recover. There is a good chance he may die from the trauma. As for his father, you are aware he was crushed to death by the falling debris."

"Yes, that is sad," Maji mumbled. "So very sad. The young man loses his father and almost gets himself killed as well. And to make it worse, he is paralyzed and may not survive. Maybe he will live like a vegetable for the rest of his life. So sad. So sad." He almost started crying crocodile tears as he shook hands with the doctor. "Thank you for the information."

Leaving the hospital, Maji decided that he and Doshi should not attempt to kill Andre while he was in the hospital. *Why bother? He is going to die very soon without our help.* Maji did not want to take any chances and make it look like murder, especially when the police were buying the theory that the falling wall was a natural disaster.

Perhaps Maji had a small spot of compassion for Andre, as he was not earmarked to die. That is this time. This is the way Maji does his business. When he has a job to do, he takes care of the person he was hired to eliminate, but not bystanders. Maji has never liked doing botched jobs. All the years he has been in this business, he has never accepted any job if it dealt with messy torture. Or children.

The Roberson job was a bit different, however, because he didn't have the opportunity to pick who was going to work with him. *This Akram character's a worthless piece of wonder who doesn't pay much attention to details,* he mutters to himself, *and he's always late in doing things.* Another thing Maji remembers is that Akram always wore dirty old clothes and didn't smell like he ever took a bath. *Why didn't he buy some new clothes?* After each job, he was paid well by Mr. Craiger. And as for Doshi, he still wonders, *why her?* Mr. Craiger could have picked Hilde, the nice German woman who is an expert with all types of weapons, especially knives. Why Doshi? He doesn't like the stupid mini cigars she always smokes, nor does he like her clothes.

For this job, Maji had to ride a camel and sleep on the ground in the giant sand dunes, but he did the job, and now, he tells himself, he can get paid and go home. *Andre's laying somewhere in a hospital bed,* he thinks, *half alive. Akram and I should have done this job right.* It still bothers him, even though Andre cannot talk or move. *There is no need for us to expose ourselves,* he thinks.

Chapter 78

After Andre's long and successful recovery, he and Jing Xian travel to San Francisco and schedule a visit with Stacey. It's time for him to review some of the long overdue proposals the company board has made for the change in ownership of the company. The two boys are staying away from corporate headquarters until every item in Andre's father's will and all company issues has been reviewed and voted on by the board of directors.

After arriving in town a couple days earlier, Andre and Jing Xian are now riding the Bay Area Rapid Transit (BART) from the Powell Street Station heading east to the Embarcadero Station in San Francisco. Andre is sitting at the window and gazing out at the passengers who are waiting to board other trains. Suddenly he yells out to Jing Xian, "Look!" He points to a man and woman standing in the waiting area. "Did you see them?" They both look back as their train pulls away.

"Yes, I saw them," Jing Xian replies. "That was the couple that was on our camel ride in Morocco. They're from Pakistan."

"Hmm." Andre thinks for a moment. "I think they said their names were Maji and Doshi. Last name? I don't remember. I'll bet you a thousand dollars those aren't their real names."

"You're probably right. But are you sure that was them?"

"Yeah, I'm sure. That's them. I haven't forgotten the way she wears her hair and dresses. Those strange colors. And the rich-looking clothes that guy always wore. I'm sure it was them."

"Then what the hell are they doing here?" Jing Xian asks. "Do we need to contact the police?"

"And what are we going to tell the police?" Andre replies. "Come on, there's no way we can point a finger at them with no proof. All we have are speculation and innuendos."

Jing Xian nods his head. "Yeah, you're right. That 'accident' took place close to over a year and half ago and ten thousands miles from here. Did they see us?"

"No. They were looking at someone else standing by the escalator."

Are you sure they didn't see us?"

"Yes," Andre says, "I'm positive. Why are you so concerned about their seeing or not seeing us?"

Jing Xian smiles. "I was hoping they did see us. They think you're dead. Maybe seeing you alive would give them a heart attack."

Andre is giving the appearance of these two villains deeper thought. "Jing Xian," he says, "do you suppose those two live in the Bay Area? Or are they here on business? Maybe they're here to kill someone else? Maybe, just maybe, they know I'm alive. They might be looking for us to finish what they didn't finish in Morocco. What if they know where we're staying?"

The two boys look at each other, lost in their thoughts, until Jing Xian notices they are pulling into their station. He pokes Andre in the side.

"It's our stop. Let's get off."

"Let's call her right now," Andre suggests as they exit the train. "While everything is fresh in my mind."

"Call who?"

"Let's call Stacey. I have an idea. We're going to need her help."

Chapter 79

"Hello, Stacey. Have we got some news to tell you!"

"Andre! What's up?"

"Guess who we saw a few minutes ago." He pauses. "No," he says, "you'll never guess. I'll tell you. You remember when we were on the camel ride and there was this odd couple named Maji and Doshi? Well, we just saw them in the Powell Street BART Station. There was no way we could have followed them, because our train was leaving the station and they were going somewhere, we don't know where."

"Andre, is Jing Xian with you?"

"Yes. He's eye-balling this pretty girl who's eating her lunch in a sidewalk restaurant." Andre laughs. "Stacey, if I had a camera right now, I think I would be able to get the Pulitzer Prize in photography right now. Jing Xian's tongue is hanging out to his chin."

"Will you guys get serious?"

"Okay. We'll tell you everything tonight. Stacey, how about having dinner with us tonight in North Beach? At the same place about seven. We'll have a table in front."

After a brief pause, she says, "I think I can squeeze you two crazy guys in tonight. I'll see you then." She hangs up.

At seven o'clock, Stacey walks up to Andre and Jing Xian's table. She's wearing a nice summer dress that shows off her slim figure very nicely.

"What do you want to drink?" Andre asks.

"I'll have a glass of that excellent Napa Merlot." She sits down at their table. "Well, guys, what do you have for me about the sighting in the BART?"

Andre fills Stacey in on what Jing Xian and he saw earlier. Then he admits to the helplessness they felt, knowing there was nothing they could do.

But Stacey has other ideas. "Guys," she says, "we need to do something to draw Maji and Doshi out from wherever they're staying. Have you guys thought that maybe they don't live here in the Bay Area? Maybe they're here on business. Or vacation? Also, have you thought that maybe they know you're both in San Francisco? That they're planning to finish their unfinished business?"

"Yeah. That's what we were just thinking," Andre says. "They looked like they knew where they were going,"

"How long did you see them for?"

"Maybe a couple of seconds. Our train was pulling out."

"Guys, let's look at the positive side first. Hopefully, they don't know anything about you right now. Let's look at it this way. If they've been living or staying around here for some time, that's good, because if they're only here for a short time, it will be almost impossible to plan anything."

A tall young man with black wavy hair comes up to the table. "Hello, my name is Kevin," he says, "and I will be your server this evening. Our house specialty for this evening is baked mahi-mahi with house sauce, roasted red potatoes, and a fresh spring mixed salad and bread of your choice for only eleven eighty-nine this evening."

Andre smiles. "We won't be eating dinner tonight. Only a few simple things."

"Very well. Here is our menu for our hors d'oeuvres and drinks."

"How about some garlic fries?" Andre asks his friends. "And artichokes hearts with a dip?"

"That sounds good," Jing Xian replies.

"And if you add some bacon and cheese-stuffed mushrooms. I'll be happy, too," says Stacey.

"And, Kevin," Andre says, "bring a bottle of your Napa Merlot."

Kevin acknowledges the order with a nod of his head. "I got that. Your order will be out shortly." He walks away.

Chapter 80

Jing Xian turns back to Stacey. "So what you are saying?"

"Let's see if they'll reveal themselves to us without knowing they're doing so."

Jing Xian nods. "Okay. That's a good idea. What would draw them out?"

Andre thinks for a minute. "Maybe we can publish something in the newspaper that states that an attorney in the Bay Area is going to open up the case due to some new incriminating information that's just turned up. Like there's the possibility of an eyewitness."

"No," Stacey says, "that won't fly. If this thing was an inside case, we'd never be able to keep it a secret without the person on the inside finding out. And our eyewitness might disappear. There has to be another way."

"Witness protection program?" says Andre, but when she shakes her head and mutters, "No way," he concedes. "Yeah. Bad idea."

"How about something with Andre?" Stacey asks.

At this point Kevin returns with their appetizers and drinks, and they stop talking and concentrate on eating and drinking.

"I've got it," Stacey suddenly says, holding an artichoke leaf in one hand. "We can say that you've had a mental recovery and you suddenly remember seeing Maji and that other guy push the wall over onto your father."

Andre shakes his head. "No ... I'm not sure...." He thinks for a minute. "I don't think anyone is going to believe that right now. How am I going to explain my recovery? Is anyone going to believe me when I say I got hurt? I think we need to plan to have them commit to something. Like trying to kill me to keep me quiet."

Nodding, Stacey takes a mushroom. "Yes! That's the idea. Let's continue on that thought," she says. "We don't want them to kill you, though. We like having you around." She gives him a playful jab in the ribs and smiles at him.

After several more drinks and more appetizers, the evening starts to slow down.

"Guys," Stacey says, "it's getting late and I have to get home. I've got to work tomorrow. You guys go back to your hotel. Let's get back together Wednesday night. You two talk about what we've talked about tonight. Who knows? You may come up with some more ideas. We'll talk the ideas through and come up with a plan.

After she leaves, the two boys order more wine and stay at the table, still talking. The threesome has come up with eleven ideas, but they are not sure how to implement any of them.

Chapter 81

For the next two days, Andre and Jing Xian walk around the BART stations in the area of San Francisco where they saw Maji and Doshi. They are hoping to see the assassins again. With any luck, they will be able to follow them to wherever they are staying. But though they have been going from station to station, they have come up with nothing.

On Wednesday morning, Andre telephones Stacey on her private line.

"Hey, Stacey. How have you been?"

"Andre, there's something that just came up with the company. I was planning to call you. We definitely need to get together this evening. I'll explain what I know then. I have to go now," she says before he can reply. "It's extremely busy today. Same place? Seven tonight?"

"Okay."

That night, they meet again.

"I wasn't sure if I was going to get here this evening," Stacey says as they sit down. "Traffic is horrendous tonight. I got the last parking spot in the neighborhood, and that was only because someone was leaving."

"I'm glad you made it," Andre says. "I ordered you a glass of your favorite wine."

"Thanks." She picks up the glass and takes a sip. "Before we get into anything else," she continues, "I have something I must share with you. First thing this morning, I received a personally addressed envelope from Mr. Craiger. He's the man who owns almost half the company's stock. The letter's addressed to you." She looks at Andre. "Your father and Mr. Craiger never agreed on anything. Now this whole thing with the company and your father's death has everything in a turmoil, and this guy Craiger thinks that since he is the person alive with the most stock at this time, he can ramrod a proposal through." She pulls out several letters out of a manila envelope and lays them on the table. "Let me explain."

"Me?" says Andre with a surprised look. "Why should he be sending me anything?"

Stacey picks up one letter. "This whole mess with the company hasn't been straightened out yet," she says, "but one of these days, you'll own fifty-seven percent of the stock. You'll have the controlling interest. So now Craiger is already starting to take the same attitude toward you that he did toward your father.

"I need to explain this very sensitive issue that your father and Craiger were having." She moves the letters around, as if lining them up for inspection. "There's this issue about x-raying sea-land containers right after they're offloaded from ships. It's for security reasons. There could be illegal things being smuggled inside the containers. Like weapons or a nuclear bomb." She indicates a letter. "There's another issue about x-raying the containers *before* they're shipped out of foreign ports. The U.S. Transportation Safety Agency has mandated that we have to come up with some sort of schedule of inspections before the end of the year for the protection of the ports in the United States."

All of this is new to Andre and Jing Xian. They nod and wait for her to continue.

"Well, what I make of this problem with the x-raying is a money thing," she says, "and maybe there's some kind of smuggling operation going on. The board of directors is still squabbling over these issues and the money. The directors are currently recommending x-raying every tenth container going out and coming in. Mr. Craiger is complaining very loudly that a list should be published to identify which containers, using their trail numbers, will be inspected in advance. He feels there might be some goods in containers that might be affected if they are x-rayed. Things that could be destroyed." She pauses and gives a significant look to her two companions. "Now, what I think doesn't matter. I'm not on the board of directors—"

"Wait a minute," Andre says. "What do you think?"

"I think they should have a small team at the loading site that will open containers that can't go through x-raying. On the shipping manifest, it can specify containers to be inspected by hand instead of being x-rayed. It can also identify suspicious containers. There is a right thought on that, and there is a questionable thought as well. If someone in our company, especially in a high position, knew which containers were going to be inspected, he could make arrangements to ship things in the uninspected containers and never get caught. I'm not saying anything about anyone, of course. I want you guys to know that. I'm only saying 'what if.' That would be a perfect plan, though. If someone knew which container to use.... Well, it's just a thought." She pauses, then looks at them. "Okay, guys, I'm finished. You can speak now."

Andre and Jing Xian are looking at each other. After a moment, Andre sighs, starts to say something, then stops. "I don't know where to begin," he finally says.

Stacey nods. "Okay. Let's start with these guys. I'm starting to get a feeling there's some connection between Tim's death and this problem with x-raying containers." She turns to Andre. "Your father got a visit from some thugs, I'd have to look it up, but it was sometime ago. They looked like they were from the Middle East. I had never seen or heard of them before. Your father didn't keep me informed of everything that was going on. Now the strange thing is to see these same two characters, Maji and Doshi, in town when they're supposed to be living in Pakistan. And now I get this strange letter from Mr. Craiger addressed to Andre." She picks up a letter. "There's this other possibility. We know that Mr. Craiger doesn't know where you are." She looks at Andre again. "Where you live and what condition you're in. As far as the board is concerned, you, Andre, are still in a paralyzed state, and I'm your personal secretary handling all business affairs for you by proxy. But Mr. Craiger has recently hired an attorney to look into the possibility of taking over the company. I don't know where he's going to take this issue. It's in an early stage, and I'll keep you posted on his progress. Everyone assumes you're living somewhere out of the United States. In some kind of rehabilitation. That's all the information that has been released. Another thing I'm thinking," she is on a roll now, "is that Andre should start living a more sheltered lifestyle while he's in San Francisco."

"No," he says, "I can't do that."

"Well, if you don't, and Maji or Doshi or maybe that other guy that was at the kasbah sees you, this whole thing we are going to put together is out the window. And you might find yourself going out a window, too, with someone helping you. Get my drift?"

"She's right," says Jing Xian. "You're going to have to stay in the hotel and not be going out on the streets. You can't be seen."

Andre gives this some thought, then grudgingly replies, "Yeah, I guess so. You guys are right. I know that has to be done or this idea will go up in smoke."

Stacey makes a firm statement. "We might want to start tonight."

Andre gasps. "Are you sure it should be tonight?"

"Yes. And I think Jing Xian should stay in the hotel as well." She turns to Jing Xian. "Maybe you don't have to stay in your room as long as Andre does, but I really think it would help. Everyone that was on the camel ride knows both of you and what you look like. Andre is considered to be a possible eyewitness to the 'accident.'"

"Okay," Jing Xian replies, "I'll stick around the neighborhood."

"I really think it would be an excellent idea if you would stay *inside the hotel*," Stacey tells him. "And that goes for both of you. And you need to let the front desk know you're staying inside. Tell them you're novelists and you're writing a book together. Or whatever. Don't worry about the hotel bill. It'll be covered."

As they both nod, she picks up her glass. "Before we disband our little meeting tonight," she says, "let's toast our new and hopefully successful plan. And let's put it into motion tomorrow"

They toast their plan, then start going into specifics. Stacey will start implementing it tomorrow by phoning her point of contact at the San Francisco gossip tabloid, *The Probe*.

Chapter 82

"Hello? Is this Christina?"

"Yes, it is."

"This is Andre Roberson, the guy you and your girl friends were talking to while you were on vacation in China last year."

"Yes?" She sounds very hesitant.

"On the river cruise?" He prompts her memory.

After a minute, she says, "Yes. Yes, I remember you. You were that good-looking guy with your friend trying to sell Chinese souvenirs to us while we were on the boat ride on the Li River. I think I bought a little Chinese horse from you. Right? I still have it on my bookshelf."

Andre blushes a little as he hears her say he is good looking. "How have you been?" he shyly asks.

"I've been very good," she says. "I'm surprised you're calling me now. You know, that was about a year and a half ago."

"Yes, I realize it was some time ago, but I do have an honest excuse for not calling earlier."

"You do?" She giggles. "Okay, let me hear it."

And so Andre tells her about his accident in Morocco, though he says only that he had a broken arm and there were some serious complications with its healing. Then he tells her that he had missed place her business card and just recently found it again. As he makes up a story about falling off a stepping stone, he is thinking to himself, *I don't want to get into the real reason for not calling earlier because of my paralysis. It would be too hard for her to understand what happened in the monastery.* This story will be fine until he meets her again. Then he will be able to explain what really happened. He will be able to tell her about the situation he is in right now.

"You know," Christina says, "you and I seem to have a knack of communicating when I'm on a vacation, and you call me only when we are far away from each other. As it happens now, my girl friends and I are getting a sun tan on Waikiki Beach. Hawaii's such a lovely place. Beautiful hotels, nice sunshine, lots of places to shop, a lot of good-looking guys. It's just a totally beautiful place. I've been thinking I need to get myself a condominium here so I can come more often and just relax."

"Say," Andre blurts out, "do you girls need someone to put sun tan lotion on your backs?"

"Well," she replies, "I'm just thinking how nice that would be. It's not much fun when you have your girl friends do it. It's better when it's a good looking guy."

Andre blushes again. He is glad she cannot see him through the phone.

"Andre," she says, "can you wait just a moment? There's this totally handsome guy walking by in one of those European bathing suits that hardly leave anything to the imagination. If you know what I mean." She starts laughing.

"Wait, wait," Andre yells into the phone. "I'll be right there!"

Christina comes back to the conversation. "Seriously," she says, "that'll take too long. You're five or six thousand miles away. There are passport and visa problems."

"No, no, no. I'm not in Morocco or China," he says. "I'm in San Francisco. I'm inheriting my father's corporation. And there are a lot of other things happening right now, too. I'd love to come over to Hawaii right now and rub tanning oil on your back, but I have to stay here for a while. I really hope you understand my situation."

"Yes, Andre, I understand," she says. "I really feel you're sincere in what you're saying. Let me change the subject. How is your friend? The one who was with you on your little boat when I met you on the river. Is he still living in China? The reason I'm asking is that I have a very good friend who is lying right here beside me. She's very interested in your buddy."

Andre can't help but smile. "That's great," he says. "I'm sure he'll be excited to hear that. His name is Jing Xian. He's here with me in San Francisco. Well, he's not right here right now, though. He's out doing some errands. I can have him call you when he gets back."

"That would be great," Christina says.

"What's her name?"

"Her name is Missy. You know, I was thinking, maybe we might be able to have a lay over in San Francisco for several days before we go on to Colorado."

"That would be fantastic," he replies. "But what happened to Chicago?"

"Oh, you don't know. Two of my friends and I were transferred to our Colorado office about a year ago. Andre, it would be great to talk with you longer, but I have to get going right now. Call me later and we can talk longer."

"I'll call you again. I promise."

Chapter 83

Maji is sitting in his leather chair in his elegant condo overlooking San Francisco Bay, lazily looking down at the clock tower pier, where a gargantuan cruise ship is maneuvering itself alongside the dock. *How is that guy going to park such a big ship in such a small place?* he wonders. At the same time, he is watching a San Francisco 49ers game on his forty-two-inch plasma television. The phone rings. "Damn it!" He picks up the phone. "Hello," he barks.

"Maji, this is Mr. Craiger. How are you?"

"Oh, I'm doing fine, sir."

"I'm glad you didn't plan anything for today."

"Well I was going to—"

Craiger cuts him off. "Maji, I was reading this gossip tabloid called *The Probe* this morning. I noticed this article by this columnist named Bertolino who writes for this rag. He's writing about this guy named Andre Roberson, the son of the late Tim Roberson. This Roberson guy is starting to get under my damn skin. I thought he was so deathly ill in Morocco, he was going to die. That was over a year ago." Craiger pauses, and Maji can hear the rustling of the newspaper. "What I'm reading today is that he didn't die. This famous doctor here in San Francisco has come up with a new revolutionary procedure for back surgery. This columnist says the doctor can repair Roberson's back and cure the paralysis he's been suffering all this time. He has been living like a vegetable for over a year. The column says he's very excited about the surgery."

Maji does not say a word, but continues to listen carefully.

"Well, hell," Craiger yells, "so would I if I was in his situation! If he's in a state of paralysis and can't talk, or maybe he can talk, you know he would be excited. Well, I don't give a damn about his well being." Craiger pauses, then goes on. "Hell, maybe he can blink his eyes in Morse code, or something. You know, if he *is* able to talk, you and I and several other people are going to be in a very serious situation. You know that. Right? And you also know that I hired you, Doshi, and Akram to do a simple job. Well, you bumbled it. I'm starting to get a feeling I may have to get someone else to correct your screw-up. Maybe you three need to have some special training."

As Craiger continues to lecture he starts chewing his cigar and his words become garbled. Maji is straining to understand what he is saying, but does not dare say he cannot understand him. Through the crunching and distorted sounds, what he hears are the words "shot dead" and "hit man." Suddenly Craiger's voice is clear and Maji can understand him. He must have spit out the cigar or ate it.

Starting to get nervous, Maji replies. "Yes, Mr. Craiger. You don't have to worry about a thing. I'm well aware of the situation. We will take care of everything."

Craiger reads from the newspaper, then says to Maji, "There hasn't been a date set for the surgery. It's hard to tell by reading this column. They write just enough to bait someone, and they never finish what they're talking about. Well, I want you to contact this guy, Bertolino. Do you think you can do that without screwing up? Find out where he got this information. Find out where this guy, Andre, is. The article says he's been living in Yancooooo—hell, I can't pronounce it. It's Chinese. I wish the Chinese would learn how to speak English."

He reads another paragraph aloud. "This columnist says it's someplace in southern China. Well, we're not going to China. The language is too hard to speak and impossible to read, and forget the damn writing. We need to know when this Roberson guy is planning to return to the United States for this surgery. Then you and Doshi can take care of him before he makes any miraculous recovery."

"Mr. Craiger," Maji asks, "do I have to bring Doshi?"

"Yes, you damn well have to bring her. Two are better than one. Do you want Akram to come with you, too?"

"Oh, please! Not him!" Maji begs.

"Okay, then you and Doshi get your butts down there and find out what's going on. I'm going to contact an associate of mine in the travel section of my company. That's half of my company. Hopefully, it will be all mine very soon." Craiger pauses. "See if you can find out if a visa application has been submitted for Roberson to return to the United States."

"I'm on top of everything as we speak, Mr. Craiger." Maji is starting to get very nervous.

"I've already given you way more money then you deserve," Craiger bellows at him. "I'm not going to advance any more until I see a headstone with the name of Andre Roberson on it. Have I gotten through to you this time? Maybe I can have a friendly talk with the dead father's secretary, too. She might slip up and tell me something about the whereabouts of Andre".

"Mr. Craiger, you won't have to worry about a thing."

Chapter 84

It has been two days since Stacey had a meeting with Mr. Bertolino, who writes a weekly column in the gossip tabloid, *The Probe*. She told him what happened to Andre and his father and revealed part of the plan she, Andre, and Jing Xian have put together. Through the years, Bertolino has written several pleasant columns about Mr. Roberson and his business. About five years ago, he wrote a very touching article about Mr. Roberson's wife, Vanna, who fought cancer for several years and had a happy and charming personality up to the last days of her life.

Vanna and Tim got along very well, and after her passing, he missed her deeply, especially after Andre went away to college. Mr. Roberson's personal life was starting to haunt him to the point of compromising important decisions he had to make at work. He struggled for a while, but managed to get his life back together with the help from his personal secretary, Stacey.

It has been nearly twenty months since Mr. Roberson was killed in Morocco. The police there wrote it off as an accident and closed the case. Now that Andre has recovered, he and Stacey are going to make someone pay for Mr. Roberson's death.

After Vanna's death, Stacey became more involved in the operation of the company and helped her boss at home by hiring a full-time housekeeper to take care of things, including cooking his meals. Stacey had eventually convinced him to buy a spacious condominium in a nice high-rise in downtown San Francisco, where he had all of his friends nearby.

Bill, Mr. Roberson's devoted limousine driver for the last forty years, was also close by to take him anywhere he wanted to go. Occasionally, they went to Scottsdale, Arizona, where they enjoyed several days on the golf course and lounging around the swimming pool. When Mr. Roberson and Bill were out of town, Roberson treated Bill like a good old friend. They played golf together and lay around the pool drinking scotch and water, though Bill almost always drank fruit drinks. Bill never drank alcohol if he was going to drive within six or seven hours. His employer respected him for his conviction.

Mr. Roberson also used to sit on his penthouse balcony with his telescope, looking out over the city. He enjoyed watching boats come in and out of the Bay, and he also saw quite a few pretty women sun bathing topless on their balconies on nearby buildings. When he was not girl-watching, he kept an eye on his investments by watching the container ships sailing in and out under the Golden Gate Bridge.

Chapter 85

"Hi, Stacey," the voice on the telephone says, "This is Bertolino, you know, the columnist for *The Probe*. We spoke last week."

"Sure. I have you in my Blackberry," Stacey says. "You know, I'd be completely lost if I didn't have it."

"Stacey," he says, "you owe me big time."

"What do you mean? Do you have good information for me?"

"Well, sort of. My secretary told me she received a call from someone who said his name was Dr. Maji. He wanted to know how he could get in contact with Andre Roberson or his doctor."

Stacey cannot help but smile. "See? I told you it would work. He's out there. We just have to make him expose himself. Please pardon the figure of speech."

"Let me tell you what he said." Bertolino sounds excited. "This guy says he read my column and was fascinated with the concept of exploratory back surgery. He wants to know more about it. My secretary didn't feel like he was telling the truth, though. He didn't sound like a doctor. You know how doctors talk. They pause a lot and use technical terms, especially if they're talking about medical procedures. Very professional. I'm very lucky to have an extremely talented secretary. She's great at noticing things about people."

Bertolino pauses. "My secretary told this so-called *Dr.* Maji called while I was out of the office. He told her he was calling from a business phone not far from here, and maybe he would stop by to talk to me. She told him I'd be back at two-thirty this afternoon, but that was a lie. I have no plans to talk to him. What would I tell him?"

Stacey and Bertolino both laugh, then he continues. "So what we're planning to do is have someone wander in from another room and take a picture of him when he arrives downstairs, you know, without him noticing it. We're good at doing that at this paper." He chuckles. "Then my secretary will tell him something came up and I had a meeting and had to leave early. We're sorry for the inconvenience. If we had his phone or cell number, we could call and let him know when I'll be back in the office. That sort of thing, you know.

"I'm sure he's going to be frustrated. Maybe angry. Hopefully, he'll give us a phone or cell number just to get the information he wants. You know, Stacey, in the tittle-tattle business, I've been contacted by every type of person you can imagine. Everyone wants to see their name in print. We're pretty sure this is the guy you're looking for. One of the photographers here owes me a favor, so he'll be waiting for this guy to show up and—*zappo*, we'll have his picture. If there's anyone with him, we'll get their picture, too."

"That sounds great," Stacey replies.

Chapter 86

Several hours later, Bertolino telephones Stacey again. "Stacey, you'll need to talk with my secretary, Kathy, in about an hour. I have her on a couple of errands right now. Oh, and I forgot to ask you—please call me Bob. Most of my friends and close associates call me that. You know, it sounds so formal when you call me Bertolino."

"Okay, Bob," Stacey replies. "What does she have for me?"

"Kathy can tell you exactly how Maji acted. And he's not a doctor. How he talked, what he said. She received another call about an hour after this Maji character called. The second guy said his name was Mr. Rajid. He said he wanted to talk with Mr. Roberson's surgeon and would call back later. He hung up and didn't call again. Does his name ring a bell?"

Stacey thinks for a moment. "I have to refer to my notes," she says. "I think I've heard that name before, but I can't place it right now. But thanks. I'll let you know."

Chapter 87

"Hello, is this Mr. Bertolino's secretary?"

"Yes, this is she. My name is Kathy."

"I'm sorry, Kathy. This is Stacey. I was talking with your boss, Mr. Bertolino, a couple hours ago about a phone call you received from a so-called Dr. Maji."

"Oh, that guy." Kathy laughs. "I'm being professional. We've received several calls about the column yesterday. You never know what these people will say. I have to be prepared for any type of trick they might try."

Stacey can hear her open and close some cabinet drawers then Kathy goes on.

"Yes, I remember Mr. Maji very well. He spoke with an accent, probably Middle Eastern. Arab? Pakistani? When he was talking, he had this air about himself, kind of a pushy and cocky. He was trying to impersonate a doctor, but he was also having problems in pronouncing some of his words. His English isn't all that good. You know, he really gave me a creepy feeling. He definitely sounded like a phony. Some of these strange people will use other people to do their calling. That's how they try to get past the secretary."

"You're absolutely right," Stacey says. "I'm a secretary, too."

Kathy's voice levels out now. "Stacey, my boss has a photographer here waiting for this guy who says his name is Dr. Maji. When we take his picture, we'll rush it through developing and get it to you so you can have either Andre or Jing Xian identify him. I just got this freaky flash in my mind. I don't know why I didn't ask you earlier, it's such a simple thing, but now it's starting to bother me."

"What is it, Kathy?"

"Can you give me a description of this guy Maji? Just in case he walks into our building unannounced and starts snooping around?

Who knows, maybe he's already been in our building and we haven't seen him, but he knows who we are!"

"Calm down, girl," Stacey says. "I'm sure everything is fine. I'm sure he knows you have surveillance cameras in the building. I'm sure of it. They're positioned everywhere.

Chapter 88

On Thursday, Stacey calls Andre in his hotel room. "Are you staying in your room?" she asks him. "Or at least staying in the hotel?"

"Yes, I'm being good," he says. "I'm staying in. But it's no fun."

"I understand," she says. "Well, I have good news and bad news. I won't give you a choice of which one you want to hear first. Here's the good news. After we get off the phone, I want you to give Bertolino secretary, Kathy, a call."

"Who is Bertolino?"

"Bob Bertolino. He writes a scandalmonger column in a tabloid called *The Probe*. His secretary's name is Kathy. She is a very attractive, tall woman. You like talking with tall women?"

"Yes. How old is she?"

"I think she's about twenty-six, but don't tell her I said so."

"Okay."

"Give her a call. She wants descriptions of Maji and Doshi. She's worried that they might get into her building and no one will recognize them. There's no telling what they might try to do. I told her there's no need for her to worry. Those thugs don't know what we're planning. All the paper did was publish a column using the information we gave them. All Bob and Kathy have to do is come up with some fictitious name and phone number for their source if they are pressured to give one."

"Okay, I'll give her a call."

"Give her your cell number, just in case someone comes into the building and looks suspicious to Kathy. She can call you with a description."

"Gotcha."

"The so-called Dr. Maji called Bertolino's office this morning using his cell phone. He told Kathy he wouldn't be able to come in person.

He said some urgent business had come up and he'd be out of town."
She pauses to clear her throat.

"The bad news," Stacey continues, "is that the phone he was calling
on had its number blocked, so we didn't get anything. The sting we
were going to initiate won't work for now. Kathy told me she didn't
think Maji had caught on to our plan, though. She said he said he'd
try calling again tomorrow. That will be Friday. She said he sounded
cautious. Or maybe nervous. Got to go now. I'll keep you posted. Say
hi to Jing Xian." And she hangs up.

After thinking about her phone conversations with Bertolino and
Kathy, Stacey makes a decision. On her next visit to their office, she will
use a side door instead of walking in the front entrance. *Who knows?*
she thinks. *This Maji and his friends could suspect something. I can't take
a chance. I must play it safe. Using a different door each time is a safe idea
for the time being.*

Chapter 89

Several hours later, the telephone in Andre's hotel room rings again.

"Hi, Andre, it's Stacey again. The more I think about it, you and Jing Xian need to stay right where you are, at least for a while. If someone sees and recognizes you, this whole thing will be a wash. If you have to go out for something, wear a cap and sun glasses, just to be safe. Where is Jing Xian?"

"Oh," says Andre, "he went across the street to get some ice cream, I think some spumoni."

"Why is he over there? Don't you guys realize how serious this could get? Someone could find out where you're living and send someone over and have you both killed right in your hotel room."

"We're terribly sorry."

"You really need to pay attention and be one hundred percent on what needs to be done. Andre, we're hoping that Maji will slip up and call on a land line and then we would be able to find out where he is calling from, but he didn't do it. He called on a cell phone, but the number was blocked. But we don't think he's caught on to what we're doing."

"Well, Stacey, is there anything we might be able to do while we're cooped up here? Maybe we can do some kind of detective work or something like that?"

"No, Dick Tracy," she says with a laugh. "You guys just stay there and don't get in trouble. If I come up with something, I'll give you a call."

Later that day, Stacey visits the Majestic Dragon Hotel where Andre and Jing Xian are staying. She feels bad about keeping the boys pinned up in the hotel and talking so rough at them and has decided a visit with a couple of pizzas might cheer them up. When she starts telling the boys about her latest plans, Andre interrupts her.

"I have an idea," he says.

"Please let me explain my idea first," she tells him, "before you jump in with another one. Okay?" She is not smiling. The pressure is starting to take its toll on her. "First, Andre, you are confined to the hotel for the time being."

Andre and Jing Xian are surprised by her sudden outburst.

"Stacey, Stacey, hold up," says Andre as he gently places his hand on her shoulder. "What's happening?"

She looks down at the floor. "I know it's hard to be cooped up here for this long," she says in a gentler tone, "but, guys, just hang in there. Maybe you don't have to stay in your room all the time, but you do have to stay in the hotel. Why don't you use the exercise room? That would be good for you. But please be very careful about exposing yourself to new people who check in. You never know who will be checking in."

She is starting to smile. "Andre, I'm working on making hush-hush arrangements through our transportation office to have you flown back to the United States from Shanghai. I'll have you land at San Francisco International Airport in our corporate jet. But this is where I run into some problems. I haven't figured it out how I'm going to get you into an ambulance at the airport from the jet, without you *really* being aboard." She is starting to show a gloomy face. "I was thinking on taking a chance on smuggling you into the jet after it lands at SFO. But that's when it gets tricky. Someone might see us. You see, smuggling you aboard would not be real hard, but getting your bed and all the life-support equipment aboard and hooked up would be difficult. You see, we have to make it look like you're still in a vegetative condition."

"How am I going to be in China and be here at the same time?"

"Please hold your horses for a moment. I will explain," she replies. "I'm focusing. Early this morning, I was thinking, maybe I'll have you fly back to Shanghai, but not on our jet. On a commercial jet. Then have you returned to the States on the company jet."

"Stacey," Jing Xian says, "you sure did a good job in your selection of pizza." He eats another slice.

"Thanks," she says. "I'm glad you like it. But," she continues, "that plan won't work."

"Why not?" Andre asks.

"For starters, we don't have enough time to apply for and receive a visa for you to enter China. I've used up all of my favors in China. I think we could put everything else together except for the visa. Wait— there's one more possibility. It just might work."

"Here we go again," Andre says with a smile.

"Yes, maybe this one might work," Stacey says. "We'll have our corporate jet returning from Singapore diverted into Shanghai and supposedly pick you up. We must make it very discreet. We'll load the bed and all the life-support equipment, and someone else will be in the bed pretending to be you. Then on its way back to the States, we'll have the jet diverted into Honolulu. To pick something up that's urgent. It'll be something like a covert mission. I can create some paperwork spelling out something that has to be picked up for security and urgency in Honolulu. We'll want to coordinate the timing of when the plane leaves Shanghai, so when it lands in Honolulu it'll be late at night. That's what we need, a late-night landing. The fewer people around, the easier it will be to get you aboard. Andre, that's when you replace the imposter in the bed. He'll get off the plane in Hawaii. The imposter will be part of the flight crew, which will bypass the visa needed for Andre. The plane won't stay overnight, just refuel and fly on to California. I have a few friends working in the Transportation Department, and I'm positive they'll work with us on this. Then, once the plane arrives at San Francisco International, there won't be any problem getting you off the plane and into the ambulance."

Chapter 90

"That sounds like an excellent plan," Andre says. "I was just thinking, maybe we should have someone we can trust to be close to me in case someone catches on and decides to take me out. Can Jing Xian be my aide on that airplane trip? It won't cause any suspicion because he's already my best friend. Everyone knows that."

"That's an excellent idea," Stacey replies. "I think it can be arranged. He's had the training that will be beneficial for your protection, if needed."

Jing Xian looks up from his fourth or fifth slice of pizza. "That means I'll be going to Hawaii with Andre to make it look like I'm returning to the States with him." He laughs. "Yeah, I knew I'd be going to Hawaii." He laughs.

Stacey gives him a close look. *What's he got in mind?* "Okay," she says aloud. "Jing Xian, you'll be part of our clean-up team in Honolulu. You'll board the plane and tidy it up. You know, like picking up trash, wiping down the restrooms, stuff like that. Make sure you look like you're doing something and stay aboard when you finish. Andre, I'll be trying to locate an ambulance company that can transport you and your bed and all your life-support equipment from the air terminal to the hospital. I'll talk with someone at the hospital to see if we can rent one of their units. Now, let's see." She's walking through the steps. "The ambulance will take you and Jing Xian to the San Francisco General Hospital, where you will be staying for the duration of this operation. If that's what we want to call it."

Andre says to Jing Xian, "Hey, see if you can think of a name that we can call this operation, okay?"

Stacey gives the boys a smile, knowing they are finally starting to laugh again. Then she continues. "I'm still working on the next thing, and that is how I'll get you a hospital room on the surgical floor at the hospital. While all this coordinating is happening, you'll be artificially hooked up to an IV. We'll get you a respirator for your breathing, just like the way you were hooked up after your mishap. I like to use the word 'mishap' because I'm convinced it was *not* an accident. It was attempted murder. You'll have to act like you're in a comatose condition, almost dead. You and everyone helping must make it look real. We don't know who they are and who they might be using.

"There's one more thing I have to ask you. Will you feel comfortable if we hook up an IV so you won't get dehydrated through all this? You won't need to be hooked up to the IV until you arrive in San Francisco and removed from the plane and loaded into the ambulance. We're not sure how close some of the on-lookers are going to get to you. One of them could be our killer. We're going to try our best to get you in the ambulance and whisk you off. You are supposed to be in a comatose condition, and you won't be able to ask for water, especially if someone we don't know is standing nearby. But remember, having an IV in your arm will raise the threat level of someone putting something into the IV bag and killing you."

"That's a frightening thought," Andre responds.

"I think it would be a good idea. If we don't do this right, someone might see through our plan, and it'll all be in vain. Remember, I don't think you'll have to have the IV in your arm while you're in the hospital room. We'll be able to monitor who comes into your room before they arrive."

Andre looks at Jing Xian. "You're going to have to keep a close eye on me when someone we don't know is in the area."

"You can bet I'll be there."

"One more thing," Andre says to Stacey. "What if I have to use the restroom when someone is close to me?"

"Well," she says with a smile on her face, "the doctor in Hawaii can give you a device that you can hook on to yourself, and you can urinate into a plastic bag while you're lying in bed. You can have the device lying between your legs on the bed. Very simple. No problem."

"Who's going to help me put it on?" he asks her with a devilish look.

"Don't even go there."

And Jing Xian quickly says, "Buddy, you're on your own on this one."

Andre looks vaguely disappointed. "Well," he finally admits, "it seems like it will work."

"You won't be able to be moving around, even if you want to," Stacey tells him. "You won't be talking. We won't know who might be watching." She pauses as if she hears someone at the door, then shakes her head. "I think I'm beginning to get paranoid," she says. "I've got to get a hold of myself.

"If they suspect that we know something," she says in a softer voice, "it doesn't matter how much we know, because they won't know how much we know. I hope I haven't confused anyone with all the if's. Anyway, if they think their identity might be compromised, everything could get deadly. Remember, we already know two of them from the camel ride. I'm almost positive whoever is out to get you won't use those two again. Maji and Doshi. But there have to be several others you didn't see in Morocco. You know, the man who drove the Land Rover that picked those two up after the murder. Why is Maji snooping around? There's something going to happen, and we have to be ready. We don't know if they wanted to kill you in Morocco, but they've tasted blood and it won't be hard for them to kill again. You guys understand?"

"Yes," Andre and Jing Xian reply in one voice.

For the first time, the two young men are starting to understand how serious this whole thing is becoming.

Chapter 91

Jing Xian is thinking about the training he received at the monastery as he quietly stretches his body into a kung fu stance. Andre is sitting backwards on a straight-back chair, with his arms dangling down over the back. He sits motionless, just nodding his head, saying nothing. He, too, is thinking about the detailed training he received at the Shaolin monastery from the visiting grand master, Da Ming. What he learned about the secret art of using his hands to inflict pain may be of use to extract information from unwilling people like Maji and his associates.

Andre focuses on the technique for inflicting pain. Suddenly and from nowhere, he feels an unexplained twitching in his face that escalates until within seconds, the muscles in his face and down his neck begin to spasm. His eyebrows begin to stretch down over his eye sockets, then quickly retract, his vision becomes blurred, and he is blind for a few seconds. The sides of his mouth stretch extremely wide, almost to the point of tearing the skin. Within seconds, however, his face returns to normal, though the muscles are still aching.

During the fifteen seconds of this occurrence, he could not move or see or hear or speak. Stunned, he manages to mumble, "What just happened?" as he uses his hands to massage his face. His mumbling voice is not loud enough for either Jing Xian or Stacey to hear. *What did I just experience?* he asks himself. *Am I going crazy? Did someone slip me a drug? I know this is crazy, but I felt like something or someone else was alive in my body.*

Stacey, who is walking back to her chair after getting a bottle of water out of the refrigerator, says to Andre, "You know, I don't think I have ever told you about what I did when I was a college girl."

Andre makes no comment. He is still sitting in his chair with his head hanging down.

She notices this. "Hey, is there a problem?" she asks.

Andre raises his head. "No. Why?"

"You just had this real ugly expression on your face, something I've never seen before. For a quick second, you looked sort of like the Hunchback of Notre Dame, and I was just wondering if something evil happened to you a minute ago." She gives a nervous laugh.

"Oh, no, I feel fine," he says. "Just a little bored, staying here in the hotel for so long. Are you going to tell us a secret about your life? Is it going to be a sexy story?"

"No, no, I'm serious. Did you know I'm in the sheriff's reserve here in town? I took several semesters of criminal law in college. I used to want to be a policewoman. Or work somewhere in criminal law. But after going through all those classes and trying to keep up with the dating scene, it got difficult for me to keep up my grades. I had to drop a few classes to be able to graduate."

Jing Xian looks at her. "How good are you with a nine millimeter Beretta?" he asks.

"I'll tell you what I can do with it. Why don't we get a cigarette and put it between your lips? I'll see if I can shoot it out. Would you be game for that?"

Chapter 92

Two hours later, Stacey is looking for a parking spot in the parking structure at San Francisco General Hospital. The dreary San Francisco weather is starting to clear up, and on her way to the hospital Stacey felt optimistic enough to stop and have her Jaguar washed and waxed, making it glimmer in the temporarily perfect weather. Just before leaving Andre and Jing Xian, she told them she was going to the hospital to walk the halls and get a feel for the place.

Entering the hospital lobby, Stacey is trying to imagine Maji, Doshi, or the other man entering the hospital. Which way would they go? Would they stop at the front desk to find out where Andre's room is? Would they risk compromising themselves? *Disguises!* There is a possibility they might come with fake beards, dyed hair, wearing hats, hospital whites ... there are a million ways they could enter the hospital in disguise. Maybe they would use different names. They might seek help from the volunteers at the front desk. There is a chance they might come through the back doors of the hospital, though there are many video cameras located in the back of the hospital, mainly to control unauthorized equipment and supplies from going out of the hospital. They might not want to give themselves away by coming through the back unless they come late at night. The hospital doors are locked at night and can only be opened from the inside by the security guard.

Stacey is trying to imagine how Maji and his associates will be approaching Andre's room. Which way will they exit the hospital? "But that's not going to happen," she whispers to herself. They might come up or go down the stairs to the fire exit. The stairs are busy with foot traffic because workers become impatient waiting for the elevator. Other staff members want to keep themselves in good physical condition by using the stairs.

Stacey steps out of the elevator on the surgery floor. How is she going to get a room for Andre? She slowly walks down the hallway, heading in the direction of the nurses' station, when a conservatively dressed woman approaches and asks if she can help her. Stacey can tell by the woman's nametag that she works here.

"Is there a patient I can help you find?" the woman asks.

Stacey looks more closely at the women. "Have we met before?" she asks.

"I don't think so."

Stacey is still thinking about Andre and Jing Xian and how she is going to help them, but suddenly she remembers looking at some of the photos Jing Xian took on the camel ride in Morocco. He had many pictures of Marrakesh and several group pictures of the members of the tour getting ready for their ride across the Sahara. This woman looks like one of the riders in the group.

"I know this really sounds stupid," Stacey says to her, "but about a year, close to two years, ago, did you take a camel ride in Morocco?"

The woman gives Stacey an astonished look. "Yes I did," she says. "How do you know that? I know you weren't on the trip." She looks more closely at Stacey. "Are you following me?" she asks, her voice starting to rise. "What do you want?"

"Whoa." Stacey backs away. The woman's reaction has shocked her. She has to calm this woman down fast. "I was a good friend of Mr. Roberson."

The woman gives Stacey with a blank look. Then, in a quieter voice, she says, "You were a friend of Mr. Roberson."

"Yes. My name is Stacey. I was his personal secretary at world headquarters here in San Francisco."

"Poor man," the woman says. "Such a tragedy." She extends her hand to Stacey. "My name is Jodie," she says, and within a minute, she is telling Stacey what happened on the camel ride.

"Yes, I was on that ride," she says. "Everything was going great. We saw beautiful buildings, we were enjoying ourselves. We all got aboard several horse-drawn carriages at our hotel and headed for the old part of the city, you know, when the French were there in Morocco at the turn of the century, they planted a lot of palm trees, which really give a unique appearance to that section of town. We also walked through the old section of the city and saw many interesting things, like snake charmers, and we ate some wonderful meals. The next day we boarded our Land Rovers and headed out into the Sahara Desert."

"It sounds like you were having a great time in Morocco," Stacey comments.

"Yes, we were. I don't remember if it was the second or third day in the desert when the tragedy happened. The trip was cancelled after the accident. It was awful. That man, Mr. Roberson, he was your boss?"

"Yes, he was. Please go on with your story."

"Well, after I got home, I saw a story in that gossip tabloid, *The Probe*, about Mr. Roberson. It said he was one of the wealthiest businessmen in the Bay Area. I didn't know that."

Stacey has an idea. "Jodie," she begins, "are you aware that Mr. Tim Roberson was the largest financial contributor to the San Francisco General Hospital? That new wing added to the hospital a couple years ago was financed one hundred percent by him. He donated money to this institution for a long time."

"That's fantastic," Jodie says. "He was having a great time with his son and his son's friend on the safari. I guess he left business behind for a couple of weeks."

Stacey nods her head. "I pretty much do all the fundamental things at the company right now. I'm keeping things running until his son, Andre, returns."

"I remember him," says Jodie. "The boys were having a great time on the trip, too. Mr. Roberson didn't act like he was worth millions. Well, I guess some people like to flaunt it, and some people are just normal people." Jodie pauses as she looks at her beeper, then continues. "Andre was also crushed by the falling wall, you know. He was almost dead the last time I saw him, just before they took both of them to the hospital in Marrakesh. I don't know if Andre died or not. It was a real tragedy." She takes a handkerchief out of her pocket and wipes her eyes. Then she remembers something else about the camel ride.

"I need to tell you about this strange couple," she says. "They were on the camel ride, too. I heard they were from Pakistan or somewhere. They were very distant and peculiar, always together, not talking to the rest of us, maybe because their English was not too good … I don't know what their problem was. The woman got into an argument with the tour guide. His name was Ajijine. He was a very nice man, always ready to help anyone. Well, she insisted that she was not going to ride a camel, not ever. She was calling the camels the most despicable things that walk on this earth. This happened on the first day we rode the camels. Our tour guide wasn't sure what set her off, and neither was anyone else, including her husband. Why would someone pay for a camel safari and then insist on not riding? It doesn't make sense. She insisted on riding in the Land Rover.

"Then, to make this whole thing really crazy, this couple … I believe their names were Maji and Doshi … they disappeared at the exact same time Mr. Roberson got killed by the collapsing wall. This couple not only disappeared, but they had their own vehicle pick them up at the kasbah where the accident happened. Is that a coincidence? I don't think that wall collapsing was an accident. There were too many strange things happening around this couple.

"When the police arrived," Jodie continues, and Stacey is all ears, "Mr. Roberson and Andre had already been transported to the Marrakesh hospital, and half of the people on the tour had already been driven back to town. It took the police many hours to get there. I don't know why. It's a very popular place for the tourists to visit. The police didn't seem to believe anyone had made the wall collapse. They didn't ask anyone for any statements or even look closely at the footing of the wall, maybe to see if there were any digging marks, showing someone was chiseling away on the wall. The police thought Mr. Roberson was in the wrong place at the wrong time, and that's what was put on the official report.

"Our tour guide did an excellent job in helping us out. He got us rooms at the same hotel we'd stayed at when we started the trip. He told everyone that the camel safari was cancelled and our money would be refunded, except for the amount covering the first couple of days of the tour. Several people on our tour wanted to continue on the ride, but it was too traumatic for most of us. Our guide got with another camel safari and made arrangements for some of the people to hook up with them."

Jodie pauses to look at her beeper again. "I have to take care of something down at the nurses' station. Why don't you walk with me? It won't take long. I want to talk with you more about this whole thing. It's been nagging inside of me for a long time."

After Jodie finishes her business at the nurses' station, she turns back to Stacey and continues her story. "I understand that Andre was an eyewitness to his father's death. Now, I can tell you what I remember, maybe it won't be exactly what they said, it has been well over a year ago or a year and a half, but I think it'll be close. There were several other people on the ride, I think their names were Allen, and Charlie and his wife, who said they heard Andre's friend, he was the good-looking young fellow from China, I can't remember his name, it was Chinese … well, they said they heard him say he heard Andre call out to his dad, and try to pull him out of the collapsing wall. Then the Chinese fellow heard Andre say, 'What are you guys doing?' before he was crushed, too."

"Jodie," Stacey says in a smooth voice, "it sounds like you would like to see justice done for Mr. Roberson."

"You're right, I would."

"There is a plan in the beginning phase right now," Stacey says. "I can't tell you too much because I don't have enough answers right now, but just in the few minutes I've listened to you, I've begun to feel you will give me one hundred percent effort in trying to bring this mess to closure."

"That's right."

"With the information we have, our main suspects are that couple, Maji and Doshi. I believe they have a leader. Maybe an employer. It seems to me that they're not bright enough to coordinate everything that's been happening. Right now, we haven't got a clue who's giving them orders, but there's a possibility that there are one or two more conspirators in the city right now. You didn't by any chance see Maji or Doshi talk with anyone else who was not on the ride, did you?"

Jodie thinks for a minute. "No. But there was something that happened. At the time I didn't think too much about it."

"What was it?"

"The last night when we were at our hotel in Marrakesh, I couldn't sleep very well. You know, with all the excitement and sleeping in a new bed. Well, late that night or early the next morning, I heard Maji and Doshi arguing. Their room was next to mine, and they were really loud. Then I heard someone leave the room, and about forty-five minutes later, I heard someone come back into their room. The reason I knew someone had left and returned to the room is the floor was weak, I suppose, right outside their door. Every time anyone would walk on that spot, it would squeak. Very annoying. After I heard their door open and close, it was quiet until it opened and closed again, almost an hour later. Maybe one of them went outside for a smoke. But it doesn't take an hour to smoke a cigarette, or even two cigarettes. Or maybe one of them was visiting someone else inside or outside the hotel."

"That does sound a bit peculiar," Stacey says.

Jodie's pager beeps again. "Stacey, I have to go now," she says. "Here's my business card with my cell number on it. Please give me a call tonight. We can talk more about this. Don't forget."

Stacey takes the card. "Jodie, there's one more very important thing I want to pass on to you. You know Andre? Well, he is alive and in excellent health. There's nothing wrong with him."

"Thank God," Jodie responds. "I have to go now. Please call me. I'll be home all evening."

Chapter 93

At seven o'clock that evening, Jodie's telephone rings. It is Stacey, making her promised call.

"How was the rest of your day?" Stacey asks.

"To tell you the truth, it was miserable," Jodie replies. "After you left the hospital, I kept thinking about what you told me. I've been hoping you'd call. I forgot to get your phone number, and if you'd decided not to call me, it would have driven me totally insane. I'm serious."

"I'm sorry for messing up your day," Stacey says. "I needed to talk with someone at the hospital about Mr. Roberson and Andre."

"What's the problem? Oh, before you tell me the problem, I have to tell you this—it's driving me crazy. You told me Andre wasn't dead and is in fine condition. How can that be? When I saw him, he was on a stretcher being loaded into a Land Rover headed for the hospital in Marrakesh. I checked him out myself and couldn't find a pulse. He was not responsive to any stimulus. I couldn't check his pupils because there was so much dirt in his eyes and on his face. Stacey, he was in extremely critical condition. Maybe he was already dead! They had to dig him out from under heavy bricks, roofing tiles, and dirt. It was terrible. The dust was so thick I could hardly breathe. I'm positive that most of his bones were broken, and it was very obvious that his back was broken in several places."

"Jodie, you are correct. All of those things did happen to him."

Jodie's voice is now choking up. "I don't understand. You tell me all these things are true, and then you turn around and tell me he's alive and in fine condition? I'm really not sure if I should be having this conversation with you. I'm starting to think you're some kind of kook."

"Wait, wait," says Stacey. "Please let me explain. Believe me, I'm no kook. All of this is true, and I can prove it. Please give me a chance, okay?" There is no reply, and Stacey wonders if Jodie has hung up. "Hello? Jodie, are you there?"

There is a long pause, then Jodie finally speaks. "Okay," she says, "I'll give you a chance. But, believe me, the very first time I feel you're trying to pull something on me, you are gone. I will definitely report you to the police."

"That's fair," Stacey replies. Then she begins to tell Jodie about the meditation process Andre underwent at the monastery. "I'll take you to see Andre for yourself," she concludes. "Jing Xian is the Chinese man who was with Andre and his father. He made arrangements with my help to have Andre taken to the Shaolin temple in a Buddhist monastery in southern China. Andre's soul traveled in his body, and when he found a problem, like a broken bone, he repaired it as he was taught by the grand master. I hope I'm not confusing you. It's hard to describe. The process put his mind and soul into a state of enlightenment. The first time I heard of this process, it almost blew me away."

"Wow," Jodie says, "is this the truth you're telling me?"

"You better believe it, girl. It's a lengthy, complicated, gruesome process. Month after month, the monks patiently worked with Andre. There were times there seemed to be no progress at all, but perseverance paid off. No one gave up.

"We didn't notify anyone of Andre's whereabouts or his condition for fear that someone might want to make sure he becomes permanently dead. At the time of the 'accident,' we were sort of thinking he was in the wrong place at the wrong time. But after putting things together, we decided that Mr. Roberson's death was not an accident. The possibility that Andre was an eyewitness made us keep his location a secret.

"What helped Andre recover quicker is his experience with meditation and his understanding of his zen. He lived in the monastery for about a year prior to the tragedy and studied under the guidance of the temple's grand master and other highly advanced teachers. When his father suffered a mild stroke, he and his best friend, Jing Xian, took a leave of absence from the monastery and came to San Francisco. They didn't know he had planned a camel ride across the Sahara. They were having a great time together before the mishap. Whoever is responsible for the death of Mr. Roberson and almost killing Andre, he knew about the camel ride and where they were going. Mr. Roberson always made his travel arrangements through the travel section of the company, whether he was traveling on business or for pleasure."

"Maybe the travel agent is in on it?" Jodie asks. "I have to see Andre. I just have to. I can't believe all this has really happened."

"Jodie, I'll call Andre and have him give you a call. You can ask him any question you want to. You can ask him what hotel you guys stayed at in Marrakesh. Name the people in your group. What did you guys have to eat for breakfast? You know, anything to prove he really is Andre. We're going to have another planning meeting, and I'm inviting you to it. Most likely, it'll be in the next day or two."

"That would be fine," Jodie responds. "I have nothing planned for this weekend."

An hour later, Jodie's telephone rings. "Jodie, this is Andre Roberson. Stacey just called me and wants me to talk with you about the tragedy on the camel ride."

"How are you, Andre? Oh, my God, you're alive!"

They talk for two hours.

Chapter 94

After her long talk with Jodie, Stacey starts filling her tub so she can soak in hot water highlighted with a splash of Eaglewood Body Oil, the most stunning and expensive aroma of the orient. It's one of those little extras she picked up in Shanghai on one of her business trips with the company. "Ahhh, this is perfect," she purrs, swirling her hand through the hot water. The tub almost full when the phone rings.

"Who can that be?" she says aloud. "It better be important. I've already gotten the boys taken care of. Already talked with Jodie." She answers the phone.

"Hello Stacey," a voice says.

It takes her a few seconds to recognize the voice. "Oh, hi, Bob," she says. "Hold on for a second." She goes back into the bathroom and turns off the water. Then she puts a small pan of water on the stove to heat up a cup of chamomile tea, which is good for getting a good night's sleep.

"Hi, again," she says when she returns to the phone. "Sorry about that. I'm getting everything ready for a nice soak in the tub."

"Sounds great," he says. "I should try that myself. Say, you don't need your back scrubbed, do you?" he asks with a sly laugh. When Stacey does not respond, he adds, "Sorry. I just had to say that." Then he speaks more formally. "I called earlier and left a message on your cell."

"I'm sorry," she replies. "I was tied up all afternoon and just got off the phone, not more then ten minutes ago. I haven't checked my messages."

"Well," Bob Bertolino says, "we had a visit from the infamous Maji this afternoon. I had my photographer take a picture of him. Of course he never knew we took it. He didn't quite look like the person Andre described to Kathy, but when you're on a camel ride in the Sahara, things are different. I suppose your appearance changes drastically when you're strolling around in a cosmopolitan city like San Francisco. We're going to have it developed ASAP and have it sent to you the first thing tomorrow morning."

"That's fantastic!" Stacey exclaims. "How is Kathy holding up?"

"She's doing fine," Bertolino replies. "It was sort of a fluke, what happened when he came into the office. It was almost time to close. She was taking something down the hall to the storage room, and I was up at the front desk doing something, I don't remember what, but we'd already turned off the buzzer at the front door. Anyway, this handsomely dressed Middle Eastern man comes in. I'll tell you, this guy looked like he was loaded, and I mean with money. Several expensive looking rings, a real nice silk suit, nicely coordinated tie, fancy cuff links. To top it off, he was wearing a fedora." Bob laughs. "Who wears a fedora nowadays?"

"Now, Bob, he might have been going to an opera."

"Yeah. In the middle of the afternoon." They both laugh.

Bertolino continues. "There was a woman with him who also looked Middle Eastern. The first thing that caught my eyes about her was her extremely long, decorated fingernails. I think maybe they were fake. I don't see how a woman would want such long nails. Hell, you can't do anything with those things on your fingers."

"Now, now, Bob," Stacey says. "Be nice."

"Well, that's my opinion," he replies. "And she had her hair all fixed up, with brown and gold highlights, sort of the way you would braid a rope. And a lot of jewelry. And a full-length fur coat. I don't know who did her makeup. Maybe she did it herself. But whoever did should be run out of town. It was horrible."

"Maybe she's a very ugly women and that was the best they could do for her."

"Stacey, what kind of business are these people in?"

"I haven't told you yet, but I will later."

"Is it legal?"

"I will tell you later."

He continues. "Well, I told Maji just what you had told me to say, that I had gotten the information for the column from a telegram from a man who called himself Shibo from the city of Guilin in southern China. I told him the telegram was sent to me personally, so it was meant for me. I had never heard of this man, Shibo, before, and I don't have any associates in China. There was no return address or phone number to reach him. I think Maji bought it. I also told him I sent a telegram back to Shibo, notifying him I had received his message. I asked him, Shibo, when Andre is scheduled to return to the States. I told Maji that I also requested a reply no later than Monday."

"That's good."

"While I'm talking with this guy and his wife," Bertolino continues, "Kathy comes walking into the office. She turns right around and walks back out of the office. I don't blame her. I had it all under control, and it was almost quitting time. He didn't seem to notice her. He was to busy stressing a point about his busy schedule, and the woman with him was becoming irritated. She kept asking him questions in what sounded like Arabic or Urdu or something while I was trying to talk with him.

"Maji told me he was a very busy man, traveling all around the world, and he would appreciate it if I would have the information ready for him exactly at one o'clock on Monday. He also told me he has some scheduled surgeries for, I think he said, intra-cranial atherosclerotic disease. He was having problems pronouncing the words, so either medical terms are new to him or his patient had better watch out."

When Stacey laughs, he says, "I'm trying to make a point. This guy, well ... he seemed confused about the telegram I showed him, I don't think he knows much about telegrams. It was obvious he had never seen one before. And that's weird. Nothing about this guy seems right. Whatever you're putting together, you need to have an answer for him before he comes back on Monday. He may start suspecting something if I don't have an answer."

"Okay, Bob. Did I get your home number when I was in your office last time?"

"Yes, you did."

"I was just checking to make sure. Yeah, here it is on my Blackberry. I'll get back with you before Monday, and that's a promise. I have to go now. I don't want my bath water to get cold."

Chapter 95

It is early Sunday morning when Stacey calls Andre and Jing Xian at their hotel. Jing Xian answers the phone, and when she asks how he and Andre are doing, he tells her they are getting bored.

"We just got back from the hotel exercise room," he says. "Working up some sweat. They have some real nice equipment here, and there's a nice buffet breakfast in the hotel dinning room, but this daily routine is starting to get boring. Tomorrow we're going to try the steam room. I'm not too fond of steam rooms, but Andre likes them."

"Well, I have some good news for you guys," Stacey says.

"I sure hope it's good."

"You and Andre are flying to Honolulu tomorrow afternoon."

"Hey, that's great!"

"We're not going to our regular place in North Beach tonight," she says next. "It's such a popular place. We want to keep a low profile until all of this is over, so I found a small, cozy place in the East Bay, a small café on Washington Street called O B's. It's in downtown Oakland, across the street from the Oakland Police Department."

Jing Xian laughs. "Yeah. Across the street from the police station. That sounds like a real safe place."

Stacey laughs. "I hadn't seen the owner of this place for a while, but a couple weeks ago, she stopped in at our office. She had received something, I think it was furniture, from China, and needed a copy of her bill of lading, or something like that. She gave me an invite, so I called her yesterday and made reservations for us."

"So you think that would be a good place to have our meeting?" he asks.

"Yes. We know Maji and Doshi are out there somewhere in San Francisco, so I think Oakland might be a better place to have a meeting. Did I tell you the owner's name?"

"No, you didn't."

"I'm sorry. Her name is Barbra. She and her husband own the place. I can't remember his name, it's sort of a hard name to remember. You know, Jing Xian, I think I'm starting to lose my mind these last couple of weeks. I'm forgetting things." She pauses to remember why she called, then continues. "Anyway, I've talked with Mr. Bertolino's secretary, Kathy. You and Andre haven't met her yet. Andre talked with her on the phone a couple days ago and gave her the descriptions of Maji and Doshi. She will be driving over the Bay Bridge from work. And Jodie, you remember her, the cute lady from the camel ride? She'll also be coming from San Francisco General. I'm just a little concerned for both of them. We won't have a long meeting tonight because Kathy has a long drive home up to Mill Valley, and Jodie has to drive way out to Napa.

"Getting back to when I'll pick you guys up, make sure you're both ready and waiting in the lobby. If you get down to the lobby early, don't make yourself conspicuous. People are checking in and going through the lobby at that time of the day, and, please, don't be waiting in the picture window."

"Okay, Stacey, we'll be careful."

That evening, Stacey pulls up in front of the Majestic Dragon Hotel in her Jaguar XJR. A couple of well-dressed businessmen standing at the curb give her car a looking over and flash their best smiles at her. Ignoring them, she waits for the boys to come out of the hotel.

When they reach Oakland, Stacey motors down the street. Andre is sitting in the passenger seat and feeling proud to be riding in such an elegant car. He's holding the driving directions. "We're in the correct hundreds block," he says, looking up from the paper.

"Where are the numbers on these buildings?" Jing Xian asks from the back seat, studying the buildings as they pass them.

"Here we are, guys," Stacey says. "Washington Street. I guess we go left, and there's the place."

"There it is." Andre points at the café, "Hey, we're lucky this evening. An open parking spot right in front."

"Well, look at that," Stacey remarks. "Jodie and Kathy are pulling in behind each other across the street. I like it when everyone arrives at the same time. It's a good omen."

Chapter 96

"Stacey, good evening," Barbra says as they enter the café. "How are you? I see you brought some friends with you. That's great. Let me get you something to drink, and I'll have my husband put two tables together for you. Here's the list of drinks. I'll get you some water, too."

Stacey makes the introductions while Barbra serves them, and after everyone is seated and has ordered their food and received their drinks, they begin to relax.

"What a nice place you have," Stacey says to Barbra and her husband.

"Thank you," Barbra replies. "It really keeps us busy at times, but it's worth it. It's very nice of you to have dinner here tonight. We hope you'll come back."

"Well," Stacey says, "it was quite a distance out of our way to get here tonight, but we had to get out of San Francisco for business reason, and your place suits us perfectly." After the owners walk away and they have eaten for awhile, Stacey calls the meeting to order.

"Okay," she says, "everyone knows what we're planning to do this evening. Right?"

"No, I don't know." Kathy raises her hand, then lowers it again. "I feel like I'm still in school, raising my hand." She chuckles. "I'm still in the dark about what you're planning. All I know is what's happening with this strange guy, Maji. And his wife, Doshi."

"This is what we're going to do in the next couple of days," Stacey says. "If everything goes as planned. Last week, after Jing Xian and Andre saw them on the BART, we made plans to try to bring them out of the woodwork. Kathy, I got with your boss, and he ran a column about a so-called doctor who claims he can perform a new type of surgery that can correct all of Andre's spinal problems, which have him paralyzed. Pretty soon, this Maji fellow and Doshi appear. Why wouldn't their employer use someone else? They'd already exposed themselves in the desert." She gives a shrug and looks around the table. "Maybe they think because it happened almost two years ago no one will remember them. Or maybe these two are the ones who killed Mr. Roberson and are planning to kill Andre. It may be just a matter of time. Once they know where Andre and Jing Xian are staying, maybe they're going to murder them to keep them quiet.

"What they don't know is that Andre has recovered. They think he's still in a comatose condition. I'm sure there's someone else involved in this plot. I have my own suspicions, which I won't share right now. I hope I'm wrong.

"I might add that Jing Xian has been with Andre the whole time, assisting him every minute. In fact Jing Xian was one of the Shaolin monks who assisted in Andre's recovery."

Everyone around the table looks at Jing Xian, giving him thanks for what he has done for Andre. Jing Xian looks embarrassed.

"Now everything is starting to fall into place," Kathy says, and Jodie is also nodding her head.

Ten minutes later, after Stacey has drunk her wine and eaten more of her shrimp salad, she is ready to continue. "Kathy," she says, "we need to generate a false telegram for Maji. When he comes into your office on Monday, this telegram has to convince him and his friend that Andre will be coming in on our corporate jet late Wednesday evening. He will be loaded into an ambulance outside our terminal, then transported to San Francisco General Hospital.

Stacey turns to Jodie. "And I have to get with you about tonight about getting Andre a room in the hospital."

Jodie makes a slight frown. "But I'm not sure I will be able to get you a room for something like this."

"I realize that." Stacey pauses to think. "I wish we had talked more before this meeting. I was thinking … if you analyze what Mr. Roberson has done for the hospital these last ten years, I'm sure it should have some weight on the right person's decision." She pauses again. "One more thing. Andre Roberson, who is sitting right here in front of you, is going to be the new owner of the company. At the present time, there's a lot of wrangling going on among the company's major players, but eventually it will be ironed out. I will almost guarantee that your hospital will receive even more money next year from our company.

I'm the president's personal secretary. Monday morning, I'll have a commitment drawn up to prove our sincerity."

She looks at Andre, who gives her a nod of approval.

Jodie nods, too. "Okay, I'll talk with the right person Monday morning. I'll give them your phone number so they'll be able to verify our meeting."

"This is the way I have put this plan together," Stacey says. "If anyone has a comment or a different idea, please bring it up, even if it sounds corny. Okay?"

Chapter 97

Stacey begins. "First of all, before we go any further, I want to know for sure if everyone is comfortable with what we're planning to do. This is the time to speak up. There won't be any reprisals or bad feelings if you don't like the idea. Maybe a few people will be disappointed, but don't let that change your mind. Okay? There's a possibility it may not work and all this planning will be in vain. There's also a slim possibility something may go wrong or someone might get threatened or beaten up. Or even killed, God forbid." Stacey is feeling good now. "Looking at everyone, it seems that we have a way to go. I don't hear any objections. Yes, Kathy. I can see some nervousness. Are you sure you're okay with this?"

"Yes," Kathy says. "I'm okay. It's just that I never thought in my wildest dream that I would ever be sitting in some off-beat place with four other people, plotting something that could get someone killed. I feel like I'm in some mystery movie." She looks around the table. "I'm in one hundred percent."

Stacey looks at her notes. "First thing Monday morning, I'll be calling Luis at my travel agency, TTT. I use this company for my personal travels. I don't want to have any conflict of interest. I'm also concerned about security with the company. I'll get the tickets for Andre and Jing Xian to fly to Hawaii on Monday afternoon. I've already made reservations for them to make sure we could get them there on time. I don't want anyone to think I'm doing anything without everyone's permission. I just had a premonition that everyone would like the idea and go along with it."

When the others nod, she goes on. "They'll be returning on our company plane, arriving at San Francisco International late Wednesday night. Andre will be in the life-support bed with an IV in his arm." She looks at Andre, who nods his head. "You remember, we talked about this?"

"The IV will be in my arm for real," Andre says. "It'll keep me from getting dehydrated. Jing Xian will put it into my arm once we're airborne out of Hawaii. He learned the procedure while he was studying in the monastery."

Jodie gets Stacey's attention. "I know two people who can help drive the ambulance from the airport to the hospital. Their names are Claudia and Jeremy. Jeremy is an ophthalmologist who's been with the hospital for many years. He's a hard worker who's always ready to do something exciting. Claudia is an extremely reliable nurse. She's been with the hospital over thirty years and is an excellent driver. Believe it or not, she has a hobby of stock car racing on weekends and has the respect from the male racers when she races. They're two very trustworthy people who have done many favors for me."

"Good. Get with the two drivers," Stacey tells Jodie, "and make sure they're available late Wednesday night. And please make sure there's an extra ambulance available at the hospital just in case an emergency comes up. We don't want to get stuck without one."

"Consider it done."

"I'll give you a call sometime tomorrow and let you know for sure what time the plane will land. We need to have Claudia and Jeremy at the airport at least one hour before the plane arrives. There's no telling what could happen, with traffic and everything."

Stacey takes another sip of her wine and turns the page in her notebook. "Kathy, could you get with your boss tomorrow morning and see what you can find in your video and audio department? I'm thinking we'll want to be able to video in a room that could be almost pitch dark. If it's possible, we'd like to get two systems. Tell Bertolino to put it on my company charge account. First, have him give me a call on my cell and I'll explain. Then see if you can find a camera with infrared capabilities. While you're talking with these camera experts see if you can locate—I'm not sure what you would call it—what I'm looking for is one of those machines that's in a hospital room, showing the line of your heartbeat on the screen. If you can find one, we need to have an expert hook a hand device on a ten-foot cord that can change the heartbeat line to a flat line, as if the person died. When they put the switch on the cord, make sure it's a silent switch. We don't want the switch to make any noise when it's flipped. We'll be using this machine in Andre's room, simulating his heart rhythm."

"I'll work on it," Kathy says.

Chapter 98

Sitting in his chair and getting sleepy listening to the women making their plans, Andre is surprised when his cell phone rings. "Hello?"

"Good evening, you handsome, good looking stud," a sultry voice says.

With a sudden jerk, he is wide awake and sitting straight up in his chair. His face has no expression as he is waiting for the next words from this mysterious caller.

Stacey notices. "Who is that?" she asks. But when she asks if they would call him back, or he can return their call, he says nothing.

"What are you doing?" the sexy voice on the phone asks.

He clears his throat. "Hello? Who is this?"

"Oh, this is your favorite dream, the one you get every once a while at night. Don't you remember me?"

"Uhhhh, I don't think I know you." He is trying frantically to place the voice.

"Well in that case, I must have the wrong number."

"No! Don't hang up!" Everyone in the café hears him.

Kathy nudges him in the ribs. "Who is it?"

By this time he is blushing.

Kathy looks at Stacey. "I think it's a girl."

Jing Xian, also half asleep, hears the word "girl" and perks up. Getting up from his chair, he walks over to Andre and tries to listen in on the call. Andre smiles and tries to push him away, but by this time, he is feeling embarrassed that he still does not know who is on the phone. He decides he has to say something.

"Hey, sweetie," he finally says, knowing that everyone in the café is listening. "I'm in an extremely important meeting right now. Can I have your phone number so I can call you back? That's a promise."

"Well," the voice says, "I'm not sure if I will be available. There is so much going on here."

"Please." He is begging now, and starting to feel pretty stupid.

"Okay," she says, "if your meeting is that important, here's the number." He writes it down, thinking, *I've seen this number before.* "Have I seen this number before?" he asks aloud.

"Yes, dummy. This is the girls in Hawaii. Have you forgotten us already?"

"Oh! The girls from the river cruise in China." He is starting to get excited, and Jing Xian is still hanging on his arm and trying to listen in on the phone. Suddenly he again realizes that everyone can hear him. "It is so exciting to hear from you guys again," he says. By now, Jing Xian is almost standing on top of him, practically tearing his arm off to get to the phone. "We really need to go now," Andre says. "Everyone sends their wishes. I'll call you back, say, in about two hours. Bye-bye."

He has to explain this to his friends at the table. "That was the girls Jing Xian and I met when we were living at the monastery in China," he says. "They're in Hawaii."

"I gathered that," Stacey says, and she gives the boys a big smile. "We need to finish this meeting. Hey, you two, why don't you split up for a while, at least until the meeting is over? Sitting on top of each other right now is not a good idea."

Jing Xian goes back to his chair, laughing to himself.

Chapter 99

Trying to get the meeting back on track, Stacey looks at Kathy. "Please keep me informed of your results," she says. "I realize we don't have much time, but the video and audio equipment are a must." Then she turns to Jodie and asks, "Do you have a repair facility in the hospital?"

When Jodie nods, Stacey says, "Get with your contract maintenance team and see if they have a cardiac monitor." I just remembered the name of it. I had it written down in my notes.

"Yes, I believe we have one in the repair shop."

"We want a machine next to Andre's bed showing his heart rate. Make sure the technician can install a ten-foot cord with an on-off switch, and make sure it is a quiet switch. If it becomes a problem, let me know. Remember, if there's a problem with money, please charge it to my company. That is, Andre's company."

"Kathy," Andre says, "don't try to find one of those heart rate machines, I mean a cardiac monitor. It may take too long. If anyone can find one, I'm sure Jodie will, since she works right there with them. Sorry. They repair them at the hospital."

After a while, Barbra comes by the table and asks if anyone needs to freshen up their drinks or wants more finger food.

"I'm going to stick with what I'm drinking," Kathy says. "I have a long way to drive home tonight."

Jodie agrees with Kathy. "This is all I'll have tonight."

But Andre orders another Napa Valley Merlot. "I'm riding tonight," he says.

"Bring one for me, too," Jing Xian says.

Stacey adds, "Maybe we can have another order of those grilled shrimp and some more chips and dip." As Barbra walks away, Stacey looks around the table. "Does anyone have any questions so far? Is anyone confused? I hope not." When everyone tells her they're with the program, she continues.

"Okay," she says, "let's all trade cell numbers, just in case we have to contact someone for information or whatever. If you have to contact me, for heaven's sake, do not call me on my office phone. There's no telling who might overhear the conversation. Always call me on my cell."

When everyone nods again, Stacey continues. "I thought I would give you guys some up-to-date information. Yesterday, I received a message from Mr. Craiger. He left a message on my home phone, which is a bit overdoing it, especially on a weekend. I have a work phone, after all, or he could have left a message with the operator. He wants to have a meeting with me on Monday to talk about how the change of ownership is coming along. Mr. Craiger is not a nice man." She smiles. "You might say a good way to describe him is that he's a pompous ass, and that's being nice." Everyone laughs. "Mr. Roberson and he used to have a lot of verbal confrontations about how to organize the inspections of the container vans. Their meetings always ended with Mr. Craiger storming out of the office and slamming the door. Once I saw Mr. Roberson almost take a swing at him." She pauses. "Just thinking about it, I'm sure Mr. Roberson could have taken him down with a few swings. Mr. Roberson always kept himself in good shape, especially for his age. But getting back to Mr. Craiger ... this man is despicable. He must weigh almost three hundred pounds and almost always stinks. Body odor, or something. Who knows? Maybe he never changes his underwear."

She gets serious again. "There's a strong possibility, I think, being that he's one of the major stock holders in the company, that he's in some way connected with the death of Mr. Roberson. Shortly before his supposed stroke, Mr. Roberson had several meetings with Mr. Craiger. There was a lot of yelling and doors slamming. I remember these two really ugly guys came in with Mr. Craiger one day. It was a very strange meeting. There was no yelling, but after the meeting Mr. Roberson left early. He didn't talk with me about anything. That was about a week before Andre and Jing Xian arrived."

As Andre and Jing Xian look at each other, Stacey continues. "I remember these two guys from a previous meeting. They insisted on having a meeting with Mr. Roberson without an appointment. Mr. Roberson was busy at the time, but he went ahead and had a meeting with them after I told him their names."

Chapter 100

Next, Stacey begins to explain in detail about the problem the company is having with x-raying shipping containers. "Somehow," she says, "this whole thing revolves around the way the sea-land containers are inspected. The TSA is trying to have more shipping containers coming into the United States x-rayed. I feel there's something wrong with the system. Why is the TSA not looking at the containers leaving the United States just as carefully as when they are coming into this country? There's too much corruption in the United States, and they're shipping things out of the States that should be monitored and inspected. Mr. Roberson wanted to x-ray every fifth container but not list containers by their shipping numbers. Each container would be inspected according to the time it arrived at the port and loaded onto the ship. The next day, the inspection would be conducted on every fourth container, and then the next day it would go back to every fifth container. Some days, the inspection would be every third container, depending if they were ahead or behind loading the containers.

"But Mr. Craiger wanted a list of which containers would be x-rayed or inspected by their shipping number several days in advance. He claimed it would be easier to monitor and identify if a problem arose. But consider this—if the shipper of the container knew his container would *not* be inspected, then he could ship all types of illegal things and not get caught. If the list Mr. Craiger wants got into the wrong hands, it would be worth a lot of money to the right people. So the TSA is trying to sort out who is going to be responsible for the inspectors. Will it be the loading company under the rules of TSA? Or will they bring in their own people?"

Andre interrupts her. "Stacey, you know so much about the company."

"I should," she replies. "I've been with the company for quite a few years. And working with the company president as his secretary, I know

260

what's happening. Andre, let me finish about the ship's departure. I think it's really important. I'll be finished soon."

He nods and she continues.

"If a container is noted in the inspection to have a possible violation, it must be pulled aside and a more thorough inspection conducted. If the violation is bad, the lock and seal are cut and the entire container can be unloaded and inspected, which can take many hours. This inspection process slows the operation a great deal.

"Now, if a container held living beings, such as people or maybe exotic animals, this would call for immigration officers, customs, the TSA, and the police. It will most likely close down one of our loading sites for hours, maybe all day.

"So until we get the ownership of the company taken care of and review these procedures, I think there are illegal things going on and someone is profiting big time."

Chapter 101

"Well," Stacey concludes, "I hope I haven't bored you with my suspicions. I just had to get it off my shoulders, and telling everyone at the same time was the best way to do it."

Andre speaks up. "I had no idea all this was happening at the company. If I'd known, I would have come back long time ago. I feel bad that I didn't do something."

"Don't blame yourself," Stacey says. "You wouldn't have been able to help. Your dad was happy doing what he liked and what he thought was best. He wanted you to enjoy life and see the world, just like he did when your mother was alive."

Andre can't help but tear up a bit. "Thanks for the kind words," he says.

"How do you propose to prove all this?" Jodie asks.

"I don't know for sure," Stacey says. "If the plan works, and someone comes to Andre's hospital room to kill him, we definitely have to be ready for whatever could happen. We need to get them confess to killing Mr. Roberson!"

"Stacey," Jing Xian asks, "what will they confess to?"

"Corruption. Murder." Stacey pauses to get control of herself, then continues. "The problems with the x-raying thing and the death of Mr. Roberson," she says. "Let me think about that for a few minutes."

Like everyone around the table, Jing Xian notices that Stacey looks exhausted and overstressed. "Let's just pretend this is a hypothetical situation," he says. "Okay? Let's say, oh, that Andre is in the hospital bed with the IV in his arm and a fake heart rate machine showing his heartbeat." They all nod. "Maji and Doshi show up. Somehow they have portrayed themselves as friends of Andre from the camel ride. They say they saw something in Bertolino's column and they're paying their respects and they hope for a successful recovery. There's no one else in the room except them and Andre. How slick could that be? One of them could have a gun with a silencer. He could shoot Andre and be gone in a matter of minutes."

"In my opinion," Stacey says, "there are several things wrong with that scenario. First, guns with silencers do make a noise, and if hospital staff is walking by, they would hear the noise and come in to see what was happening.

"Second, when a gun fires, there's a lot of smoke. The smell of black powder will fill the entire room. When the shooter leaves the room, the smell of the black powder will flow into the hallway and follow them down the hallway. That toxic smell definitely is something you don't want to smell in a hospital. They would never make it out without being detected."

Jodie has an idea. "Here's another way they might kill him. They might insert something into his IV tube that will kill him. That way, the hospital won't know he was killed until they perform an autopsy, and the killers would be long gone. There's one other little, tricky thing we need to do when Andre is moved into the hospital room. The IV needle has to be removed from his arm. Andre's arm needs to be taped so it *looks like* there's a needle in his arm. But there's a small downside to this idea," she admits. "If the IV isn't being used, it won't show the drip in the tube. But someone with nursing knowledge, like myself, will notice that. It doesn't sound like this woman, Doshi, has any nursing skills. That's another reason the room should be kept as dark as possible. If they put some kind of solution into the IV tube, we'll have evidence, and Andre won't be killed."

"Great thought," Stacey replies. Taking a sip from her freshly opened bottle of club soda, she continues. "I have just one more idea. It's a possibility, but I don't think it will happen. They—I'm using 'they' because I don't think just one person will come in—they will probably have a lookout or someone to assist them. They know Andre is still alive and could be a possible witness to his father's death. This has alarmed them, and they don't want to miss this opportunity. They could use a pillow and suffocate him. But there are problems there, too. If someone tries to suffocate a person, it can backfire for the killer. When a person is in bed, they may be dying, sick, healthy, or whatever, but when their air is turned off, they thrash around and try to get air. People somehow get super-strength, maybe an adrenaline rush. It's sort of a mystery how people become so strong in life-threatening situations. So if someone tries to suffocate Andre, the IV tube may get ripped out of his arm, the life support system might get broken … there are so many things could happen. Killers are not smart."

Jodie interjects a thought. "Why can't we put a camera in a very obvious spot so Andre can be monitored at all times? The killers will focus on the camera and forget about if there are other monitoring devices. We can figure out a way to immobilize them so they can't kill him."

"You know," Kathy says, "I feel uncomfortable talking about the possibility of Andre getting killed. It just runs shivers up my spine."

"I know," Stacey says. "But we'll all get through this together."

Chapter 102

Jing Xian laughs. "Kathy, how do you know so much about killing? Has your boss been a bad guy lately?"

"Believe it or not," she replies, "when you work at a place like where I work, you get to know about all types of people. I've talked with some of the reporters investigating murders, and they get so detailed about a crime scene and the bodies lying everywhere, it really gets freaky sometimes. Every once in a while, a reporter will be in the office talking with Bertolino and he'll have a couple dozen pictures of a crime scene. It's so horrific. I just can't stand to be in the same room when they talk about crime scenes." She takes a large sip from her drink and continues. "Stacey has a good idea about using a thermal imaging infrared camera and an audio system to record everything that takes place in the room. These two systems must be set up where they cannot be detected. They'll be recording evidence we may need for the police." She looks at Stacey. "Isn't that right?"

"You betcha, girl." Stacey points at Kathy with the shrimp in her hand. "You'll be working on trying to rent this equipment from someone in your building?

"I'll be on it."

Stacey explains. "I'm not sure if you guys know how an infrared camera works. It doesn't show the image of a person like a movie camera. It shows the heat, the thermal image, of a person. We'll be able to see their whereabouts in the dark room. Andre will be the only person who will be able to see in the dark, using his exceptional bat senses. If we used a normal camera, it wouldn't photograph in the dark room."

Stacey points to something on Jodie's list. "Jodie, the room we need must have a connecting door to an adjoining room where Jing Xian and I will be monitoring the camera."

"That's good," Kathy says. "I was hoping you wouldn't ask me to be in the room with you. I'm not a physical person, and I wouldn't be much good if anything got physical. I could wait in the ambulance with Jeremy and Claudia downstairs and let you know if we see any suspicious people coming into the hospital. We can stay in contact by cell phone."

"Great idea, Kathy. You three can take turns staying awake," Stacey replies. "We are not sure if, or when, they'll pay Andre a visit, so it may take a long time. Remember, they may send in someone that none of us have seen before, so we want to make sure Andre is monitored all the time. And maybe a medical person might come into the room to check on something, so we don't want to jump to conclusions just because no one knows him or her."

"I will check with the nurses on those days," Jodie says, "and make sure they don't come into those two rooms."

"What we need is to run another item in your boss's column about Andre's surgery," Stacey suggests to Kathy. "Make it as low-key as possible, not a lot of attention, just enough to arouse their curiosity."

"The blurb in the column needs to make these guys act within the two days between Wednesday night and Friday afternoon," Jodie says. "That will make my job a lot easier, convincing the hospital to give us a room for two and half days."

"You want to make it *two* rooms connected for two days," Stacey corrects her. "If they won't give you two rooms, remained them what Mr. Roberson has done for the hospital in the past years. If they won't cooperate, we will pay for the two rooms at the going rate, but they shouldn't look for any donations in the years to come. There are other hospitals in the area who would love to get our money."

"That sounds like blackmail," Jodie says.

"Well, yes, it is, but we don't have much of a choice right now. All we need is cooperation, and in a few days this whole thing will be over."

"Consider it done."

Chapter 103

When the table falls silent for several minutes, Andre looks around at his friends. Finally Stacey breaks the silence. "We're forgetting Andre," she says. "You know he has the ability to travel through the darkness unscathed."

"So what will that do for us?" Kathy asks.

"Let's think about it," says Stacey. "Even if the room is completely dark, with blackout covers on the windows and no nightlight, Andre will be able to see what Maji, Doshi, or whoever is doing when they enter the room." She turns to Andre. "You know you can't move at all when they enter your room, not even a twitch of your body."

"Yes, I know," he says, "but if a confrontation builds, I'll be able to defend myself quite easily in a dark room."

"Good. Well, then, does everyone agree with that idea?"

Everyone slowly nods their heads. But some of them wonder how Andre can really see in the dark.

"Let's continue with this scenario," Stacey says. "Let's say that if they put something into Andre's IV tube to kill him, it's most likely they'll be using a syringe."

"Hey, wait a sec," says Kathy. "If the room is totally dark, how are they going to put something in the IV? Won't they need a light or something?"

"That's a good point."

Jodie speaks up. "I've done thousands of injections and worked a lot of night shifts where you don't want to wake the patient, and sometimes you are basically working in the dark. When you come into a dark room from the lighted hall, you have to slow down until your eyes become adjusted to the darkness. This could take several minutes. A lot of times, the nurses have small pen lights to see by. To make sure they're in the right room and have the right patient."

"So if they're prepared," Kathy says, "maybe they have a flashlight?"

"Yes."

Stacey speaks again. "Hopefully, by that time we'll have already detected them and be ready. Andre will have to wait for about a minute for the solution to feed back down through the tube and into his arm. But it won't work." She smiles. "After a minute, Andre will push the switch we hid under his blanket that controls the monitor. The switch will change the heart rate on the screen to a flat line and a buzzer will start buzzing. At that time, presumably if it's Maji or Doshi, they'll assume he's dead and their job is finished. They'll leave the room." Thinking about what she has just said, she adds, "They may want to pull the plug to disconnect the buzzer. They certainly don't want anyone coming in and attempting to revive Andre. We need to make sure the monitor is plugged into a socket in a location where it's easy for them to pull it before they leave the room. If this happens, there's no way we're going to get a confession for the murder of Mr. Roberson. Only the attempted murder of Andre. We won't be any closer to Mr. Craiger, and in a couple years on good behavior they all will be out of prison." She sighs. "My brain is getting tired."

Chapter 104

Andre has been sitting quietly. Now he speaks up. "As most of you know, I received special training in martial arts from Grand Master Da Ming, a Shaolin monk, while I was living at the monastery in China. This grand master is an expert in the field of inflicting deadly pain. I know this sounds morbid, but it's an ancient combat technique written in certain war books from the early dynasties when China was in great turmoil. I was chosen by Grand Master Shibo to learn this technique. Most martial arts teachers know nothing of it. When the technique is administered to an unfortunate person, the pain is so excruciating that the person is unable to sustain his sanity. Master Da Ming demonstrated it on me, and I can't even describe the severity of that pain. In the past, when the technique was used to extract information, most individuals would beg to be killed. The procedure is something like acupuncture without needles. It uses different pressure points located on the body. I only use my hands and nothing more in the traditional style by pushing and twisting my fingers in the right spots." He pauses and smiles. "It really works. Does anyone want me to show them?"

No one says a word.

Andre continues. "If things start to go wrong, and Maji and Doshi start to leave the room, I think it'll be best if I confront Maji and administer the pain technique. I'm sure he'll confess and tell us everything we want to know. At the same time I'm taking care of Maji, you two," he looks at Stacey and Jing Xian, "come in and take care of Doshi. We don't want her to get away. Or even get out of the room."

"Andre," Jodie says, "that technique sounds sick. Does it really work?"

"Yes, it does." He stands up and takes a step toward her. "Here. Let me show you."

"No, no! You stay over there."

"I'm just kidding, Jodie. I wouldn't hurt you." He sits down again. Then he looks around the table. "All kidding aside," his voice is serious now, "I can get information out of this guy. I'll be watching both of them very carefully. So don't come into the room until you see me start to move out of the bed."

Stacey summarizes their plan of action. "Once they put something into the IV, Andre waits for about a minute. He then punches the switch and his heart rate flattens. They presume he's dead and drop their guard. They might leave the room, but we don't want that to happen."

"Hey, Jodie," Kathy asks, "could we use one or two of your security guards at the hospital to make an arrest or just detain them until we can call the police?"

"I don't think so," Jodie replies. "The security guards are not used for making arrests. They don't carry guns. The hospital hires a private security company with rules written in their contract, and we can't change anything unless the contract is rewritten. They're only used to watch and report any problems they see in the hospital or on the grounds."

Chapter 105

"Okay, okay," says Stacey. "I have a couple friends that are deputy sheriffs. I've worked with them many times in the past. They are fine specimens. Tall, physically fit, and handsome. That seems to cover their requirements," she says with a smile.

"Okay, can we get back to work?" Kathy suggests.

Still smiling, Stacey continues. "The deputies love their work. They're always volunteering to help me out. I'm sure they'll be able to juggle their days off if we need to make an arrest or whatever. But for legal reasons, we can't have the deputies in the room while Andre is coercing a confession out of Maji, although I'm sure he is the guy who killed Mr. Roberson. If they have to give a statement in a court of law, they have to be honest and truthful about what they saw and heard. Andre's way of getting the truth might not be a legal way of getting information."

"He may need several minutes to extract the information from an unwilling person," Kathy agrees.

"So if the deputies wait in the car downstairs until we call them," Stacey says, "Andre will have enough time. They can wait in an unmarked car with Kathy and Jerome."

"That sounds perfect," Kathy says.

Stacey laughs. "Oh, behave yourself. I found them first. We won't be able to have both deputies here at the same time. They'll probably alternate shifts."

"You know," Kathy says, "I was just thinking. Way back in my younger days, my boy friend (can't remember which one) and I would park at lovers' point over looking the ocean. What a great time that was. Now, a few years later, I'm going to be sitting with a handsome deputy sheriff."

"Come on, girls," Jodie says, but she is also smiling.

Stacey continues, "By having the deputies downstairs, we'll have extra eyes to notify us if they see anyone entering the hospital. Just in case, I want to reiterate that if anything goes haywire, I'll have my revolver with me. Believe me, I know how to use it." She looks around the table. "Well, it looks like we got the police thing taken care of. I'll call them tomorrow to make sure they're available. I'll let you guys know."

She glances at her wristwatch and sees its ten-ten p.m. *It's getting late,* she tells herself, *and we need to end this meeting.* "I think everyone knows what they need to do," she says aloud. "The time frame is extremely important. I hope you all have each others' cell numbers. Don't worry, I've taken care of the tab. This is on me."

There are several other customers still in the café when the group gets up to leave. Barbra and her husband meet them at the door.

"You have a good evening," Barbra's husband says, "and please have another meeting here in the future. We sure can use the business."

Everyone heads for home.

Chapter 106

As Stacey and the two boys get into her Jaguar, Andre gets out his cell phone and starts dialing. When a voice answers, he says, "Hello, Christina?"

"Yes, this is her."

"I can hardly hear you," Andre says. "The music in the background is so loud."

"Yeah," she says. "My friends and I are at a night spot in Waikiki. The music's terrific here. Great to dance to."

"I can't understand you." He is almost yelling into the phone.

"Just a minute," she says. "I'll go outside. Don't hang up, okay?" A few minutes later, her voice comes back, but there is no background music now. "Andre!" she says. "I just checked the cell number on my way outside to see who it was."

"Yes, this is he. How are you?"

"I'm great," she says, "and how are you? Tell me what's happening."

"I just got out of my meeting and I'm on my way home."

"Why was your meeting so late? Or was it a real long meeting? You know, those types that go on forever and ever?"

"No, it was a long meeting with a lot of details, but I can tell you more when I see you."

"And when will that be?"

"Jing Xian and I will be flying into Honolulu tomorrow afternoon."

She laughs, then stops laughing. "That's not much of a notice," she says. "That'll be Monday evening you're arriving."

"Yes," he tells her. "We'll be in Hawaii until Wednesday evening, then we have to return to San Francisco on the company plane. The plane we're flying back on is a scheduled flight from Singapore to San

273

Francisco, but it'll be diverted to Hawaii briefly to pick up Jing Xian and me, then it'll continue on to California."

"Oh," she replies. "You have a company plane?"

"Yes. The company requires many trips to our offices, which are located around the world. It'll be used for this trip because of its significance to the mission."

"So it looks like I'll have to cancel all my dates for two days?" she asks.

"Yeah. Gee, I hope I won't be messing up all your plans."

"Don't be crazy," she says. "You won't be messing up anything. I'm looking forward to seeing you again. It's been a long time. This time, it'll be longer than eight minutes standing on the side of a boat, though two days in the land of paradise is not very long, either. And I was just thinking—how am I going to remember how you look?" She laughs again. "Are you over six feet tall? It was sort of hard to tell your height when you were standing in that little boat."

"Close," he says. "I'm six foot three."

"Oh, that's nice. You know, the weather is terrific here. My friends and I have been lying in the sun so much, I'm starting to look like the locals. Although the sun is nice and bright, it's starting to zap the energy out of us. This trip is worth everything we've invested in it. When we get back home, all our friends are going to be so envious of us."

"Hey, Christina," Andre says, "is Missy around? You remember my friend, Jing Xian? He'd like to talk with her."

"That would be nice," Christina says, "but she and Amy, our other friend, are taking in a dinner show at the Moana Sheraton this evening."

Jing Xian, who has been listening to Andre's side of the conversation from the back seat, reaches over the seat and grabs the cell phone out of Andre's hands. "Hey, Christina," he says, "this is Jing Xian. When am I going to get to talk with Missy?"

"I'm so sorry you haven't been able to talk to her when you've called," Christina says. "It just seems like the timing's off. She totally wants to talk with you. You'll be able to see her when you get here, though."

"That'll be great," he replies. "It's too bad she doesn't have her own cell phone."

"We decided to just bring one phone. We didn't think we'd be talking with many people. You could say this is a get-away trip for all of us."

"That sounds real good," Jing Xian says. "I'm giving the phone back to Andre now. Bye."

"You know," Christina says to Andre. Her voice is sincere now. "You sound like an interesting guy. I think I still have the souvenir you sold me in China. It was a hand-carved water buffalo, right? You must have been enjoying your life in China. I'm sure of it. I've been talking with you off and on for the last month, and now you tell me you've become the president of some big company with offices around the world. Are you and Jing Xian telling the truth? Or are you guys making something up just to impress us? You know, nothing happens on my first three dates with any guy! But either way, you impress me."

"I hope you believe me," Andre says. "How about having dinner with me tomorrow night? I'll tell you everything, or everything you'll believe." He chuckles.

"You are on! Call me tomorrow when you know what plane you'll be on, and the time, I'll pick you up. Hey, it's starting to get loud out here. More people are coming outside on the deck."

Chapter 107

The next morning, Mr. Craiger is punching in numbers on his cell phone. When there is an answer, he says, "Doshi, good morning."

"Who is this?" asks the voice on the other end of the line.

"Who is this, you ask! You mean you don't know who this is after all the money I've given you two? Are you that stupid, that you don't know who I am?"

Doshi suddenly realizes who she is talking to. "Oh, Mr. Craiger. My mind was on something else. I didn't recognize your voice."

"My voice hasn't changed in the last couple of days," he says. "I don't think it's hard to understand me. Are you drinking?"

"I'm terribly sorry for the misunderstanding," she says. "It won't happen again, I promise."

"Be careful about your promises. They can come back and bite you in the ass. Now, cut the crap—have you read today's *Probe*?"

"Well, no, not exactly, I was planning to get one with breakfast."

"If you wait much longer, there won't be breakfast and the papers will be gone."

"Yes, I see. I will get one immediately."

"Do you know which newspaper I'm talking about?"

"Not exactly, Mr. Craiger."

"What do you mean not exactly? You idiot, it's the only damn paper I read. It's *The Probe*. I've told you that a thousand times. Is it really that hard to remember?"

"No, sir. No, Mr. Craiger."

"I want you to buy a paper and read the column this guy, Bertolino, writes. He's writing about Andre Roberson. Who should have died over a year ago. Roberson is coming to town for some kind of surgery to recover from his paralysis from that damn camel ride in Morocco. You got me?"

"Yes. I understand. Explicitly."

"Stop that! Quit using fancy words. You don't know what they mean, and you're just showing how stupid you are."

"Yes, Mr. Craiger."

"After your breakfast, and don't make it an all-day affair, I want you and Maji to get down to the San Francisco Airport where this exporting company's air terminal is and start snooping around. Ask some questions. That shouldn't be too difficult, if you can do it without getting into trouble, I mean, stay out of trouble. Talk with some of the ground crew and see what they know of a company plane coming in late Wednesday night. If you find out something, let me know as soon as possible. You got me?"

"Yes, Mr. Craiger."

"There might be a slim chance you can eliminate him before he arrives at the hospital."

"Eliminate who?"

"What did you just say?"

"Uhh ... nothing. I didn't say anything."

"That's what I thought you said. I'm thinking once he arrives at the hospital, there'll be too many people checking him out, and all that other stuff they do at a hospital. Are you writing all this down?"

"Yes, Mr. Craiger."

"For the two days he'll be there, they'll hook up video cameras to monitor him. Or use some other means to observe him. Try to find out where they're going to take him once he's off the plane, you know, out a side door into a special truck, something like that."

Chapter 108

Maji and Doshi come walking up to the customer service counter at the corporation's air terminal and Maji addresses the clerk standing behind the counter.

"I hope you can help me," he says. "I'm checking to see if you have a plane coming in from the Orient in the next couple of days."

"Hold on," the clerk says, "and I'll check. It'll be just a few seconds. I'm pulling up the information as I speak." But as he is speaking to Maji, he also pushes a button that notifies the manager that someone is asking about that flight. "Ahh, yes," the clerk says, "here it is. I have a flight coming in from Shanghai this evening. Around seven o'clock. There might be a problem. We can't tell right now. A typhoon is approaching the coast of Shanghai, and it may affect the take-off and arrival times. We can't make any predictions right now. When there is a large turbulence like a typhoon of this magnitude, we don't attempt to fly unless there's an urgent delivery. At the present time we don't have any immediate flights, but things change all the time."

Maji turns to Doshi, who is standing beside him. "Will you quite poking me! Yes, yes, I'll ask him." He turns back to the counter. "I have another question. Could there be another plane coming from another country in the Orient?"

The clerk nods. "Let me check. Yes, there's another plane leaving Singapore in a couple of days, but we won't have any information on this flight, either, until we know what the typhoon is going to do. At the moment, this inversion is sitting still, not moving anywhere. It's just blasting the eastern shoreline of the Asian continent." When Maji frowns, the clerk adds, "Sir, I can give you a phone number that you can call that will give you an hourly update of our flights coming into the terminal."

"That would be great. Thank you." Maji accepts a card from the clerk. After he and Doshi walk away from the counter, he gets out his cell phone and dials. "Hello, Mr. Craiger, this is Maji."

"I know who you are, I recognize your voice. What did you find out? ... I see, I see. ... Are you sure that's all the flight information there was? ... Okay. ... No. Actually, no, that is *not* okay, I mean, there has to be more information than that. It doesn't make sense. There's something going on." Mr. Craiger puffs on his Cuban cigar. "There's a plane coming into the San Francisco from the Orient in the next couple of days with Andre Roberson aboard. I have to find out when. Do you understand?"

"Yes, Mr. Craiger."

"I want you and Doshi to camp out down there. But don't let those people at the terminal see you. You understand? I didn't hear you say yes."

"I'm sorry. Yes, Mr. Craiger."

"That's better."

PART VI

ANDRE AND JING XIAN ARRIVE IN HAWAII

Chapter 109

As Andre and Jing Xian pick up their bags in the Honolulu airport, Andre looks around. "Hey, Jing Xian, have you seen two good looking girls who look like they're waiting for someone?"

"You know," Jing Xian replies, "I really don't remember exactly what they look like."

"I was thinking the same thing. There sure are a lot of good-looking girls around here. Well, keep looking. We're on time." Andre glances at his wristwatch. "It's been about a half an hour since we arrived."

"Are you sure we're supposed to meet them at the Carousel 4 in baggage claim?" Jing Xian asks.

"That's what she told me." Suddenly Andre's cell phone rings. "Hello?"

"It's Christina. Are you at the airport now?"

"Yeah. We've been here for half an hour. Where are you?"

"Andre, I have some bad news, well, maybe it's not all bad."

"I bet you're not going to be picking us up."

"How did you guess?"

"Just a gut feeling." Andre rolls his eyes at Jing Xian.

"Just get a cab," Christina says, "and tell him you want to go to the Hawaiian Village Hotel Resort in Waikiki. We'll meet you in the lobby."

"Sounds great," says Andre. "See you in awhile."

When Andre tells Jing Xian about the change in plans, Jing Xian grins and says, "Hey, I've got a great idea. If we can't find the girls, we can always come back here."

"You mean come back to the airport?"

"Yes. This is the place where everyone has to come to. We can hang out here for a couple hours"

"You're crazy. Let's catch a cab."

When they pull up in front of the Hawaiian Village Resort, the boys look around and Jing Xian says, "Nice place. Is this where they live?"

283

"I'm not sure," Andre replies. "I don't remember their address."

As the boys are walking up the sidewalk and passing between two giant tiki statues, two very attractive young women approach them and ask them if they know where the outdoor bar is located.

When Andre replies, "I'm not sure, we just got here," one of the girls suggests that they ought to check it out.

"What do you think about that?" Jing Xian asks.

Andre, who is standing still and watching the girls walk away, says nothing. As they reach the entrance of the hotel, two awesomely tanned girls come up to them.

"Hi, boys," one says. "Are you looking for a good time?"

Immediately, the boys' heads turn in the direction of the voices.

"Hi," Christina says as she comes up to Andre, a big smile on her face. Missy is smiling at Jing Xian.

"Hey, there, good looking," she says. "It's been a long time. We were hoping you were the right guys, you know, we don't have any pictures, only memories."

Christina laughs. "We didn't want to make a mistake, then where would we be?"

The boys laugh as well and slap each other on the back as they gaze at the most ravishing girls they have ever seen.

"Are we in heaven?" Jing Xian whispers to Andre. "I was just joking a while ago, about going back to the airport." The boys gave the girls big hugs.

"Oh, you're taking my air away," Missy protests.

"Sorry," says Jing Xian. "I'm just trying to stretch my arms after a long flight."

Andre looks around the lobby. "This is a nice place," he comments. "You girls made a nice choice. Do you have an ocean view?"

"No, we don't," Missy says. "In fact, we don't even have a view of anything, not even a swimming pool. We don't exactly live here."

"You girls aren't staying here? Look what you're missing," Jing Xian says.

"Yes, we know that," Christina says. "Our travel agent told us stories about this place, and the astronomical prices we'd have to pay. I don't think she's ever been to Hawaii. She didn't tell us about the special package deals they have here, either. So we got this great deal, which is not much of a deal, it's too far from everything. We didn't want you guys to see our place first thing, though. The place we're staying at is not far from here … if you're a sea gull flying. It's six or seven blocks away."

"We can go there in a cab," Andre says.

"On our next trip to Hawaii," Christina says, "this will be the place we'll be staying at. Even if we have to spend a lot more money, it'll be worth it. They have a fantastic restaurant under a thatched roof out by the swimming pool. There's a view of the ocean there."

"Sounds great," Andre replies. "How about all of us get something to eat? I'm starved."

"So am I," says Jing Xian.

"That meal was fantastic," Andre says an hour later as he finishes his glass of wine. "The restaurant is perfect, and the food is comparable to none." Jing Xian reaches for the bill, but Andre picks it up first. "I can charge it to the company expense account," he says. "This is company business, you know."

Christina looks up. "So, how long are you guys going to be in Hawaii?"

"We'll be here for about a day. I mean, maybe two days."

"For only one night maybe? Or maybe two?"

"Yes."

"What does that mean?" Christina asks. "I thought you were going to be here two or more nights."

"Plans had to be changed at the last minute," he says. "It was extremely important. Possibly life-threatening. We have a company plane headed for San Francisco out of Singapore, but it's been rerouted because of a typhoon to come through Honolulu. Both Jing Xian and I have to be on that plane. So tonight is really the only full night we'll have here in Hawaii this time." He repeats, "This time. What I've seen so far, this is the place I need to return to." While he is talking, he is looking into Christina's big brown eyes.

"You know," she says, "you're more handsome than I remembered." She looks over at Missy. "You want to come to the restroom with me?"

Missy starts to say no, but she exchanges a significant look with Christina and changes her mind. "I think I have an eye lash in my eye," she says as she stands up.

As the girls start to walk away from the table, Andre's cell phone rings.

Chapter 110

"**H**i, Stacey," Andre says. The girls are still standing by the table, so he says, "This is my personal secretary calling from San Francisco. She's probably checking up on me."

"Andre," Stacey says, "I was just calling to make sure you got there okay. We have a slight change in plans."

"We do?"

"Yes. Bertolino mentioned you in his column in this morning's edition just to keep the thugs up to date. Shortly after the paper went on the street, his office received three telephone inquires about you. What time are you returning? On what plane? Who is your doctor? Where is the surgery going to take place? Where are you going to recuperate? All those questions! It's getting a bit spooky."

"Yeah. Spooky."

"Some of these callers could be legitimate," she says, "but I'm sure at least one was from the people who want you dead. I don't know how many people are involved, but we can't take any chances. We thought we'd only get one call, like we did last time you were in the column, but this time there were three. We've got ourselves deep into this. We need to proceed very carefully with some changes."

"Okay. I'm listening."

"I spoke with my deputy sheriff friend, Hallett, and he told me it would be a good idea to bring you and Jing Xian back early. If you come back early, we can make adjustments, if needed, but if you come back as planned, they could set up an ambush or be waiting somewhere for you. We need to have the advantage. Okay?"

"So … we're going to bring you guys back earlier than planned. Right now, we're looking at some time early tomorrow morning. We're still trying to find out the exact time the plane will be leaving Singapore. Our plane left Shanghai and landed in Singapore to pick up a few special items, but it may have a problem taking off as scheduled. There's that enormous typhoon approaching the coast of Singapore, you know. We're in touch with the weather bureau in Singapore to see when the plane will be able to leave. If the inversion stalls off the coast, the typhoon's too big for us to fly around it. We may have to wait it out. We should have updated information in a couple hours, but right now, we have too many questions and not enough answers. I'm sorry about the change in plans."

"Stacey," Andre finally says, "you have got to be kidding."

"No, I'm not. I'm dead serious. Look, I'm sure you made some fantastic plans, but this has priority over everything. Andre, it's your life we're talking about here. Oh—I have to go now. I have an incoming call. Please keep your cell with you and keep it on."

"Okay."

"I'm really not trying to screw your life up," she assures him, "but if we don't do this right, you may not have a life. I hope you understand what I'm trying to say. Your father was a wonderful man, and you remind me so much of him, I'll be damned if I'm going to lose you, too, to some madman."

As Andre listens, speechless, she goes on. "Plan a trip to Hawaii next month. For two weeks. You, Jing Xian, and the girls. I will personally take care of everything. Take a trip to the Mediterranean. Wherever. I have a time share on the island of Santorini. You guys would enjoy riding donkeys to the top of the mountain."

"You don't have to do that Stacey," he finally says. "Hell, I'm the CEO of the company."

"I know. And I want you to enjoy it."

"You've got a very good point. I have a lot to learn. I'm going to need your help for a long time."

"I'm sure you'll be an excellent CEO, and I'll be there as always. I want you to hang in there now. Okay?"

Andre pauses for a moment. "Yeah. You're right. I'm not putting the priorities in the right order."

"I understand your feelings," she assures him. "You went through all that mental and physical isolation for almost two years during your recovery. It must have been devastating. You're a young, handsome man, and soon you'll be out meeting some of the most beautiful women on earth. And very soon, you'll have a very demanding company to run, too."

"Stacey...."

"I'm sorry, Andre. I got carried away."

"That's all right," he replies. "I guess I needed a little personal guidance. Well, when you get the news, give me a call. I'll explain everything to the girls. Jing Xian and I don't have a lot of time, do we?"

"What's wrong?" Jing Xian asks. "Are we going back early?"

Andre slowly puts his cell phone in his pocket. "I don't know," he says. "The whole world is starting to blow up around me."

"What is it? What's going on?" When Andre still doesn't explain the phone call, Jing Xian says, "Hey, buddy, do you need some help?"

When Andre is finally able to speak, he says, "We have to leave early in the morning. Stacey will call in a couple of hours with the exact time. There's a typhoon off the coast of Singapore. They're waiting to see what it's going to do. There may be trouble at the airport in San Francisco, too. Stacey's extremely nervous. That's why she wants us to leave early."

The two girls are still standing near the table with blank looks on their faces. Christina looks down at the guys.

"Well," she says in a cheery voice, "there's no sense in everyone having a gloomy time. We don't have a lot of time? Okay, then, come on, let's just stay here in the Tiki Hut lounge and have a drink. Maybe two. Then we can go back to our place. Preferably by cab." She laughs. "You guys can shower and clean up while we do the same, and we'll go somewhere. It's not the end of the world."

Chapter 111

At Andre's suggestion, they go out under the full moon and walk on the sand by the water. The tide is out and the waves are hardly breaking on the sand, making little white, splashy reflections of the moon. The warm trade winds are blowing in from the leeward side of the island. Andre is walking slowly, holding Christina's hand, and about fifty feet behind them are Jing Xian and Missy, also holding hands. They are all walking barefoot and feeling the warm sand between their toes. No one is talking, but there are many thoughts going through the air.

Finally, Andre glances at his wristwatch. "It's getting close to midnight."

Christina squeezes his hand.

Stacey called a few hours earlier to say that he and Jing Xian had to be at the corporate air terminal in Honolulu no later than two a.m. Now Andre stops walking, slips his arm around Christina's waist, and looks into her eyes. He slips his other arm around her and pulls her closer to him as she raises her arms and wraps them around his neck. She can hardly see his handsome face in the shadows, but she doesn't need to see his face to feel the pain he is going through. So much anticipation they had, and now it is all fading away. It may be some time before they will be together again, and who knows what might happen? She raises her face to his, and lightly runs her tongue across his dry lips. He is not moving a muscle. She softly nibbles his bottom lip and runs her tongue over his lips again. They are both starting to breathe heavily. Suddenly, however, several people walk by, then a large group of tourists passes, laughing and taking pictures of each other … and the moment slips away. They look at each other for a moment, and he presses his lips against her soft lips. The desire immediately returns. Her warm lips part, and his tongue searches inside her mouth. His arms start to move down her back, sliding down, and his hands press her buttocks. Andre murmurs something under his breath: they have to start heading back to the airport. Christina slowly moves her head down to his neck.

"Just a couple more minutes?"

She starts to kiss his neck and moves to his muscular chest, kissing and running her tongue along his muscles. She hesitates when her tongue touches the scarred imprint of the crouching lion on his chest. This is starting to get Andre very excited, and he realizes he must stay in control, especially tonight. He starts to pull away from Christina.

"Honey, we have to stop. I have to restrain myself tonight. I must! We just don't have enough time."

They can hear Jing Xian and Missy also talking. They come closer.

"I just checked the time," Jing Xian says. "It's getting late, plus we have to stop by the hotel and pick up our stuff."

"Missy and I will ride to the airport with you," Christina says.

"That would be great."

Chapter 112

Mr. Weaver, the company's expediting coordinator at the terminal, turns to Andre. "This is your room," he says. "You will need to remove your clothes and put on this hospital gown. Here's a pair of hospital slippers. This is the best gown we could get you. I think we got the right size. Yes, I think it will fit. After you get changed, call out to let us know you're ready, and a registered nurse, her name is Cathy, will come and hook you up to the IV drip and check your vitals. We decided to bring a professional to the terminal just in case your helper may have a problem while you are in the air."

"Okay." Andre sounds sad.

Mr. Weaver continues. "Cathy's one of the best nurses we have on the staff. You won't feel a thing. Watch out for her jokes, though. The flight from here to San Francisco is a little over five hours, so we think you can leave the IV in until you get to the hospital. At the hospital, someone can remove the needle and make it look like it's still in your arm. Any questions?"

"No. I understand everything."

Weaver turns to Jing Xian. "Come with me, he says, "and I'll show you your room, too. Change into this jumpsuit. It's what our clean-up crew wears. Then go aboard the plane when it arrives to clean it up. There will be two other workers with you. They're aware you have no experience and you'll be staying on the plane when they're finished. On this flight, there won't be too much to clean up, so just look like you're busy doing something. Maybe you can arrange the seat belts on the seats. That always looks nice when new people come on board. When the buzzer goes off, notifying the clean-up team to deplane, slip into the restroom and wait in there until someone tells you to come out. By that time, there won't be anyone around who is not cleared for security for this mission."

"Hello," Andre calls out. He is standing in his hospital gown, open in back, waiting for the nurse. "I'm ready," he says.

"Nice," a woman behind him comments. "Nice cheeks."

Turning around, he sees a tall, voluptuous, blonde nurse standing there, one hand resting on her shapely hip, the other holding a medical bag. She fills out her flowered Hawaiian blouse, and her snug shorts compliment her tan. That is to say, she looks like no one's vision of a nurse.

"Very nice," she says again. "I thought maybe I'd have to dress you, like all the other patients that come through here. I really don't understand why they don't know how to put these gowns on. These guys that come through here always need help. I don't know why." She smiles at him again. "But you, you've got the gown on correctly, butt open," and she gives a little chuckle as she looks at his butt cheeks again. "Here, let me take care of the rest of the ties." She tells Andre to sit down at a nearby table and stretch out his left arm. "Hmm, that's a nice looking bird you've got tattooed there."

"Yes. It's a special bird I got while I was staying in the Black Hills."

"Interesting." She leans forward and looks at it more closely. "Nice colors," she says as she takes his pulse. She then puts a thermometer in his mouth and listens with her stethoscope on his chest for a few seconds.

Reaching into her medical bag, she brings out an IV tube set with a solution bag. After cleaning off his arm with an alcohol pad, she inserts the IV needle and tapes it up. She looks at him again and smiles, then hangs the bag on a metal stand so it will drip freely. She makes a couple adjustments and says, "Ready to go."

"I didn't feel a thing," Andre comments.

"Yes. Painless insertion's my specialty. You won't feel a thing." She gives him another big smile. "They'll be in to get you in a while," she says as she sashays out of the room.

Chapter 113

"The loading crew has already fastened your bed to the pallet," Weaver explains. "We'll fork-lift it into the plane. After the pallet has been moved into place, we'll bring you in a wheelchair. The lifting mechanism will raise you out of your wheelchair and set you in the special bed. We'll secure you with straps so you won't roll or fall out. You'll be fitted with a respirator when we bring you out to be loaded on the plane. After you're airborne, however, the equipment will be disconnected and you'll be able to move around in the plane at will. After we land in San Francisco, we'll transport you out of the plane in a wheelchair with all of your life-sustaining equipment attached again. Shortly before our arrival at the airport, the crew will hook you back up to the respirator. That's so everything will look realistic for your trip to the hospital. We'll transport you from our terminal to the hospital using a wheelchair ambulance."

Five hours and fifteen minutes later, the plane is in the San Francisco's air space requesting permission to land. The crew chief addresses Andre.

"We're going to land shortly," he says, "so you need to get back on the bed. We have to make everything look real. We're not sure if our workforce here has been compromised or not. Once the plane has come to a stop, we'll lift you onto a gurney and roll you down to the waiting ambulance. They decided a gurney would make more sense than a wheelchair because of your back condition. We also want to make sure the equipment is working."

PART VII

ANDRE AND JING XIAN RETURN TO SAN FRANCISCO

Chapter 114

"Hello, Mr. Craiger. This is Maji."

"I know who you are. Yeah, yeah, yeah, get to the point, will ya? Dammit, what happened?"

"We were waiting at the airport just like you instructed us. We waited and waited, but there was no plane. We started to get worried. So I went up to the terminal and asked around and found out we were three or four hours too late." Maji pauses, knowing he will be yelled at. "We missed his plane."

"You *what?* Tell me again! What did you do?"

"They said there were some changes in the flight plan because of some typhoon off the coast of Singapore. That's why the plane arrived earlier than expected. What do you want us to do now?"

"I want you to get over to the damn hospital and take care of this matter tonight," Craiger bellows. "I don't want him to be alive tomorrow. Do you understand? Get over there before they can put up monitors or security guards or any other damn thing they use to protect this guy. You understand me?"

"Yes, Mr. Craiger. Doshi and I are on our way. Right after I hang up the phone."

"Wait. Just a moment. I'm thinking. Go over to the hospital tonight, maybe about, oh, two-thirty in the morning. Yeah, that's a good time. Everyone will be tired and half asleep. It has to be done tonight."

"Yes, Mr. Craiger. We're on our way."

Chapter 115

"Stacey, this is Jack at the air terminal."

"Hi, Jack. How's it going?"

"Well, we just had an inquiry at the terminal information counter about when our plane was coming in. We gave out the information you told us to give. The individual who was inquiring had a heavy accent, though I couldn't tell what nationality he was. He was dressed very nice, though. He rushed away. He looked extremely unhappy when we told him about the plane."

"That sounds like the person we were expecting," Stacey says. "Good work, Jack. I'll be there shortly."

"We're going to load Andre into the ambulance now," Jack says. "Jeremy and Claudia are already in the wagon. Did you want to come down and see him before we depart for the hospital?"

"Yes. I'll be there right away. Don't leave until I get there."

Twenty minutes later, Stacey walks into the office. "Where do you have Andre hidden?" she asks.

"He's all set up in the ambulance with the driver and his assistant. They're waiting in the building beside the terminal. I'll drive you over there."

When they arrive, Stacey goes inside the building, Jack right behind her. The security guard recognizes them and lets them pass. As they approach the ambulance, Jeremy gets out of the vehicle.

"You must be Stacey," he says.

"Yes, I am. And you must be Jeremy. Are you taking good care of my friend, Andre?"

"We sure are. We have him strapped into the gurney. I think he's asleep right now." Claudia, the assistant driver, comes around the back end of the ambulance, and greets Stacey.

"Andre hasn't asked for any pizza yet, has he?" Stacey asks with a grin.

"Don't say that word too loud," Jeremy says. "The respirator's keeping him relaxed, but he seems to be getting tired of this whole charade."

"I don't blame him," Stacey says. "Well, let's wake him up." When Jeremy releases the door, she sticks her head in the ambulance. "Hey, big guy, are you in here?"

"Yes, we are," replies Jing Xian. He feels like a zombie.

"This whole thing will be over pretty soon, hopefully within the next couple of days," she tells them. "We got information that the thugs were here. We told them that the plane had landed a couple hours before they got here. We're lucky we arrived early. They were here earlier than we anticipated." Stacey turns to Jack. "Are you armed?" she asks him.

"Sure," he says. "I'm on duty."

"Okay, you need to ride with Jeremy and Claudia to the hospital," she instructs him. "Jing Xian and I will follow. Jeremy will bring you back after we get Andre into his room. I'll feel a lot better with some fire power."

As Jack and Stacey walk back to his car, he turns to her. "Hey," he says, "a couple of my employees coming to work on second shift saw a man and a woman sitting in a car over that way. They were looking at our terminal through binoculars. That was maybe an hour after that strange guy came in asking about an inbound plane from Asia. Those two sat out there for a couple hours." Jack and Stacey look in the direction where Jack is pointing, but there is no car there now.

"I'm sure something's going to go down," Jack says, "but I can't tell you how they'll try it. Be ready on the freeway. That's my advice. I have a hunch they'll try something before you get to the hospital."

Chapter 116

In spite of Jack's warning, the convoy has an uneventful trip through the usual San Francisco traffic from the airport to the hospital. When they arrive, Jeremy backs the ambulance up to the receiving door. Then he turns to Jack and Jing Xian and says, "You two guys get on that side of the gurney. I'll handle this side. Claudia will make sure nothing is hanging off the gurney."

Jing Xian leans over the gurney whispers to Andre. "Hang in there, buddy. We're almost there."

Kathy is also present. Stacey turns to her. "Can you go up ahead of us? Just to make sure everything looks okay? I don't want any surprises." She also sees Deputy Hallett. "Can you accompany us to Andre's room?" she asks him. "Then you and Kathy can run the stakeout in the car."

While Stacey is directing traffic, Maji, who is sitting with Doshi in their car, which is now in the hospital parking lot, lays down the pair of binoculars he has been using to observe the unloading of Andre Roberson from the ambulance.

"We were told at the customer service counter that the plane had landed four or five hours ago," he says. "Why are they just arriving here now? Did they stop somewhere and have dinner?"

"Maybe they had a problem on the plane," Doshi says. "Like passports or visas? Mechanical problems?"

"Maybe they did," Maji says, "but why did they lie to me? Something sounds fishy. But I can't tell Mr. Craiger that. He would kill us."

"What do you mean us? You are the one who screwed up. Not me."

He turns and slaps her. "Shut up. I have to think about this. There's too many people around here right now. I don't think it's safe to be this close. We better get out of here before someone comes nosing around."

300

Chapter 117

Very early the next morning, a thick fog lingers close to the ground, limiting visibility to about twenty feet. Kathy telephones Stacey from the stakeout car. "Stacey," she says, "I can just barely make out the silhouettes of two people entering the hospital together. I can't tell if they're female or male. ... Oh, they both just paused and looked around briefly, as if someone might be following them. They're going in now."

Stacey hurries into Andre's room. "Andre, wake up." She shakes him.

"Okay. I'm awake."

"Kathy just saw two people entering the hospital together. Be ready. They may be up here in a few minutes." She takes a minute to look the room over. Everything seems to be in place. Then she hurries back into the adjoining room, where Jing Xian, who is drinking a cup of hot tea from his thermos, asks her if she wants a cup.

"Yes," she says. "I can have a couple sips before the action starts."

Meanwhile, Maji leaves Doshi standing in the hospital lobby and walks quickly to the elevator. He is still looking around suspiciously, making sure they have not been seen. It is so quiet in the hospital that he is becoming more and more fidgety. *I don't see any security guards*, he tells himself. *No one at the information desk. Someone from the janitorial service buffing the other hallway. But they don't see us. Perfect.* He motions for Doshi to join him, and they both step into the elevator.

Inside the elevator, Maji quietly tells Doshi, "Push the fourth floor button," and the elevator begins to move. "Why is the elevator going so slow?" he asks as he stares at the panel. Finally, the door opens and they exit on the fourth floor. All the lights on the floor have been turned down to conserve energy. They pause and look around again. Has anyone noticed them? They can hear the nurses talking in the nurses' station down the hall. Maji listens carefully to find out what the nurses are talking about, but he cannot make out any words. He is certain they didn't hear the elevator stop.

Guiding Doshi by the elbow, he leads her toward room 409. He called the hospital earlier in the day and learned Andre's room number from a nice helpful person at the information desk. Unaware that his call had informed Stacey that someone was interested in Andre's arrival, he thought his task was going to be too easy. The floor is sparkling clean with its new coat of wax, making walking quietly impossible. Maji is walking on his toes in his patent leather shoes, but Doshi's strapless high heels are clicking on the tiles. The noise is starting to make Maji furious.

"Either walk quieter or take those damn things off," he snarls. "You'll wake the dead. We don't want to get caught. You understand? Or have you forgotten why we are here?" He jerks her elbow as they stop at the door of room 409.

"Will you stop pulling my elbow," Doshi snaps back. "I know how to walk."

"Alright." Feeling in his pocket, he pulls out his Beretta. He pulls back the slide, injects a round into the chamber, and flips off the safety. He holds the pistol in his right hand, down beside his leg. Then he nods to Doshi, and she opens the door. They leap into Andre's room and stand up against the wall.

"Why is this room so dark?" he whispers. "I can't see a damn thing."

She shrugs her shoulders and whispers, "I think they usually have some kind of night light on."

The assassins are standing motionless as their eyes adjust to the darkness in the room, which is deathly quiet except for the beeping sound from one of the machines beside Andre's bed. Also beside the bed is the illuminated screen showing Andre's heart rate, and there are some other machines with steady red, blue, and white lights and a blinking yellow light. Maji doesn't know what all these machines are used for.

He and Doshi scan the room to see if anything looks suspicious, then Doshi slowly moves over to the stand holding Andre's IV solution. She reaches into her purse and brings out a syringe filled with a deadly formula, which was concocted by a friend of Akram's who works in a pharmaceutical laboratory. It is guaranteed to kill anyone in a matter of seconds. Unable to see clearly enough in the dark, she also takes out a small pen light and turns it on to find the IV tube. Then she sticks the light in her mouth so she will have both hands free. She aims the light beam to the IV tube. Moving carefully, she takes the IV firmly in her hands and plunges the needle into the tube heading into Andre's arm. She empties the syringe. It is still difficult for her to see the tubing clearly because of the shadows created by the light moving back and forth because she is breathing so heavily. Finished, she puts the syringe and pen light back into her purse, and turns and looks at where Maji is standing. She slowly moves backwards, making sure not to run into anything, and when she is beside him again, she whispers in his ear.

"I put everything into the tube. He should be dead in no time."

Stacey and Jing Xian are waiting in the connecting room, staring at the camera and trying to figure out where Maji and Doshi are standing. Their images are hard to make out.

"Somehow this was not such a great idea," Stacey mutters.

Chapter 118

Andre, lying perfectly still in the hospital bed, can sense every move Maji and Doshi are making in the dark room. *I have to wait about a minute before I can push the button on the heart rate machine that will flat-line me,* he reminds himself. *No! I won't let them get away!* Squinting, he can see Maji with his pistol in his hand. This makes their plan riskier. *He's too far away for me to jump up and grab him,* Andre thinks. *He needs to come closer to the bed. How am I going to draw them closer?*

But Maji is becoming impatient. He starts fidgeting with his weapon. A minute has passed, and the monitor is not showing that Andre is dead.

Andre is ready to push the button. But something has gone dreadfully wrong. The monitor is not responding. He pushes the button several more times, but there is no response. The switch is not working. *What am I going to do?* In his nervousness, Andre is beginning to perspire, and Maji and Doshi are still too far away for him to grab either one.

Maji looks at Doshi, checks the illuminated hands on his Rolex, and looks at Doshi again. "It's been well over a couple of minutes since you put the poison in the IV tube," he hisses. "He's supposed to be dead already!"

At this moment, Andre accidentally drops the nonfunctioning switch on the crumpled sheet between his legs. Frantically, he starts feeling around between his legs to find the switch.

Wondering why this is taking so long, Maji starts moving towards the foot of the bed. He can see an extra pillow there.

Using his bat vision, Andre sees Maji creeping toward the bed. *Maybe it was a bit of good luck the button didn't work. Now I have a chance to grab him.*

Wait! Something's wrong! He's picking up the extra pillow. Is he going to suffocate me? Andre focuses on the killer. *No, he's going to use it to muffle the noise when he shoots me.* Andre's body tenses up, and he's sweating more profusely. *I have to find that switch!* He is still moving his fingers around between his legs. *Great. Here it is.* But trying to turn the switch over in his hand without moving his arm is difficult. *Where's the damn button?* Andre loses his focus on Maji, who is still holding the pillow and looking down at his victim.

The assassin does not raise his pistol, but quickly leans over and puts the pillow over Andre's face. But because he is still holding the pistol in his right hand, Maji is using his left hand and leaning against the side of the bed. This makes him slightly off balance. He glances back and forth, from the monitor to the door. When is Andre going to die?

Doshi, who is more nervous than ever, begins waving her hands in the air, trying to get Maji's attention. They need to leave the room. Right now! But Maji shakes his head. He wants Andre dead.

A split-second before the pillow descended, Andre sucked in a quick breath of air. *I'm in control,* he tells himself. *No panic. I'm staying calm. The palm of Maji's hand is smashing my nose and his finger is gouging into my eye. Should I start thrashing around? Grabbing his hands and making all sorts of noises? Or should I just relax my body? He'll feel me go limp and assume I've died.*

But Andre suddenly begins to experience an odd feeling of terror. Claustrophobia is awakening in his body. *Focus!* He keeps repeating to himself. *Stay calm. Stay calm. How long will this guy hold the pillow on my face? Just relax. I can't move. Regardless how hard he presses the pillow, I am in control.*

Maji is still leaning off balance, and now he is beginning to get tired. He moves his feet, then he moves his hand on the pillow. With his hand in a new position, he begins to press harder.

Under the pillow, Andre's teeth are pressing against his lips. He tastes something like salt. He immediately recognizes it. He is tasting his own blood. *The pain is tolerable! Focus! Keep your focus,* Andre keeps saying to himself. *I have enough air for a little longer.*

Then, *No way, no way. This is starting to get ridiculous. Enough of this, I'm going to stop. A change of plan. Wait. Not yet. Need to try the switch one more time, it has to work, once I press the button, the monitor will display a flat line, he will assume I'm dead, he'll relax. I have to make sure they think I've suffocated.*

At the same time, Maji is deciding that the solution Doshi put into the IV tube was no good.

I can make my move any time, Andre is telling himself. *I can destroy him any time. I can tear him from limb to limb and feed him to the wolves. I can mop the floor with his body. Stop! Where are these thoughts of annihilation and destruction coming from? I don't remember having thoughts of killing him. All I want is information. Who killed my father? And why?*

Now a peculiar feeling starts creeping into Andre's subconscious mind, taking control of his emotions. An unfamiliar rage starts to churn in his soul. He is sensing something he has never experienced before, except once when he was in China. It was at the temple. He experienced this same rage while he was recovering from his paralysis. He explained the strange feeling to Grand Master Shibo, who looked in the ancient books and could not find any reason for his feelings. The feeling of destruction never came again. Andre forgot it.

"Perhaps," Master Shibo explained, "there was some kind of spiritual entity that entered you. Perhaps it accompanied the enlightenment process and dissolved into your inner being. Under certain conditions it may be awaken and do its deed, and then go back into your inner being without your knowledge."

An unforeseen, dark, menacing haze comes over Andre's thinking and fills his mind. He is no longer rational.

One second before the haze completely takes over his mind, Andre pushes the button to the monitor. Success! The flat line appears on the screen, accompanied by a loud humming.

Maji stands up and looks at Doshi. They both smile. They have killed Andre. He motions to Doshi to get her to unplug the monitor.

Chapter 119

Suddenly, like a bat attacking its evening meal, Andre makes a swift move, yanking his arms out from under the sheet and grabbing Maji's neck just under his left ear. Andre's fingers penetrate deep into Maji's fat neck, pressing close to his jugular vein. Immediately, Maji feels horrific pain beyond imagination. He gasps but no sound comes out. Blood oozes out of his nose and mouth, and his eye are bulging almost out of his head. The grip Andre has on his neck paralyzes his whole body, like a cobra injecting its venom disabling all movement.

Maji still has the Beretta in his hand, and his fingers reflexively squeeze off two rounds. One bullet goes through the mattress and lodges in the floor under the bed. The other bullet grazes Andre's inner thigh and lodges in the wall. Still holding Maji's neck, Andre struggles to get out of the bed. He plants both feet on the floor.

Hearing the noise, but unable to see anything in the dark, Doshi starts screaming, then, totally disoriented, she freezes. When she makes a dash toward where she thinks the door is, she runs into the chair in the corner of the room, cutting a deep gash in her leg. She falls down and, completely terrified, tries frantically to crawl out of the room, clawing along the wall in search of the door.

The room has become a scene of chaos, and Andre's personality has shifted to uncontrollable madness as he squeezes the life out of Maji. He is now standing over the assassin, still pressing his neck, administering unrelenting pain to his would-be murderer. As he dies, Maji loses control of his bodily functions.

Hearing the commotion, Jing Xian and Stacey run into the dark room, each carrying a flashlight. Doshi, now crouching in the corner, sees their lights and leaps for the door, but stumbles in her fancy high-heeled shoes. Jing Xian sees her with her hands on the door handle and in one smooth motion jumps through the air. His heel perfectly connects with the back of her head, smashing her face with a loud thud against the door, breaking her nose and several teeth. Knocked senseless, she crumples to the floor. The hospital room is now filled with the smells of gun powder, urine, and excrement.

"Andre!" Stacey yells, "Andre, are you okay?" She runs across the room to him.

"Yes, I think so" he says calmly, "I'm fine."

"What happened?" Her voice trembles as she spots Maji stretched out across the bed. She shines her flashlight on his bloody face.

Jing Xian also crosses the room. "Is he dead?" he asks. He feels for a pulse on Maji's arm and shakes his head. "No pulse."

"Did he tell you who's behind this?" Stacey asks Andre. "Who killed your father?"

But Andre only gives her a blank look. "I don't remember," he says. "I don't remember. The last thing I remember is … I'm in bed." He pauses for a second. "Then Maji … he puts this pillow on my face and starts to suffocate me. Everything is still cool. Then I get dizzy." He shakes his head as if to clear it. "I don't remember anything else after that until you guys came in. What happened? What did I do?"

Jing Xian grips Andre's arm. "Hey, big guy. Let's just sit down over here." Aiming the flashlight, he guides him to the chair. "You look tired."

"Well, I haven't had much sleep for a couple of days."

Stacey is attending to Doshi, who is starting to come around, moaning as she cups her face with both hands. Blood is dripping off her chin and running down her arms. Stacey flashed her light on the woman's face.

"It looks pretty bad," she says. "You're going to need to see a doctor."

Doshi pulls back and shakes her head. "Yeah, yeah, I know what I need," she growls. "I don't need your medical advice. Get away from me." Jing Xian has finished putting the light bulbs back into their sockets, and now the room is filled with light. Doshi sees Maji sprawled across Andre's bed. "What's wrong with him? Is he dead?"

Stacey nods her head.

"You're shitting me."

"No, I'm not. He's dead."

"How did he die? Did he get shot?"

"No, he must have died from a heart attack." Stacey thinks some more. "Or he might not have been able to survive the severe pain inflicted by the master. Andre."

Doshi, a bewildered look on her face, takes a quick look over at Andre. Then she looks back at Stacey and shrugs her shoulders. "So what?"

Stacey explains. "You know, of course, that Andre is an expert in the ancient technique of administering pain without using any tools. He leaves no marks. He studied under the best master while he was in China. Maybe he needs to talk with you for a couple of minutes, I'm sure you will have a few things to tell him. We have plenty of time before the police arrive."

Chapter 120

At this point, Deputy Sheriff Hallett comes rushing into the room with his hand on his holster, ready to draw his revolver. Kathy is right behind him.

"Is everyone okay?" the deputy calls out. "Are these the suspects?" He sees Maji on the bed, then looks at Doshi and heads her way.

"What is that smell?" Kathy asks. Then she sees the excrement on the floor.

"Well," the deputy says a minute later, "it doesn't look like you guys need any help. Everything seems to be under control."

Kathy looks at Doshi's face. "You need to get some medical treatment," she says, but Doshi says nothing.

"Turn around," the deputy says to Doshi, "and put both your hands behind your back. I'm going to put these handcuffs on you just to make sure you don't decide to do any other stupid things."

Deputy Hallett calls into his station and requests an inspection team, adding that someone should take his prisoner to jail and take Maji's body to the coroner's office. He also leaves a message for Deputy Nolen to contact him. After Hallett finishes making his call, he looks around the room.

"Listen up, everyone. This room is now an official crime scene. I don't want anyone to leave. Try not to touch anything. Okay? I need to get everyone's name and phone number. An investigation team is on the way."

Stacey and Andre are still standing together in a corner. "I'm glad Deputy Hallett didn't get here quicker than he did," she whispers. "We had just enough time to tape Doshi's confession. Now we know who had your father killed. And how they did it."

"It seemed to me," Andre replies, "that she was relieved when she told you about Craiger." He gives a grim smile. "She called him an

SOB. What kind of guy is this Craiger, with his abuse and constant threats?"

"I suspected Mr. Craiger all the time," Stacey says, "but I never had any proof."

"Well, I was starting to get a little nervous, hoping I would not experience another blackout and destroy Doshi, too."

"It didn't take much to convince her," Stacey says with a chuckle. "All you did was lay your hand on her shoulder. She started shivering. She knew confession was the right thing to do, even though she's going to spend a long time behind bars. The tape from the ultraviolet camera didn't come out very well. When someone walked in front of another person, it was difficult to see who was who. We left the camera recording when we came into the room, and, wow, what a kaleidoscope of figures there is on the screen. We didn't get much in all the commotion. And it's too blurry to be useful. There seemed to be some kind of odd, strong interference. Maybe something in the building? Some electromagnetic force?"

"Well, maybe there could be some sort of macabre disturbance."

Stacey nods. "At least we have the recording of those two talking when she tells him she emptied the entire syringe of poison into your IV tube. Then they both just stood there, waiting for you to die. That is definitely attempted murder."

Chapter 121

As they are speaking, Stacey notices some blood on the front of Andre's medical gown. "Did you get cut?" she asks him, "Were you shot when his gun went off?"

"I don't know," he replies. "I don't feel any pain."

"Here," she take the edge of Andre's hospital gown in one hand and begins to move it. "Let me take a look—"

"Right here in front of everyone? Oh, no, you don't. Move your hand. There's nothing to see."

"You do have underwear on," she says, and then she looks at Andre's face and sees that he is blushing. "You mean you *don't* have any underwear on?"

"You don't have to broadcast it to everyone," he says turning a bright pink. "We were in such a big rush in Hawaii, changing clothes and trying not to be seen and all that, and ... and, well, when I was putting on the gown, someone told me to take everything off to make it look authentic, and then put the gown on, so that's what I did. We were in a hurry. When we arrived in San Francisco, I didn't know what had happened to my shorts. I was embarrassed to tell anyone that I lost them. What can I say? Anyway, I didn't think I'd be getting shot."

"Let's take a look at it," Stacey insists. As she calls Kathy over, Andre folds the hospital gown up and pulls it up between his legs, as if he's wearing a diaper.

The two women look at the wound in his thigh. "I'm not a nurse, but it does look a bit nasty to me," Kathy says with a smile. "I can't see it very well. It needs to be cleaned up. Most likely, you'll be getting at least three or four stitches, I would imagine. When was your last tetanus shot? Oh, it doesn't matter. They always give you a tetanus shot if you get shot. Let me get you a wheelchair. We'll wheel you down to the nurses' station. They'll take care of you and have you stitched up in no time."

Just then Jodie comes into the room, "I just got a phone call," she says. "I got here as quick as I could. How is everyone?" She looks at Maji's body, which is still stretched out across the bed. "Is this the guy everyone was having a problem with?" When Stacey says yes, Jodie looks over at Doshi, who is still crouched in the corner in handcuffs, waiting for the sheriff to come and pick her up. "And she's is the other one?"

"Yes," Stacey says.

"I remember her."

Stacey puts her arm around Jodie's shoulders and whispers to her, "A medical team from the hospital is coming. Nothing here is life-threatening. Kathy just took Andre somewhere, I believe to the nurses' station. He got grazed by a bullet, we think, on his inner thigh. It will most likely need some stitches."

"Oh. I hope it's not serious."

"No, it's not. Just needs some cleaning up and a few stitches. They need to look Doshi over before they transport her to the Alameda County Jail."

Chapter 122

Standing in the middle of the room, Stacey is reviewing what happened in the last half an hour. "Something's missing," she says as she stare's at the floor, "but I just can't put my finger on it." All of a sudden she lets out a squeal and rushes over to Kathy. "I just got this real freaky chill," she says. "Something's wrong! I don't know what, but we've overlooked something." But Kathy only gives her a questioning look.

At this point, two medical people arrive, and Jodie directs one of them to Doshi, the other to examine Maji's body. He takes the sheet from the bed and covers the body.

Still trying to figure out what they have overlooked, Stacey speaks loudly enough for everyone in the room can hear her.

"Has anyone been downstairs to see if anyone else might be waiting?" She gives Kathy and the deputy sheriff a quick look. "When you came into the hospital, did you notice any unusual activity? Maybe someone standing or sitting alone? A car slowly drives by? Maybe someone driving away?"

Kathy replies. "When they," she nods in Doshi's direction, "came to the entrance of the hospital, I was half asleep. The deputy was asleep. We were taking turns, sleeping an hour at a time. When I saw them, they were coming from around the corner of the building. It was impossible to tell if someone dropped them off or if they had their own car parked somewhere. There was no one else, no car around. Now I may have nodded off slightly before they arrived, I can't say for sure. I'm very sorry. After we called you, we waited for your call before coming into the hospital lobby. I noticed someone buffing the floors in the right hall. He was wearing a radio headset and didn't notice us. Wait—there's something else, I remember now. There was another car! Just as we were getting out of our car, I dropped my cell phone. After I picked it up, I looked up, and there was this dark, shiny car, really big, driving down the road past the main hospital building. It was there, and then it was gone, disappeared in the fog. The car just disappeared. I didn't pay any attention because it happened so fast and I was totally focused on getting upstairs."

"Craiger has a new Lexus," Stacey replies. "It's black. Four doors. His cars look like limousines."

Kathy starts getting choked up. "It's all my fault."

"No, no," the deputy says. "It was my fault; I wasn't thinking there would be someone else downstairs. And I'm supposed to be the expert."

"Well, maybe there isn't any one else downstairs," Stacey says. "But we need to check it out and make sure these two came by themselves."

Chapter 123

"It's a sure give away when someone is sitting alone late at night in a car in a deserted parking lot by a hospital," says Deputy Hallett. He spins on his heels and heads for the door. "I'm out of here," he yells. "Got to secure the area. Who knows what could be lurking down there?" Rushing to the elevator, he adjusts his shoulder holster. "If anyone asks, I'm calling all of this into the station right now." He disappears into the elevator.

Stepping out of the elevator in the hospital lobby, he pauses and carefully looks in all directions. The excitement of the unknown is what gets him excited. *He briefly thinks back when he was an army captain in a Special Forces Delta unit at Fort Bragg. If he had stayed in the military, he would be just about getting out now with a nice retirement, but too many trips to Columbia, the Philippines, some hot spots in Afghanistan, and Somalia had started to take their toll on him, both mentally and physically.* He focuses on the task at hand and clears his mind of all stray thoughts, then cautiously moves across the lobby, staying against the walls and in the shadows. He leaves the hospital and quickly moves to the corner of the building, still staying in the shadows.

Suddenly a cold shiver runs down his spine. "Damn, it's cold out here," he mutters through clench teeth. "That mist goes right through my clothes." The coastal fog is lingering close to the ground, hanging on top of bushes and trees, and in some spots making a total blackout. *Fog must've come in after I went inside. Can't see a damn thing. Wish I'd brought my jacket.* Another chill races down his spine, but it's too late to go back.

"This is tricky," he's grunts as he takes the first few steps out into the parking lot. The asphalt is slippery. *If I have to do any running, I've got to be careful. Wait! What was that?* He pauses, thinking he has heard something. He looks in the direction of the faint sound. *Yes, I can hear a man's voice.* He puts one hand on his weapon, and with the other pulls his high-powered flashlight out of his belt. It's a good weapon for hand-to-hand surprise moves.

The voice is coming from behind some oleander bushes about a hundred feet away to his left. He looks around to see if anyone has come to the hospital for his backup. No one is there, but he cannot take a chance and call again. Instead he makes a quiet call to Stacey to see if anyone upstairs can come down and back him up.

"We'll send someone down soon," she tells him.

After putting his cell phone back in his pocket, he heads in the direction of the mysterious voice.

Chapter 124

Crouching and dodging from one bush to another, Deputy Hallett spots the parked car and works his way up to about fifteen feet from it. Peering out of the bushes, he notices that his sleeves are wet from the fog on the leaves. Squatting behind the shrubbery, he can clearly see the black Lexus. It must be Mr. Craiger's car. He cannot, however, make out who is sitting in the car, though he can see a blurry silhouette of a big person behind the steering wheel. All the windows are up, and condensation steaming up the windows makes visibility almost impossible.

I need someone else to be here with me as backup, he gripes to himself. *How can I be sure this is the person we are looking for? Well, I have a good suspicion of who it is. I could be wrong, though. What if it's a doctor working late? I'm sure the driver would understand, especially at this time of morning, if I tapped on his window. But I'm not on duty, and I can't just come up and ask for his identification. I could show him my badge and tell him I'm a plain clothes security officer for the hospital at night. There have been many burglaries in the area lately.*

Suddenly a hand touches Deputy Hallett shoulder. Startled, he whirls around, swinging the large flashlight and almost taking off Jing Xian's head.

"Dammit," he says in a low voice, "you scared the hell out of me! How did you get over here without me seeing or hearing you?"

"I'm sorry, Deputy Hallett. I can move without sound. I didn't want to say anything and give myself away."

"Interesting, that's very interesting."

"It's an art," Jing Xian adds. "I learned it at the Shaolin monastery. I'll show you some time."

"Yeah, okay." Deputy Hallett is keeping his eyes focused on Lexus. "This fog's something, isn't it. Thick." As Jing Xian nods, the deputy adds, "I'll tell you what I'm going to do. First, I'm pretty sure the guy in that car is the one we're looking for."

"What's your plan?"

"I think there's only one person in the car. I might be wrong, but let's just hope I'm right. You wait here. I'll walk up to the side of the car. I won't draw my weapon unless he shows some kind of provocation, and I'll knock on his window. Get his attention. When I knock on the window, I want you to move quickly to the other side of the car. Stay towards the back end of the car. If he's armed and decides to start shooting, he won't be able to see you. You got that?"

"Got it."

"If there's gun play, though, you'll be in my direct line of fire. I don't want to be shooting bystanders. I want him to think I'm here by myself. He may try to get out the other side of the car and make a run for it. If he does, take him down, just like you did to that woman upstairs. Damn, you've got good feet! You'll have to show me some of those foot moves."

"Okay. You're on."

"Now, after I get his attention, I'll show him my badge and identify myself." He stops as a thought hits him. "Damn, I don't have any description of this guy. I'm gambling on his driver license to identify him. If this is him, he probably doesn't know that those two he sent to Andre's room failed in their mission. Otherwise, he would have been out of here in seconds." The deputy pauses again. "Well, just to be on the safe side, I'm going to have the safety strap on my holster unsnapped. If any shooting starts, hit the ground immediately."

Chapter 125

Approaching the black Lexus, Deputy Hallett knocks on the driver's side window. There is a long pause. The big shadow in the car is sitting motionless. Starting to get a little nervous, the deputy takes a step away from the car and puts his hand on his weapon. Slowly, the window comes down four or fives inches.

Hallett takes his badge out of his pocket. "Sir?" he says. "I'm Deputy Sheriff Hallett." He shows the driver his badge.

"Is there something wrong?" the man in the car asks. "I realize it's late. I was on my cell phone and—"

The deputy interrupts him. "Would you lower your window all the way down, sir? I need to see your driver's license and registration."

While Deputy Hallett is talking with the man, Jing Xian moves to the right rear of the car.

The driver, a big man, seems strangely nervous. Hallett can see perspiration forming around his lips and on his forehead. "Deputy," he says, "I didn't do anything wrong and I'm in a hurry. I need to get to Santa Barbara for a meeting, and you're slowing me down." His tone of voice betrays his belligerence. Digging through his glove compartment, he tells the deputy that he cannot find his registration.

Hallett uses his big flashlight to scan the inside of the car, looking for anything that looks out of place. At the same time, Jing Xian moves forward on the other side of the car, watching the driver to make sure he is not going to pull a gun out of the glove compartment.

The fat man glances out the window several times. When he spots Jing Xian, he starts breathing heavily and coughing. Then he picks up a used tissue lying on the passenger seat and coughs several times in it and then blows his nose.

The deputy decides he is stalling for time and examines his driver's license more closely. "Do you have anything else with your name on it?" he asks.

The man hesitates, then replies, "Yes, I do have something. Would a credit card be okay?" He hands a Visa card to Hallett, who now sees that the picture on the driver's license looks like the man in the car. Same color eyes, same hair color, same height and weight. The license says the man's name is Thomas Avery.

"Well, Mr. Avery," he says, "here's your license back." As he is handing the license back to Mr. Avery, he looks across the top of the car at Jing Xian and shrugs his shoulders. They seem to have stopped the wrong man.

He addresses the driver again. "Mr. Avery, I'm going to give you a verbal warning this time. If I were on street duty tonight, I would give you a citation for not having your registration with you in your car." The deputy cannot give Mr. Avery a ticket that night, anyway, because he is not on duty and does not have his ticket book with him.

"Tell me, Mr. Avery," he asks as if curious, "why are you here in the hospital parking lot at this time of morning? Lately there have been numerous burglaries reported in this area of town." Hallett is fishing to see what reason the man will give for being here before dawn. He is also checking to see if the man might be on drugs.

"Officer, I was on the freeway heading south to Santa Barbara when I received a call on my cell phone." Mr. Avery is sounding angrier and angrier. "I didn't want to talk and drive at the same time. As you well know, it's dangerous to do that, especially at this time of morning. It's against the law. When I got off the road, looking for a spot to park so I could finish my call, I got lost. Then I spotted this parking lot and pulled in just a few minutes before you arrived. Officer, I was here trying to figure out how to get back to the freeway. I really don't think I broke any laws." He is still breathing heavily and he has his finger on the button to raise the window. "So, Officer," he says in a sarcastic voice, "if everything is okay, I would like to continue my trip."

Deputy Hallett decides there is no reason for him to keep Mr. Avery any longer. "Yes. Everything seems to be in order." He steps back and away from the car.

Mr. Avery closes his window and starts his car, but he forgets to raise the passenger's side window, which he had lowered while looking for his registration. More likely, he was trying to get a better look at Jing Xian.

At that moment, Deputy Hallett hears some people running from the direction of the hospital. Not knowing what is happening, he crouches down. *Who are these people?* He doesn't recognize them because of the heavy fog, and all he can hear is the loud noise of their footsteps.

Stacey and Andre run into view. "That looks like Craiger's car."

When they are about fifteen feet from the side of the Lexus, Stacey's feet slide out from under her on the wet asphalt. Grabbing Andre's arm to keep from falling, she looks into the car. It is Craiger. He calmly returns her look.

"Oh, my God, it's him! Don't let him get away!"

Chapter 126

*G*ot to get the hell out of here. Mr. Craiger hits the gear shift and slams his foot on the gas pedal. In his haste, he thinks he has the car in drive, but he is wrong. It is in reverse. The engine screams, the tires spin on the wet pavement, and the car shudders. An enormous cloud of smoke flows out from under the rear end of the car, along with the smell of burning rubber.

The car is not moving. Mr. Craiger is frozen, hanging on to the steering wheel with both hands, his eyes staring straight ahead. Suddenly, with a hard jolt, the back tires find traction. The car jerks backwards, slamming him against the steering wheel. The impact smashes his face against the steering wheel, breaking his nose and spraying blood all over the inside of the windshield and dashboard. The G-force of the accelerating car pins him against the steering wheel as the car flies backwards across the parking lot and ricochets off the curb. It is airborne until it comes to a screeching halt in a clump of palm trees on the edge of the parking lot. The rear end is extensively damaged, the rear window is smashed, the bumper clatters to the ground, and the trunk springs open.

Mr. Craiger dazed, slowly starts to pull himself up in the seat. *What happened to the air-bags,* he wonders? *They never inflated.* He reaches down, grabs the bloody gear shift, and tries shifting the car into drive. Miraculously the engine is still running. Though the gas tank was not ruptured in the collision with the palm trees, the smell of gasoline fills the air.

Deputy Hallett, Jing Xian, Stacey, and Andre are starting to recover from the shock of watching Craiger's attempt to escape. As they start running toward the car, Deputy Hallett yells out to his friends.

"Don't run up to the car! Get away from it! It could explode!"

The fog, steam, and smoke covering the parking lot make visibility impossible, and the car's engine is still racing. His foot still pushing the accelerator to the floorboard, Craiger smacks the shift lever into drive. Suddenly the car violently lurches forward at top speed. Tires screech, smoke bellows out of the fender wells. The car rockets across the parking lot again.

"You won't get me, you bastards!"

The broken back bumper scrapes the pavement, casting off a stupendous array of sparks. Suddenly the back end of the car explodes into a ball of flames. The explosion is so powerful it brings the back end of the car three or four feet off the ground. The blazing car hits a tire stop and careens in another direction. It is heading at high speed for a giant redwood tree at another edge of the parking lot.

Stacey is already dialing 9-1-1.

The car slams into the giant redwood tree and explodes a second time, engulfing the tree in an enormous fire ball.

Both doors of the Lexus are blown off their hinges, and the witnesses can momentarily see the fat man inside being incinerated. His burning, bloody body is thrown through the windshield, but the heat is so intense no one can get close enough to even try to rescue him. People come running out of the hospital, some of them carrying fire extinguishers. It is too late.

Chapter 127

As the morning sun peeks through the fog, droplets of water form and drop from the tree branches, giving the illusion that it is raining. Police and sheriff's cars are parked everywhere on the hospital parking lot, their radios squawking. The daily grind of people begins flowing in and out of the hospital, some people visiting the hospital for medical care or on business, others on law enforcement business. Additional fire engines arrive to mop up the gasoline spewed on other trees when the Lexus hit the redwood. Workers from the crime lab and the coroner's office are taking photos of the burned-out car and removing pieces of evidence. Soon the fire department begins removing the charred body from the wreck as investigators begin taking statements, photographers recording the scene, and press and television reporters continue jockeying around to see who can get the most information. Kathy has already phoned her boss, Mr. Bertolino, and he soon arrives with several of his cameramen. Special agents are inspecting the remains of the car crash, police technicians are measuring the parking lot, and the fire department mopping up.

Deputy Hallett has finally been joined by Deputy Nolen, who is sipping a hot cup of coffee. Stacey walks up to them.

"Hey, Nolen," she says, "you missed all the action."

"I sure did," he replies. "I was on the other side of town, trying to take care of a family dispute. You know the drill. The man has a few drinks, and the women wants to throw him out while her secret lover is standing by, shooting up. You never know what it's about until you get there, and then half of it doesn't make sense."

"Come on, guys," Stacey says. "Let's check out the others." They walk to where the rest of their group is standing. "I think it's all over," she says to them. "Except for that guy I believe rigged the wall to fall at the kasbah. We don't know his name, so we can't identify him. Who knows, he might have been one of the locals in Marrakesh." She shrugs her shoulders. "I don't think we're going to get any more information out of Doshi. One of these days, we'll get him, though."

As everyone nods, Jing Xian has an idea. "Let's call Hawaii!" He and Andre step away from the crowd and start dialing Andre's cell phone.

"Hey, Christina," Jing Xian says. "Can I speak with Missy?"

As Jing Xian starts talking with Missy, Andre starts looking through his wallet and finds a business card from the Yangshuo Hotel with Jing Ling's name on it. He begins to think about the wonderful, if brief, time he had there.

"Hey guys," Stacey says as she walks over to where they are standing. "We've got a lot of work to catch up on at the office. Andre, you're the president of the company now."

Printed in the United States
By Bookmasters